The Passions of War

"Mrs. Bent asked me to put in for a special commendation," Peter said stiffly. "She says your work during the emergency was above and beyond the call of duty, and suggested I thank you personally—on behalf of myself and the staff."

Denise stared at him, open-mouthed. Her magnificent body began to sag as tension left her. Her face was pale. It was like watching a candle flickering out. And her eyes filled as she swayed, catching hold of a chair.

He rounded his desk to catch her in his arms. When she lifted her tear-dewed face, his concern became something more.

"Denise—don't—"

And then he was kissing her, finding the sweetness of her mouth beneath the salt of tears, feeling the thud of her heart against his own, the rounded curves beneath the stained uniform pressed too closely to his.

Books by
Aola Vandergriff

Daughters of the Wild Country
Daughters of the Far Islands
Daughters of the Misty Isles
Daughters of the Opal Skies
Daughters of the Southwind
Daughters of the Shining City
Daughters of the Storm

Published by
WARNER BOOKS

Daughters of the Storm

Aola Vandergriff

WARNER BOOKS

A Warner Communications Company

WARNER BOOKS EDITION

Copyright © 1983 by Aola Vandergriff

Cover art by Jim Pietz

Warner Books, Inc.,
666 Fifth Avenue,
New York, N.Y. 10103

 A Warner Communications Company

Printed in the United States of America

First Warner Books Printing: October, 1983

10 9 8 7 6 5 4 3 2 1

This book is lovingly dedicated to—
Chrystal
Mikey
Tiffany
and Tammy

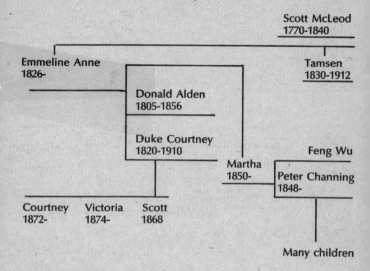

Scott McLeod
1770-1840

Emmeline Anne
1826-

Tamsen
1830-1912

Donald Alden
1805-1856

Duke Courtney
1820-1910

Martha
1850-

Feng Wu

Peter Channing
1848-

Courtney
1872-

Victoria
1874-

Scott
1868

Many children

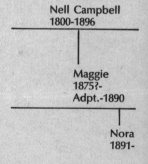

Nell Campbell
1800-1896

Maggie
1875?-
Adpt.-1890

Nora
1891-

Daughters of the Storm

April 15, 1912, 2:15 A.M.

Electric lights blazed from every cabin of the great ship. Lights on all the decks and on her mastheads glittered, reflected in still waters, smooth as glass. A sound of music from the ship's band wafted over the sea.

The melody the musicians played was called "Autumn."

The *Titanic* was a luxury vessel on her first cruise, ideal for lovers, for honeymooners. One couple, seemingly isolated from the confusion around them, appeared to be newlyweds from a distance; he, tall and broad-shouldered; she, small and slender, with dark hair swinging to her waist.

The situation was not as idyllic as it seemed. A portion of the ship was submerged, the lights still glowing in the sunken section suffusing the water around her with an eerie green radiance. Lifeboats, some overfilled, others cast off half empty, were fragile shells on the bosom of the North Atlantic. Those left aboard were silent with the knowledge of their plight.

Only the band played on.

Upon closer inspection, the couple who kept to themselves proved to be no longer young but of inderterminate age. The man's hair was brushed with wings of silver. Shining threads spangled the silken strands of the woman's black hair and her small oval face was peach-soft with time. One hand rested on the man's arm. A guiding hand.

For the man was blind.

"Tamsen," he said softly, "you should have gone on without me. Maybe there's still time—"

Tamsen Tallant shook her head. There were no longer cries of "Women and children first." In any case, she had no intention of leaving her beloved's side. And she wasn't the only woman to stay behind. A few feet away stood Mrs. Isidor Straus, holding fast to her husband's hand. They exchanged understanding smiles.

"I got you into this," Dan Tallant groaned. "Dragging you all over Europe, seeing eye specialists when I knew it was a lost cause—then changing our reservations so we could travel in style—"

"It's been wonderful," Tamsen told him. She thought of the tender nights in which they'd reaffirmed their longtime love. "And I'm glad!"

"Glad? When we're due to sink any minute! Good God, Tam!"

"Would you want to leave me like Em? Or Arab?" the question silenced Dan. Both Tamsen's sisters had been widowed within the last six years. Duke Courtney, Em's husband, had died quietly in his sleep. Juan

Narvaéz, married to Arab, was a victim of the San Francisco quake, killed by crumbling masonry as he pulled an injured child to safety. The two women, one faded and tottery, the other childlike and fretful, lived on, attended by Maggie and Sean Murphy, adopted children of their longtime, deceased friend, Nell.

Tamsen and Dan were quiet for a moment, each imagining the loneliness one would know without the other. Then Tamsen spoke.

"I couldn't live without you, Dan," she said in a small voice. "I wouldn't want to. This way, we'll go together."

His hand went out, seeking and touching her hair in a gentle caress. "Then I'm glad, too. As long as you're not afraid—"

"Not when I'm with you," she whispered. "Let's just wait—and listen. Listen to the music." She began to sing along with the ship's band in the husky, breaking little voice for which she'd once been famous.

"Hold me up in mighty waters,

"Keep my eyes on things above—

"Righteousness, divine atonement—"

She paused as the band missed a beat, the musicians seeing what she saw, a gigantic swell of water like a wall of glass lifting, towering against a starry sky as the ship nosed downward.

"Hold me, Dan," she whispered. "Hold me."

The band recovered in time to play the melody to the end. Her cheek against her husband's heart, Tamsen sang the final words.

"Peace," she sang, her eyes wet with tears of mingled sorrow and happiness.

"Peace, and everlasting love."

---- *chapter 1* ----

Brussels, August 20, 1914

Liane Wang woke, confused and disoriented for a
few moments. The dream she'd just experienced
seemed very real. Far more so than this Belgian
hotel room with its ornate decor, golden cupids
decorating the high ceiling above her bed.

It had been two long years since the sinking of the
Titanic. And during those years, Liane refused to
admit Tamsen and Dan went down with the ship.
She would have known it, she insisted stubbornly to
her confidante, Jo Blaine. She would have felt
something.

This time, her odd intuitive nature had failed
her. Now she could stop hoping. Now she could
cry—

The golden cupids blurred above her as she wept—
not from grief, but because their passing had been so

15

beautiful. They'd gone as they would have wanted, in each other's arms.

She must tell Jo!

Rising, still a little weak from a mysterious fever that had kept the whole party stranded here in a country at the brink of war, she pulled on a robe and went to the connecting door.

They were already awake, and talking excitedly in there. Jo—and Denise.

Her hand faltered on the knob. Denise would laugh at her fancies and then Jo would go along with her, teasing her about being weird, like Aunt Luka.

Why did Denise have to join their tour? She'd spoiled everything!

Em Courtney had financed this trip, wanting her great-granddaughter and great-niece to "do Europe" and meet their unknown cousins. Liane and Jo had set off in the company of Maggie and Sean Murphy and their daughter, Nora, looking forward to a wonderful adventure.

Now it had all been spoiled.

Denise Dugal, of the Scottish branch of the family, insisted on coming with them. She intended to go all the way to America, to become a movie star—

There'd been a row with her parents, who didn't want to lose their only daughter. And then a rift between Liane and Jo, who was dazzled by the glamorous older girl. Jo was ambitious, desiring to become a writer like her parents; a big-time reporter. Denise, with her movie aspirations, was someone she could talk to.

And Liane was only fourteen, acutely couscious of the Oriental blood in her veins. Her silky black hair was straight as a string. She hated the almond shape of her eyes, seeing the creamy tint of her skin as sallow. And she was always doing dumb things, spilling tea, tripping on the stairs, getting lost in the hotel—

Timidly, she turned the knob and entered the room, her slim shoulders braced. Jo and Denise were at a window, looking out into the narrow street below.

"Jo," Liane whispered, "I've got to tell you. I had a dream. Aunt Tamsen and Uncle Dan—"

"Hush!" Denise snapped. "Listen—"

Silenced, Liane obeyed. She heard a sullen roll of thunder that puzzled her. The sun was shining—

The thunder was followed by a low crackling and popping, like popcorn over an open fire.

"What is it?" Liane wanted to know.

"Gunfire!" Denise's bright face was blazing with enthusiasm. "The Gerrrmans! They've coom! Isna it exciting?"

The news was not unexpected. The German troops had crossed the Belgian border and Maggie was frantic, not wanting to move on until Liane was fully recovered, and terrified that they'd be trapped in the middle of a war. Now it appeared that they had waited too long. Liane went white.

"I think it's awful! Men—men are dying out there!"

"Dinna be a ninny!" Denise turned on her. "I'll wager ye believe those tales! That the Gerrrmans kill priests and eat babies!"

"Don't tease her," Jo said. "She's just a baby herself, and she's probably scared. Denise, do you realize I'll have the scoop of the year? Imagine! News from occupied Brussels! Dad will have a fit!"

"I ken the Gerrrmans are fine-looking men," Denise added, turning again to the window. "How lang, d'ye think, afore they tak the city?"

"Denise," Jo gasped, smothering a giggle, "you're terrible!"

"There's naething wrong wi' a little rrromance," Denise shrugged, preening before the younger girl's open admiration. She was scared, too, probably as frightened as the wee Liane, but she'd be domned if she'd show it—'

The door flew open behind them, admitting their chaperones, Maggie and Sean Murphy, along with their daughter. Maggie had once been a wispy urchin of the streets in Liverpool. Adoring the woman who adopted her and found her a fine Irish husband, she'd spent years patterning herself after Nell Wotherspoon. Now she was a reasonable facsimile. Short, obese, rouged, her straw-colored hair dyed black when it began to show gray, she managed a strong family resemblance. Only the eyes, hidden in layers of fat, were different; hers were green grapes, where Nell's had been raisins. Her language, too, had been faithfully copied, with an added accent of the streets.

"'Cep'n I don't cuss," she told anyone who would listen. "Damn's awright. Goddamn ain't."

Her husband, Sean, worshiped her as he had worshiped Nell, adoring every pudgy pound of her. He remained always in the background, secretly apologetic that he did not resemble the burly, peg-legged Sim Blevins, Nell's last love, in any way.

He was still in the background as Maggie barged into the girls' room, face pasty beneath her rouge, jowls quivering.

"Bin down to the depot," she barked. "Got tickets to Paree. We gotta git the hell out. Train's leavin' in a few minutes. Leave all yer junk. don't take no more'n 'ee kin tote—"

"We are in nae dangerrr," Denise said mutinously.

"This is the fierst exciting hoppening in my whole life! and I winna leave my luggage—"

Maggie screwed up her face and thrust her jaw forward pugnaciously. "When 'ee 'orned in on this 'ere trip, I tolt yer ma I was th' boss. Now, gitcher butt in gear afore I kick it up ter a 'unnert an' sixty!"

Then Maggie turned to Jo. "An' 'ee! Yer leavin' that typewriter be'ind."

"I won't—"

"'Ee will, by damn!"

Jo fled before her menacing advance.

Nora was sent to help Liane dress. When the last button on her green traveling suit was fastened, Liane looked hopelessly about her room. She must leave the pretty dresses her mother had sewn for her; her sketchbooks filled with wild Scottish scenes from the Dugal lands; the steep green hills, the burn; a drawing of Rory, the Dugal's youngest son—

Stuffing her handbag with a change of underclothing, she hesitated. There was room for one more thing: the book Jo's mother, Missie, wrote about the McLeod sisters—Tamsen, Arabella, and Em—

It was heavy, but she could carry it. Liane knew her own shortcomings. She was small and timid, but she could borrow from Tamsen's courage in these pages—

The firing sounded closer as they left the hotel in haste. Belgians were fleeing the city. The narrow cobbled streets were crowded with shawled women. They pushed wheelbarrows and prams filled with supplies. Children clung, crying, to the skirts of mothers blank with shock. One woman carried a birdcage, bumping blindly into Liane, bruising her arm. Doggedly, the travelers fought their way through the exodus to the crowded train station, reaching their transport just as it was ready to pull out.

A grim-faced conductor pushed them into a crowded compartment, Maggie, purple with rage, protesting all the way.

"Dammit, I paid fust-class, 'ee cheatin' bastid, an' 'ere 'ee are, packin' us in like sour-deens! Hell, I'll go all the way t' th' top! 'Eads is gonna roll afore I'm done!"

At last they were jammed in, standing as the train started with a jolt that sent Maggie off her feet and into the lap of an astonished Belgian gentleman. The gap she left filled rapidly as passengers sought more space. Grinning, she settled herself.

"Gonna be a long ride, luv," she told the uncomprehending man in a conversational tone. "Hell, might ez well be ez comferble ez we can."

She gave a broad wink at Sean, who smiled back in admiration.

One thing about Maggie, she always came up smelling like a rose.

The train, after several false starts, picked up speed and steamed out of the station, its whistle blowing. The small cortege was on its way to safety. Behind them, the big guns were silenced.

There was only a crackling of small arms as the Germans moved into Brussels, executing the *francs-tireurs*—the civilian snipers—as they came.

chapter 2

A few miles northeast of Mons, the overloaded train shuddered to a halt. The dazed, half-smothered passengers were ordered to disembark. They stood in an open field staring dismally at their captors and at the twisted, damaged tracks ahead. Armed men, faces set, walked along the rows of refugees, questioning, occasionally asking for identification.

As they approached the girls and their chaperones, Denise made a discovery. Some of them were British soldiers.

"I be damned," Maggie said loudly. "Hey, you—"

A young officer turned in surprise that became shock at the sight of the painted, obese little woman. "Americans?" he asked hesitantly.

"Most of us," Maggie said cheerfully. "Me, I wuz 'atched in Liverpool. Mebbe you've 'eared of me mum. Lady Wotherspoon, she wuz, afore she passed on. My man 'ere's a Irisher. "Er," she pointed to Denise, "is fresh outta Scotland. A Dugal, she is. Now, sence we're kinda all related, so ter speak, 'ow the hell do we git outta this 'ere mess?"

Confused by Maggie's language, the young officer stalled for a moment. Then he looked regretfully at the pretty girls accompanying the rather amazing woman. One was small, rather Oriental in appearance, with silken blue-black hair, little more than a child. Another was statuesque, crowned with glorious red curls. A third was tiny, dainty, with rumpled black locks, blue shining eyes filled with curiosity. Even the fourth, with straw-colored hair, freckles, and steady gray eyes, wasn't too bad.

Four of the sweetest-looking lasses he'd had the pleasure of meeting. And right in the middle of a bloody war! Pity! He suppressed a groan.

"All I can do is give you direction. We have word that thousands of refugees are coming this way, leaving Brussels afoot. We must pass them through quickly, because the German army is on their heels. The B.E.F. is to hold the line at Mons, if possible, and this"—he waved a hand at the pastoral scene around them—"will be a battleground.

"I suggest you make all possible haste, through Mons, then to Le Cateau. Sir John French has his headquarters there. Perhaps he can help you on to Paris. From there, it might be possible to find a way out of France which I highly recommend."

"You mean walk?" Maggie's voice rose to a disbelieving squawk. "Yer outa yer gourd!"

"I am afraid there is no alternative," he said stiffly. "I cannot spare men or transportation at this time."

"Well, if we gotta, we gotta," she grumbled. She turned and plodded off, Sean and Nora following.

Denise, Jo, and Liane waited to thank him, and he took each of their hands in turn. "Pairhops we will see you again," Denise smiled. But Liane saw something in his eyes, a haunted darkness that made her shiver.

They would not be seeing him again. What's more, he knew it. And he wasn't much older than Rory.

Standing on tiptoe, she touched his cheek with her lips, then fled. He turned scarlet and put a hand to his face. "Jove," he said.

Denise and Jo looked stricken. "She's just a child," Jo said hastily. "I don't know what got into her!"

He smiled ruefully. "I'm rather pleased, actually. Do thank her for me."

He watched as the small group formed and moved out of sight. It would be something to remember when the Germans came. the B.E.F. had been ordered to hold the line at all costs.

He had a premonition that he might have had his last kiss from a pretty girl.

"I say, Charles, how did you rate that?"

The young officer straightened his nineteen-year-old shoulders and turned to his friend with a very un-British grin. "I don't know, old man," he said in a deprecating voice. "I suppose some of us have what it takes, and some of us do not—"

His last words were drowned in the sound of an explosion. The defenders of Mons had dynamited the train, to keep it from enemy use. The cars left the rails, jackknifing like toys flung by a massive hand. The members of the small scouting party, sent to intercept the last train out of Brussels, returned to their posts to await the force of the German thrust.

The train's former passengers turned at the detonation, seeing their earlier transport rise and tumble earthward in destruction.

"Bastids," Maggie grumped. "Coulda let us git on through afore they blowed th' tracks. Hell, we look like Booshees?"

"They had no time," Sean said, a new note of authority in his voice. "And neither do we. The man said we must hurry."

He rushed his reluctant wife and the girls in his charge to the rear of the column. The Belgian refugees had stopped only briefly. Now they were plodding drearily on, leaving their old lives behind, heading for an uncertain destination.

It was late afternoon when they reached the fortified city of Mons. Here they were challenged and passed on with a warning to keep moving, to get behind the lines as quickly as possible. Beyond the town, an emergency mess had been set up to feed the fugitives. Belgian businessmen, shopowners, and peasants stood in a long line to receive a bowl of nourishing stew.

"Hoomiliating," Maggie said righteously. They come to this place as toorists and now, by damn, they was beggin' in th' streets. Nell would flop over in her grave, she would!

Her scruples didn't keep her from wondering if she could get in line for seconds.

There was no opportunity. As they finished their stew, hands touched their shoulders. "Move along there. You've got to leave the battle zone! Hurry!"

They wearily obeyed, moving out into the dusty white roads. To either side, the setting sun shone down on rolling, golden early autumn fields. Jo, in her excellent French, offered to carry a woman's child for a time. The mother looked at her blankly and finally shook her head. Each family unit seemed to cling together in fear, too shocked at their uprooting to understand in what direction danger lay.

They passed deserted cottages flanked by neat stone walls and terraces; open-ended barns with a sweet scent of fresh hay. Liane imagined the former occupants bringing in cows for milking, then going to their tables for a supper of bread, home-made wine and cheese—

A British observation plane buzzed overhead, and the picture changed in her mind. The cottages became blasted ruins, the walls tumbled, and over the landscape like a cloud hung the smell of blood and death—

The war would follow on their heels, devastating this peaceful landscape. She already felt its fetid breath—

Maggie, though her feet were killing her, was alert to the well-being of her young charges. Liane was still in a convalescent stage. The girl's face was white, and she stumbled. Maggie stopped dead, her hands on her hips.

"Awright," she said decisively, "we ain't gonna try to keep up with this bunch. See that place over there?" She pointed to a small farm, stark against the far horizon. "We're gonna stop there fer th' night, git us some shuteye, an' rest our dawgs. Anybody got any objeckshuns?"

"Let's go on," Liane said, urgency in her voice.

"And I vote tae bide," Denise overrode her. "A body told me it was twenty-six miles to Le Cateau. 'Tis a grrreat way, yet. I canna take another step!"

"And I want to get my impressions in my notebook while they're still fresh," Jo added.

Sean and Nora saw no reason to dissent. They

were surely out of the danger zone. It would be better to pause for the night and get a fresh start in the morning.

They left the road, Liane lagging behind. For some reason, the thought of approaching the deserted farm made her tremble. It was farther than they'd thought and darkness was swiftly falling. Liane could hear her cousins, who walked ahead, their voices carrying in the still evening air.

"Why d'you suppose the old warhorse decided to stop? Because her feet hurt?" It was Jo who spoke, Denise who answered.

"I heard her tell Sean 'twas because o' wee Liane. It seems she stumbled—"

Jo chuckled. "Doesn't she always? She's at that awkward age. And doesn't she do the strangest things?"

"Like bussing that yoong mon, ye mean? I canna imagine what got intae the child."

"It was embarrassing," Jo agreed.

Liane's face was hot in the darkness. It seemed like a miracle when they finally reached the abandoned farm. In the distance, haycocks were featureless mounds against the night sky. Sean stopped them. They waited while he explored the interior of a large, open-ended barn with a ladder leading into a loft.

"I do not like entering a stranger's house," Sean admitted. " 'T'would not be bad, sleeping here in the sweet hay—"

"Hell, no," Maggie said. "I'm fer a bed, long ez there ain't a strange man in it."

Overruled, Sean Murphy knocked at the door of the house, then opened it reluctantly.

"Anybody to home?" Maggie sang out. "Speak up, er ferever 'old yer pieces!"

There was no answer to her cheerful, booming voice. Sean struck a match on the seat of his trousers. There was a smell of sulfur and a small light flared. It revealed a table and several candles. As Sean lit the tapers, Maggie expelled her breath in a whoof of relief.

Candles in hand, they looked through the house. This was a plain household, with stone walls and a fireplace at one end. A scattering of meal indicated that the food shelves had been hastily emptied. Maggie looked at the bare cupboard in disappointment.

"Dammit, I'm 'ungry! Don't git somethin' t'eat, I'm gonna fade away ter nuthin'!"

The others hid their smiles. The likelihood of a dwindling Maggie was too remote to consider. But they ignored stairs leading upward to a sleeping loft in favor of steps that led down to a cellar.

Here, there might be food.

There was. Maggie screeched with delight at the sight of a huge yellow round of cheese.

" 'Ot damn! Looka that! Looks like we're gonna git t'feed our faces after all!"

"Give us a minute, luv," Sean said uneasily. "I want to check this place out, first. You girls take a look at that side room. I'll have a look-see upstairs."

"The hell yuh will," Maggie said firmly. "Think 'ow long it's been sence we et! Me knees is weak, an me stomach thinks me throat's cut. We gotta keep our strength up! Saw off a 'unka that!"

The girls, laughing at Maggie's childish greed, decided food could wait until they'd explored the place. They crossed the cellar floor to a door in the earthen wall. Nora tugged it open. Denise held her candle high and gasped at what she saw. Then they disappeared.

Sean Murphy, searching for his pocketknife, heard Denise's indrawn breath and wondered what the divil she'd seen. He was a bit put out with Maggie for holding him up. He was the man of the family, wasn't he? It was his job to protect those girls. Bejabbers—there might even be a body in there!

His knife slid through the cheese like butter, and he handed a slice to his salivating wife.

"There ye are, me love."

Maggie, never one to stand on ceremony, downed half the chunk in one enormous bite.

"Dad!"

The urgency in Nora Murphy's voice jerked Sean's attention from his wife. Nora stood in the doorway, candle in hand, her face white. The other girls crowded behind her.

"Dad—we gotta get outa here. We found—" She stopped uncertainly, staring past him. "What's the matter with Mum?"

Maggie was clutching her throat, her green-grape eyes bugging out of her head as she looked pitifully at her husband. "Gawd 'elp me," she whimpered. "I'm dyin', Sean."

Indeed, she had every appearance of it. Her face was like tallow, her lips coated with foam, her body heaving uncontrollably. Sean put his wiry arms about her quivering frame, his voice squeaky with fear.

"Maggie! What is it, me darlin'?"

"I bin pizened, Sean! Them bastids pizened what they ain't tooken!

Poison! Holy Mither! Why hadn't he thought o' that! The people here had cleaned out all else before they left—and they'd left that cheese for the flaming Germans—

Maggie clutched her stomach and burped, more

bubbles appearing on her foam-flecked chin. Her eyes rolled upward as she verged on fainting.

"Help me," Sean barked. "We got to lay her down easy—"

"We can't," Nora said. "We gotta git outa here! Oh, Mum! Mum!" She burst into tears as she moved to Maggie's side, and Denise took over for her.

"She's trying tae say we maun move alang." The Scottish girl's burr thickened with excitement. "This is—some kind of Gerrrman post. There are Gerrrman rations i' that room! Equipment. A lanterrrrn, still warrm!"

"Hells bells," Maggie choked. "Bin pizened, an' gonna be kilt by sojers, too—"

Murphy was torn between two horrors. Maggie leaned on him heavily, moaning and strangling. They'd found themselves in a spy-nest, and he, the only man, was responsible for a group of females, including his beloved wife, who might be dying on him— and without whom he didn't want to live.

He stared helplessly at the offending cheese. If only he knew what kind of poison it contained. And—the thought struck him like a thunderbolt— Sure, and why hadn't the damned Germans eaten it? Except for the slice he removed it was untouched—

"I'm gonna try something," he said hoarsely. "If something happens to me and Maggie, you girls head out fer the road. Go on to Le Cateau, and don't worry about us. Understand?"

The knife trembling in his hand, he cut another slab of cheese.

Maggie caught at his wrist in alarm as he raised it to his lips. "Naw, Sean," she burbled. "Dammit, don't—"

He chewed a morsel and gagged at the taste, his eyes lighting with relief.

" 'Tis only soap," he said.

"Lor' lumme!"

Maggie was silent for a moment. Soap? An' Sean, th' sweet sonofabitch, tasted th' damn stuff when it coulda been pizen. He risked his life, fer her sake. Her face screwed up in a grimace as she tried to stop an onset of tears. No sense gettin' sloppy about it, like Nell allus said—

Batting her wet lashes, she managed a sickly grin. "Mebbe it'll clean up me langridge," she said ruefully. "Now, let's get th' hell outa 'ere, afore them Boshees comes back."

chapter 3

When they left the cottage, the moon had risen enough to illuminate their surroundings. Its light was eerie on a landscape where mists were beginning to form. To one side, the barn stood, skeletal, deserted. Small chicken houses were black humps that seemed to shift and move.

"I ain't goin' out in that," Maggie grumbled. "I'm sick to my stomach. Feel like I'm gonna puke. Hell, them Boshees is long gone. Mebbe we skeert 'em off. Les' go back in, an try out them beds upstairs—"

"Maggie—Sean—Look!" Liane's voice interrupted them. She pointed into the distance. Three lanterns bobbed, diffused in the mist, heading toward the farmstead. And the quiet night was shattered by the sound of a dog's barking.

For a moment, the small group stood frozen, unable to move.

"Mebbe them's the folks what lives 'ere, comin' 'ome," Maggie whispered.

"And maybe it's German soldiers," Sean interposed. "And there's a dog. Sure, and they'll track us down if we run! Quick—in here—"

He shepherded the women into the barn, feeling for the ladder that led to the loft. "Up there," he commanded. "Hurry. And pray to the Holy Mither there's fodder there!"

The girls scurried up the ladder. The dog's barking was ominously close as Sean pushed Maggie's enormous rear upward, finally reaching the loft floor himself.

"Dig down in the hay," he ordered. "And not a peep out o' ye!"

"If I only had a gun," Denise mourned.

Small, freckled Nora clapped a hand over the Scottish girl's mouth. "Shut yer yap," she threatened. "You get me mum and dad kilt, I'll throw you down to 'em!"

Denise fought away. "Ye dinna tell me what tae do," she threatened. "Ye and yer folks are joost serrvants—"

Nora's wiry fist swung and connected. Denise's gasp was drowned out as the dog dashed, yipping, into the barn, followed by the sound of boots crunching on straw.

In the loft, the intruders were suddenly still, holding their breath, unable to move. The moon shone through a wide, oblong opening through which hay was pitched to animals on the ground. It touched pale, frightened faces. Liane, facedown, eye to a crack in the loft floor, shivered at the sight of German uniforms.

"*Nur keine Aufregune,*" came a guttural voice from below. "*Alles ist in Ordnung—*"

"Don't get excited. All is in order." Jo, with her proficiency in language, translated the conversation. She closed her eyes prayfully. Please God, let the speaker be believed—

"*Nein,*" another male voice persisted. The dog was barking at the foot of the ladder, crazed with the scent of its prey.

Jo's heart sank as she listened, trying to sort out what they were saying from the noise the maddened animal was making.

"*Es gefällt mir nicht.*"

"I don't like it." Still another man. He continued on to say that there was certainly someone in the loft above. The first speaker laughed. "Then you will climb the ladder, Hans?" he said in his own tongue. "Go!"

"Perhaps you are correct. There is no one there," the suspicious soldier said after some hesitation. "We have our orders to dismantle the equipment and leave before dawn." He whistled at the dog. "*Kommen, Fritzi!*"

There was an almost audible sigh of relief from the loft as the dog's frenzy subsided to a whine and booted feet moved away. Then Maggie's traitorous stomach, outraged at the enormous ration of soap she'd forced into its empty cavern, erupted in a low, rolling rumble.

The exodus of the Germans stopped instantly.

Only Liane saw a soldier reach for the pistol on his hip, pointing it upward. Her mouth opened in a silent scream as he fired toward the direction of the sound.

Maggie! Dear God, Maggie!

A hush followed the explosion, and Liane saw the soldier approaching the ladder, gun still at the ready. She closed her eyes.

He would kill them all. He must be stopped—but how?

She forced herself to relax, and thought of her beloved pet at home, the way they carried on long conversations in cat language.

The men below heard a plaintive mew, ending on a complacent purr.

In an instant, they were laughing. "*Katze!*" one cried gleefully. Slapping a sheepish companion on the back, they made their way out of the barn and to the house.

It was a long time before those hidden in the loft dared to speak. Nora broke the silence with a frightened whisper.

"Mum—you all right?"

"Fine ez frawg fuzz," Maggie affirmed. "Well, we all 'ere? Good. Liane, that wuz a purty smart stunt you pulled off. Hell, thought they was a damned cat up 'ere, meself. Say, Sean, you dumb bastid, you ain't said nuthin'!"

"Dad?" Nora asked, her voice trembling.

"Sure, and me gifta gab was skeert right out of me," Sean said weakly.

Maggie grinned. "That figgers. Now you all skooch over close-like, an' les' figger what we gonna do."

Jo delivered her interpretation of what had been said. The Germans were preparing to move out in the night. It would be too risky to attempt an escape until they were gone with their dog. They'd have to wait them out.

"Two of us can keep watch at a time," Nora said

briskly. "The rest can sleep. Denise and I will take the first shift."

"I prefer tae watch wi' Jo," Denise said cuttingly, the memory of Nora's blow returning. She lifted a hand to her bruised lips.

"And I choose Liane," Nora said, her neck stiff with resentment. She and the willful Scots lassie had clashed since Denise Dugal joined the party. Denise, older by several years, sandwiched between three older brothers and a younger one, was hot-tempered and spoiled. In addition, she'd latched onto young Jo Blaine, more or less cutting Liane out of the picture.

To Nora, with her San Francisco background, Liane and Jo were family. Denise had no business pushing herself in where she wasn't wanted.

Denise and Jo moved close to the oblong aperture and lay on their stomachs, watching the house. They were both ecstatic over their adventure; Denise, because it was exciting after the monotony of life in the Scottish hills; Jo, planning the article she would write when she reached Paris.

Moonlight lay along the stone walls below in golden puddles. The scent of new hay was clean, sweet. Denise wished one of the German soldiers would step outside so she could see him. She wondered if any of the men were handsome. Denise Dugal had been ripe for love for a long time. Only her stern Scottish will had kept her from succumbing to one of the neighboring lads at home. She wanted more from life. Adventure, excitement—

Dreaming a little, she concocted a movie script in her mind. In it, the Germans returned to the barn. Heroically, Denise climbed down the ladder, sacrificing herself to save the others. She wished she'd had the idea, earlier. The others would have seen her as a heroine—

Instead it had been that—that bairn, who saved the day!

"What are you thinking about?" Jo asked suddenly.

Denise blushed in the darkness. "About Liane. What the lass did."

"She didn't sound like a cat to me," Jo said. "She could have got us all in trouble!"

"I wish she was at hame wi' her mama," Denise said sourly. "We can handle dangerrr, but she's much tae yoong."

Jo agreed. She knew she'd put Liane down in order to gain Denise's approval, and she felt a little sick inside, as if she'd betrayed her best friend. She changed the subject.

"What if—what if those Germans found us? If they did and we escaped, it would make a great story!"

"Oonless they—ye know," Denise said with a delicious little shiver. "Jo, ye dinna suppose they wad—?"

"Rape us?" Jo Blaine, daughter of a newspaperman and an emancipated lady writer, was accustomed to straight talk and called a spade a spade. "Maybe."

"I'd dee," Denise said. "I'd joost dee! Jo, hae ye e'er—?"

"Been raped?" Jo asked. "No!"

Denise's face flamed in the darkness. "Nae, nae that! just—the otherrr!"

"Slept with a man, you mean? Have you?"

Denise was tempted to weave an impressive tale about her experiences, but she—she couldna lie.

"I hae nae," she said, disconsolately.

"Me, either," Jo said.

They had another bond in common. For a long

time, they sat in silence, dreaming their dreams of lovers waiting for them somewhere in the world; a lush redhead who wished to be a movie star, and a future New York ace reporter, trapped in a barn loft—and thinking of men.

Liane, lying in her bed of hay, was unable to sleep. She still had a haunted feeling, a premonition of something wrong. The sensation had been with her since they left the roadway. How she wished they'd gone on!

She was exhausted, weak after her long illness. And tomorrow they would be on their way again.

Twenty miles to Le Cateau, or more. And after that—what?

She wished she were in her own bed—at home.

She was still wide-eyed when Nora touched her arm. The two of them crept to relieve Jo and Denise, who'd grown rather tired of their bargain.

Denise fluffed her glorious hair, and yawned. "Hae nae seen a thing," she said. "Deadly dool. Ye'll probably enjoy yer watch."

Nora looked after her as she crawled to make a nest for herself in the hay, Jo right behind her.

"I'd like to smack her a good one," she said angrily. "The bitch! And Jo's going right along with her! She needs her bottom tanned!"

"They're all right," Liane said. "I don't think Denise means to be—unpleasant—"

"Ho, ho, ho!" Nora said sarcastically. "I just wish me grandmum Nell was still alive. I bet she'd handle her!"

Liane smiled, remembering the ebullient old woman, her life story contained in the book Jo's mother, Missie, had written about Tamsen Tallant.

The book was in her portmanteau. She crept to the

place she'd lain in and retrieved it, holding it close. It made her feel that Tamsen was near. With it, she was not quite so frightened. Her heart, which had been going pit-a-pat, slowed, and some of the cloud of apprehension she felt faded. Tamsen would watch over them—

It was nearing three in the morning by the small watch Liane wore pinned to the breast of her chic green traveling suit, when the door to the farmhouse opened. She and Nora counted. Three dark figures, burdened with gear, made grotesque shadows against a lighter night. A motor sound announced a lightless vehicle. The Germans—along with their dog, thank God—boarded, and within minutes they were gone.

The silent girls heaved a mutual, happy sigh. The danger was over. They could wake the others and be on their way before the heat settled in.

Liane crawled toward the spot where Sean Murphy lay making odd, moaning noises in his sleep. Poor man. He was exhausted. She wished she could let him rest.

"We can go, now," she whispered, her hand on his knee. "Wake up—"

Her fingers encountered something wet, sticky. Bewildered, she jerked away—then touched him again, an awful suspicion forming in her mind. She reached for his shoulder, shaking him. The only response was a whimper of pain.

There was no longer any need to be silent. Liane's voice rose shrilly, her voice bordering on hysteria.

"Maggie! Nora! Oh, God, help me! It's Uncle Sean—

"He's hurt!"

Sean Murphy had received the bullet fired through the loft floor. Knowing his loving wife, he feared that she would "raise hell and put a chunk under it," as she was fond of saying. He'd padded his wounded knee as well as he could with a handkerchief, and clenched his teeth, waiting the Germans out.

Now, he was semiconscious, due to pain and loss of blood. Maggie held him in her arms, blubbering her head off.

Jo and Liane left the loft and entered the farmhouse, returning with lanterns. Nora located ropes and a pulley, rigging a device to lower the injured man to the barn floor. It was Denise who worked over him, deftly cleansing and binding his wound with strips from her petticoat.

Just like home, she thought wearily. On the Highland farm, life was one dreary grind of sick animals and minor accidents. It had been her job to help her mother at the nursing and veterinarian chores. And her father wondered why she spurned the neighbor lads who came a-courting!

This was a miserable end to her great adventure!

"I hae doone a' I can do," she told Maggie. "We maun seek a prrroper doctor."

Maggie's face was the color of lard, her day-old rouge streaked with grimy tears.

"You think we're gonna be able t'save 'im?"

"I dinna know," Denise told her truthfully. "I dinna know."

chapter 4

When Sean Murphy's wounds had been cleaned and bandaged, the five women held a conference.

There was no food in the house. In the direction of Mons they could hear occasional explosions. They could not remain here until the battle caught up with them, and the wiry little Irishman was in no shape to travel.

"Then we maun leave him behind," Denise said. "He said that if anything should hoppen, we—"

She stopped as four pairs of eyes fastened on her face; eyes that held shock and anger at her remark. Even Jo was staring in disbelief.

"I dinna mean that," Denise floundered. " 'Tis ainly that we maun find trrransport—"

Maggie sat down on the barn floor beside Sean. "Ain't gonna leave 'im," she said stubbornly. "Be damned ef I will! 'E, stays, I stay! Ye wanna go, git th' hell on down th' road!"

Tears began to pour down Maggie's face as she cradled Sean's head in her arms. Nora squatted beside her.

"It's all right, Mum. Nobody's gonna leave Pa, er you, neither!"

"O' course nae," Denise added, her cheeks crimson. "I ainly thocht tae gae for aid—"

Nora glared at her. "You ain't got no say-so! Nobody asked ye to come along! You invited yerself, and ye ain't nothin' but trouble! Why don't ye keep yer bloody mouth shut?"

Denise opened her mouth, then quickly closed it again.

Nora moved quickly to take charge. Ignoring Denise, she sent Jo and Liane into the house to find any linens that were left behind. These were to be torn into strips and baked in the oven to make sterile bandages. The covering they had placed on Sean's wound was already soaked through with blood.

As for Nora herself, the pert, snub-nosed freckled girl went foraging. Behind the barn, she found a neat pile of discards. Among them, Nora located two ancient bicycles with bent spokes and tireless rims, along with a cart lacking wheels, and with a broken axle.

She set to work.

Em Courtney owned one of the first automobiles in San Francisco. When Maggie and Sean moved into the Courtney home after Nell's death, Nora gravitated to the garage. Fascinated by the shining, high-topped vehicle, she spent hours polishing it as a child. She could be found beneath it, her face smeared with grease, or with her head inside its hood. She had the heart and soul of a mechanic.

It stood her in good stead now, as she reinforced the broken axle with a bedpost, and fitted the bicycle wheels to the cart.

Denise, her cheeks still hot, walked off alone. In a small walled enclosure near the rear of the house, she found a bonanza: a wee kitchen garden. It had been hastily gleaned by the departing owners, but she managed to locate several turnips, some carrots and onions that had been overlooked when they left in haste.

Her humiliation was eased as she considered the vegetables with satisfaction. They'd had nothing to eat since the stew they were given at Mons. This would certainly prove her value to the party! And she could do more. Growing up in the Scottish Highlands with four brothers had taught her a lot.

Taking a small round stone from the garden wall, she set off across the fields, whistling a Highland tune.

Late in the afternoon, as Nora finished the last touches to her makeshift cart, a delicious scent wafted from the house. Maggie's eyes bulged, her stomach taking precedence over her heart for a brief second.

"I be damned," she said.

When Denise proudly carried out a bowl of stew, made from garden gleanings and the rabbit she'd killed that afternoon, she was soundly praised. The edge was taken from her euphoria when she overheard a conversation.

"I don't think Denise meant what she said, Jo," Liane was saying.

The wee snip, Denise thought, her anger rising. She had nae need tae be defended by a mawkish fourteen-year-old! Then she stopped, stunned, as Jo Blaine answered.

"I think she's spoiled rotten. She only thinks of herself!"

"But she really doesn't know Uncle Sean, yet," Liane offered. "She doesn't love him like we do."

"Would you have left her, under the same circumstances?"

"Well—no. But I think it's because of Aunt Tamsen. No matter what the problem was, she always found a way—"

"Denise wouldn't think like Tamsen. She's more like Aunt Arab—"

Denise backed from the open door, her face flaming. She'd met Tamsen only once, on that ill-fated trip before she and Dan embarked on the *Titanic*. But she'd read the book about her life over and over, seeing herself in Tamsen's role. Arab, indeed! Though Denise was her granddaughter, she'd always thought of her as self-centered, maybe even selfish.

Arab might have deserted a wounded man. Would she, Denise?

Hands to her hot face, she had to confess that she honestly didn't know. She'd only repeated the instructions Sean had given them the previous night. And she'd lost the respect of Jo, whom she loved like a sister.

She would win it back, she told herself resolutely. She would win it back again!

It was nearly dusk when they loaded a tick into the cart and carefully placed Sean's small wiry body atop it. They set out immediately, since the sound of artillery seemed ominously close. Denise insisted on pulling the cart, the others taking turns at pushing. The wheels wobbled on the rough terrain that let to the road, and the world had darkened into night. Behind them, the sky held a red glow, with intermittent flashes that might have been lightning in a more peaceful time. Ahead, the white dusty road was a moonlit ribbon.

It led to Le Cateau.

It was a quiet group that labored along that road. Liane could feel Sean's suffering, and hurt with each jolt of the makeshift cart. She also felt the horrors that lay behind them, beneath the fire-spangled sky over Mons. She thought of the young British officer, trying to remember his face, his reserved smile.

She could not summon his features to her mind's eye. Instead, there was only a sense of loss, of desolation.

Jo, too, was silent, not her usual enthusiastic self. Later, she would be able to describe the trip in the most perceptive detail: the way the dust hung in the night air, stirred by the now departed refugees; the scent of blood; Sean Murphy's blood as it soaked through a fresher dressing; the riven sky behind them, the thudding of shells, more felt than heard.

Maggie plodded along, deaf, dumb, and blind to everything around her. In her mind, she'd gone back to her wedding day; a little street thief, pregnant by an unknown man, standing beside the husband her adoptive mum, Nell, had won for her in a poker game.

He'd really lucked out, Sean told her later. 'Twas the luck o' the Irish.

Now, it looked like the luck of Sean Murphy was running out. Maggie had never been much for praying, and this was a helluva time to bother God, with a war going on, and all, but she'd be damned if it wasn't worth a try!

Dawn revealed the roadsides littered with debris. The fleeing refugees had lightened their loads. There were tipped barrows, a perambulator holding a tall wooden clock, pieces of worn luggage, bags of meal, a heavy Bible written in a foreign tongue—

The burden that slowed their own progress was not one that could be discarded. And there were still many miles to go.

The girls were wan, their faces gray with dust. Only Maggie seemed serene.

"It's gonna be awright," she said cheerfully. "I done made arrangments. Hell, I wouldn' be s'prised if 'E didden send us a angel er sump'n."

Jo and Denise exchanged worried glances, and Nora's freckled face puckered with concern.

"You wore out, Mum? Maybe we oughta rest awhile."

Maggie laughed. "Hell, no! Keep goin'. Somewheres up there, we're gonna find us a gen-u-wine mirrycal!"

And find it they did. A mile further along, something hulked against the horizon. It turned out to be a British truck with a high cab and a canvas-topped bed. The cab was empty.

It was Nora who spied the boots sticking out from beneath the truck. A dead man? She shivered at the thought, then gave one bootsole a hearty kick.

"You, under there! You awright?"

There was a muttered curse, and the hidden man inched himself out. He was slight in stature, his face smeared with grease, and he had a wrench in his hand. He stared at the women surrounding him, blankly. Hot damn! These were no Belgian peasants!

"Who the hell—"

"Watch yer language!" Nora spat. "They's ladies present! And I might ask th' same question! Who the hell are you!"

The man's blue eyes lit up as he grinned impishly. "A Yank—like yourself, I'd say!" He thrust out a grimy hand. "Lucky Looper, here. New York, Brooklyn."

Nora ignored the hand and looked at him with suspicion. "That ain't no Yank uniform!"

He grinned again. "Deal myself in wherever there's a fight." He jerked his head in the direction of Le Cateau. "Hell, somebody's gotta help them dumb bastards." His grin faded as he saw the wounded man in the cart. "Looks like you could use some help."

"Looks like you could, too," Nora said crossly. "Gimme that wrench."

Jerking the tool from his startled hand, she crawled under the truck.

Johnny (Lucky) Looper, soldier of fortune, adventurer, jokester and ladies man, found himself at a loss for the first time in his life. Four beautiful babes! Four of them! All sizes, shapes, and ages, and his for the taking! They didn't call him Lucky for nothing. Within seconds of introduction, he picked the redhead for himself. He liked his women tall and bosomy, and he'd bet her passions matched her hair. Still, the others weren't bad—

Except for the old lady. God, what a woman! Looked like someone from the red-light district for sure. Still, he bowed gallantly, greeting her in the Frenchie style.

"Hiya, ma'am. Pleased t'meetcha!"

To his shock, the woman began to blubber.

" 'E done it," she said, wiping her nose on her sleeve. "Damned ef 'E didn't! 'E sent us a bloomin' angel!"

Johnny Looper had never been called an angel before. Again, he was at a loss for words—a most unusual condition. Then the freckled girl crawled out from under the truck.

"Fixed it," she said briskly. "Let's go."

Before he could question the legality of carrying civilians in a British military vehicle, the women had loaded Sean Murphy into the covered bed, four of them climbing in beside him.

All but the redhead, who had seemed to stand a little apart from the crowd.

"D'ye mind if I rrride up front, wi' ye?" she asked, with a charming smile.

He did not.

He aided her into the cab, cranked the vehicle, then ran around to slide beneath the wheel.

"I do hope ye're gangin' to Le Cateau," she said in her soft, husky voice.

He was. But looking at that lovely face, at the petal white flesh revealed by the open throat of her demure gown, he lost his heart.

"Listen, doll," he said hoarsely, "just say the word. We're gonna go just as far as you wanna go!"

chapter 5

As they plowed along the dusty road toward Le Cateau, Denise filled her companion in on their adventures, telling him how they'd been trapped by German spies; how Sean Murphy was wounded. She played up her role in the affair a bit—after all, it hurt no one—and he looked at her with admiration.

Sir John French would want to hear this story. To think the damn Boche could infiltrate like that! And the girls were lucky to have got safely away. The thought of a lousy squarehead laying hands on the girl beside him made him sick.

"You know what they'd of done if they found you," he said, his voice hoarse. "A good-looking doll like you! God!"

Denise smiled deprecatingly. "I've a'ways thocht m'sel rrrather plain—"

Plain! This gorgeous creature? "You look like a movie star," he said in an awed voice.

Denise bounced on the seat with delight. "How did ye ken?" she asked. "That's why I'm gangin' to Califorrrnia! Tae be in pictures, wi' th' Gish sisters."

"Then you've already signed a contract?"

She smiled enigmatically, and shrugged an affirmative answer.

"I'll be damned! I did a stint in Hollywood once."

"Ye—ye did?"

He looked away from the road, his brown face crinkling in a devilish grin. "Stunt man. Climbing buildings, jumping off cliffs, running through fire. That kind of stuff—"

"Then y'ken soom o' the starrrs and producerrrs?" she asked excitedly.

It was his turn to smile and shrug.

Johnny (Lucky) Looper had never faced a camera in his life. And rarely had he ever told the truth. But if it impressed the lady—

He rounded a curve, and Denise slid against him. Gallantly, he put an arm around her, and, blushing, she let it remain.

Denise Dugal had always been the shining star of the Dugal household, indulged by her older brothers, worshiped by Rory, the younger one. Now, out in the wide world, insecure, a little frightened, she needed Lucky's admiration like a wilted flower cried out for water. He was not her type; too short, for one thing, but the warmth in his bold blue eyes made her feel important again. Safe. And he just might give her a list of contacts in the movie business—

"What the hell!"

Swearing, he released her. On the outskirts of Le Cateau was a barricade that hadn't been there when he left to take a truckload of ammo to Mons. British Tommies approached, their rifles at the ready, gaping at the red-haired girl beside him; the other feminine faces that peeped from beneath the canvas to see why the truck had stopped.

Lucky Looper slid from the vehicle and jerked his head toward the sergeant in charge, indicating that he wished to speak to him privately. There was no need to identify himself. He was known as the lucky Yank, the toughest, most daring, fighting man in the outfit. It was considered an honor to be paired with him. And they knew he'd volunteered to take a load of high explosives to the front.

Johnny Looper laconically rolled a cigarette as the sergeant waited, his eyes bugged with curiosity.

"Well, Looper? You're late. Thought you'd bought it."

The soldier cast a glance toward the truck. Four women, all beauts! "What did you do this time? Raid a bloody fancy house?"

"The ladies," Looper said, "were captured by German spies, and were facing a fate worse than death. The husband of the older woman is wounded." He paused modestly, allowing a puff of smoke to escape slowly through his lips. It formed a perfect ring. "Naturally, I did what I could. There were only three of the enemy. The ladies were—most grateful."

He asked to see Sir John French, at once, and they were waved on past the barricade. Within an hour, the story of Lucky Looper's latest exploit had spread through the camp. It seemed that he had taken on a small army of Germans, single-handed, and rescued a bevy of beautiful girls who had gratefully bestowed their favors on him in turn.

That was their Johnny Looper, their lucky Yank!

Sir John French, a pedantic gentleman, was not in the mood to deal with a nebulous report of German spies behind his lines. He had had great plans to smite the weaker side of the oncoming Boche. His army of one hundred thousand men formed a front hinged on the coal-mining center of Mons, extending east-west for twenty-seven miles. Unfortunately, the various parts of his army were not linked by telephone.

All hell had broken loose.

The Germans had swung wide, attacking the French Fifth Army all along its front. Its bridgehead guarding Namur at the strategic point where the Sambre joined the Meuse was destroyed. Both rivers were falling—and fordable.

Sir Charles Lanrezac of the French Fifth had requested that Sir John launch a flank attack at the enemy columns. Sir John, to protect his own position, refused. He agreed to hold at Mons for twenty-four hours, and his decision to retreat had come too late to stop the carnage.

This post, with the falling of Mons, would be overrun. The only recourse was to withdraw, though it was possible the Germans had already moved to his rear.

His headquarters had been plagued with a swarm of refugees. They had been hastily fed and sent on their way. This, however, was a different situation. These people were Americans. It was important to maintain good favor with people from the States, with this bloody war rapidly assuming such dimensions. Moving the troops out, it would be impossible to provide protection for a group of ladies—or hospital procedures for a badly wounded man.

It was best to move them on to Paris. And Private Looper was a good man to see them through.

Food was provided for the small group; a place to wash away some of the dust of the road. A harried surgeon took a look at Sean's wound, cleaned and rebandaged it.

"'E gonna be okay, Doc?" Maggie asked hoarsely.

"It's possible that he will lose that limb."

"But will 'e be okay?" she insisted.

The surgeon's face reddened. The angry red streaks fanning out from the man's wound did not bode well. Dash it all, he was trained for surgery in the field, not dealing with frantic wives.

Maggie, seeing the doubt in his face, decided to go back to praying. Her and Him was on pretty good terms, back there along the road from Mons. Hell, He worked one mirrycal, might ez well go fer broke—

Finally, they left Le Cateau.

The roads were packed with a gray horde: refugees with stricken faces, moving toward an unknown destination. Dully, silently, they plodded, paying no attention to the vehicle that repeatedly sounded its Klaxon.

Finally, Looper left the road, running over autumn gold verges, the truck jolting as if it would fly apart. Maggie pounded on the back of the cab until he stopped, going around to see what the touble was.

"Yer givin' Sean one helluva beatin'," she screeched. "Dammit, git back on the road."

He rolled a cigarette and glared bluely through its smoke. "Needs a doc, don't he? In a hurry?"

"Hell, yes!"

"Then take a look." He gestured toward the choked thoroughfare. "Make up yer mind. Do we go on, or sit and wait?"

"Keep goin'," she said in a subdued voice. "Yer the boss."

They paralleled the River Oise, passing through a
lovely, serene land of small cottages and walled gardens, mounded haycocks and fruit-filled orchards.
The owners of those pleasant little farms stopped
their work to watch the terrifying exodus from the
north, calling out for news. Aproned women fetched
water pails and ladles, trying to alleviate the misery
of a parched people, less fortunate than they.

Liane again felt a *frisson* of foreboding. She wanted
to call out to the good farm folks to join them, to run
for their lives. The neat farmhouses would become
blackened ruins, orchard and gardens blasted, walls
toppled—and among the devastation would lie the
dead—

"Gimme some water," Maggie said. "Think 'is
fever's up some."

Liane jerked from her nightmare world and obeyed.

As Liane, Nora, and Maggie hovered over Sean, Jo
took out the small notebook in her bag. In it, she had
scribbled her random thoughts. In the front was a list
of the places she wished to see in Paris, to write
about for her father's newspaper chain.

The Grand Opera House of Paris, with its eight
tiers of galleries for ropes and drops and backdrops;
its cavernous cellars, four stories underground where
a trapdoor opened to reveal a black, subterranean
river.

Notre Dame, the Louvre, the tomb of Napoleon,
with its purple sarcophagus incribed, cryptically, *ICI
GIT . . . POINT DU NOM*.

Here lies . . . No name.

She snapped the book shut, sighing. The excursion
that had begun so merrily had turned into a bad
dream. She was suddenly homesick, missing her
mother and father, her lame half-brother—

Conscious that someone had moved to sit beside her, she turned to look into Liane's lovely, Oriental eyes. They were filled with a soft compassion and understanding.

Dear Liane!

How could she have forgotten how close they'd always been, almost like sisters. Liane had always been there, confidante and friend, when she needed her. Not like—Denise, who would have left Uncle Sean to die, and who now was flirting madly with a strange young man. Jo's heart welled with love for her young cousin, once removed.

"Liane, I—I've been teasing you a lot. Belittling you, I guess. I didn't mean to do it. I don't know what got into me. I'm sorry—"

"It's all right," Liane said gently.

"No, it isn't! I guess—I guess it's because Denise is older, and you're so young—"

"I know."

Unaccountably, Jo burst into tears, putting her arms around Liane, holding her tightly.

"Please forgive me!"

"There's nothing to forgive. I—I am young, I guess. But I'm growing older every day."

It was true. This was Liane Wang's fourteenth birthday, and no one had remembered. It didn't matter, now that she and Jo were friends again.

In the cab of the ammunition carrier, Denise's head dropped. Finally, she slept, her blazing curls resting against Lucky Looper's shoulder. He drove more carefully, at last outdistancing the refugees who clogged the road, and picked up speed.

It had taken nine hours to make the journey from Le Cateau. Nine jolting hours of misery for Sean Murphy. But Looper could not be glad it ended.

He touched the cheek of the sleeping girl with a gentle finger.

"Wake up, doll. We made it. There it is."

He waved a hand to encompass the view before them, the dark, huddled mass pinpointed by winking lights—that was Paris.

chapter 6

Nearly a month after reaching Paris, Denise Dugal and Nora Murphy were escorted to a table at Maxim's, 3, rue Royale. They were waiting for Johnny Looper and a date he was bringing along for Nora.

Denise, sensing that every eye in the room was on them, was glad she'd shopped so carefully. Her chic green gown brought out the color of her eyes; the tub-shaped matching hat was larger, more ornate than any in the sumptuous room. She could only wish Nora looked a little less frumpy and plain.

They'd arrived in Paris in the clothes they stood in, and it was necessary to purchase new wardrobes. Nora could have bought anything she wished, and Denise would have been glad to aid her in her selections. But the girl refused to leave her father's side for more than a few minutes at a time. She wouldn't be here, now, if Maggie hadn't forced her, and the dress she wore was borrowed from Liane. It didn't suit her at all.

Denise sighed. There was no point i' greetin' o'er what couldna be helped. At least she had a date, and she could thank the present state of the war for that.

The battle to the north had become a stalemate. In the Vosges Mountains of Alsace-Lorraine, French troops had fallen back to concrete-and-steel fortresses built prior to the war. Between the forts, the poilus had dug rifle pits and trenches. Some two hundred to three hundred feet away, was a parallel line of German trenches.

Further west, the Germans had pressed toward Paris, only to be driven back at the Battle of the Marne. They rallied, digging in on the ridges behind the Aisne and Vesle rivers, again with French trenches opposing them. As the armies tried to outflank each other, the trenches stretched farther north, almost to the sea.

Jo Blaine kept up on all the action, explaining what she had gleaned from talking to people in the streets. It meant little to Denise, who was only bored with Paris, impatient for Sean Murphy to recover so they could be off to the States.

But the stalemate had provided one benefit. Johnny Looper had obtained leave. Today, he'd come to the Meurice, on the rue de Rivoli, where they were staying, and asked her out.

Maggie, conscious of her status as chaperone, refused to allow Denise to go alone with a strange man.

"Strrrange mon!" Denise had raged. "A mon that brocht us tae safety? Ye thocht he was an angel—"

"Sometimes, angels is men," Maggie said cryptically. "But men ain't no angels, if you git what I mean. Promised to look after ye, and by damn, I'm gonna do it, hell er 'igh water. One of the girls goes with ye, er ye don't leave this 'ere ho-tel!"

Denise would have chosen Jo. But under Maggie's rules, Jo Blaine had not been allowed to see the sights of Paris without a companion.

Jo's choice had been Liane.

That rankled with Denise. She had little liking for the abrasive Nora, but she'd asked her to come along. Though, there might be something to be gained there. Lucky said he'd find a friend for her. And that friend might be taller than Lucky Looper, someone more Denise's style. She'd foist Lucky off on Nora.

"Heavens," she said now, looking at Nora Murphy. "Canna ye summon oop soom sperrit? Ye leuk like ye've coom frae a burying!"

"I'll probably be goin' to one," Nora said morosely. "Me dad's sinkin' fast. Dammit, I should have stayed to the hotel with Mum!"

"Dinna be a silly fule! They wadna let him leave the hospital, if he wasna better—"

Denise stopped, evading Nora's steady gray gaze. It was true that Sean Murphy had been released, but it had probably been to free a bed. He'd been in a French hospital, and wounded soldiers filled the rooms and the corridors. Sean, abed at the Meurice, was conscious now, but gray-faced, emaciated, alternating between chills and fever.

"I still think he'd be best off at hame. If we teuk ship—"

"He would die on the way."

The girls sat in silence after Nora's pronouncement, Nora thinking of her father, Denise inwardly bemoaning the situation. It was true that Sean Murphy had little chance of survival, and though Denise felt bad about it, 'twas a pity the rest of them had to be trapped here in wartime Paris. It was not as gay as she had hoped, what with Maggie keeping such a tight rein on them all.

"There's Private Looper," Nora said suddenly.

Denise turned to look, her eyes widening when she saw his companion. He was in French uniform, an officer! And he was tall and handsome, with a small mustache and soft brown eyes.

The two men approached the table, Looper with his devilish grin, the young Frenchman looking stunned, as if he'd seen a vision. Denise was shocked when she realized that he was looking beyond her welcoming smile, his eyes fixed on Nora. When Lucky Looper made the introductions, Jacques Leceau gave Denise a cursory nod, then bent over Nora's hand.

"Mademoiselle," he said huskily. *"Enchanté de faire votre connaissance! Parlez-vous francais? Non?* Then we shall speak the *anglais—"*

The men seated themselves, and Leceau ordered expertly from the menu, then turned to Nora.

"You have the look of sadness," he said gently. "Is it that you have lost someone in the fighting? A husband, lover?"

Lover! Chaste, tomboyish little Nora had not even been courted before! Her freckled face reddened.

"Hell, no," she blurted. Then, wishing she had bitten her tongue, she said, "It's me dad."

Seeing his eyes darken with sympathy and understanding, the dam of her shyness was breached. She began to tell him of the flight from Brussels, the German spies, how Sean Murphy had been shot; the way the hospital had taken him in, treated his wound, then turned him out again.

"There are other hospitals," Jacques Leceau said thoughtfully.

"Full up," Nora said. "Ain't no room, nowhere."

She stopped, suddenly realizing that he was holding her hand. She jerked away, her face scarlet again.

"Pardon," he said in a quiet tone. "I forgot myself in my concern. And you are so very like someone I once knew."

Indeed she was. Jacques Leceau came from a wealthy French family. His parents were frequently abroad, and the lonely litle boy had been reared by a series of governesses, tutors, and maids.

The one he'd loved the most, more than his mother, had been a small Irish girl—a girl like this one, with hair like the sun on ripe, uncut hay; with eyes like gray mist, and a tilted, freckled nose.

Moira had looked like this when they sent her away, replacing her with a male tutor on Jacques's eighth birthday. She'd had this same expression, as if she were losing a loved one—

He would find a way to help Nora Murphy, Leceau vowed to himself. But, for now, he would make her smile!

He set out to be his most charming, and Nora, dizzy at his nearness, her hand in his again, was enchanted, bemused—in love.

Denise, piqued at his lack of attention, was furious. What a man like that could see in a girl of Nora's appearance and class, was a mystery. Unable to penetrate the invisible wall that seemed to surround the couple, setting them off into a world of their own, Denise turned to Johnny Looper. She flirted outrageously, hoping to attract Leceau's attention with fluttering lashes and inviting smiles.

Looper was tickled pink. He'd brought Leceau

along to cover his own inadequacies in French society. He could get by in the barracks or in the field. He could even order *un verre de bière,* and he was at home in some of the dives on the Left Bank. But, hell, he didn't know which wine went with what, or which fork to use—

Too, he'd wanted to show Denise he had aristocratic friends. But he'd been afraid the guy would take over his girl.

Encouraged by her flirting, he took Denise's hand. She let her fingers remain in his, hoping no one noticed. Nora had the full attention of a French officer, and she was left with an—an uncouth American, a private in the British army. A beat-up, cocky little man who was half a head shorter than she!

She was grateful when the food was served and she had an excuse to remove the hand he stroked suggestively.

Over coffee, Looper suggested they take in a show; see some of the nightlife of Paris.

Nora, torn between her worry over the dying man at the Meurice and the thought of perhaps never seeing Jacques Leceau again, said she felt she must return to the hotel.

"That, I will not allow," Leceau said firmly. "He will not regret that you have a few small hours of pleasure, and he is not alone."

"But, dammit, I can't—"

He put his finger to her lips, as if to seal off her refusal.

"You can," he said softly. "And you will." The finger moved up to her tilted nose, pressing it in an affectionate gesture.

Nora Murphy, drowning in warm brown eyes, felt a weakening in her knees, a disconcerting warmth spreading through her body. She fought for words to express her reasons for going home. Maggie might need her—

Denise, Johnny Looper's hand having moved under the table to capture her knee, was ready to leave.

"Dinna be a ninny, Nora," she said sharply. "'Tis nae fair tae spoil the nicht for us a'—"

Johnny Looper agreed. Voted down, Nora consented. To Looper's delight, Jacques Leceau picked up the check. Then they moved out into the Paris night.

Wartime Paris was thronged. It was too late to get theater seats, which should have been purchased in advance. They settled for a small chansonnier on boulevard de Clichy.

Leceau explained to Nora that chansonnier meant singer, and that such places were true Parisian institutions. The little theater was much like a tiny smoke-filled nightclub. Surrounding them were poilus and their girls, the French soldiers mostached, bearded, with long blue coats over red trousers. They were vivacious, noisy, determined to make the most of their leave.

The entertainment consisted of a fluid series of acts—singers ad-libbing their way through what appeared to be naughty songs; comedians, entertainers of all sorts. Their barbed, ribald wit was extremely Gallic, and the audience participated from time to time, roaring with laughter at the antics of those on stage.

Most of it was incomprehensible to Nora and Denise. Nora did not mind. It was enough to sit in blissful proximity to the young French officer; enough to feel the warmth of his shoulder touching hers; to watch his sensitive mouth twitch in a smile; to have his eyes meet hers in sharing a joke she didn't understand.

Denise was miserable. She didn't understand a word of what was going on, and Johnny Looper wasn't faring much better. Though she was by far the best dressed woman in the room, the recipient of admiring glances, there wasn't a man there she would have—

Except Jacques Leceau, who had no eyes for anyone but Nora Murphy.

To make things worse, Looper's hands had grown more insinuating in the darkness, and she could feel her body begin to react in a most peculiar way. Was it possible to want a man, without loving him?

She stiffened, pushing his hands away. There was no place in her life for a man like Johnny Looper. She didna intend tae be caught i' a trrrap o' her ain emotions!

They finally left the chansonnier and returned to the Meurice. Johnny Looper managed to place a kiss on Denise's cheek. It was cool against his lips as she said a formal good-night.

"Looky here, doll," he said, "this ain't no way to send a hero off to war! How about a real smackeroo, right here—"

He pursed his lips and closed his eyes in anticipation.

"I didna ken I was expected tae pay for my evening," she said in a chilly voice. "I hadna thocht o' rrromance!"

His furious blue eyes popped open. "Romance, hell! All I asked for was a kiss—!"

"I dinna kiss a mon if I maun bend doon tae do it."

Denise swept into her room, shutting the door. Looper spun to see if Nora and Leceau had witnessed his dismissal. They had not. They stood before the door to the suite Nora shared with her parents, oblivious to anything but each other.

Nora's heart was in her wide gray eyes. "It—it's been real nice," she whispered. "I had a real good time."

Leceau caught her hands in his, holding them against his heart. She could feel it beating, hammering within his muscled chest.

"I have only tomorrow," he said, his voice heavy with regret, "then I must rejoin my unit. Perhaps we might meet for *déjeuner?*"

Nora felt again that trembling sensation of weakness at his touch. This night had been like a dream, a beautiful dream. She would wake at his leaving. Perhaps it would be best to say good bye here, tonight, while everything was still perfect; something wonderful to remember.

"I don't think so," she said helplessly. "Me Dad—"

"Then I will see you if I have another leave?"

She didn't know where they would be staying. They'd wired home for funds, but had received no answer, thus must move to less expensive accommodations.

"I understand."

Leceau raised her hand to his lips and left her. Nora stepped inside the door and stood for a long time, hand against her cheek. The small suite she shared with her mum and dad was dark and quiet. They were both asleep.

She could let her tears flow unchecked, here, with no one to see. For one night, she had been a lady. And she had loved—

When Jacques Leceau and Johnny Looper parted, Looper headed for a sleazy district of the city. His passions inflamed by a red-haired girl who teased and didn't follow through, he went to the sordid apartment of a young art student—who would.

Leceau had a different destination. He made his way to the luxurious Hotel Claridge. If what he heard were true, there might be something he could do for Nora Murphy. More than anything in the world, he wanted to watch over her, to take care of her for the rest of her life.

But this was wartime, and life was uncertain. She had been wise in saying adieu after this one perfect evening.

There was, however, no reason he couldn't try to help her. And it would give him the opportunity to see her one more time.

chapter 7

Nora Murphy was to have little rest that night. She got into her flannel nightdress and into bed, wanting only to go over the wonderful evening in her mind. And then her father woke, lapsing into the intermittent chills and fevers that seemed to be increasing in their frequency.

She and Maggie worked over him, alternately sponging his burning body and covering him against the tremors that rattled his bones.

It was dawn before his seizures eased, and Nora could return to bed.

At seven in the morning, there was a pounding at the door of the Murphy suite. Maggie, clad in a voluminous nightgown, her rouged face raddled in the dawn, padded to the door and poked her head around it. She blinked at the sight of a young French officers in a trim uniform.

"This 'ere's a helluva time to go wakin' folks up,"
she growled. "Gotcha a wrong number, sonny! Dammit, go check at th' desk!"

Leceau was taken aback, but only for a moment.
He bowed graciously.

"Madame—"

Maggie's eyes narrowed suspiciously. "You sellin'
somethin'? I ain't buyin'!"

The young Frenchman laughed nervously. "No,
madame. I wish to speak with Mademoiselle Murphy."

Maggie's glowering inspection was replaced by a
knowing grin. She recalled that, as they worked over
Sean, Nora mentioned her date had been with a
Frenchie. And here he was, all hot an' bothered, at
this ungodly hour!

Mebbe she'd been sellin' Nora short.

"Nora," she bawled, "gitcher butt in 'ere. Somebuddy
to see yuh—"

Nora struggled from the deep sleep of exhaustion,
unable to come fully awake. Her first thought was of
her father. She stumbled to the door of her room,
barefoot, clad in her long white flannel gown, hair
rumpled. Stopped in her tracks at sight of Jacques,
she refused to believe her eyes.

"Who," she whispered inanely, "who—"

Maggie's eyes crinkled, and she winked at the
newcomer. "Just one a' them damn frawgs," she
boomed coyly.

Nora drew a shuddering breath, then escaped back
into the privacy of her room. Leceau was left to wait
uncomfortably in Maggie's presence until she returned,
decently dressed, her face pink.

She apologized for her previous appearance.

"You looked very beautiful," Jacques Leceau said
sincerely. He meant it. Just so had young Moira

looked when she appeared in the night to quiet a small boy's terrors; to smoothe his brow with her capable, square little hands; to erase his nightmares with fanciful tales of strange and wonderful things—

The sight of her had driven his errand from his mind. Reluctantly, he tore his gaze from her and launched into the reason for his early arrival.

He had located a hospital where Sean Murphy would be cared for.

Maggie sat down heavily, her eyes welling, jowls quivering.

"This ain't jest a damn windy?" she asked finally. "You sartin-sure?"

"I have already made arrangements, if you agree."

"Ef I agree? Hell's bells! Right now I'd settle fer a damn vet!"

"The physicians will be women."

Maggie was suddenly a mask of indecision, and Leceau held up a staying hand.

"Let me explain."

A Women's Hospital Corps was on its way from London. They would be working with the French Red Cross. The luxurious new Hotel Claridge was being transformed into a hospital, workmen being aided by a group of Belgian refugees occupying an upper floor.

There would be space there for Maggie and the girls. If they wished, they could volunteer for nursing duties and thus defray the cost of their lodgings. He had talked with Red Cross representatives, and a bed was being prepared for Sean Murphy now—

"'Ow we gonna git 'im there?"

Leceau flushed. "I took the liberty of providing an ambulance. It is waiting at the rear entrance—"

Maggie was instantly on her feet. "Nora, wake up

them girls. Tell 'em to get their butts in gear. We're gonna git this show on th' road!"

Within the hour, Sean Murphy was taken, by litter, to the Hotel Claridge. The structure was in a state of turmoil as workmen raced against time. The windows were still whitened, the walls still wet with paint. Plaster and debris covered the floors. Everywhere, there was a sound of hammering. Sean Murphy was put to bed in a corner of one of the great salons on the ground floor, a young French Red Cross nurse hovering over him.

She did not speak English, and Leceau translated her words for Maggie.

Sean Murphy was a very sick man. But Madame Murphy was not to worry. He would be made well, as soon as the lady doctors came from England.

"I be damned," Maggie said in a voice choked with tears, "ef 'E ain't gone an done me a mirrycal again."

Maggie's euphoria was such that, when Leceau requested the pleasure of Nora's company for the remainder of the day, she practically shoved her into his arms.

Nora protested in vain. Then she said, "I will see if Denise—"

"Denise, hell! You two go on, 'ave yerselfs a 'igh old time."

"But you said—"

"I know what I said," Maggie told her testily. "But Jack, 'ere, looks like a gennulman, and you ain't gonna git in no trouble in the daytime!"

Nora, dazed, found herself out in the street on the arm of Jacques Leceau.

Instinctively, he knew that much of Paris would be of little interest to a girl like Nora. With her simple directness, she would view ostentatiousness as fool-

ish waste; historical sites as something over and done
with; artistic creations poor replicas of nature.

He took her, instead, on one of the little river
steamers known as *bateaux mouches*, fly boats. The
steamer moved along the Seine from station to station, making brief stops at floating landing stages.

As they glided across the water, he pointed out the
beautiful facades of the Louvre and the Tuileries; the
tower of Notre Dame; la Tour St.-Jacques; the domes
of the Institut and the Pantheón.

Finally, with a basket containing cheese, bread,
and wine, they paused at the Pont Neuf, the "New
Bridge," actually older than any of the others spanning the Seine.

Behind the statue of Henry of Navarre, steep steps
led down into a lovely, peaceful garden, the Jardin
Henri IV. The triangular little park was once a separate island, a sandspit called l'Isle des Treilles, joined
to the larger island of La Cité in 1604 when the
foundations of the bridge were laid.

Jacques explained all this to Nora, smiling to himself as she was more interested in a silver fish that
broke water at the end of an old fisherman's line, and
a burst of late-blooming wild flowers at the base of a
gnarled tree.

Finding, a secluded corner, he spread a checked
cloth on the fall grass, and they sat down together to
enjoy the picnic he'd provided.

Warmed by the wine, Nora lost some of her shyness. She was soon telling him about her family and
their attachment to Tamsen, Em, and Arab, descen-
dants of Scott McLeod; of Nell, her long-dead adopted
grandmother who, along with Tamsen, had operated
a brothel; how Nell had found her own mum, Maggie,
taking her away from a life as a street waif and

pickpocket. She told him of Nell's first husband, Dusty, whom she'd never met, but who had made a lady of Nell. Nell's second spouse, Sim Blevins, well-to-do former crimp—

"Crimp? I do not know this word."

Nora blushed. "He shanghaied crews for ships. You know!"

Leceau did not, but it sounded fascinating. He moved closer, slipping an arm about Nora.

"Tell me about your father. What does he do?"

Since Nell's death, Sean and Maggie had cared for the two widowed McLeod sisters, Arab and Em. "But he's not really me dad, you know."

Leceau sat upright. "Then—where is your natural father?"

Nora was scarlet again. "Damned if I know."

Leceau shouted with laughter at her forthrightness. It was so beautiful, this honesty of hers, so refreshing after his experience with French coquettes. So like Moira.

He put a finger beneath her chin, tipping her face to his. "You are much like a girl I once knew," he said huskily. "Someone I loved—and lost a long time ago."

Nora's heart plummeted. She hadn't thought of other women in his life.

"Did she—is she dead?"

"*Non*. She just—had to go away."

"I—I'm sorry."

"Do not be." He grinned wryly. "It is all well, now. I have recovered. At the time, I was only eight years old."

Her heart soared again, and she leaned into his encircling arm while he told her of Moira, the peaceful haven of her love for a frightened little boy.

"You have those same qualities, Nora."

"But you're grown up now. And I don't reckon you're scared of nothing—"

"You are very wrong in that," he said moodily. "Perhaps I am even more afraid. Afraid of what this war will bring; that I might never see this garden again; afraid of—losing you!"

She lifted gray eyes to haunted brown ones, her lips slightly parted in surprise at what he'd said. Then his mouth was on her own, tender, sweet, seeking—and finding an answer.

And finally he rested his head against her breast and she held him, keeping him safe against his fears, as Moira had.

It was dusk when they returned to the Hotel Claridge, and nearly time for Leceau to rejoin his men. There had been no talk of future plans. Leceau had, almost superstitiously, avoided it. And Nora understood.

At the door of the hotel, he held her close for a moment, as if drawing on her strength. Then he was gone.

Nora did not look after him. Instead, she entered the structure, shoulders sagging as the great door closed behind her.

He needed comforting. She had been the comforter. When all the time, it was she who was so terribly, desperately, afraid.

chapter 8

The time of waiting for the British doctor-ladies to arrive was a busy one. Denise was petulant, missing the luxury of the Meurice, certain that they were going to be stuck in this madhouse of construction forever. Doggedly, she mopped and scrubbed at the French Red Cross representative's direction. Just like hame, she thought, wringing a mop into a bucket. Just like hame!

Nora, expert with hammer and nail, worked along with the Belgians, converting the ladies' cloakroom into an operating theater. Liane pasted paper over the glass partitions separating the great salons. Jo set up a filing system in a small cubbyhole, converting it into an office to handle records.

Maggie remained at Sean's side, alternately cursing the British ladies for taking so long to arrive— and fearing they would. She wasn't certain she trusted female doctors. But, she supposed, anything was better than nothing. Sean had been weakened further by the move. His flesh was dry to the touch, parchment over bone. His eyes were deeply sunken, and most of the time he didn't know where he was.

"You gonna be awright," she kept telling him. "Soon as them wimmen git 'ere."

One morning she was sponging his wasted body when she was suddenly conscious of someone behind her. She spun, one hand yanking up Sean's sheet to cover him.

Facing her was a trim woman in a greenish gray uniform, a small cloth hat fringed with a veil of the same color.

Maggie thrust out her jaw. "'Oo the hell are you?" she asked truculently. "Ain't a sick man got no privassy?"

The newcomer met her angry gaze with steady eyes. "Not if he is my patient," she said in a chilly British voice. "I am Dr. Louisa Garrett Anderson. I have just arrived. If you will excuse me—"

She inclined her head toward the door of the salon in a gesture of dismissal.

"Now, lissen, dammit, 'e's my 'usbin'—"

Maggie's voice trailed off and she backed away. Dr. Garrett pulled off her gloves and was bending over the sick man.

Meekly, Maggie left the room.

The hotel was full of women, all in the same uniform type of clothing, carrying luggage, boxes of medical supplies. One of them, giving orders, looked like she might be the boss.

Maggie approached her.

"I'm Maggie Murphy," she said. "Got me a sick man, 'ere. You in charge?"

The woman, ticking off items on a clipboard, nodded without looking up. "I am Dr. Flora Murray," she said absently, "administrator. Can I help you?"

"That there Doc Anderson. She any good? Hell, she jest barged in an' took over like she—"

Cool blue eyes stared at Maggie from either side of an aristocratic nose.

"She is the best, madam. Our chief surgeon, and a most capable one. Now, as you can see, I am quite occupied."

Maggie backed away and stood waiting helplessly outside the door to the great salon. The lady doctors from London moved around her like a fluttering of cabbage moths, efficiently setting up their new hospital.

She was still standing there when Dr. Anderson emerged, bypassing her, hurrying to Dr. Murray. They spoke in low tones, and Maggie caught only snatches of the conversation.

"It is much too early. We need several hours—"

Dr. Anderson shook her head. "It must be done immediately."

"But you should rest. At least a cup of tea—"

"You forget, Flora! As a member of the medical profession, I insist—"

"Very well."

The administrator, Flora Murray, snapped out several names. When those she called stood before her, she began to give orders, and Maggie heard these clearly.

They were to prepare the operating room, immediately. Surgical instruments were to be sterilized. This person was to assist Dr. Anderson. That one—

The room began to spin around Maggie. Dr. Anderson, returning to her patient, saw his wife's blotched face and dazed expression. She paused, led

Maggie to a chair, and seated her, talking to her in a quiet, straight-forward way.

Sean Murphy's leg must be amputated. There was infection in the bone below the knee. Without surgery, the infection would spread throughout his body.

Maggie flinched under the impact of her words, her bulk seeming to shrink. "Wot's 'is chances, Doc? I mean, takin' it off an' all—?"

"None too promising," the woman said honestly. "If he does recover, the process will be slow."

Maggie's head bowed, her hands tightening into pudgy fists. Finally she looked up, her green-grape eyes dull with misery.

"Git on with it," she said hoarsely. "An', Doc—do a damn good job, willya?"

"I shall do my best," Dr. Louisa Garrett Anderson's voice was gentle. "I promise you."

There was no time to sit beside Sean's bed, to hold his hand and tell him how much she loved him. Maggie watched, quivering inside, as Sean Murphy was lifted to a litter and carried into the one-time cloakroom that was now an operating theater.

The door closed against her.

As word spread throughout the hotel, the girls joined her. Nora's face was white, freckles prominent, her gray eyes glazed with tears.

"Oh, Mum! What if he—" Her voice died away.

"'E's gonna be awright," Maggie told her. "Now go find yerself some work to do. Them folks need 'elp movin' in."

"But, Mum—?"

"Dammit," Maggie said testily, "I druther set 'ere by meself. Got enough t'think about, without you girls a-caterwaulin'. Now git!"

She glared around at them: at Nora, Liane, Jo, and Denise. "Go make yerselfs useful!"

They left reluctantly. When they had gone, Maggie leaned her head against the operating room door. She could hear nothing but her own heartbeat as it shook her heavy body; her own breath, short, gasping as she breathed through her mouth, her nose clogged with tears.

She'd never told the shrimpy little Irisher how much she loved him. Mebbe there wasn't no words fer it. Sean had always just been there, standing by her when she was delivered with another man's child, taking that child as his own.

And Maggie took him for granted. Her adoptive father, Sim Blevins, had seemed to be the man of the family; tough old Sim, with his bearlike body and peg leg. When Sim died, her mum, Nell, had been solid as a rock, moving into his place; someone to lean on.

She thought of that now, the way Nell stood up to her tragic loss.

All her life, Maggie had patterned herself on her adopted mother; trying to look like her, talk like her, be her if she could.

And now she knew she'd fallen short of the mark. She was made of weaker stuff. If Sean Murphy died, she couldn't live without him—

"Oh, hell," she gasped, wiping her face on her sleeve. "Hell an' damnation!"

She wished they'd never come to this bloody country, that they was 'ome, back in their small apartment in Em Courtney's 'ouse!

She stiffened. Did she hear Sean groan? There was a scurrying sound in there. Please, Gawd, don't let nothin' go wrong—

"God! She'd plumb fergot to ast 'Im about this thing. 'E stepped in afore, so why not now?

" 'Ere goes," she whispered grimly. "It's me, 'ere, Maggie Murphy. 'Ate like hell t' bother Ye again, but it's a 'mergency sitchiashun. Reckin I ain't been no bloomin' angel, but Ye pull Sean outen this, an' I'll never do nothin' but good th' rest o' me life! Deal?"

She paused, listening. Seemed like there oughta be an answer. But she heard nothing, just her own heartbeat and shallow breathing.

Waiting outside the operating room, Maggie grew old on the outside, cheeks sagging, eyes dull, shoulders drooped. But on the inside, the layers of years peeled away. Once again, she was the skinny frightened little waif Nell Wotherspoon had taken into her arms and her heart.

Except now, there was no Nell to watch over her, to love her, to protect her.

Nell was long dead. Sim Blevins had passed on. And now she might lose the man who, though she hadn't allowed herself to see it, was the most precious thing in her life.

She began to blubber, hands to her face, tears spurting through her fingers.

"Lemme 'ang onta 'im a little while longer," she prayed. "They's things I gotta tell 'im!"

The door to the operating room opened, and two of the gray-green-clad newcomers backed from the room, carrying one end of a litter.

Maggie stared in agony as the litter slowly emerged. Sean's foot made a hump in the sheet that covered it—only one foot. Maggie scrubbed at her eyes. The sheet dropped off below the amputation, and there was a small bloodstain.

There was a pause as the women got a gresh grip.

Then she could see Sean's shoulders, and at last his face. It was gray, his mouth bloodless, his eyes closed.

Maggie went down into spinning darkness.

Sean Murphy was dead.

chapter 9

For once, Maggie Murphy was wrong. And she was happier about it than anything that had ever happened in her life.

He lived. Sean Murphy lived.

True, he hovered on the brink. But, as Maggie said, "Where there's life, there's 'ope!"

She settled herself beside him, blind and deaf to anything but the sound of his breathing, the lift of the sheet over his slat-thin ribs, while chaos boiled around her.

A doctor at the American Hospital at Neuilly had sent over a batch of badly injured British officers. They arrived before the remainder of the corps' baggage was extricated from French Customs. Beds and pallets rapidly filled the salons of the converted hotel, converting them into gigantic wards. All through the night, nurses and doctors worked over the wounded while orderlies and volunteers unpacked and sorted equipment.

Jo, Liane, Denise, and Nora were among those volunteers. Nora, still pale with worry, opened crates and boxes while Jo checked off lists, and Denise and Liane put supplies in their designated places.

Denise pushed back her damp hair and looked down at her soiled gown.

"I hope we dinna hae tae be here lang," she said petulantly.

Nora fixed her with a cold eye. "We'll be here as long as me dad is ailing. Dammit, if you don't want to help, go to bed! We don't need the likes of you!"

"Ye dinna ken what I'm like!" Denise burst out, her eyes welling with tears. "I hae nae intention—"

"Then keep yer damn trap shut!"

The girls squared off at each other: the lovely redhead's eyes flashing; Nora's face like freckled marble. Jo stepped in between.

"This is silly," she said angrily. "We're all tired and worried, but we've got a job to do! Denise—those men out there—what if one of your brothers was hurt! Wouldn't you want someone to—"

"My brothers are tae auld tae be callit up!" Denise said sulkily. "They are hame and family men—"

"Not Rory."

"Rory is tae yoong!"

"But he's growing older. If this war lasts another year or two—"

"It canna!" Now, Denise was pale. The thought of her little brother in uniform, wounded, was like a knife-thrust. "I' any case, I hae nae intention of slacking my worrrk! There's nae harrrm i' wishing!"

"Ladies!"

A voice from the doorway of the supply closet

stopped them. The administrator, Dr. Murray, was regarding them crisply.

"We are shorthanded in the wards. Have any of you had any nursing experience?"

"A wee bit," Denise said reluctantly.

"Then come with me." Flora Murray paused and looked at Liane. "Some of the men are feverish, thirsty. Perhaps you would see to it that they have water?"

The girls followed her to one of the large wards. A small woman in the gray-green uniform the doctors wore called out to them.

"Over here. I need some assistance—"

Denise went to her, feet dragging as she saw what was at the end of an arm the woman held. The patient's hand was a pulpy crushed mass, with splinters of bone protruding.

"This must come off," the doctor said briskly. "Will you help me?" She lifted her eyes for a moment, seeing Denise's pallor. "You are not a fainter, are you? Can you do it?"

Denise drew a deep shuddering breath. The patient was only a boy. He looked no older than Rory.

"I can do it," she said.

Liane was immobile for a moment, stunned at the sights, sounds, and smells around her. Bristle-faced young men, many of them stripped almost bare beneath the nurses's searching hands, moaned and groaned, gasped and whimpered. The odor of blood and infection was overpowering, overriding the harsh scent of hospital disinfectant. Only a whispered request for water galvanized her into action.

She hurried to the supply room and picked up an oddly shaped pitcher, filled it, and ran back to the man's side. She was pouring water into a cup when a passing nurse stopped her.

"What in the world are you doing! My word—"

"He asked for a drink," Liane said defensively. "Isn't he supposed to have—"

"Not from that," the nurse said, scandalized. "That is for elimination!"

The roar of laughter from patients in nearby beds sent Liane from the room, her cheeks crimson. It took a great effort of will to find a proper pitcher and return. She hoped Denise hadn't seen her make a fool of herself—

Denise had seen only a hand, amputated, dropped into a bucket—to be thrown away like so much refuse. She looked toward the far end of the room where Maggie sat, her bulk shielding Sean Murphy from view.

She hadn't thought of what a terrible thing it must be. Sean Murphy's leg had gone the way of that hand. Part of a human being. Poor Maggie! Poor Nora! She regretted the hard words they'd had earlier, wishing she could call them back.

As the days passed, Sean lay silent, still closer to death than life. Maggie sat beside him, often praying in her own inimitable way. The girls were all pressed into nursing service as more and more men were brought in.

They were often in shocking state. Some of them had lain on platforms in tiny railway stations for days. Others had been placed in barns, roofless sheds, lying in rows of misery on dirty straw. When they arrived at the Hotel Claridge, they were dirty, starving, wasted, burning with fever; their wounds septic.

"Blimey," one of the emaciated Tommies said to Liane, seeing a pretty face and, above him, the gilded ceiling of the hotel, "I've been and died and gone to 'eaven, I 'ave."

The young man did die. Liane wept, but not for long. There was no time. Soldiers were being sent in from all over France and the French empire: Bretons, Alsatians, Provençals, Moroccans, Zouaves. They suffered and sometimes passed from life, unable to understand the comforting words of those who cared for them.

Mingled with the grimness of illness and death were brighter events. Strangers brought gifts of money and warm clothing to the hospital; shopkeepers sent their wares; flower women brought bouquets. Silk-hatted, tailcoated elderly men often aided in carrying stretchers. Emotional Parisians turned out to reward their heroes in every possible way.

Short, pale M. Casanova, the hotel's manager, greeted every arriving convoy of patients gallantly and assiduously, as though he were hosting a party of tourists.

His eyes were often filled with tears, however, and his trim black beard quivered with the trembling of his chin.

Subjected to more horror than they knew existed, the girls worked long hours, catching snatches of sleep at intervals. The differences they'd had earlier were now forgotten.

"Remember the patient we worked with this morning?" Jo asked Denise. "The one with the—the thigh wound?"

Denise remembered.

"Did it bother you?" Jo asked. "Seeing him like that? You know what I mean."

Denise did. The patient had been young, handsome, well built—and, of necessity, exposed. This

sort of thing had been the greatest shock to the
well-brought-up young women. But they had grown
used to it by now.

"Do ye mean, did I hae rrromantic thochts?"
Denise asked. "Tae be honest, I didna. I thocht ainly
of the job tae be doone."

"Me, too," Jo said ruefully. "Oh, Denise, do you
think we'll ever feel romantic again?"

Denise's eyes welled with tears, and Jo's watered
in sympathy. They put their arms around each other
and were sobbing when Liane came in. She looked
downcast, and they reached out and drew her into
their circle and she, too, began to cry.

Nothing she'd done all day had been right. Just
now, she'd put a perfect cast—on the wrong leg. Dr.
Murray had given her a terrible scolding.

It was good to let go, to feel a closeness with the
other girls.

In a short while, they pulled themselves together.
Their weeping session had felt good, a safety valve.
Now they could laugh at their silly behavior.

It was a good thing that they'd had those few
moments to let down. Another convoy was coming
in.

chapter 10

By late November, Sean Murphy had improved enough that he could be moved from the salon-ward to the living quarters upstairs. He was reduced to a shadow of his former self, but his stump was healing though his spirits were low.

"Ye deserve more'n half a man, Maggie, me darlin'," he said in a somber tone. "I wasn't all that much t'start with, ye know. If ye'd rather find a body with two good legs—"

"'Ee tryin' t'git ridda me?" Maggie asked fiercely. "'Ee knot-headed little bastid! Mebbe one o'them lady doc's tryin' t'cut me out?"

Sean raised himself to a sitting position in his bed, wincing in pain as he did so.

"Ye know better'n that! Sure, an' there's never been nobody but you!"

"Then what the hell we argifying about?"

"It's just—t'ain't fair, you bein' saddled with a cripple."

Maggie gave him a baleful glare. "'Ee callin' Sim Blevins a cripple?"

Sean looked blank. The old man who had become Nell's husband and Maggie's adoptive father in the process had a peg leg. Yet he was so strong, so rugged, he'd never thought of him as handicapped.

"Gawd, no!"

"Don't cuss," Maggie said sternly. "An' now 'ee done spoke yer piece, lemme get my two cents' worth in. What I'm tryin' t'say, is wimmen ain't like men. Diffrent things give 'em—uh—'eartburn. 'Member Jack Smaul, to home? Ears like a damn rabbit. Reckin his wife likes ears. Me, I got a thing fer peg legs. Makes me go all weak in th' knees, like a sappy kid."

"Maggie, you don't mean that—"

"Try me!" She blew her nose with a honking sound. "Jest try me!"

Sean Murphy broke into a slow grin. "Sure, an' maybe I'll take you up on that." He caught at her pudgy hand and pulled her down beside him. "Never managed with one leg afore—"

"Sean Murphy! Blimey! 'Ee'll 'urt 'eeself!" Maggie, in her emotion reverted to the speech of her childhood.

Murphy buried his face in the soft rolls of her neck, loving her, soothing her, until at last he had his way. And he discovered he'd lost nothing that really counted. He was all man, again.

"I wonder what that hoity-toity Dr. Elizabeth Garrett Anderson would say about what 'ee just done," Maggie said, much later.

Sean Murphy managed a perfect, Irish leer. "I dunno. I'll give 'er a try, an' ask her opinion."

Maggie giggled at the thought of the starched lady surgeon in her position.

"Try it, 'ee damn fool, an' th' doc'll need a doc."

Sean grinned to himself. Maggie had been wrong in only one thing she said: that cock-and-bull about wimmen being different from men. Personally, he liked them like Maggie, soft and full and round. If all men liked the same kind of female, they'd all want his wife.

In the meantime, he was beginning to feel a lot better about himself. All his married life, he'd kind of been in Sim Blevin's shadow.

Hell, with all he had going for him now, and a peg leg, too, he'd be irresistible!

As Sean Murphy recuperated, he seemed to become more masculine, more in charge. Maggie was quieter in her happiness, her cheeks beginning to bloom beneath the rouge she still assiduously applied. Dr. Anderson managed to see him daily and was pleased with his progress. If Maggie eyed her with occasional suspicion, refusing to allow her to examine Sean alone, only Murphy knew why.

Maggie was jealous, and he reveled in it.

In the wards, the tempo had slowed somewhat: the two opposing armies at an impasse. In the field, the soldiers spent their time digging communication trenches; dugouts for command posts, supply storage and telephone switchboards that linked the frontline commanders with supporting artillery and commanders farther to the rear. Many of the casualties were men sent on patrol, to try to obtain information about the enemy. Others were shot while stringing barbed wire in huge coils to stop surprise enemy attacks. Those who died in the trenches were usually victims of high-explosive shells that churned the earth into a sea of mud.

These men were beyond help.

Those who were brought in were verminous, filthy, and often almost mindless from the horrors they had endured; memories of the sleek fat rats that fed on corpses in no-man's-land brought more than one patient awake and screaming in the night.

They spoke little of their experiences, however. It was as if, by ignoring them, the ugly happenings would go away and life would be beautiful again. Young boys with old faces, the patients flirted with the pretty girls who tended them; who brought them food, drink, and medications, and helped them write letters home.

Jo, with her proficiency in languages, assisted the poilus and French officers. Liane wrote missives for the British officers and Tommies. The text of the letters varied little with nationality. Parents were informed their sons were well—and happy. Young husbands wrote yearning, stilted notes to wives and children. Lovers blushingly declared their affections for their special girls.

Christmastime approached, and with it a flurry of activity. There was no longer fuel to serve the five huge boilers in the hotel basement, and the wards were freezing. In spite of their discomfort, the lady doctors from London were determined to make the holiday a festive occasion.

Allied flags were fastened to many beds. In one ward, the Union Jack was fastened to a large blanket, with "The Flag of Freedom" embroidered beneath it. Packages had come in for some of the long-term invalids; jars of marmalade from Britain; woolen scarves for men who might never walk the streets of Paris again; rounds of cheese from French farms; warm gloves for a boy who'd lost a hand.

As though the two opposing armies had recognized the season, few new patients were brought in. The girls were given leave from duty on Christmas Eve.

In the rooms Maggie, Sean, and Nora occupied, the spirit of Christmas reigned supreme. Nora had found a tree, decorating it with yarn, candles, and tiny, tinkling silver bells she'd found in a little shop. A small charcoal fire burned in the fireplace, giving out a delightful warmth. Maggie had set a long table down the middle of the room. The usual fare of stringy boiled beet, turnips, and cabbage was present. But, in addition, Maggie had commandeered the hotel kitchen, making a gigantic plum cake.

As Maggie finished the final preparation, the girls clustered about the fire, warming toes and noses that had felt the chill for a long time. Each was lost in her own thoughts.

Jo and Liane were thinking of home. On Christmas Eve, there was always a family gathering at Em Courtney's. Em would play carols, and they would sing.

Denise, too, was thinking of home. Her mother kept Christmas in the American way. Her older brothers would all be there with their wives and children. And young Rory—

I do believe I'm hamesick, she said to herself in amazement. Her eyes filled with tears.

Nora did not think of home. She thought of a young Frenchman with warm brown eyes; a boy-man, who needed comforting. Where was he this night? Somewhere in a damp trench, eating iron rations, watching the burst of shells against a dark sky?

And did he think of her?

"Come an' git it," Maggie shouted cheerfully, "afore I throw it out!"

Laughing at her familiar words, the girls moved toward the table, Nora and Maggie helping Sean balance on his crutch until he reached his place at the head.

"Merry Christmas, ladies," he beamed.

Maggie's face broke up, quivering with emotion as she thought of how sad this Christmas might have been.

And there was a knocking at the door.

"I'll git it," Maggie said briskly. "You all set." But Nora was ahead of her. She swung the door wide and made a small stricken sound.

"Jacques!"

Jacques Leceau, with a two-day leave, stood there, his arms laden with packages.

"*Joyeux Noël*," he said to the room at large.

But his eyes were only for Nora.

chapter 11

On Christmas morning, Jacques Leceau called for Nora. The day had dawned crisp and bright, and he looked with approval at the small girl in a blue coat with coordinated scarf and mittens. The garments had been gifts from Sean and Maggie. Jo had selected them, and they suited Nora perfectly.

More important, Nora felt beautiful, today.

They left the hotel and paused, realizing they'd made no plans for this wonderful day—except to be together.

Perhaps the Jardin Henry IV? Where they had first discovered their love?

Nora shook her head. The little park was a special place. If they returned now, it would be cold, the sun not reaching its warm fingers into the shadows. The leaves would have fallen, dead and leathery, on frosted grass. It would be best to remember the way it

was, to hold that memory safe in her mind. They had
so little time.

Instead, they just walked, still a little shy with
each other. Heads turned to watch the handsome
French officer and the small girl with hair the color
of ripe straw. Parisians loved lovers, and especially
now in wartime when life could come so quickly to
an end.

Little, black-shawled peasant women smiled at
them; men in baggy trousers beamed around their
curved black pipes. Passing soldiers looked at Jacques
with envy. A new young widow turned to hide her
tears.

Jacques and Nora saw only each other.

They wandered, hand in hand, along the rue de
Rivoli, stopping to view the gilded equestrian statue
of Jeanne d'Arc.

"She must have been much like you," Jacques said
tenderly.

Nora gave him a flashing smile. She had no idea
who the woman was, but it had evidently been a
compliment.

They moved from historic place to historic place.
In the garden of the Palais Royal, they saw the
statute of Camille Desmoulins, depicting his speech
that led to the destruction of the old Bastille—and
fired the fuse of the French Revolution.

Nora listened as Jacques talked, her mind not on
his words, but on his sensitive mouth, remembering
the way if felt on her own.

We have only today, she thought. Just today. She
shivered and he put an arm around her.

"Are you cold, my love?"

"No," she whispered. "No. But let's walk on."

Every step they took sounded a message in her ears.

Only today!

Jacques Leceau was equally troubled. He'd snatched at the first leave he could get, hurrying to Paris, certain that Nora would have already gone. And he had found her! It had been pleasant last night, invited to join her family at dinner; doubly pleasant for a man who'd never really known a loving home. But he'd wanted Nora all to himself.

And now they were together, but there was no place he could hold her, tell her he loved her—

And even if there were, it would be wrong. Death had come close to him many times these last weeks, and he could foresee no future. He could not even ask Nora to wait for him. It would be unfair.

He broke from his reverie and looked at their surroundings. "This is 'Le Théâtre Français,'" he told Nora, "the National Conservatory of Dramatic Art. And this," he moved closer to another sculpture, "is the poet Alfred de Musset."

Nora traced the lines engraved on the pedestal with a mittened hand.

Rein ne nous rend si grands qu'une grande dolour—

Le plus desesperes sont les chants les plus beaux—

Et j'en sais d'immortels qui sont de pures sanglots.

"Is this one of his poems? What does it say?"

Jacques cleared his throat. "It translates, roughly:

'Nothing can make us greater than a great, great grief—

The sweetest songs are those of hopelessness—

And I know some immortal ones that are pure sobs of deep distress.'"

Nora burst into tears.

Jacques led her into a small alcove and held her head against his chest.

"*Non*," he whispered, "do not weep, please, I beg you!"

But the tears would not stop. Nora cried for her father, for all the wounded men she'd cared for—and for Jacques Leceau, the love she'd only just found; a man she might not see again.

He held her for a long time. Her hair, as he'd thought, held the clean ripe scent of autumn wheat. Dazed, hurting for both of them, he was at a complete loss. Beyond the shadows in which they stood, he could see the bright sky; an old woman feeding pigeons.

It was a picture he would remember as long as he lived.

Finally Nora's sobs subsided. He lifted her face and solemnly wiped away her tears.

"I'm sorry," she whispered. "Dammit, I didn't mean to spoil our day!"

He grinned at the language that was Nora's own. "You have spoiled nothing. but now you must tell me what I can do to make you smile!"

Nora's wet eyes hardened into a look of resolve.

"You mean that? Whatever I want?"

"Anything to give you happiness."

"You got a room somewhere? I mean, while yer in town?"

The muscles in his arms began to quiver at the import of what she was saying.

"I do not understand—"

"You ain't sleepin' in the street?"

"I have a small room in Le Marais, on le rue Brise Miche, but—"

"Then let's go there."

"We cannot," he said hoarsely. "It is better that we walk—in the open. Perhaps dine at a sidewalk cafe—"

The glow left her face, the gray eyes lifeless. "I'm sorry. Hell, I guess I got th' wrong idea. I figgered that we—we—"

"*Mon Dieu!*" he said hoarsely, "I am only a man! I think of you, of your reputation! I would not be able to resist—"

"Didn't ask you to," Nora said.

Within moments, Jacques Leceau had hailed a horse-drawn cab. They sat apart, not daring to touch, to look at each other, conscious of fire coursing through their veins. When they reached the quaint, narrow street peopled with artists and vagabonds, Jacques assisted Nora from the carriage. He could feel a trembling in her that matched his own. Her hands were like ice.

"There is still time for a change of mind," he told her quietly. She shook her head numbly, unable to speak.

Entering an ancient building, they climbed steep steps that led to a room looking down on the house-tops of older Paris. It was spacious, sparsely furnished, the ceiling slanting with the angle of the roof. Along one wall was a fireplace, charcoal still glowing. A bed, a table, two chairs.

Jacques went to replenish the fire while Nora removed her coat. She stood, her hands twisted together, looking about. Piled on a small chest was the clothing he'd discarded upon coming from the trenches. A rumpled uniform, splashed with mud and blood; a pair of mud-caked boots; a dented helmet—

And he was going back to that.

He rose from fanning the fire and turned, startled at the sudden passion in her face; the way she flew toward him, putting her arms around his neck. He lifted her, feeling the way her body fitted into his—in all the right places.

"Nora," he whispered, "oh, Nora!"

"Love me, Jacques!"

His hands went to the buttons of her gown, slipping it away, marveling to see that her shoulders, too, were sprinkled with freckles like golden dust on cream. Later, when he'd satisfied his terrible, draining need, he would kiss them—every one!

He lifted her slim small body and carried her to his bed. Even then, he paused.

"You still want—this to happen?"

For answer, she raised her arms and pulled him down to her. I must make this good for her, he thought. I must keep my senses—

Then all was forgotten as she arched to him with a small cry. As they consummated their love, Nora heard him say her name, an exultant shout. And then he said it softly—like a prayer.

Later, his head cradled against her breast, he said, "It should not have been like this, in the day, in a small poor room. You should have had flowers, stars, soft music—"

"We'll have that someday."

She felt him stiffen in her arms. "If there is a someday—"

She put her finger to his lips. "Don't talk like that, dammit!"

Nora! His dear, funny, passionate Nora! So many

girls packed into one lovely little body. He had to grin, then his smile went away.

"I wish to marry you, Nora. I wish a home. I wish many children. But if that does not happen, promise me that you will remember. This one day, you are my wife."

"This day, and always—"

"I do not ask for always. Just for today."

"Then, dammit, what you waitin' for? We're wastin' time!"

Late that night they took a cab back to the Hotel Claridge. Now, they sat close together, holding, touching. The driver, a sentimental man, kept his eyes straight ahead and reined his horses to the slowest possible walk.

When they reached the hotel-converted-to-hospital, Nora looked at Jacques in panic.

She hadn't thought. There was talk about moving the entire hospital, perhaps even to another city. her dad, of course, was still being treated until his stump healed. If the hospital closed and they were somewhere else, how would Jacques ever find her—

He grinned at her sudden terror and held her tightly. He had already considered their plight. His own unit was being transferred; where, he had no idea. They would communicate through M. Casanova, leaving their various addresses.

Nora had to be satisfied with his answer, though somehow, not knowing what was ahead of them made their parting seem more permanent. She held to him until he was forced to pry her fingers from his sleeve.

"I must go, Nora."

"Yes," she said brokenly. "Yes."

He walked her to the door of the hotel and kissed

her once more, a long and lingering gesture of love. Then he walked away.

She watched him go, then hurried to her room. When she finally slept, her fists were clenched tightly, as if she held a tiny piece of the day in each hand.

chapter 12

Nora Murphy seemed to bloom in the days following Jacques's visit. She threw herself into nursing with renewed vigor, seeing each man as Jacques in similar circumstances. Sensing her concern for them, the men turned to her; feverish voices calling for Nora in their delirium; the admiring eyes of those recuperating following the small girl with straw-colored hair and a pert nose.

"I dinna think what they see in her," Denise said spitefully.

"She's a very good nurse," Jo told her.

Denise snorted, tossing her flaming hair. "I am the ane t'do the dirrrty work! A' she has tae do is check their fevers and smoothe their beds!" She glared at Jo. "'Tis a case of haeing one mon, and leuking for another—"

"What in the world are you talking about," Jo gasped. "Nora hasn't—"

"Hae ye nae seen it? The way she's been, all saft and daft? She and that mon o' hers did mair than see the sights that day—"

Jo clapped her hands over her ears, her face red with anger. "I won't listen to this! Denise, you're vile!"

"I hae no behaved like a strrrumpet," Denise stormed.

"Maybe it's because you haven't had the opportunity!"

Again, Jo turned to Liane for friendship. Nora moved serenely in a dream of love, and Denise was once more on the outside of their small circle.

It was only that she was smarrrter than they, she comforted herself. Wiser in the ways of the worrrld!

Denise wasn't the only one who noted Nora's glowing face, her absent-mindedness, her preoccupation with the wounded. Maggie needed only to look at her daughter, and she knew—

Remembering herself as a street waif, new life burgeoning beneath her apron, she felt a terrible fear; a fear she dared not share with Sean in his condition.

Her Nora was not a girl to give her love lightly. She placed no blame on either of them, the boy or the girl. Mebbe, she thought, holding Sean's thin hand, I might of did the same damn thing, in their circustances! It's their bizness—

But she prayed that nothing would come of it.

Nothing did.

Weeks passed. In February came the expected move. The Corps opened a hospital in a large, deserted villa called the Château Mauricien, at Wimereux, near Boulogne.

Maggie, Sean, and the girls were given a choice. Sean was still not strong enough to chance a journey to the States. Boulogne was a seaport, the fourth in importance in France. Dr. Murray would see that they were transported to England, there to sit out the war—or they could remain with them in Wimereux. Their skills were sorely needed.

If we maun go to England, Denise thought mutinously, I shall be sent hame. Wars sometimes lasted years. She would be auld and gray, her brow brent—

Besides, there were men here! They might be short a leg, an arm, an eye, an ear—but they were men!

She voted to remain in France.

Jo, too, was unwilling to leave. She'd learned the secret of sending wires. The French telegraph system was under government ownership, and if one really wanted a message transmitted, one paid for a *reçu*, or receipt. This system was insurance against having one's money pocketed and the wire deposited in a wastebasket.

She had sent her first article home, directly to her father, Matthew Blaine. It contained a description of the hospital, along with whatever news she could glean from the patients. They often lost their shyness with a young girl who had heavenly blue eyes and could speak their language fluently. There would be other items to follow.

Besides, it was from Boulogne that the Romans, in A.D. 43, set sail for the conquest of Britain! There might be sights even more exciting than the sewers and catacombs, and abattoirs of Paris!

Seaports were vulnerable to attack, weren't they?

There, she might write the story that brought her fame!

"I think we should stay," she said eagerly.

Nora said nothing, but Maggie could read her answer in her eyes. If they left France, there was little probability Nora would see Jacques Leceau again.

"Well, what the hell we waitin' fer?" Maggie snorted. "Pack yer duds. We're movin' t' this 'ere shat-toe."

Nora found a moment to speak with M. Casanova, leaving a forwarding address for Jacques. When she tried to pay him for his services, he shook his head and kissed her hand.

It was a delight, he told her ecstatically, to serve young love.

Nora, blushing, escaped to tend the needs of the men who would be transported on litters to the train for Wimereux.

Wimereux proved to be a disappointment. The Château Mauricien was not in sight of the sea, but had all the disadvantages of a coastal atmosphere. The weather was cold and damp, the skies gray and dismal. Many of the wounded who'd made the move recuperated and were released, one by one. The military stalemate brought a drop in serious cases, and the Mauricien became little more than a casualty clearing station.

A cook and maid had been brought from London, and a staff of Belgian girls employed for the kitchens. There was little work for the girls to do; none of the pressures they'd felt at the Hotel Claridge, with its influx of wounded and dying. Jo champed at the bit, feeling they were lost in limbo. Denise complained. Liane was intensely homesick, now with time on her hands. Nora, perhaps, felt the inactivity more than

the others. It gave her time to think, to wonder
where Jacques might be at the moment—

To worry.

Hospital facilities had now greatly expanded in
France. There was talk of closing the Château
Mauricien, of finding new quarters in London.

When the senior doctors, Anderson and Murray,
left unexpectedly, crossing the Channel to England,
the rumors increased.

"Mum, d'ye think we'll have to leave?" Nora asked
Maggie.

Maggie looked at her daughter, thin and haunted-
appearing, blue shadows smudged beneath her eyes,
and searched for words to comfort her.

"Don't reckin that'd be too turrible," she said with
false cheerfulness. "Arab done writ and said we oughta
visit her girl Luka. Never met up with 'er, but hell,
Jo an' Denise is fambly, an' we come purty damn
close—"

"I don't think so, Mum." Nora sought for reasons.
"She's married to a lord, ain't she. Pretty high-toned,
I guess."

"Pshaw!" Maggie elevated her nose. "Y'fergit me
mum was a lady. I been thinkin' on takin' a trip back,
anyways. See me ancesstral 'ome! Hell, like me mum
uster say, we're makin' mountings outa mole 'ills.
Give it a bit! See what 'appens—and mash yer ol'
mum a cuppa, whilst we're waitin'!"

Nora forced a grin and went to do her bidding.
Her mind on Jacques, she made the tea too strong.
Maggie took a sip and grimaced.

"Somethin' wrong?" Nora asked.

"Hell, no. It's just right. 'Its the spot, it does."

Sean, offered a cup, was not as charitable. "What's
th' lass tryin' t'do? Pizen me?" he asked plaintively.

Maggie shushed him.

"Sometimes, girls is got other things on they minds. Men don't unnerstand. Leave 'er be."

Sean Murphy conceded her the point. He'd never understood how a woman thought, not even the one he was married to. She was continually surprising him.

When the doctors returned from England, the rumors became reality. They had made arrangements for a five-hundred-bed hospital, converting the old workhouse of St. Giles, Bloomsbury, into a medical facility.

"That's the one described by Mr. Dickens, in *Oliver Twist*," Jo said excitedly. "It's supposed to be an awful place."

"It is being renovated, according to our wishes," Dr. Murray said dryly. "We intend to call it 'The Endell Street Hospital,' and we will have a sizable staff."

"Then you won't be—needing us, anymore?" Nora's voice trembled.

"No, indeed. Though, of course, you will travel with us. I understand there are relatives—

Nora interrupted her. "When will we go?"

Dr. Murray pursed her lips; the same gesture she used when admitting a dying patient. "Late March or early April, I would say. The reconstruction will take some time. And I must go to Paris to tie up a few loose ends before—"

"Doc," Maggie said hoarsely, "these 'ere girls needs a break. You wouldn' consider lettin' 'em git a last look at Paree, wouldja? I mean, hell's bells, bein' stuck 'ere ain't bin no fun. Give 'em a chancet to kick up their 'eels, so t' speak—"

"I suppose they could accompany me—"

"Hot damn," Maggie said. "Fer a bloody saw-bones, yer one helluva lady!"

Several weeks later, Maggie saw them off on their holiday in the company of the starched Englishwoman. Liane had elected to remain behind and help Maggie pack for their journey to England. Denise was shining in anticipation of the visit to Paris, Jo intent on picking up a great story.

Only Nora seemed pale and strained. Her eyes were too large for her face and filled with a desperate hope. And Maggie knew what that hope was.

Nora was praying that she would see Jacques Leceau before she left the country; meet him on the streets of Paris, where they had found their love.

And there was just about as much chance of that, Maggie thought glumly, as of findin' a snowball in hell.

This damn war! And wars was sump'n men whomped up. Wimmin, Maggie thought virtuously, is peace-able-like.

If she could just git aholt of that damn Boshee kaiser, she'd tell 'im so.

An' then she'd beat th' hell outen 'im!

---
chapter 13

The small entourage disembarked in Paris and went directly to the Hotel Claridge, where Dr. Murray intended to take rooms for their two-day stay. The hotel had lost its antiseptic atmosphere. It was filled with refugees. Where soldier-patients once bled and died, children ran and played, their mothers' voices lifting shrilly above the din. Walls were smudged and carpets stained.

Dr. Murray, tilting her nose at the less sanitary atmosphere, introduced herself to a clerk at the desk and managed, arguing, to obtain private space for her group.

"I must admit, I find the situation here appalling," she flung over her shoulder as she left to go to her room. "I should not be surprised at finding lice and fleas! Come, girls!"

Nora lagged behind, hearing the red-faced, mustached clerk mutter under his breath. She approached the desk timidly and asked the whereabouts of M. Casanova.

With rolling eyes and Gallic shrugs, the old man stated that he hadn't seen Casanova in some time, and he had been left with this towering monument of insanity.

"But how long has he been gone?" Nora insisted.

The clerk spread his hands. "Who knows. *Pour une semaine? Deux?* A day would be too much! with such as Madame Murray—"

A week, perhaps two. And Jacques might have been here in that time! Nora blinked back tears of frustration. "Can you say when M. Casanova's comin' back?"

Again the shrug.

"Mebbe," she moved closer to the desk, "mebbe you might have a message for Nora Murphy. That's me—"

He shuffled among some papers under the counter and shook his head. Nora's knees sagged, and there was a touch on her shoulder.

"Are you well, miss?"

She turned to see a pretty girl in uniform, with a saucy face and dancing curls.

"Just sorta disppointed," she said, trying to smile. "I thought my—my friend might of left me a note. I ain't sure where he is?"

The girl laughed wryly. "It appears we're in the same case, luv. These bloody thoughtless men!" Remembering her manners, she touched Nora's freckled hand with rough, red fingers.

"I'm Violet Tremm, VAD." She inspected her hands. "Horrors, aren't they. They comes from being stationed in a flaming field hospital. Now, it's me for home and jolly England! If Pierre has not made arrangements, it is his loss! Quite likely we will never meet again!"

She cares, Nora thought. She's hurting, too.

"I'm Nora Murphy," she said quietly. "I've been workin' in the hospital at Wimereux, and I'm leavin' for England, too. I reckin I know how you feel. Maybe your—Pierre—couldn't make it. You know how things are.

"I should," Violet Tremm said, her eyes huge with memories. "When you have seen what I have seen! But I am leaving while I am still sane."

She smiled bravely and slid a glove on her reddened hand, then raised it in a salute.

"Ta," she said.

Then she was gone.

Nora followed the others to their quarters.

That night, she didn't sleep, but lay thinking of Violet Tremm, whose problems paralleled her own. Violet was going home, probably never again to see the man she loved. Maybe she'd been smart enough to give her Pierre her home address. Jacques knew only that Nora lived in San Francisco. He would never find her.

She cried for Violet and Pierre, for Jacques and herself.

The morning brought one of those beautiful, misty, watercolor days known only to Paris. Dr. Murray bustled to handle her unfinished business, and Jo left the hotel, wishing to explore corners of the city she hadn't seen.

She did not invite Denise along, and the red-haired Scottish girl took it to heart. They hadn't really been friends since she made her unfortunate remark about Nora's intimacy with her Frenchman. She'd counted on this Paris trip to heal the rift.

"I dinna care," she lied to herself. Reluctantly, since she had no wish to spend the day alone, she approached Nora.

"I thocht we might leuk at the fashions, hae lunch at a cafe—"

"I got other plans," Nora said vaguely.

Denise's cheeks flamed. Stiff-necked snobs, they were! Let them gae their ain way! She didna need them!

Slipping into her belted green velvet coat, she left the hotel, feeling miserable, deeply sorry for herself. She had gone only a few blocks when she heard her name called in a hesitant voice.

"Denise?"

Her head jerked up and saw him, standing a little way off, a wariness in his eyes as though he were uncertain of his welcome.

"Johnny! Johnny Looper!"

And then she was running to meet him. For the first time, she kissed a man for whom she had to bend down.

Meanwhile, Nora checked at the desk again. There was no message, and M. Casanova had not returned. She checked again within an hour. And then she made a decision.

Leaving the hotel, she found a horse-drawn cab. Shabby, an aged driver, it might have been the same one she and Jacques occupied a lifetime ago. In a trembling voice, she gave the address.

"La Marais on la rue Brise Miche—"

It was a stupid notion, she told herself. There was no reason Jacques should be there on this one day out of a year. But it was the only hope she had left—

Reaching the narrow street with its ancient buildings, she asked the driver to wait.

Then, heart beating in her throat, she climbed the steps that led to a room that touched the sky. There was movement beyond the door, and she began to tremble, finally forcing herself to knock with a gloved hand.

"*Entrez!*"

Nora froze at the sound of a woman's voice, her impossible dream crashing about her ears. And a man flung the door open; beret atop a bearded face, black brows knit together. Beyond him she could see a lovely girl standing by a window.

She didn't have a stitch on.

Nora's face flamed. "I—I am sorry," she whispered. "I made a mistake—"

The man's face cleared. "Ah—*américain!* You weesh a painting, *un petit souvenir?*" He pulled her into the room, pointing at a gaudy canvas. "*Cinquante— non? Trente?*"

Now Nora could see the paintings lining the walls; an easel on which stood a half-finished portrait of the nude girl. A model. It was not—what she had thought.

In her newly acquired, badly accented French, she finally made him understand that she was seeking news of a former tenant.

He shrugged and spread his hands. He knew nothing.

Nora left the building and ordered the driver to return her to the Hotel Claridge. The room where she and Jacques had truly known each other had been her last hope of finding him. She was sorry she'd gone. There was nothing there to remind her of what had been.

"Mademoiselle—"

The driver's hesitant voice brought her awake.

They'd reached the hotel, and she remembered nothing of the drive.

Alighting, she paid him and entered the building. She would leave a message with the clerk, telling Jacques she was leaving for England—and giving him her San Francisco address. There was little chance he would receive it, but she would give the man a sizable tip—

The face behind the desk had changed. The pallid face and long black beard belonged to M. Casanova.

With a glad cry, she hurried toward him. Reaching across the counter, he took her hands, kissed them, his warm brown eyes filled with tears of emotion.

"The little mademoiselle! Ah, yes—"

"You have a message for me?"

The mobile features went suddenly still.

"You will come with me, *oui*? Into my office—"

She followed the breathless little fat man, suddenly terribly afraid as he seated her.

"I have been ill," he said, averting his eyes. "This was brought to me. I kept it with my private papers—"

He took a brown envelope from his desk and held it, seeming reluctant to give it into her hands.

"Jacques gave you this?"

"*Non*, mademoiselle." His voice was so gentle. "This man, I do not know, but he was—*bien amiable*. His friend died in the trenches. The letter survived—"

He watched the light fade from Nora's face, saw it grow old and unbeautiful before his eyes, closing against him like a knobby fist.

"Please," she said in a tight voice, inclining her head toward his office door.

M. Casanova left and closed the door behind him. He was not a cursing man, but he struck the counter top with his fist and released a stream of expletives in graphic French.

In his office, Nora opened the brown envelope with icy fingers. It contained still another, this one tattered and smeared with dark stains. It was addressed to Mademoiselle Nora Murphy, in care of M. Casanova, the Hotel Claridge, Paris.

Jacques's handwriting, Nora thought dully. She had never seen it before. She would never see it again—

She opened the second envelope to find a ring: Jacques's ring. A single sheet of paper was folded around it. On it was a hastily written note.

There is little time, my Nora. And I have a premonition. If the worst should happen, remember Musset's words. "Rien ne nous rend si grands qu'une grande dolour." Nothing can make us greater than a great, great grief—

In this message, I place my ring and my heart, praying they will reach my love, my wife.

It was signed, *Your adoring Jacqu*——
The signature trailed off in a scrawl that was lost in a dark blotch. It could only be blood.

Nora made a harsh, retching sound, then hunched over in an agonized, dry-eyed misery. She sat that way for a long time, then rose, methodically placed the letter in its brown envelope, and left the office.

Violet Tremm was at the desk again. She smiled hopelessly at Nora.

"Still no word from Pierre. I suppose I must forget him." She looked curiously at Nora's set face, then at the envelope in her hand.

"It would seem that your man is not going to meet you, either—"

"No," Nora said, her voice alien to her ears. "He—he couldn't make it."

Violet Tremm was a kindhearted girl. It was clear that Nora was taking her man's defection much harder than she. She looked almost—frozen.

"Walk with me a little way," Violet said impulsively. "I think we'd both feel better for it."

Violet chatted as they walked, talking to the rigors of life in a field hospital close behind the trenches. Here the wounded were brought for immediate attention, to be sent to proper hospitals—if they lived. Here, surgery was often butchery, due to lack of time and personnel. She had lived in a tent, inadequate in winter.

"I do not know if I shall ever be warm again," she said.

Sometimes when the wind was right, they could smell the stench of the decaying dead.

Nora shivered and Violet stopped talking.

"Perhaps you should go back," she said. "You don't look well. Cheerio, luv. Maybe we will meet across the Channel—"

"Wait!" Nora put a hand on her arm. "Wait!"

Violet Tremm's voice trailed off and she stared at her new friend. She did look—odd!

"Tell me," Nora said hoarsely, "how I can join the VAD. I'm stayin'!"

Violet looked at her curiously. The poor girl had it bad! She wanted to tell her no man was worth all this, but she was wise enough to hold her tongue.

chapter 14

All the girls were unusually quiet as they boarded
the train for Wimereux. Jo had tramped the streets of
Paris, not wanting to waste a moment. Denise had
spent her time with Johnny Looper, alternately inviting his attentions—and fending them off. He had
taken her to exciting places on the Left Bank, showing her a side of life she never knew existed. He
pointed out ladies of the night who roamed the
mysterious fringes of Paris, with their black-rimmed
eyes and mouths like crimson gashes; the men who
let these women work for them. And, slinking in the
shadows, the Apaches (pronounced Apash), the night-
prowling criminals who waited in dark streets to
strike down and rob an innocent passerby.

It was all thrilling to a girl from a Highland farm.
One day, Denise told herself, there might be a movie
made of such a place. She thought of herself as a

siren, in a slit skirt—of a dark-clad actor, who would spin her into his arms.

The script she considered was so real that she allowed Johnny to go much further than she'd intended. In the horse-drawn cab, heading back to the Hotel Claridge, she succumbed to his kisses. They became more insistent, and his hands began to roam.

Denise felt herself warming inside, beginning to melt in a haze of dizzy euphoria. Then Johnny Looper leaned forward to give the driver a change of address.

She sat up in alarm, pulling her clothing together. "What are ye oop to! I maun go back—"

He laughed cockily. "You want it as much as I do," he said. "Hell, another hour or two won't matter—"

She was now in full control of her senses, her face flaming. "Dinna hark to the mon," she called out to the driver. To Johnny, she hissed, "I am nae that kind of wooman!"

Johnny Looper settled back, his face grim. "You coulda fooled me, sis," he said nastily. "You'll tease the wrong guy one of these days, and you'll pay the piper—"

"Dinna be angrrry wi' me, Johnny—"

"Hell, I ain't mad. Just should have recognized the breed. Wine me, dine me, tell me I'm gorgeous—but don't touch!"

"I'm nae like that—"

"Ain't you? Well, I ain't stickin' around to find out. Here's yer damned hotel. Find yer own way in."

"Johnny—"

He sat, adamant, his arms folded, staring straight ahead as she climbed from the carriage unaided. The minute her feet touched the paving, the carriage drove on.

She stumbled into the hotel, embarrassed, humiliated at his leave-taking. And those awful things he'd said to her, making her seem egotistical and self-centered!

The thoughts plagued her all night. By morning, she had justified the situation. Johnny Looper had been much too forward, and she only defended her virtue as a decent woman should—not like Nora Murphy, for instance!

On the train, she seated herself by Dr. Murray, leaving Jo to sit with Nora. Nora looked ghastly in the morning light, probably sulking because her lover didn't show.

Denise had no idea what Jacques Leceau saw in the lass, anyway. She was whey-faced and skinny, built like a lad!

She looked down at her own ripe curves complacently, remembering the touch of Johnny Looper's hands—

Jo busily transcribed notes. Nora sat stiffly upright, Jacques's ring on a chain around her neck, hidden inside the neckline of her dress. Later, she was to remember nothing of the return to the château. Like a wounded man who woke to find his legs missing, she knew only that something was gone. The pain had not yet settled in.

When they reached the hospital, they found a state of chaos. Maggie, overseeing the crating of medical supplies, looked searchingly at Nora, who was white and unusually quiet.

"Didden run inta that Jack-feller, I reckin?" When Nora didn't answer, she plowed on with forced cheerfulness. "Ain't nothin' to fret about. 'E'll find us when this mess is over, effen 'e's got a mind to.

Other'n that, 'ow'd ye find Paree? Git some writin'
stuff, Jo? You be'ave yerself, Denise?"

Denise reddened. In the cover of her confusion,
Liane reached a hand to Nora. "You must be tired
from sitting on that train," she said quietly. "Let's
take a walk."

They left the chaotic atmosphere of the château
and went into the garden.

It was a misty day, rainbows puddling on the
cobblestone path, drops collecting on shrubs just
beginning to green. The girls walked in silence for a
while, then Nora turned to Liane. Her companion's
eyes were dark with sympathy beneath a sheen of
tears.

She knew! Liane with her strange, perceptive
mind knew!

Nora's mask shattered into a thousand pieces and
she drew a shuddering breath. Liane put her arms
around her, and the tears came in a flood that would
not stop.

When they finally ceased, Nora wiped her wet
face. The tip of her nose was red, her face blotched
and swollen, but the old Nora looked out of her gray
eyes.

"I'm all right now," she said. "You—know, don't
you."

"I guessed," Liane said soberly.

"I don't want to talk about it. D'ruther nobody
knew. You understand that?"

Liane nodded gravely.

"Oh, Liane, I wish—oh, damn, damn, damn!"
Nora struck out at the garden wall with her fist, then
laid her forehead against the damp stone.

Like the patient who lost his legs, her feelings
were returning. And it hurt, ah, God, it hurt!

They returned to the château, and Nora looked at the work in progress, rolling up her sleeves to reveal wiry, capable wrists.

"Where do you want me to start?" she asked crisply. "What do you want me to do?"

Before long, the hospital was swept clean of its apppurtenances. The patients, including Sean Murphy, were prepared to be moved to Boulogne for transport. Maggie was in a state of elation.

"Never figgered I'd wanna see England agin," she chortled. "An' 'ere I am, lookin' forward to it. Got a letter from Luka sayin' we was welcome. Mebbe she'll find you girls a 'igh-toney 'usbin' like she's got—"

"Mum, I ain't goin'."

Nora's statement dropped in the middle of Maggie's chatter like a bombshell.

"What the hell—"

"I ain't goin'."

Nora had moved away from the small group, her back to the wall, her chin raised against the storm she knew would come. "I'm goin' to a field hospital, up behind the lines. I joined up with th' VAD."

Maggie's green-grape eyes were a study in anger, hurt, and bewilderment.

"Yer crazy," she said. "It's that damn frawg lootenant, ain't it! He talked ye inta this!"

Nora flinched, but she answered quietly. "No, Mum, he didn't."

"Don't give a damn 'oo done it," Maggie said, getting control of herself now. "But yer goin' with us effen I 'afta 'awg-tie yuh! Ef you think I'd leave yuh 'ere by yer lonesome—"

Liane moved to her side. "I'm staying with her, Aunt Maggie."

"Th' hell yuh are! Yer folks said I was th' boss, an' dammit—"

Jo stepped forward to join them. This was just what she'd been looking for, an opportunity to be in the thick of things, not just—handling bedpans.

Maggie's frowning gaze turned toward Denise, still at her side. "Looks like only one of you damfools got any sense—"

Denise had been appalled at her sister-travelers. Then she thought of the alternative: being stuck in a rural part of England, or returned to a Highland farm.

She, too, went to Nora's side. Together, they faced Maggie Murphy.

Maggie's eyes moved from one to another; Nora's face implacable and set; Liane, quietly determined; Jo eager and glowing, and Denise—willful and stubborn.

She knew she had lost control of her daughter and her three young charges. And she still had Sean to worry about. What in the hell was she going to do?

Arab an' Em was gonna be mad as the devil. So would Jo's and Liane's folks. The Dugals would probably know she couldn't do a damn thing to stop Denise—

As for Nora, her own girl had become a stranger these last days. Mebbe it was time to let go.

"Suit yerselfs," she said, screwing her face into a ferocious grimace to hide her threatening tears. "Yer gonna do it, anyways!"

A general without an army, she tramped upstairs to check on Sean.

---------------- *chapter 15* ----------------

In late April, a small motor convoy drew up at a cluster of tents, all well marked with red crosses, set about a tiny stone house that had once been the heart of a little farm.

This was a field hospital, behind the lines at Ypres. The driver of the first vehicle began hastily unloading supplies. The driver of the second gallantly aided his cargo, a number of well-dressed young ladies, to the ground.

Seeing their faces as they stared at the scene, he smiled humorlessly, his expression hidden behind his bushy mustache.

He was a seasoned soldier, but even his gorge rose at the sight of men lying on the ground, waiting for medical attention. Outside of the cottage was a pile of amputated limbs, waiting to be carted away. There were so many wounded that the newer victims, those who lay on blankets, faces blue, coughing their lungs out, must wait.

For some time, the Germans had bombarded Ypres with monstrous mortars, decimating its heart—the cathedral and the Grand Place; reducing the roads to areas pocked with craters. A steady stream of wounded had poured into this small hospital, the few doctors working around the clock.

Then the mortars had inexplicably stopped their every-twenty-minute pounding on a sunny golden morning. At five o'clock, the bombardment began again. This time, it was accompanied by a hissing sound, and a greenish cloudlike mist wafted toward the village of Langemarck—drifting, settling, while the soldiers in the trenches remarked on its beauty.

Gas!

Some men died where they stood. Others stumbled away. And the mortars began again, chewing up the land, spitting it out with great exhalations of fetid breath.

The four girls, awed by the immense horror before them, stood uncertainly as the driver off-loaded their luggage.

"I suppose," Jo said, "we should report there." She pointed to the cottage. "It seems to be the—"

"Aye," Denise said distastefully, not waiting for her to finish her sentence, "that it does!"

Leaving their bags, they walked toward it, trying to close their ears to the pathetic moans around them; the shrill retching whoops of men fighting to breathe.

They reached the door as a bandaged soldier backed out, carrying one end of a litter. The occupant's face was covered. The girls watched as the body was rolled off the stretcher beside a long line of blanketed forms and another lifted on.

Then the figure of a man appeared at the door of the cottage. Tall, broad shoulders stooped with fatigue, the man had unruly blond hair above shadowed blue eyes, and a face covered with the golden down of a week-old beard. His clothes were stiff with blood.

"Get cracking, you bloody bastards," he shouted at the orderlies. "What in hell do you think this is? A flaming picnic?" Then he saw the four young women and his jaw dropped.

"My word!" He rubbed his tired eyes and looked again, then snapped at the stretcher-bearers. "Get him on the table. I'll be right there. Now," he turned back to the girls, speaking with exaggerated patience, "I don't know how the hell you got here, but if you're looking for someone—father, brother—he's either here," he waved toward the tents and the wounded on the ground, "or there." He gestured toward the long lines of blanketed dead. "Or out there." He pointed toward the horrendous noise of war.

"Now, excuse me."

"That isna why we are here," Denise said, her cheeks bright with anger at their summary dismissal. "We wish t' gie aid and comfort to these men—"

"I'm afraid most of them are not up to what you have in mind. I suggest you return to your—tea parties—or whatever the hell you do for fun and stop wasting my time!"

Jo Blaine stepped in front of Denise, her hands balled into fists, her blue eyes snapping. "I would suggest you watch your tongue! We are here because we were sent for! I demand to see Dr. Peter Carey—"

For a moment he looked utterly confused.

"I am Dr. Carey! I asked for medical aides, yes! But, for God's sake, not women! Not here—"

"Your request was turned over to the VAD," Jo said in a professionally cool tone. "Now, if you will tell us where to change—"

"Change, hell! I ask for help and they send me this! Since you're here, dammit, we'll get on with it. I dare not hope one of you might have experience in surgery?"

Denise, furious at his arrogant manner, stepped forward. He shoved her toward the door. "Prep the man on the table." He turned to the others. "Until I discover your talents—if any—see what you can do with the men out here. I do not suppose you can harm them."

"The man's an insufferable monster," Jo raged as he left them. "If he thinks he can treat us like— like—" She stopped, at a loss for words.

"He don't matter none," Nora said practically. "It's them that needs us. We come here t'work. Reckin we oughta git at it."

Jo conceded she was right. She and Nora, protective toward the younger Liane, worked among the surgery-bound patients. Here was a man whose hands grasped his midriff, holding his bulging intestines in place. All they could offer him was reassurance. There was a boy with empty eye sockets; his pulsating brain visible through a large hole in his shattered skull. And this man—his wounds were already septic, smelling, his foot half gnawed away by trench rats.

"Dear God, Nora! There was nothing like this at the Claridge—or at Wimereux!" Jo was almost crying as she worked over a man who bled and bled. "Do you think we can stand this?"

"We can do anything we have to do," Nora said serenely.

It was Jacques Nora tended, just as the man before had been. She did for others what she could not do for him.

Jo set her teeth and went on working. And when the stretcher-bearers appeared again, she pointed to the man who was bleeding to death and said, "Take this one."

Liane would almost have preferred the wounded patients. There was so little she could do for the blue-faced, black-lipped men who had inhaled the deadly fumes. Their lungs were seared, their skin blistered. Finding a bucket of clean water, she made folded packs to cool burned, blinded eyes; lifted men to a more comfortable position as they coughed their lives away.

In the cottage, Dr. Peter Carey completed an amputation, thrusting needle and thread at Denise Dugal. "Sew up the flap," he said tersely. "I'll help over here." He moved on to another table, where another doctor was needing advice.

Denise stitched away, her fury overcoming her nausea. True, she'd helped with surgery at the Hotel, but that had been—different. Though Peter Carey's hands were skilled and deft, the conditions under which they worked were barbaric. She'd managed to hold on to her nerves through the entire operation, and he hadn't even complimented her on her aid.

"Domn him," she said under her breath. "Domn him for a Sassenach!"

Then the flesh beneath her fingers began to quiver and the patient moaned. She swallowed hard.

'Tis ainly a lamb I'm mending, she told her exhausted

brain. 'Twas the way she must think of this work if she were to survive.

That night, Dr. Peter Carey gave the girls their assignments. Since Jo was experienced in hospital records, she had the job of recording the patients and listing the dead. Liane—he frowned at her and she felt suddenly guilty, sensing he'd guessed she lied about her age—Liane was to aid the less injured and the convalescents in feeding, watering, changing bandages, and the like.

Nora, he intended to train to work with him in surgery. Denise would aid young Dr. Percy.

Denise opened her mouth and closed it. The stuck-up mon! Sae she wasna guid enough for him! She'd like t'gie him a piece o' her mind.

They would alternate duty, each operating pair taking two hours on, two off. He suggested Denise and Dr. Percy get some food and rest.

Young Dr. Percy, an effeminate fussy little fellow, still somewhat short of medical education, needed no coaxing. He had operated steadily for thirty-six hours and he was asleep before he finished his tin cup of watery soup.

Denise had no appetite after her day's work. She looked into the tents. They were filled with patients. Finally, she rolled herself into a blanket on the ground, miserable as the night mists soaked through it.

She'd quit—even if she maun gae hame. Except that was exactly what that arrogant bastard expected her to do!

In the cottage, Peter Carey, reeling from fatigue, was patient with Nora. She did not have the knack for surgery the redhead had, but she was capable enough to obey his orders well.

He wished he and the girl, Denise, would work as a team. But Percy, nervous and none too competent, needed her more.

He grinned to himself as he thought of Denise Dugal catching Percy in a careless mistake. He had an idea she'd keep him up to snuff—

In spite of a constant stream of incoming patients, the efficiency of the newcomers began to be evident. Peter Carey ruefully admitted it to himself, though he didn't say anything to the young ladies.

Women had no business being this close to the front. They should be protected from the ugliness of war. He had asked for surgeons, dammit! Not a petticoat brigade. How they expected him to handle this load with no one but a pip-squeak like Percy—

Percy was male, however. And his performance in saving lives wasn't exactly to be applauded. Denise Dugal, with only practical experience, was proving to be a far better doctor than he.

If only she weren't such a damned distraction! The times when circumstances forced all to be in surgery at the same hour, he'd found himself unable to keep his mind on his work. As for Percy, it was obvious the man was gaga about her.

There was no place for women in the field!

Peter Carey was worked to the limit. Inside, he felt a smoldering anger at man's inhumanity to man. Worn out, frustrated in his efforts to save every patient, he vented his irritability on Denise—who retaliated with lofty disdain.

"Damned insubordinate wench," he growled, writing a letter to headquarters in his mind.

"You misjudge her," lisped the adoring Percy. "She is a fine woman—"

"They sent us women," Carey said stubbornly, "and we need men!"

He needed help desperately. There had been four surgeons attached to the hospital in the beginning. Two had been transferred to another along the long line of trenches. In this time of direst emergency, Doctors Carey and Percy had been making do with two incompetent French orderlies, a Belgian cook, and a number of walking wounded.

He had to concede that Nora was capable and willing. However, something about the girl bothered him. She was calm and unflappable, handling the most gruesome cases with aplomb. He sensed some kind of tragedy in her background. Something so terrible that all that followed was an anticlimax.

Pert Jo Blaine he liked. He had an idea she was a square-shooter. She'd straightened out his records in no time at all, even helping to search the dead for identification. And Liane Wang? Here was another puzzle; she was obviously very young, still at the awkward stage. He grinned a little, thinking of how many times she'd tripped over tent ropes, dropped medical trays. He wondered if she were old enough to be a volunteer. With her Asian blood, it was hard to tell her age. And how the devil could these girls claim to be kin?

Their relationships didn't matter, as long as they did their job. But, Jove, the Dugal woman was an irritating female!

His feelings toward Denise were reciprocated. "Bluidy slave drrriver," she snorted, tossing her fiery mane.

"He's a damn good doc," Nora said indignantly. "And he works harder than we do, don't he?"

"Ye should ken that better than I," Denise said suggestively. "Yer wi' him a' the time. Pairhops ye prefer the British tae the French? Or wull any mon do?"

Nora was red with anger, her gray eyes rock hard. There might have been a real altercation had Liane not appeared.

"I need some help," she said frantically. "I—I think I just put a splint on the wrong leg—"

Shaking her head, Nora went to check, and, if necessary, to cover for her.

There was little time for idle conversation. At the front, the mortars still blasted away, the hospital serving only to repair the victims of battle enough to send them on to other facilities or across the Channel, should their condition permit. There was no time to form friendships, to learn to know the battered men except in relation to their injuries.

In the meantime, attack and counterattack continued. The citizens of Ypres were evacuated, men swearing in coarse Flemish accents, children wailing. The sky beyond the city was aflame. Poplar trees along the avenues quaked and rustled in the shock produced by falling shells.

The German attack reached within twenty-five hundred feet of the town's perimeter—and hesitated. In the brief pause, the Canadians and reserve battalions from two British units pressed forward, holding the line.

While the armies met in mortal combat, another battle was being fought in the skies.

Earlier, planes and great gas balloons were used by both sides for reconnaissance. Now they had become weapons of war. A German Taube had dropped bombs over Paris shortly after the beginning of hostilities, but the action was little more than a propaganda ploy. Later, pilots carried any weapon at hand: pistols, rifles, shotguns; grenades suspended below the aircraft. Now, planes buzzed above the war zone like hornets, equipped with a deadly sting: the cumbersome British "Gunbus"; the Morane-Saulnier Ns; Nieuport 10s, Bristol Scouts, and Sopwith Tabloids.

And most recently produced by the enemy, the "C" class of airplane: armed two-seater biplanes of more than 150 miles per hour. These included the Albatros CI, the DFW CV, Rumpler C IV, and Halberstadt CV.

These planes were capable of aerial fighting, and bombing, in addition to providing ground support, reconnaissance, and artillery spotting.

Jo listed the planes, learning to identify them all. Two pilots had been brought into hospital, one British, one French. Too badly burned to transfer, they both were able to speak. She took voluminous notes before they died, sending an article home, entitled "These Brave Winged Men."

She felt good about it. It deserved publication on a national scale.

When she heard the faint buzzing sounds that

indicated a dogfight overhead, she would leave her records and run to gaze into the skies.

"Watch him," she would mutter. "He's on your tail—oh, oh! A bad loop! Pull out—get your nose up—you're going to stall—"

The walking wounded teased her about her fixation. "This will be our first woman flier," they said.

"You just might be surprised," she answered, laughing.

But when a Bleriot monoplane with a wounded French pilot managed to land, intact, in the vicinity of the hospital, she was stunned at the flimsiness of its structure. It looked as if it were made of matchsticks wired together with baling wire. Old handkerchiefs had been sewn to cover the wings and the fuselage where the pilot sat, the remainder left naked to facilitate the replacement of brace wires—

In this, a young man, little more than a boy, had dared to fly above the earth, a shotgun his only weapon.

"Are they all like this?" she asked the flier, once his wounds were tended.

They were not, he said, though many flew this craft. He thought the new German Fokker with a single Parabellum machine gun mounted to its cowl might be the best—

Jo hadn't seen one, but she recognized it instantly when she did. It came barreling out of the north one early morning, dropping a series of exploding shells along the road the ambulances traveled to the front. The pilot dipped low over the huge tent that was well marked with a red cross on a white ground, close enough that she could see his blowing scarf, a wave of his gloved hand. Then a small bush at the perimeter of the grounds exploded in a shower of dust and leaves as his machine gun chattered.

Another pass over the hospital, and he was gone, a sliver dot winging away in the blue sky.

"The bloody bastard!" Peter Carey swore, shaking his fist at the disappearing plane. "The unmitigated jackass!"

Denise was not so sure. There had been something thrilling in the pilot's flamboyant actions. And after all—he had hurt no one.

"Just whose side are you on, Miss Dugal?" Carey asked testily.

"I was joost pointing oot that he did nae harm. And he could hae!"

"This is a hospital! In there," he pointed to a large tent, "are men who have gone through hell! Your heroic friend just reminded them that it is still out there."

"I didna think—"

"Don't try," Carey said, turning on his heel. "It would probably not be worth the effort!"

It developed that Dr. Carey was justified in his concerns. Within the hour, several of the more severely wounded patients worsened rapidly. A French soldier with a head wound went suddenly, completely, mad.

He somehow got hold of a pistol and backed up against the wall of the hospital tent, pointing it erratically around the vast room.

Liane, bent to change a bandage, stood. Her heart was pumping wildly, and she took a step toward him.

"No," she whispered. "No! Put it away—"

He fired, the bullet striking a support near her head. Another shot went through the roof, a third through a side wall. The fourth struck a water pail with a clanging sound. The fifth and sixth went into the dirt floor of the tent, and then the man was grabbed by two of the more lightly wounded patients.

"Get the doc, hurry—"

With one glance at the madman, bull-strong in his insanity, Liane fled for help.

Peter Carey subdued the man and sedated him, cursing the German pilot under his breath. This patient had been on the ragged edge for some time. Evidently the strafing had driven him over the brink.

And little Liane had narrowly missed being killed.

He couldn't guess her fears at reentering the tent, nor that only the thought of Tamsen Tallant, a woman long dead, had given her the courage to do so. Tamsen would have faced up to the problem.

Carey saw Liane going from patient to patient, calming them after the frightening episode, acting as though nothing of moment had happened. In his view, she was a very brave young lady.

All of them were, for that matter. He'd been so busy considering them a nuisance that he'd refused to consider their true value. Even that redheaded witch.

He was sorry he'd spoken to her as he did. She couldn't have known the effect the German plane would have on the patients. For some reason, he was always ready to read her off when she opened her mouth.

He supposed he owed her an apology.

Word of the madman and Liane's miraculous escape had already reached the little house that served as surgery. Denise felt a sense of guilt as she remembered the quarrel she and Carey had earlier in the day. Why did I nae hae the sense to keep my mouth shut, she wondered. Noo the mon hae been proven richt—

She gave a small cry as a spray of blood soaked her apron. She should have been paying attention! Dr. Percy had botched another job, cutting too deeply, severing a major vein—

Dear God!

Together, they fought to stanch the flow; a white-faced bumbling young man and a frightened girl. And then it was too late—

"I—I was looking at you," Percy stammered foolishly. It was a mistake—"

Denise stared at the dead man. She had become accustomed to death, grimly closing her mind against the horrors she had seen. But this had been needless. She burst into tears.

Percy came around the table and put his arms around her. "Don't cry," he said. "It could not be helped. He was a surgical risk—"

Then, the feel of her warm body driving all thoughts of what had happened from his mind, he lost his senses. He forgot his bloodstained hands. They were suddenly all over her as his mouth sought her lips— and struck her chin.

"You're so beautiful!" he said passionately. "You don't belong in this terrible place—and neither do I. I've done my duty for my country, and I intend to request assignment back to London. I can get a discharge! My father will go to bat for me.

"I'm a wealthy man, in private life. I can give you everything—"

Dr. Peter Carey, all primed for an apology to Denise Dugal, walked in on the tender scene. His eyes went from the embarrassed couple to the bloodless features of the corpse, his mouth tightening in a granitelike face.

"He—he died. I was comforting Miss Dugal," Percy said inanely.

"That's quite evident," Peter Carey said harshly. "And now I wish to make a statement. This is a hospital. You are a physician, and this young woman is a volunteer. While you are in my surgery, you will remember that. Of course, I have no control over your—intimacies—on your own time."

"It wasna—" Denise began.

Carey interrupted her. "You are excused, Miss Dugal. Not you, Percy!" A hand on the shoulder stopped that young man as he prepared to follow Denise from the room.

"You and I," Peter Carey said ominously, "need to have a consultation—about a former patient."

Denise went to the little tent that had been set up for the girls, her face hot.

The fule, she fumed. The bluidy fule! Tae think she'd gie a second glance at a—a wee squeakie mouse like Percy! He was spying on them, that he was! Walking in, all saft-footed and sly—

Raging, she stripped away her bloodied apron, hanging it up to see if it could be sponged. Then her eyes caught the location of several bloody handprints and her face flamed again.

She put her hands over her eyes. Nae wonder the mon thocht as he did! She was sae humiliated she could dee—

Sitting on the edge of her cot, she sank into a puddle of misery that was only lightened when she replayed the scene.

Poor little Percy, probably on tiptoes, hunting her mouth and hitting her chin.

Why did she hae sooch a fatal attraction for shorrrt men?

chapter 17

In the days that followed, Dr. Wilmoth Percy pressed his suit. Denise could hardly endure him, but the knowledge that it bothered Peter Carey was an incentive. She felt his angry eyes on them as they worked together in surgery. Whenever there was an opportunity, she smiled adoringly at Percy and fluttered her lashes.

"There, Doctor," she would say. "I think ye did an excellent job."

She learned his first name, Wilmoth, and addressed him that way at every opportunity. The little man's chest swelled, and he took to walking on his toes in order to appear taller.

Then suddenly, there was another glut of patients. Savage fighting erupted as the opposing armies battled for possessions of villages between Ypres and Arras. A combined British-French offensive had been arranged; the British to attack at Festubert, the French at Souchez.

Britain's attack gained no ground, due to a shortage of ammunition and the continuing German attack at Ypres. The skirmish lasted for only forty-five minutes—and cost ten thousand men. The wounded filled the hospitals directly behind their lines, and spilled over into those as far north as Ypres. Dr. Carey sent a message to headquarters, urgently requesting another surgical team and as many orderlies as could be spared.

Again, the wounded came in by every available means of transportation. The two ambulances—Ford trucks with covered beds—jounced along the shell-pocked roads carrying their cargo of grievously injured.

Then one day a single vehicle came limping in. Petrol ran freely from its gas tank, and water spurted from the radiator as it pulled up before the hospital tent—to die. The driver half climbed, half fell from the cab, his elbow almost blown away, his clothing covered with blood.

While his load of patients was removed and his arm tended, the man gasped out his story. It had been a plane. A German plane took one low sweep, machine-gunning as he came.

"Dammit," Carey swore, "those trucks are well marked as ambulances!"

The pilot couldn't have missed the red-cross symbol, the driver averred. He was so close he could see the devil laughing. One sweep, and he waggled his wings and took off again.

The driver had brought the ambulance on in, but apparently the second one hadn't fared as well. He was still out there with a truck filled with wounded, several miles down the road.

Nora's face was bleak.

"We'll have to bring them in!"

"How?" Carey asked sourly, "piggyback? Look at that bloody thing!" He gestured toward the truck.

"You got a pocketknife?"

Brows raised, he reached into his pocket, handing her the implement. She flipped it open expertly, selected a blade, and picked up a tent stake. Hauling the toolbox from the truck, she found a hammer. She whittled a stake and made a plug for the gas tank, then moved to the front.

"Fill the damned tank," she shouted, "while I fix this thing. Liane, bring a bucket of water!"

The emergency repairs finished, she cranked it. Nothing! Swearing under her breath, she lifted the hood and poured gasoline in the carburetor. Then she ran around to crank it again. This time it caught. Dr. Carey ran toward her.

"Get out. I'll drive—"

"Ye'll do no such a damn thing! Yer needed here. And, hell, this is a automobile we're talkin' about, not a busted leg! You a mechanic?"

Carey had to admit that he was not. Perhaps Dr. Percy?

Dr. Percy had no mechanical aptitude, nor inclinations to be on the shell-pocked road at the mercy of a mad German flier. He begged off. He, too, was indispensible, with the mob of patients who had just arrived.

"But you cannot go alone. I will not allow—"

Jo ran forward and climbed into the cab beside Nora, her eyes shining. Another experience to write home about—

The truck choked, backfired, and was off down the road in a cloud of dust. Carey looked after it, his brows creased with worry, his eyes alive with admiration.

"By God, I hope they make it! But—my word! I've never seen anything like that!"

Denise opened her mouth to retort, thought better of it, and went to Wilmoth Percy's side.

"I'm sure," Percy whispered to her, "that the—the young lady's talents are acceptable under the circumstances. But her actions are not quite—feminine. I cannot imagine a man being attracted to her—"

"Oonless he has a likin' for mechanics," Denise said sourly.

Dr. Carey was watching, so she swallowed her jealous thoughts and turned on the charm. Percy responded satisfactorily.

As they bucketed toward the stranded truck, Nora steered skillfully around shell holes. Jo studied her. She knew there had been some problem with Nora's Frenchman, though she'd never dared to ask. Nora, for all her tomboyish exterior, was a private person. She hoped whatever it was didn't bother her any longer. She did look relaxed and happy. Jo put a hand to her hair, which was blowing in the wind.

"I like this," she confided. "I'm so sick of being shut in a dark little room with records—"

"And I'm sick of diggin' out shrapnel, and tryin' t' piece them sojers back together! Hell, I just ain't got th' knack fer it. Jo—I think I oughta take up amb'lance drivin'. Reckin it's more my style." She turned to look at her friend, her gray eyes anxious, narrowly missing a crater.

Jo gulped, then smiled. "I'd like to be your aide, if you'll have me."

"You ever drove?"

She hadn't.

"Then I'll learn you."

"Dad," Jo said dreamily, thinking of her newspaperman father, "will just die! This sounds like something Aunt Tamsen would do—"

The only hitch would be Dr. Carey. He was shorthanded, and they couldn't leave him now. Then there were the other girls, Liane and Denise—"

Nora chuckled, wrinkling her pert, freckled nose. "Liane is dangerous enough without wheels! Didja know she ran smak-dab into Ol' Prissy Percy last night. She was carryin' a bedpan." The chuckle erupted into laughter. "There was you-know-what all over his front—"

Jo was laughing, too. "It couldn't happen to a nicer guy," she said, wiping tears of mirth from her eyes. Then she leaned forward.

"There it is."

The ambulance sat off the road, the driver sprawled half out of the cab. A number of wounded had dragged themselves from the stifling canvas-covered rear of the vehicle, and lay dazed and exhausted around it.

"Looks like a damn battlefield," Nora said, her face somber. "Jo, get any that can walk into this'un. I'll take a look at th' truck."

The ambulance had fared better than its driver. Aside from a number of bullet holes, there were only two flat tires to contend with. Nora and Jo moved the patients from one vehicle to the other, then Nora jacked up the truck and changed the tires, quickly and efficiently.

When she had finished, she was covered with dirt, her hands black, her nose smudged. Jo had to laugh.

"You're a sight," she grinned. "And now that the ambulance is operable, what do we do? You can't drive them both back."

It was Nora's turn to grin. "You," she said gleefully, "are gonna drive the other."

"I—oh, Nora, I can't!"

"Gotta," Nora said practically. "Come on. I said I'd learn you—"

Had an observer plane been overhead, the pilot would have seen a strange sight. In Jo's amateur hands, the empty ambulance seemed to frog-hop across the terrain. At one point, approaching a shell hole, Jo took both hands from the wheel and covered her eyes. Then, sensing that Nora did not intend to help her, she clutched the wheel grimly, slewing away to safety.

After one or two more satisfactory trials, Nora climbed down from the cab.

"Yer on yer own."

"Oh, dear God!" Jo killed the engine in her fright, but Nora climbed into the loaded ambulance and drove off without a backward look.

Gritting her teeth, Jo got down and spun the crank. The engine caught and she got back into the driver's seat, mentally planning ways to even the score with Nora. To her surprise, she managed to level out after a few near-catastrophes due to oversteering. Though her knuckles were white from gripping the wheel, she began to feel euphoric as she approached the field hospital.

Ahead, Nora had already stopped. They were all out unloading the first vehicle: Dr. Carey, Percy, Denise, Liane—

She would pull up evenly beside the other truck and come to a smooth stop. She would show them!

There! Synchronize clutch and brake! Simple! Slip the gear into neutral, release the clutch—

She got it almost into neutral, but not quite. The truck jumped forward, popping her neck. Before she could collect herself, it leaped again. It stopped before the little tent she shared with the other girls, and she climbed out, straight-backed, pretending she'd done it on purpose.

Hearing the laughter behind her, she gritted her teeth. She just might not ever speak to Nora Murphy again.

chapter 18

The little group at the field hospital worked throughout the night. Then relief arrived the next morning in a transport straight from Paris. In the group were two doctors. Dr. Ian Stacey was bald, the age spots on his head giving him the appearance of a large speckled egg. Dr. William Butts had a bushy head of hair and a short pointed beard. Obviously both had been recently dyed. One had been an obstetrician, the other a pediatrician, and neither would ever see seventy again.

"Scraping the bottom of the barrel over there," Stacey said cheerfully. "Saw the chance to do our bit for jolly old England, what? Volunteered, and here we are."

"And hoping to see some action, I might add," Butts put in, his eyes roving boldly over the girls who stood behind Peter Carey. "I say, may we select our own assistants?"

God forbid, Nora thought. She would tab Butts as a pincher and fondler. She'd seen his kind before.

In addition to the aged doctors was a young man, Ned Burns. He was fragile and wan, his health having kept him from the armed forces. He had a brief stint of medical school to recommend him.

There were also four orderlies with various ailments that kept them from service. One had a withered arm, another a twisted foot. The other two were obviously dull-witted.

Peter Carey was fit to be tied. He'd waited a long time for additional support, and they'd sent him a motley crew. He felt better upon questioning Stacey and Butts and discovering they had general practice in their backgrounds. Ned Burns, though frail, seemed bright enough.

At least he would be able to get females out of his surgery!

He turned to the girls. "These gentlemen will take over in my department. You will be assigned to patient care—"

Nora lifted her chin. "Hell, no," she said. "I plan to drive the amb'lance from now on. Me and Jo done decided on that."

Jo looked horrified, then she gulped and nodded.

"That," Carey said frostily, "will be the occupation of these gentlemen. He turned to the orderlies. "I will need two of you for that purpose. If you will volunteer—"

None of them stepped forward. None of them had ever been behind a wheel.

"I refuse to allow—"

Nora squinted up at him, her eyes like stone. "Don't look like you got no say, Doc. And right now, me an' Jo's headin' back fer another load."

She walked toward the trucks, Jo following. Carey hastily sent two of the orderlies, one to ride with each girl. Jo started her vehicle and prayed she would make a dignified exit.

She did.

Behind them, William Butts laughed, an old man's high-pitched giggle. "Looks like the little ladies won out, Dr. Carey. I would say they have brains as well as beauty."

His eyes were fastened on Denise, and she cringed. If he touches me, she thought, I'll scream!

The arrangements worked out well. The aged doctors proved to be hardworking and capable. Young Ned Burns was an apt pupil, and more adept at his work than Dr. Wilmoth Percy.

Percy was relegated to the background, routine care of patients and the like, called upon only in emergency. He was irritated, feeling he hadn't been given his due.

It was because Peter Carey was jealous, he told Denise. Jealous, because he, Percy, had attended a more prestigious school. He did not tell her that his moneyed grandfather had insisted his grandson have a profession, else he would not inherit.

He did not have to take Peter Carey's insults. He had written to his father to have him transferred home. It was only a matter of time. And he intended to use that time to woo the lovely Scottish redhead, and convince her she must go with him.

Denise, piqued at having been banned from the surgery and put to work bathing patients, changing bandages, and emptying bedpans, was irritated, too.

She knew her work in surgery had been excellent. Yet, she had been relegated to a slavey—because she was a woman.

Liane listened to her grousing, but it was clear she was none too sympathetic.

"Somebody has to do it," she pointed out. "And the men are all so nice, no matter how ill they are. They try not to complain."

"They dinna like me! They're a' asking for you!"

"Only because I've been here longer," Liane said gently. "They know me better. Did you know Sam"—, she pointed to a young man in a full body cast,—"Sam has three children. He showed me their pictures. And Thomas, over there, was only married three days before he went to the front. Joshua—"

"Oh, stop yer minchy prating! If ye are trying tae mak me feel guilt—"

"Oh, no," Liane said, wide-eyed. "I wasn't!"

Denise left her and went to tend a young boy who looked very like one of her older brothers. He had a mop of red hair, deep blue eyes—and he was dying.

He held tightly to her hand through most of the night, calling her Laura.

Then finally it was over.

She left the hospital tent and went out into the night, leaning against the rough canvas of the tent, crying. She was crying for the boy—and for herself. Why was it, she wondered, that no one understood her. She was nae the witch they all thocht her to be. Her mother had always said she was like Granny Arab, tae full o' her ain sel tae be luving and gieing.

And a' the while, she wished tae be like Tamsen.

She was suddenly fiercely jealous of the unknown Laura she had replaced for just a little time—

"My word, what luck. I thought it was you—"

Wilmoth Percy. Denise was suddenly glad the darkness hid her grimace of distaste. His soft, pudgy hand closed over her own, attempting to turn her to face him. Instead, she kept her eyes on the distant flashes of exploding shells.

"'Tis a bonnie sight, if ane didna ken 'twas a battle," she said.

"Yes," he said distractedly. "Miss Dugal—Denise—I must speak with you. Only today, I have received mail from home. My father—"

"I had mail, tae," she interrupted, trying to pull her hand free. "My mum wrote, sending alang a note from my granny—"

Percy was not to be deterred. "My father has arranged for my transfer to London. I told him all about you; that you are Lord Dugal's daughter—"

"My father is a farrrmer, a second son. My uncle is The Dugal—"

"No matter! He is delighted with my choice. My mother is arranging a series of social events in your— our honor; teas, balls. I took the liberty of saying I thought you preferred the color green, and she is decorating our room in—"

"Dr. Percy, I hae gien ye nae reason tae believe—"

"You have not said yes," he told her fondly, "but is it not true that actions speak louder than words? When you look at me, I see it in your eyes! Your hand is trembling in mine—"

"Oh, lordy," Denise moaned, closing her eyes. "Oh, lordy!"

"Denise—"

It was Liane's voice, calling her. The younger girl had come out of the hospital tent, on her way to empty a bedpan. "Denise, will you take a look at number four? He seems—"

Her voice broke off as she saw Dr. Percy standing so close to Denise. In her embarrassment, she tripped over a guy wire. For the second time, the good doctor received an unexpected shower.

Denise fled into the tent, holding her hand over her mouth to keep from laughing. When Liane returned, red with embarrassment, she hugged her.

"Liane, I luve ye!"

Liane looked surprised, then her soft amber eyes filled with pleasure. Again, Denise Dugal felt guilty. She had never been friendly with Liane. For the first time it dawned on her that the girl must be lonely. She had nothing in common with tomboy Nora, or Jo with her modern upbringing. Her age and her Asian blood somehow set her apart. Denise, too, was lonely. She needed someone to talk to.

"Liane," she said, "I wad like us tae be friends."

"I would like that, too," Liane said shyly.

"Pairhops we could hae a gossip, then."

"That would be nice. Right now, I must see to Sam—"

She went to the man's cot, and moved him a little, easing his position. Denise heard him mumble something, and Liane's answering laugh.

Denise had offered the hand of friendship and had been left standing. She tossed her head, her impulse fading. There was nae reason to worrit aboot Liane. She maun think o' herself.

In her head, she kept hearing Wilmoth Percy's declaration of love, visualizing a round of social events, teas, balls; the life of a queen. That would show them

all that she was someone. Jo and Nora, Liane; that—
that domned bluidy Carey!

Unfortunately, Wilmoth Percy went with the
package.

chapter 19

Dr. Percy went to his tent and removed his clothing. He wondered if that damned little Chink had purposely drenched him with the foul contents of the pan she carried. That she would manage it twice in one day seemed a bit preposterous.

Maybe, he thought smugly, she was trying to attract his attention. She was possibly envious of his devotion to the lovely Denise. Women were like that.

Scrubbing up, he liberally patted on lavender water from a bottle that had been a gift from his mother. The scent always evoked a wave of nostalgia for his home, where he was awarded the love and respect he deserved.

Reaching for a clean uniform, he paused. His transfer was already valid. There was no need to do Carey's dirty work any longer. He must speak to the man in the morning, tell him he was going. It would be wise to have a good night's sleep, and be fresh for what might be an awkward interview.

Pulling on a flannel nightshirt he crawled into his bunk. For a long time, he lay smiling at the tent roof, imagining Carey's face when he learned he was losing not one, but two of his people.

At dawn, Percy rose and dressed in an immaculate uniform, then went to find Peter Carey. Carey was sitting on a low wall outside the cottage, a cup of coffee in his hand. He was rumpled and unshaven, his jacket stiff with blood, his blue eyes bloodshot and shadowed. He and young Burns had worked throughout the night. Now he had a brief respite, since Stacey and Butts had taken over.

"My word, man, you look dreadful."

Percy's voice was higher than he'd intended. He lowered it somewhat on the last word.

Carey looked at him somberly, and took a sip of coffee.

"And you," he said pointedly, "do not."

Percy stiffened. "I must tell you that I am no longer attached to your staff. I am sorry to deprive you of my services—"

"I think the hospital will survive," Carey said dryly.

Bloody bastard, Percy thought. Well, he'd get his comeuppance! With a ring of triumph in his voice, he finished his sentence.

"And the services of Miss Dugal, who has consented to become my wife. She will be leaving for London with me."

Peter Carey jerked, the coffee in his cup spilling over his hand. For a moment he stared at the self-satisfied expression on the foppish little man. Then he called out to an orderly.

"Tom, bring Miss Dugal here, will you?"

Denise, exhausted from a night on duty, emerged from the hospital tent, trying to straighten her hair. Carey thought this was a true test of womanhood, the ability to look so lovely in dishevelment. The morning light touched her hair with a finger of fire, and he felt a sharp pain in the region of his heart.

"Ye sent for me?" There was still defiance in her voice. She was willful, stubborn, strong-headed—but that was not a bad thing in a woman. And all this was to be wasted on—that.

His eyes moved to Wilmuth Percy, who seemed to shrink before his appraisal, then back to Denise.

"I understand congratulations are in order," he said quietly. "A courier is coming through shortly, then proceeding to Boulogne. I would suggest you effect your packing immediately."

Standing, he took Denise's hand, feeling it tremble in his own. "I wish to thank you for your assistance. It has been invaluable. We—we shall miss you."

Denise was too stunned to speak. Congratulations in order? Dear God! What had Wilmuth Percy done! Peter Carey was turning away. She caught at his arm.

"Wait! Ye dinna understand—"

Peter Carey had regained his equilibrium. "There is no need for further discussion. Luckily, neither of you are indispensable. Now I must check on a patient. If you will excuse me—"

He strode away, not looking back. Denise watched him go, with disbelieving eyes. The bluidy idiot! Tae write her off like—like a kitchen maid, after a' she'd doone! Tae push her at this wee squeekie-mouse o' a mon! Nae indispensable! She'd like tae wrrring his flaming neck, she wad!

Wilmuth Percy touched her arm. "The man is rude," he said with a touch of pique. "Did you note that he said nothing about my services here? Unmitigated gall! But he is unimportant. Come, my dear, we have preparations to make."

Jerking away from his possessive hand, Denise fled to her tent. She was seething with fury, shedding angry tears.

Domn the mon! Domn him! And Wilmuth Percy, tae! As soon as she calmed hersel, she'd gie the twa o' them what for!

But did she want tae?

She was twenty-four, ganging on twenty-five, and wi' no prospects i' sight. Her ain cousins didna like her. She wasna wanted here, and she wadna gae hame! In London there would be teas, balls, a social whirrrl—

And there would also be Wilmuth Percy, wi' his fawning ways and clammy hands.

For now, she had nae choice. She had as much as been told tae gae. She wasna indispensable.

She began packing furiously. Liane came in, yawning after her all-night stint, and looked at her with wide eyes.

"What are you doing, Denise?"

"Minding my business," Denise snapped, "which is mair than ye do, ye meddling snippet!"

Liane backed from the tent. She'd learned there was no dealing with the Scottish girl when she was in a towering rage. She had no idea what was wrong, but she was worried. She wished Jo and Nora would hurry back.

In answer to her wish, a cloud of dust appeared on

the road. The ambulances were returning, and at an unusual speed. They braked in front of the hospital tent, and Nora called for help. They must unload quickly and retrace their drive. The British had made an attempt to press forward again, and with disastrous results. Men had been scythed down in a deadly fire. They would be bringing them in by the hundreds—

Peter Carey swore and began issuing orders. The more severely wounded were to be placed before the surgery, taking priority. Butts and Percy were to work as a team. Burns and Stacey. He—and Denise Dugal—

Denise moved to his side, but Percy stood fast. "I'm not on duty," he said squeakily. "And neither is my fiancée. You forget, we're not officially—"

Carey looked at him, his eyes cold as January. "I did not forget. This is an emergency situation."

"It is your emergency, old boy," Percy blustered, "not mine. Come, my dear."

The scorn in Carey's eyes was echoed in Denise Dugal's.

"I shall stay."

"I will not allow my wife to—"

"I am nae yer wifie, nor do I intend tae be."

Percy was still fussing when she turned her back to help lift a litter, and disappeared into the cottage. Sometime during that long day of blood, sweat, and tears, he disappeared. Denise was never to see him again.

She stood by Peter Carey, slapping the instruments into his hand, often closing wounds as he moved to aid one of the other doctors. There was no time to think of Percy, or of anything else for the next thirty-six hours.

Butts and Stacey were finally given a short time to
rest. When they returned, Carey finally capitulated.
He was reeling on his feet, blind with fatigue.

Denise led him, stumbling, to his tent, where he
fell across his cot, fully dressed. He was asleep when
she pulled off his boots, lifted his feet into the bed,
and drew his blanket up under his chin.

He leuked like a wee lad lying there, his brow
unworrited and smooth. A' the cares and anger were
wiped awa. He'd said naething about her staying, nor
the work she'd doone this day, and mair likely never
would, but she was glad she had—sae glad!

She smoothed back his tumbled blond hair, touched
the downy beard that had gone unshaven these last
days. She hadna noted his lashes, sae lang, curling
against blue-shadowed hollows beneath his eyes, nor
how tender was his mouth wi' its lang British upper
lip—

Impulsively, she bent to kiss him. He stirred and
smiled a little.

Did he dream it was her who kissed him? Or some
other lass, waiting for him in his ain country?

Denise Dugal had come a long way toward growing up, this day, but her tendency toward jealousy
had not improved.

chapter 20

At two in the morning, Denise and Peter Carey were called to replace two weary old men. Dr. Stacey's bald head was ashen beneath its age spots. Dr. Butts was too exhausted to sneak his customary pinch as Denise passed by. Seeing his reddened eyes, she was almost sorry.

All the long day, she and Carey worked together. Oddly enough, she felt no fatigue. Instead an odd new energy hummed through her veins, regenerated as Peter looked up with an occasional smile, or the words "Well done!"

When their stint had ended and the other physicians took over, Peter Carey reached out unexpectedly to take her arm.

"I'm too tensed up to sleep. Would you care for a short walk?"

She would.

They didn't go in the direction of the road, but out into the fields, now a profusion of blooming wild flowers. Reaching a grassy hummock, Carey sat down, pulling Denise down beside him.

Neither spoke for a long time. It was good to just be still. In the distance, there was an occasional explosion, red and blue lights flickering in the sky, but the sight and sounds of war had become the norm. They might, Denise thought, have been two peacetime lovers enjoying the evening.

Her face turned pink at the notion and Peter Carey looked at her curiously.

"It's odd," he said. "You've been here for some time, and I know nothing about you. Just that you're Scottish, and have a talent for surgery. How did that come about?"

She recounted her life on a Highland farm, the need for handling emergencies, both human and animal, from time to time.

"I envy you," he said. He had grown up in London. His father was a prominent doctor, and he followed in his footsteps. He had four sisters—

"And I hae four brothers," she laughed.

"The other girls, Jo Blaine, Nora Murphy, Liane Wang. I understand there's some kind of relationship?"

"Jo is my cousin. Nora's people are"—she started to say servants, but changed it—"old family friends. Liane is my cousin's daughter's daughter—"

Peter Carey held up his hands in helpless confusion. "This is too much for me! Liane is of Asian blood, is she not?"

"Her gransire, and her father. There is a story, a buik aboot the family. It a' began wi' thrrree sisters, Tamsen, Arabella, and Emmeline McLeod . . ."

She wove her way through the tale of the family

forebears and he watched her, enchanted. The sun's last light glinted on her hair. Just beyond, two butterflies hovered over a mass of yellow bloom. She twirled a blossom in her fingers as she talked. He wanted to take it from her, kiss those deft small hands—

"Leuk!"

He followed her gaze. In the distance, too far to hear the sound of their engines, two planes were involved in a fight to the death. As they watched, one of them spun from the skies, twirling like a falling leaf.

Their idyll had ended. The war intruded on them even here. Peter Carey got wearily to his feet. "I suppose we had best return. They will be calling us at two."

Denise took the hand he extended to her and stood, brushing grass from her skirt. He had not released her hand and her heart was beating much too fast.

"This has been very pleasant," he said quietly. "Thank you."

"I hae enjoyed it," she admitted.

For a moment it seemed that he might bend to kiss her, and she swayed forward, lost in his blue gaze.

"Peter—"

It was as if a shutter closed over the emotion she'd seen in his eyes. Releasing her hand, he stepped away.

"I'm glad we've had this chance to know each other better," he said in a remote tone. "It will make it easier to work together—professionally."

Walking beside him, scorning his helping hand, Denise held her head high. Domn the mon! She'd

near made a fule of hersel, for cerrrtain! She maun
see that it didna hoppen again!

Peter Carey, too, was cursing himself. He'd loved
only once before, and it had ended badly. The girl,
learning how he wished to pursue his life's work,
walked out on him. He'd suffered for a long time
until he saw her as she was: selfish, shallow, vain—

The atmosphere of war precipitated relationships.
And he had no desire to repeat his first mistake. He
would watch himself carefully from this time forward.

There was no need. Denise Dugal was as circum-
spect as any orderly might have been. She handled
her duties promptly and with dispatch. The warm
flower-scented evening in the fields might never
have been.

Working around the clock, no one noticed when
the patient load began to slack off. One day it seemed
there was more than they could handle, the next
there was time on their hands.

Here in the immediate area of Ypres, the fighting
had become a holding action. The bulk of both
armies had moved southward, each side seeking a
spot to break enemy lines.

The French, seeking to take Vimy Ridge, some
fifty to sixty miles below Ypres, failed in their efforts
and lost two hundred thousand men.

Peter Carey chafed at the orders that kept his field
hospital at a distance from such furious battles. He
was treating trench foot, minor wounds, and an
occasional case of syphilis—while men were dying
down the line, for lack of care. Again, he fired off an
angry letter to headquarters.

No answer came.

Now, the ambulances driven by Jo and Nora were
filled, not with the wounded, but with the dead.

With the easing of battle, bodies were collected from the trenches, bagged, and carried to a central point to be identified for the record, then transported for burial.

Nora was able to handle the more grisly details. Jo admired her courage. She seemed to be made of steel! As for Jo, she was placed in charge of personal effects, a job she could handle physically but not emotionally.

Often, she wrote far into the night, letters to go along with a packet from a young man's pocket; a packet which might contain a picture of a child; a watch with a cracked crystal; a love letter to a girl.

"I think these are the hardest," she told Nora, trying to smooth out an envelope stained with mud and blood. "It means they've never had a chance to live."

Nora looked at her with eyes that were suddenly blank with grief.

"I know," she said dully. "I know."

"Nora!" Jo rose, upsetting a bottle of ink that unnoticed, ran down the side of the table she used as a desk. "Oh, Nora! Why didn't you tell us!"

"It wouldn't of helped him," Nora said.

Jo burst into tears, and the small freckle-faced girl put her arms around her. It was Jo who must be comforted.

On September twenty-fifth, the British took the town of Loos and fought on to Lens, where they were driven back by a savage counterattack. The French fought to the top of Vimy Ridge, but suffered twice as many casualties as they inflicted. The Allied total of killed, missing, wounded, or captured had reached a total of one million five hundred thousand men.

Then, along the lines, there was a waiting. The rains began, turning trenches into seas of mud; making shell holes into tiny lakes in which a man could drown. Men shivered through November in clothing that was never dry. Food was scarce, even more so at Ypres, since most supplies were diverted to the trenches. The staff of the little hospital were always hungry—and cold, as wintry winds billowed the walls of their tents.

A wood stove was kept stoked in the cottage, but still the surgeons had to work in shifts, warming their cold, stiff hands in turn.

"I keep thinking of those poor devils out there," Peter Carey said mournfully. "It must be hell!"

"It's not so bad when you are young," Dr. Stacey said. "I remember once, years ago, I had a patient out in the country—"

He drifted off into one of his interminable yarns. It had to do with delivering a baby, and the snowy night on which it was born. The story proceeded to give the child's name, its subsequent illnesses, such as measles and diptheria, its schooling and its present occupation.

Denise yawned, excused herself, and went to bed.

Sleet slanted against the tent walls with a million tapping fingers, and she shivered for a long time. Finally, the blankets began to hold the warmth of her body and she slept.

It was odd that she dreamed of lying in a field, still warm from a day of sun. And that lying next to her, holding her, was Dr. Peter Carey.

The next day, a day when there was no sound carried from the front, when the world seemed frozen into eternal silence, mail arrived by courier.

Included in the mail were many small boxes and

packages, gaily wrapped inside their plain brown traveling garb.

Stunned, the girls realized it was almost Christmas. They did not wait to open their gifts. In the parcels were edibles from Maggie in England and the Dugals in Scotland; note paper and pens from Jo's parents; an assortment of candies from Liane's— and last, but not least, flannel gowns trimmed with lace, and heavy underwear from Em Courtney and Arab Narvaéz.

I do hope you girls remember you are ladies, read an admonishing note from Em. *We sewed the nightdresses ourselves. The garments in the stores are shocking!*

There was a rush to don the underwear. The two elderly ladies had done exactly the right thing—for the wrong reasons.

The girls were still half dressed when Peter Carey rushed into their tent, waving a piece of paper.

"It's come!" he shouted exultantly. "We're moving out in February! We're going to"—he paused and squinted at the paper—"to a spot on the Somme River, between Albert and Chaulnes. And why the bloody hell we're going there, I haven't a clue!"

chapter 21

The edibles the girls received in early December were shared with staff and patients. Again, the specter of hunger stalked the compound. With little to do, the girls talked of other, happier holidays.

"I keep thinking of Gran-gran's turkey," Liane said. "The way she cooks it, all brown and crusty, with corn bread dressing."

"And sweet potatoes piped around it," Jo put in. "And cranberry sauce, and succotash!"

"With three kinds of pie," Nora added. "Apple, with cheese, pumpkin with whipped cream, mincemeat—"

"A saddle o' mutton," Denise said dreamily, "wi' boiled potatoes—and haggis."

"*Yucch!*" Nora said. The other girls made wry faces.

"I hae as much richt tae what I like as ye do!"

173

"It sounds like garbage," Nora said, wrinkling her nose.

Tempers were short, and the conversation gave promise of becoming a full-fledged argument until Jo intervened. "Maybe we can think of something we're all hungry for. A baked hen, maybe roast duck or goose . . ."

In this, they all concurred.

In those last weeks before the holiday, in addition to hunger and cold, they faced another enemy, this one unknown.

The girls worked different shifts, and it was not unusual for one of them to be alone in their tent at some hour of the night.

It was Liane who woke to see the figure of a man bending over her, a dark shadow against the dim light from the tent flap. She began to scream, twisting away as the intruder tried to put his hand over her mouth—and he fled.

It would be impossible to discover his identity. Peter Carey questioned the orderlies, the ambulatory patients to no avail.

"I don't think you will have any more trouble," he told the girls grimly. "But if we catch him, I'll personally beat hell out of him. This is what happens when women are in a place they shouldn't be! One smile, and a man thinks he can—"

"Are ye faulting us wi' this?" Denise glared at him, her eyes sparking fire. "'Tis nae the mon's doing? Joost that the wee Liane led him on?"

"I did not say that!" Peter Carey's face was red. "I only said that women in a man's world can expect—"

"Expect what?" Jo stepped to Denise's side. "To take blame for being raped?"

Carey's red face deepened into crimson. "You are deliberately misunderstanding me," he said.

"I dinna think sae!" Denise faced him squarely, as Nora and Liane moved up to join them.

He looked helplessly from one to another. Nora's jaw was set and stubborn. Denise was obviously ready to do battle. Small, outspoken Jo had her fists clenched. Liane looked at him gravely, with a pitying expression.

"Oh, hell," he said. "All I'm going to say is that I'll do my best to protect you!"

"We," Denise said icily, "wull prrrotect oursels!"

Peter Carey scowled, turned on his heel, and walked away. He was both embarrassed and seething. He'd only said what he did for the sake of their own safety, and they'd managed to twist his words into an insult. If they wanted to think like that, they could go to hell!

"We dinna need help frae the likes o' him," Denise said loftily. "I dinna think th' mon wull gie it another try, noo that we're alerrrted."

"Who do you think he could be?" Nora asked. "One of the orderlies? A patient—"

"It might even be a German spy," Liane said, her eyes wide.

Jo laughed. "I doubt that. He would have more on his mind than molesting little girls! No, I would say it's someone we know, someone connected with the hospital—who knows when only one of us is off-duty."

"Pairhops the high and mighty Dr. Carey himsel," Denise said, red flags of color still flying in her cheeks. "He seems tae think we're fair game!"

"Oh, Denise!" Liane gasped, her face paling. "You surely don't think—"

"I think we maun keep an eye on them a'! And it wad be wise t' be canny, and stay together."

The first day, the girls were jumpy, scrutinizing any male who was able to walk. The second day, they began to feel more secure. And on the third night, Liane was on duty; Jo and Nora leaving with their ambulances before dawn. Denise saw them off, then secured the tent flap tightly and crawled into her cot, secure in the knowledge that it was almost morning.

She woke to an odd, gnawing sound.

A rat, she thought, sitting upright. She reached for her boot, and cowered against the wall. Where was the domn thing! She drew back the boot, ready to let fly as she searched the tent with frightened eyes.

The tent flap opened, and a shadow blotted out the gray morning light. Liane?

It would not be Liane. She had fastened the flap tightly. The sound she'd heard was that of a knife sawing away at rope!

She waited.

The body of a bulky man shouldered his way through the opening. She couldn't see his features, but his head seemed too large, grotesquely shaped. He stood for a moment, as if adjusting his eyes to the darkness, then cautiously felt his way toward her cot.

Denise let fly with the boot, along with a stream of Scottish invective that would have put any of her father's cottagers to shame. The intruder caught the boot somewhere in his midsection and staggered backwards. Then he fumbled wildly for the opening and ran out onto the compound.

Denise ran after him, the other boot in her hand. "Ye bluidy flaming cowarrrd," she shouted, "stop where ye are!"

He disappeared around another tent, and the door

to the surgery opened. Peter Carey stepped out, his eyes widening at what seemed to be an apparition. Denise Dugal stood in her long white flannel gown, barefoot on the icy ground, a boot raised to hurl like a missile.

"What in the name of God!"

She turned to face him, breathing hard, the beating of her heart thundering in her temples.

"'Twas—joost a rat. I thocht t'kill him."

"You are more apt to kill yourself," Carey said grumpily. "Out here in the cold in your nightdress."

Denise looked down, gasped, and fled, her cheeks burning.

Again, the girls held a consultation, reaffirming their intention of handling the man themselves. The shadow Denise had seen, with its odd, misshapen face, pointed to a stranger; maybe a Belgian or Frenchman, driven mad by the war, roaming the countryside—

"I dinna think sae," Denise insisted. "He came straight for my bed. If he's a strrranger, he hae been spying on us."

It was a shivery thought. That night, no one slept.

"I don't know which is worse," Liane said disconsolately, "being cold, scared—or hungry." The others agreed with her statement. Mess had become almost unpalatable, with rancid bully beef boiled into a thick broth, served up with hardtack.

The next day, Nora came back from an ambulance run. She was shivering and beaming. She had taken her coat off, and it was wrapped around an object she carried like a child in her arms. When the coat was removed, it proved to be a large goose. She had already attached a cord to its foot, and it flapped and squawked before finally settling down to be admired.

"Christmas dinner," Nora said proudly.

"Good show!" Peter Carey said. "I'll have one of the orderlies prepare it now. In this weather, it will keep—"

Denise stepped forward. "We cannot kill the creature! It is a living thing."

"But—Denise!" Carey lost his formality as he stared at her. "A goose is intended for—"

She stamped her foot and burst into tears. "After a' the bluid and hurt we've seen, you wad want mair? I couldna eat a bite of this birrrd!"

Liane swallowed. "I don't think I could, either." Jo agreed, and Nora looked longingly at the booty she'd snatched up along the roadside. She was a practical girl, and it seemed Denise was being ridiculous, but, hell—they all had to stick together. She'd argue it out with her later, in private.

Peter Carey watched them go toward their tent, four pretty girls leading a Flemish goose. Reared in the city, he had a special liking for all birds and animals, wild and tame. He would not have cared to kill the feathered creature, but they had been on short rations for a long time. He couldn't help admiring Denise Dugal, seeing a side of her he didn't know existed.

He wished they might have met at another place, another time.

Tethered inside the tent, the goose, now dubbed Gus, calmly nibbled away at hardtack, broken and scattered on the ground. Nora took the opportunity to present her argument.

"Dammit, Denise, you can be noble if you want, but them things is to eat—"

"Aye," Denise smiled. "But there is soomthing ye dinna ken. A goose wullna let a body slip by wi'oot gieing an alarrrm!"

"I be damned," Nora said in awe. Then, "And mebbe we'll catch the sonofabitch by Christmas!"

Several days later, Liane slept alone again. She slept soundly, with Denise's assurance that Gus would sound an alarm. She woke to a terrible clamor, a honking, a hissing, a beating of wings.

In the darkness, she could see the goose in midair; a white blur, a shadow fighting it off, then turning to run, crashing through the entrance, knocking a tent pole down on his way.

Liane rose, trembling, and lit a lantern. The tent looked as though a snowstorm had struck, covered with feathers, but Gus was well, alive, and still hissing with indignation.

In his beak was a triangular piece of cloth.

Nothing was said to Peter Carey. It was Denise who discovered the source of the scrap of material. Dr. Butts, bending over a patient, displayed a sizable mending job, pulled together with surgical thread.

Denise looked at him closely, squinting her eyes, trying to imagine what he would look like in a darkened tent. His stiff black hair—white now at the roots—and beard would make a grotesque silhouette.

This was their man.

The girls held a consultation.

"Do ye ken the spot across the field, where there's a bit o' hedge?" Denise asked.

They did.

"Then here is what we'll do—"

All that afternoon, Denise flirted with the roguish old doctor, fluttering her lashes and smiling, much to Peter Carey's bewilderment. Carey was even more mystified when, following the end of surgery, Denise invited Butts to walk with her.

"Joost as far as the hedge," she said.

The doctor was delighted. His chest expanded, and he turned to give Carey a suggestive wink as he followed Denise from the room.

The damned old fool, Carey thought. And what had got into the girl? Hell, it was none of his business what she did on her own time!

Butts waddled along after Denise, admiring her shapely figure. If he had known she was attracted to him, he needn't have risked his neck last night. That bloody bird! He'd volunteered for service just to escape the kind of charges that would have been brought against him if he'd been caught. And here, the lady seemed ready and willing.

He was puffing a little when he reached the hedge. Denise maneuvered him until his back was against it, then gave him a seductive smile.

"Have ye nae guessed what I want o' ye?"

He laughed, heavily. "No need to apologize for your feelings, my dear. I want the same thing—"

He reached for her and she took a step backward. At that moment, the other girls rounded the hedge and stood blocking his escape. His eyes darted around the circle and he tried to bluff it out.

"What the bloody hell—"

Denise drew a pistol from her pocket, and handed it to Nora. Then she carefully withdrew a surgical knife, removing it from its case.

"I thocht ye might want tae instrooct us i' a lesson i' surgery."

Her eyes began at his head, ran along his body, and then stopped.

"I ken the best place tae begin—"

Dr. Butts fell to his knees, blubbering like a baby. Before his ordeal ended, he confessed his sins to four implacable faces, promised to reform, and Peter Carey would never know what had happened here today.

On Christmas Day, the soup was thinner than ever. Again, the girls talked of happier times; of turkey and mutton, of three different kinds of pie. But never once did anyone mention roast goose. They shared their hardtack with Gus, as he pecked away happily on the floor.

---------------------------- *chapter 22* ----------------------------

The Forsythes, in their palatial manor on the English moors, had no such compunction. Maggie looked at the roast goose gracing the center of the table, and then at her hostess.

"Best-lookin' damn bird I've seen in a coon's age," she pronounced. "Luka, you done yerself proud. Ye got yerself a good wife, 'ere, Alastair, y'lucky bastard."

Alastair Forsythe smiled at his wife. When he and Luka married, she'd been a fairylike creature, with silver hair and eyes. Age had not changed her, except to give her a calm serenity that he loved. His own hair was white, and he still marveled that this woman loved him. He began to carve, and Maggie turned to Sean.

"Some folks is luckier than others. Like me. Look at Sean 'ere, good ez new an' twice ez feisty with that peg leg of 'is."

Sean grinned. Maggie was proud of his new leg, almost to bursting. She swore it gave him a resemblance to old Sim Blevins that was "plain spooky." He would never be the man her adoptive father was, but he was glad Maggie thought so.

The groaning table was surrounded by Luka's children and grandchildren; all of them rosy-cheeked and sturdy. There were, however, several empty places. When the meal was finished, Alastair stood and raised his glass to them in a toast.

"To those of us who are missing," he said huskily. "And may they come safely home from the war."

Luka lifted her glass, smiling, though tears trembled on her lashes. "They will be safe," she said serenely.

After dinner, Maggie insisted on washing up. As a guest in this house, she wanted to earn her keep. It didn't dawn on her that this was normally servants' work, and that Luka joined her in the chores to ease her feeling of indebtedness. Together they cleared the table and carried the dishes to the kitchen.

Throughout the family, it was known that Luka, Arab's youngest daughter, had a strangeness to her; that she knew things other folks didn't. Her remark about her boys being safe intrigued Maggie. She approached the subject in her usual fashion.

"Whatchu said in there about yer boys. Howja know?"

Luka shrugged her frail shoulders and smiled. "I—just do."

"Then y'reckin y'could say the same about all them girls we left? 'Ow they're doin'?"

Luka closed silver eyes, then opened them. "They will be safe. Nora—"

She stopped, her smooth brow wrinkling. Maggie

felt a sudden irrational fear. "Sump'n wrong with Nora—?"

Luka took Maggie's pudgy hand in her slim fingers. "Your Nora is well. Her grief is behind her."

Maggie was stumped for a moment, then she said, "That French feller, Jack, that's 'oo yer talkin' about, ain't it? 'E dump 'er?"

Luka shook her head, and Maggie read her answer in her changing eyes.

Maggie blinked back tears. The Frenchie had been a nice boy, fer a frawg. Look what he done for Sean. She'd figgered Nora stayed behind, 'opin' t'patch up a argument, or something. She must of knowed the boy was dead. Why the hell didden she say so?

All Maggie could do now was pray that Nora had a happy Christmas. She wished to hell they was all back home.

In California, the place the Murphys called home, the two elderly ladies, Em Courtney and Arab Narvaéz, were having their annual family dinner.

Missie and Matthew Blaine were there with Matthew's son, excused from service due to a lame leg. Petra and Lee Wang sat close together for comfort. Liane was their only child, too young to be plunged into the horrors of war, and they were half out of their minds with worry. The empty chairs at the table haunted them all.

Em's turkey, as usual, was a superbly done bird: golden and crackling. She had insisted on doing the cooking herself, with her aged, blue-veined hands. And there was enough for a crowd.

"So many of us gone," she said wistfully. "Duke, Juan, Tamsen and Dan—"

Arab reached to touch her sister's velvet-clad arm.

"We can't fret over what we cannot change," she reminded her. "We must think about the living. And after all, Maggie and Sean are with Luka, and the girls all write—"

Em looked stubborn for a moment. "I swear, if Maggie and Sean weren't almost family, I'd discharge them! To let those children get mixed up in a war! They should have dragged them home, if necessary."

"You forget our escapades," Arab said in a small voice. "Em, maybe we should read Missie's book again. I suppose, if we were in the girl's place, we would have done the same—"

Em's face cleared, her remembering smile bringing back a trace of her girlhood beauty. "I guess we would," she admitted. "I'm just glad we can depend on them to behave like ladies in any circumstance!"

She stood, preparing to go to the kitchen. "I'm certain they're having an absolutely splendid Christmas. Now, who's ready for dessert? There are three kinds of pie—

In Scotland, Ramona Dugal beamed at her noisy brood. Once almost a mirror image of Tamsen, she had settled into a matronly woman with huge dark eyes; a motherly woman, with a lap for grandchildren and soft arms to cuddle them. Her rawboned Scottish husband worshiped the ground she walked on, as did her crew of redheaded sons.

Outside, it was cold; the burn gurgling beneath a coat of ice, the very hills frozen to the sky. But in Ramona's kitchen it was toasty warm, and smelled of good things. A long trestle table had been covered with her best linen cloth. It nearly bent beneath the weight of Ramona's cooking. Here, there was no dearth of mouths to feed.

She tapped on a glass with a spoon and shouted above the din. "Jason! Mike! Stop tussling! You forget you're grown men! Sean, have you washed up for dinner? Where's Rory?

Turning to her daughters-in-law, busily moving food from stove to table, she said distractedly, "Find the children. Everything's on."

After a lively racket as they enthused over the beautiful dinner, they seated themselves. Denis Dugal bowed his head, giving thanks for their blessings, and asking God to watch over the lamb who was absent.

Ramona's face crumpled a little as she thought of the headstrong, spoiled lass who was her only daughter; for whom the love surrounding her had not been good enough; who was set on having her own way.

She said her own little prayer for her daughter's safety, and asked that the girl find what she wanted from life.

Food was passed, rapidly disappearing from platters and bowls. The lusty, brawling family attacked it with their customary gusto, without slackening their noisy conversation. It was some time before Ramona became aware of Rory, who stood, trying to make himself heard above the din.

"Mum, Dad, all o' ye! Hark! I hae something tae say—"

Ramona smiled at him. She wished him luck, but her youngest son had little chance to get a word in, with all the commotion going on.

Finally, he used her trick, snatching a spoon, tapping on a glass. The conversation finally ground down to a halt as they looked at him curiously.

He looked so pale, Ramona thought, suddenly alarmed. And his forehead was beaded with perspiration. Perhaps it was too warm in the kitchen, after all—

"I hae something tae say," Rory Dugal said again, stumbling a little over his words. "I hae joined the arrrmy. My rrregiment is leaving on the morrow—"

The kitchen wasn't too hot, Ramona thought inanely, it was cold. She began to shiver uncontrollably.

chapter 23

The weather was bitter as the little hospital moved to its new location near the Somme, again using an abandoned farmhouse as a center for surgery. Skies were clear, but the temperature was low. The ground was frozen, iron-hard, resisting tent stakes as the orderlies drove at them with sledges, their curses almost tangible in clouds of smoking breath. Finally the tents were up and patients began coming in. Here, there were a few wounded, but the majority suffered from influenza, frostbite, and the like.

Again they seemed to be in the midst of a holding action. A case of "Hurry up and wait."

The Butts affair had drawn the girls closer than they had ever been before. They had time to talk now, to really get to know one another. Jo, strongly influenced by her mother, Missie Blaine, was a strong advocate of women's rights. They discussed the heroism of nurse Edith Cavell, executed by the Germans for her work in the underground; Mairi Chisholm and Mrs. Knocker, the Heroines of Pervyse, who had been given the star of the Order of Leopold II. And, most exciting of all, the story of Sapper Dorothy Lawrence who, as a lark, managed to dress as a soldier and get herself into the trenches at the front.

"Nae wi' men like Peter Carey aboot," Denise laughed.

"One of these days," Jo said sturdily, "he won't have any say about it! They'll discover a woman can do anything a man can do! There will be women in the army, women who fly. I plan to learn, if I ever have the chance."

Nora grinned. "If you learn like you learned to drive, I don't wanna be nowhere around."

The memory of Jo's first attempt brought laughter, and Jo joined in good-naturedly.

Except for the cold and hunger—always hunger—the interlude of waiting was not unpleasant. And finally they discovered what they were waiting for.

There was fighting all along the line, particularly at Verdun. Pressure there was relieved by an offensive along the Somme.

The British were moving ahead.

In mid-June, British troops marched along the road near the field hospital. Trucks carrying heavy guns and ammunition rolled past, obscuring the blue sky of France with dust. Carey, talking with an officer, was able to ascertain that the bulk of the troops under Field Marshall Haig were units of the New Army, or "Kitchener's Army." General Sir Henry Rawlinson's Fourth, General Sir Edmund Allenby's Third; General Sir Hubert Gough with a newly formed Reserve included, as well as General Marie Emile Fayolle's French Sixth Army.

Peter Carey returned to his people, his face drawn and pale. "I don't know what's set up," he said, "but there's going to be one hell of a fight!"

The whole crew worked at preparing for a massive crisis. A truckload of new medical supplies was uncrated and situated to handle an emergency. Surgical instruments were prepared and wrapped in sterile cloth. Cots were set up close together, with only room to slide between. Nora spent her time beneath the ambulances, or with her straw-colored head under the hood.

"Damn things gonna be ready when we need 'em," she said grimly, "er I'm gonna know the reason why!"

For a day or two, there was no sound. The dust settled on summer flowers, larks sang. And then, somewhere on the horizon, the cannonade began. For five days, there was no cessation as light and medium artillery smashed at the German frontline trenches. Other medium and heavy artillery reached farther, bombarding positions deep in the German rear.

On June 26, as though the firing had pierced the sky itself, it began to rain, a steady drenching rain that turned trenches into running rivers of mud and delayed Haig's attack.

On July 1, the sun shone. One hundred thousand British soldiers began a shoulder-to-shoulder march across the territory they'd reduced to no-man's-land.

And Germans rose from shell craters and dugouts, firing with machine guns, rifles and cannon, throwing grenades, sending flares to signal support fire from the German artillery.

There were fifty-seven thousand British casualties.

The small hospital was the recipient of a massive wave of wounded. They were brought in every type of conveyance. Nora and Jo drove their ambulances as close to the front as they were allowed, picking up walking wounded; men carrying the shattered bodies of their friends—bleeding themselves, but pleading "Help him. He's my chum!"

Her VAD uniform covered with blood, skirts draggled with mud, Nora exchanged her clothing for that of a soldier: pants, tunic, trousers, heavy boots. Jo followed suit. Two diminutive women, with the help of a pair of slow-witted orderlies, they worked night and day.

In surgery, Dr. Stacey worked along with the lame orderly, Dr. Butts with Ned Burns, Denise with Peter Carey. The patients were no longer people. Faceless, they passed through the surgical area as injuries; shrapnel; jaw blown away; splintered, shattered, ripped, torn—

Two days and nights of steady surgery. And the stream never ended. Hold a tin cup of soup in one hand, a bleeding artery with the other—

"I canna," Denise wept. "I canna—"

"You can," said Peter Carey.

Dr. Butts dropped first, midway through an amputation. Ned Burns looked dazedly at the fallen man, then at his patient, spreading his hands in a hopeless gesture. This one was over his head.

Carey, working over a man whose crushed ribs had pierced his lungs, glanced at Stacey. He, too, was unable to leave his work. Burns was incompetent by himself. Carey looked at Denise.

"Get over there! Finish the job!"

Denise went white. "But I'm nae a doctor! I—"

Carey gestured toward Butts's patient. "Do you

think he cares? For God's sake, the man's bleeding! You've watched me enough! You know how!"

Denise stepped over Butts and took his place at the table. Her hands were trembling, her eyes blurred, but somehow she managed to finish the job as Carey's patient was being exchanged for another.

Carey inspected her work, and put an arm around her, hugging her close to him.

"Good girl," he said.

It was the finest compliment she'd ever had.

Then he knelt to take a look at Butts, who had not moved since he'd fallen. He felt for a pulse, and lifted a flaccid lid. Finally, he got wearily to his feet.

"Gone," he said tersely. "Heart. I've suspected it for some time. Pity. Fine doctor—"

Denise watched them carry Butts's body from the room, feeling a kind of sick horror. The man had been pale and quiet since that day in the corner of a hedge below Ypres, his lips rather blue.

Maybe they had killed him!

Late that night, emergency assistance arrived in the form of four young British doctors in crisp, clean uniforms. With them were orderlies and ambulances. Peter Carey greeted them, his own clothing stained and rumpled; his hands shaking, his eyes red-rimmed.

His people, he told them, had been on duty for more than sixty hours without sleep. Give them twenty-four hours, and then he would return to proper shifts.

He stumbled off to his tent without waiting for an answer.

Denise stepped under an improvised shower that had been rigged for the women. It consisted of a bucket of water, tipped into still another with a perforated bottom. She scrubbed her body with the strong disinfectant soap they used in surgery, trying to erase the smell of blood.

When the others came in, she was lying wide-eyed, staring at the tent roof. Nora was grumbling, certain that the newcomers would damage one of her beloved vehicles.

"Oh, shut up," Jo scolded. "Me, I'm going to fall into bed and sleep for a hundred years!"

"Until the prince wakes you with a kiss," Liane laughed.

"That," Nora drawled, "will probably be Doc Butts."

Denise began to shiver a little. She turned over on her stomach so they couldn't see her face in the lantern's light. She couldn't tell them Dr. Butts was dead. Not tonight.

She kept remembering the way he dropped, how she'd stepped over him, her terrible fear as she finished the surgery he'd begun.

And then Peter Carey's arm about her shoulders. "Good girl," he'd said.

And she wasn't, she thought drearily. Really, inside, she wasn't good at all.

In the corner of the tent, Gus, fed and watered after a too-long period of neglect, made a small contented sound and preened his feathers.

---------------- *chapter 24* ----------------

To Peter Carey's surprise, Dr. William Butts had no records. There was no one to inform of his death. Dr. Stacey knew no more than anyone else. He had met the man on a train from Paris, and had been surprised that, mentioning his destination and profession, they had much in common—even going to the same place. Concerned, he wondered if the man had a record of malpractice.

Peter Carey shook his head. He was a damned fine doctor, no matter what his other problems might have been. He was certain of that.

Apparently ineligible for burial at Britain's expense, with no one in England to claim to body if it were returned, Carey made arrangements for burial in the cemetery of a small French village, the name of William Butts to be inscribed in the records of a little church.

Denise didn't mention the dead man's heart condition, or the fact they might have hastened his death, to the other girls. The frightening of Dr. Butts had been her idea, and she felt guilty enough without seeing that guilt reflected in other eyes. In retrospect, he seemed a harmless little man, addicted to pinching and sneaking into their tent after dark. Maybe he'd had nothing more in mind than just looking.

Luckily, there was little time for conversation. After the first mandatory time for rest and recuperation, they faced a grueling schedule.

The summer sun blazed down as one advance after another was repulsed. Water in rain-filled shell holes steamed, evaporated, diminished, disappeared, leaving bloated bodies to disintegrate in the sun. The smell drifted behind the lines when the wind was right.

The word that drifted back was more frightening. The wounded had an aura of hopelessness, of defeat, unnatural to the British soldier. This was not the old, regular army dying out there, not a cross section of population as with the French, but the cream of British youth. From Verdun, rumor had it that the French armies, though they had fought so bravely, were at the edge of rebellion. Their uniforms were ragged, their food below the level of sustenance.

Unless some new method of warfare—or some new weapon—were introduced, there was fear the war was lost.

It was Nora who produced the first hope. Coming back from a collection point behind the trenches, she'd been forced to pull off the road as a military convoy passed by.

Among the trucks and troops were a number of

monstrous machines, gun turrets thrusting from their snouts and sides—looking like prehistoric monsters.

A new weapon had entered the fray.

Damn! She would like to see the insides of one! To see how it worked!

The armored vehicles were a surprise to the Germans as well. Shipped this far by railway, they'd been covered with canvas and listed on the railroad's manifest as "tanks," to imply they were water tanks.

Mechanically unreliable, the vehicles—called tanks, for want of another name—failed to accomplish their hoped-for purpose. They were too small in number and spread too thin for efficiency.

Another hope gone glimmering.

The Battle of the Somme had cost the British 475,000 men, the French, 195,000. The Germans lost 500,000 before the fighting shivered to a halt late in November. A blizzard raged across the field of battle, coating barbed wire and the remnants of shattered trees with ice, softening the land about the shallow, pleasant, winding little Somme—where blackbirds once thrived and herons nested on its marshy banks.

The backlog of patients was such that the crew sent to fill in during the emergency did not leave until late December. The girls were surprised to discover they had known them as faces, never as names or personalities. The workload had been too hectic to become really acquainted.

"It's just as well," Nora said crossly. "You know where them bastards are headin'? To Paris, to have a big whoop-de-do over th' holidays. Heard 'em talkin'. Wine, wimmen, and song. Wanted Carey t'leave Stacey in charge and take off with 'em."

Denise paled. The thought of this desolate place

without Peter was rather frightening. "He wadna—"
she began.

"Hell, no! Said ez long as there was folks t'keep
keer of, he was stickin'. Wasn't goin' back unless he
was ordered to."

"It wad be nice," Denise said wistfully, looking
down at the men's clothing and heavy boots the girls
all wore now, "tae dress like a lady, and hae a real
Chrrristmas dinner."

"Well, dammit," Nora said, "what th' hell's stoppin'
us. Reckin them men," she gestured toward the
hospital tent, "would apperciate a change of scene!"

Her idea was a welcome one. The girls dug to the
bottom of their lockers, dragging out gowns that
hadn't been worn for a long time, hanging them to
shake out. They'd been hidden from view for so long,
they seemed new and lovely. Liane had a problem.
In the year they'd spent in the field, she'd grown.
Her dress had to be let out at the bosom, taken in at
the waist, let down at the hem.

And Nora went foraging.

In a village far behind the lines, she found cheese,
a huge sausage, several jars of preserves, and a dozen
dusty bottles of wine. Recklessly trading military
property—two pairs of army boots and a number of
blankets from stores, she acquired an ancient piano.
Its keys were yellow, one ivory missing, but it wasn't
too much out of tune.

The girls were ecstatic when she returned with her
acquisitions. They hid them out until Christmas Eve,
moving the piano into the hospital tent while Peter
Carey was in surgery, covering it with a canvas tarp.

Then they dressed. Denise wore a green gown
with a tightly fitted waist, and straight skirt; her
glorious hair falling in a cloud over shoulders empha-

sized with puffed long sleeves. Jo's dress was blue, beautifully tailored to her slim figure, echoing the color of her eyes. Nora wore a plain dress of brown piped with cream.

"You should really have jewelry with that," Jo told her. "A lavaliere, or a pin—"

Nora fingered the ring she wore on a chain, hidden beneath the neckline of her dress. "Hell," she said, "I ain't tryin' to win no beauty contest."

When Liane finally donned the dress they'd altered, her companions looked at her in surprise. It was obvious that the slim young lady in the muted melon shade was no longer a child. The style and color of the gown seemed to emphasize her Asian look.

"Something's wrong, though," Jo decided. "It's your hair. Liane, why don't you wear it like your mother does, with straight bangs, the rest down your back?"

"It would make me look more—more—"

"Chinese? Are you ashamed of it?" Jo, as usual, was straight-forward and to the point. Liane blushed.

"No—"

"All right, then!"

Jo went for a pair of surgical scissors and cut Liane's silken hair straight across the forehead. The others gasped at the change it made. Liane was no longer a coltish, awkward girl, but an exotic stranger.

The sausage was sliced and laid in rings on a medical tray, alternating with wedges of cheese. As an additional touch, mounds of preserves on hardtack added color.

There were no wineglasses. Tin cups would not suffice for a gala event. Denise brought a number of small beakers from the hospital stores.

· Liane balked. "We don't now what those have been used for—"

"They hae been sterrrilized," Denise said haughtily.

The bedridden patients in the hospital tent looked up in amazement as four lovely ladies in pretty dresses entered. The girls moved from bed to bed, smiling.

"Merry Christmas!"

Those who were able to respond answered, forgetting their hurts for a moment. A blind man, hearing the cheerful greetings, reached out to catch Jo's skirt.

"I smell perfume," he said wonderingly.

The tarp was pulled off the piano, and Liane sat down to play, her slim fingers caressing the keys. "Silent night," she sang in a voice like bells, "holy night—"

The others joined in; Denise's voice soaring, Jo's deep and full, Nora's a whispering, husky tenor.

And from the cots, set side by side with little room to pass between, those men who had the strength to sing joined in.

In the surgery, Doctors Carey and Stacey finished with their patient. Stacey accompanied the orderlies who carried the still-unconscious man to the hospital tent. But Peter Carey, tired, and for some reason depressed, walked toward his own tent, hands shoved in his pockets.

He'd never wanted to be a doctor, he thought wearily. The job had been passed down to him, a family heritage. All he wanted from this life was a little peace—

Peace on earth, good will toward men!

A damned lie, he thought morosely; a false premise! At the moment, a good part of the globe was engaged in chaos! He'd seen enough of man's inhumanity to man to believe peace was never possible.

The front was quiet at the moment. He wondered if the Germans felt as the British did, that on this night of all nights, slaughter was a sacrilege?

It seemed so still out there, with nothing but a white landscape against the darkness; the softly falling snow.

Silent night—

He flinched a little and shook his head. Now, by God, he was hearing things! Maybe he should have gone to Paris for a little rest and recuperation. His nerves were stretched too thin—

Holy night—

Female voices! The sound of a piano! It was coming from the hospital tent—

His brows knit, he hurried toward the entrance, stepping inside, his lashes covered with snow. And then he saw them: four beautiful young women. And a piano, in this place?

Impossible!

The music ceased and a girl in green, a girl with Denise's glorious hair, her eyes, came toward him. His heart seemed to stop beating at the sight of her, and his breath caught in his throat. For a moment he was unable to speak as his helpers greeted him one by one with a holiday salutation.

Only when he saw Liane did his voice return. And Peter Carey made the greatest mistake of his life.

"Liane! You grew up when I wasn't looking. My word, if you aren't the prettiest girl I ever saw!"

He didn't see Denise's mouth tighten, or her eyes narrow. Carey had looked beyond her at Liane. He passed her by and didna say a word!

No one noticed, as the tent rang with carols and

good cheer, that Denise was quieter, more reserved than usual.

Within the next week, she suggested that Nora's relationship with Jacques Leceau had made a mark on young Liane; that the girl was too conscious of her sex, and should be sent to Maggie, in England.

Jo, knowing Jacques was dead, having promised to keep it to herself, was furious.

"You don't know what the hell you're talking about!"

"Ye dinna need tae shout at me, Jo Blaine! For a' I ken, yer nae better than they are, a'ways flirrrting wi' the men—"

"Flirting!" Jo squalled. "Denise Dugal, for two cents, I'd—"

"Ye'd what?" Denise had her hands clawed, ready to attack.

Peter Carey, coming around the corner, backed hastily away. There was no peace on earth at the moment, or good will toward men—

He wondered why the phrase had not included women.

chapter 25

In mid-February, orders came to empty all hospital beds, if possible, and to gear-up for emergency conditions.

Nora and Jo made trip after trip to the coast, their ambulances laden with severely wounded men—now bound for British hospitals—and home.

Often, they lingered on the docks, watching the great ships that crossed the Channel, wondering what it would be like to join Maggie and Sean at Luka's; to lead fairly normal lives until they could return safely to the States.

At the moment, that return was a remote possibility. After the sinking of the *Lusitania* in 1915, American opinion was so outraged that the Germans pledged to adhere to international law. Now they'd announced resumption of unrestricted submarine warfare. All approaches to the British Isles were blockaded, any ships subject to torpedoing. The hated pigboats roamed the waters unseen, sinking vessels at will.

"Reckin I'd go home, if I could," Nora said. "But I don't see no use settin' the war out at Luka's. Don't know how much good I'm doin' stayin' here. But there ain't nothin' else I can do fer Jacques."

Her gray eyes were wet, the color of the winter sea, as she thought of him. Jo put an arm around her. "I can't go either," she said frankly. "Dad's been publishing the stuff I send home. He said a New York paper picked up on a thing I did about the Somme. I feel like you do. It'd be okay if we were heading for San Francisco—"

"Denise could go home if she wanted."

"Don't I wish!" Jo said with exasperation. "She's kept us all in a turmoil since Christmas. And she's always picking on Liane! Now, Liane's the one who should go to Luka's. Do you suppose if we talked to her—?"

"I tried, dammit. But she insists she'll stick with us. Says it's what Tamsen woulda done."

"I suppose she's right. But, Nora—do you ever get the idea the Allies are losing?"

"Ever' time I haul a load of wounded in," Nora said grimly.

With one last look at a departing ship, they returned to their ambulances and made their way back to a collection of tents that had become home.

The expected offensive came at last, along an eighty-five-mile front from Arras to Rheims. It reached a stalemate in May. The small advances the Allies made were not worth the cost in lives.

And to add to the horror, the French were near mutiny.

The weather again sided with the enemy, and a

late spring snow added to the misery of the fighting men. The little cottage serving as surgery reeked with blood, the hospital tent was filled, and wounded men lay on the ground or leaned against the cottage walls waiting their turn—while the virgin snow turned crimson around them.

Denise, two days without proper food or rest, finally broke.

"I canna take it anymair," she wept. "I canna!"

Peter Carey did not look up from his work, but asked an orderly to take her to her tent. She sat for a while on the edge of her cot, her face in her hands, then finally rose and went doggedly back to the surgery.

It was good that she did. The red cross of the hospital tent was hidden under a blanket of white. A lone German flier, ranging over Allied territory, evidently thought he was over the enemy trenches. Leaning out of the cockpit, he tossed an explosive shell, then hummed away toward the German lines.

It destroyed the girls' tent and one end of the hospital tent.

In the cottage, the noise was stunning. The building seemed to tilt and the stone floor shivered beneath Denise's feet. She looked at Peter Carey, her eyes wide with apprehension, frozen in place.

"We have to finish here," he said quietly. "Then we'll see."

Within minutes, they were out into the night. Denise gave a small cry when she saw the tent was gone, then saw Liane. She ran toward her, screaming.

"Jo? Nora?"

"They're all right," Liane said. "Hurry, we need help—"

One end of the hospital tent had collapsed, and all

who could move were trying to pull the canvas away from those buried beneath it.

There were only four dead; the first was a boy of seventeen who, since he was brought in, had called constantly for his mother.

His mother could not help him now.

The second man had been one of the lucky ones, with a good chance of survival—and return to his wife and children.

His luck had run out.

The third had been brought in from the trenches, insisting God had saved him for a purpose. He survived shellfire, only to bleed his life away beneath a stretch of smothering canvas.

The last was a middle-aged career soldier, blessedly with no one to mourn him. He had been wounded trying to save a fellow soldier entangled in the Boche's barbed wire.

There was no great outcry from the other patients. They lay silent, accepting, awaiting whatever disaster fate had in store for them.

The attacker did not return. Several hours were lost as all hands worked desperately to jury-rig the hospital tent, protecting the wounded from the cold and falling snow. As they worked, a courier arrived, handing Peter Carey a message. He glanced at it, his face brightening briefly, then shoved it into his pocket. Everyone would be elated to hear the news—but not now. There was no time. He and Denise finally returned to the surgery to find there had been several more deaths, due to lack of immediate care.

Denise shook her fist at the sky. "Ye bastarrrd!" she screamed, "I pray ye rrrot i' hell!"

"There's no time for that," Carey said quietly. "Come on, give me a hand—"

Watching him work, his sensitive mouth compressed as his deft long-fingered hands performed their work, Denise had a cold sensation. What if the shell had landed on the cottage—and she had been in her tent. What if Peter Carey had been killed! The thought filled her with horror.

Peter Carey looked up with tired blue eyes. He saw her ashen face and sought for words to comfort her. Suddenly he remembered the message he'd received. It contained a few scrawled words, but those words might change the progress of the war in France.

"This," he gestured around the blood-spattered room, "may all be ended soon. The United States has declared war against Germany. We have another ally."

It wasn't until later that Denise realized the import of what he'd hold her. Ships would be plying back and forth across the Atlantic, carrying troops. Those ships would be armed, and they would return—

Traffic would be moving both ways.

In mid-June, replacements were sent for the entire staff of the little hospital, along with a letter of commendation for the work of Dr. Peter Carey, Dr. Stacey, and their aides. They were to take a month's rest and recuperation, then report at headquarters in Paris for reassignment.

Carey and Stacey left immediately for Paris, determined to work out the logistics of the next move. There had been a shortage of thermometers and catheters, in addition to a paucity of food supplies. This time, they planned to be better equipped.

He didna even say good-bye, Denise thought as she watched them leave. And it was likely they might not meet again. Peter Carey could be ordered

to return to England. There was every likelihood she
and the others would be assigned to different posts.

As far as Denise was concerned, they ought to
think about returning to the States. She broached
the subject and, surprisingly, the others agreed. They
were all tired, sick of the scenes of pain and death
they'd lived with these last years.

"How many articles can you write about a field
hospital?" Jo asked petulantly. "Most of the time, we
don't even know what's going on on the Eastern
Front—or other places in the world, for that matter.
Just bodies and bedpans—"

"I miss my mother and father," Liane said softly. "I
know they worry—"

Even Nora felt the terrible yearning for home.

Before they went to Paris, they would go to Le
Havre, see if it would be possible to engage transportation on a troopship headed for America. If they
could, they would wire Maggie and Sean to join
them.

On the trip to Le Havre, there was a general
feeling of euphoria that faded when they checked
into the hotel that night. Due to the crowded wartime conditions, they were forced to share one room.
Each thought the others asleep as she lay awake
thinking of their upcoming journey.

I've grown up here, Liane thought drearily. Could
she ever go home and be the quiet, obedient child
her parents still thought her? Up at six, to a day of
sewing, reading—perhaps a trip to the bay for sketching
or water-coloring. It had been a peaceful existence
for a little girl. Now, would it be—enough?

Jo also had doubts. It was true that the articles
she'd written were good; graphic descriptions of life
in a field hospital. But if she stuck around, something

bigger might break. Maybe she was giving up her only chance at fame.

Nora hugged a pillow to her wiry little body, trying to soothe the ache of memories. Jacques was in France. Leaving here made her feel as if she were turning her back on him, rejecting him. There would be nothing at home to remind her of his love. Finally, she soaked the pillow through with silent tears.

Denise, to quell the uncertainty that still gave her a shaky feeling inside, mentally created a dream script in which a new, talented star took Hollywood by storm. She visualized herself in gorgeous gowns, appearing before the cameras, descending stairs to meet the hero—

Who, for some strange reason, resembled Peter Carey.

The next morning they went to the docks. Here, there was chaos, confusion, as the Corps of Engineers hammered away at wood brought in from the forests of southern France, extending the piers for off-loading of men and supplies.

A huge ship, its length camouflaged, sidled against the dock. It flew the American flag. Jo, looking at it, found it suddenly hard to swallow.

"I know it's silly," she confided to Nora, "but I feel like saluting! Oh, look—"

Down the gangplank came a horde of fresh-faced boys in leggings and puttees, carrying their gear, their caps tilted at a romantic angle. They marched by, eyes slanted toward the bevy of pretty girls in the watching crowd. From somewhere in the ranks, a wolf-whistle sounded.

Jo's eyes filled with tears. "I'd like to whistle

back," she whispered. "Look at them! So young, so brave, so confident! And before long—"

"They'll be at the front," Liane finished for her.

They were silent for a long time. It was Denise who finally voiced their unspoken thoughts.

"I canna leave," she said firmly. "I feel we wull be needed mair—"

"And I'm staying, too." Nora's face was firm with decision.

Jo raised her eyes to the flying flag above them. "I couldn't go, now."

And Liane, unaccountably relieved that the decision was made for her, said that she, too, would remain on French soil.

They left Le Havre and headed for Paris, feeling almost as if they were going home. And at VAD headquarters, they found Dr. Peter Carey had been there before them. He had recommended them all highly, and asked that they might be assigned to his new unit, since they were a successful working team.

They were all too excited to notice Denise's swift change from euphoria to thoughtfulness. The man had been furious when they joined him at Ypres, and had consistently voiced the opinion that they intruded in a man's domain.

Therefore, it could only be that he was attracted to one of them.

Liane, Jo, Nora? Only one thing she knew for sure. It was certainly not Denise Dugal! Nor, she said to herself haughtily, do I want it tae be!

chapter 26

The girls occupied themselves in various ways during their Paris leave. Liane and Nora went to the banks of the Seine, where Liane captured the scenes in delicate watercolor, and Nora, wrapped in the warm embrace of the sun, dreamed of Jacques.

Jo hung around a newspaper office, thirstily drinking in the news. There was rumor that Russia was withdrawing its support on the Eastern Front. And in the United States, women were coming into their own as auto mechanics, streetcar conductors, elevator operators. They worked on factory assembly lines, as traffic cops, delivered ice, and plowed fields, replacing their men who had gone to war.

It's about time, thought liberated Jo Blaine. It's about time!

Denise, left on her own, went shopping. She purchased a lime green traveling suit that brought out the glints in her fiery hair, with a skirt just short enough to reveal a pair of exquisite ankles. How she wished Peter Carey could see her in it!

But that, of course, was impossible. She had no idea where he was staying. And, of course, she didn't really care!

Her actions gave lie to her defiant thoughts. Each day, she was led, irresistibly, to the *terrasse* of the Cafe de la Paix; the corner regarded by boulevardiers as the center of the world. Here, it was said that if one sat long enough, anyone in Paris would pass by in time.

The lovely woman at a corner table attracted much whispered comment as she sat sipping at a cold drink and scanning the passersby.

No one had heard further word from Peter Carey. He would just show up at the last minute, Denise told herself, irritated at his thoughtlessness. At least he might inform them of their destination. But, then, he thocht of nae ane but himsel!

She almost didn't go to her accustomed place, then changed her mind at the last minute. She took her usual table and was staring gloomily into her glass when she heard her name.

"Denise?"

She jerked upright to see Peter Carey standing over her. But it was a new and rejuvenated man she saw, dressed in a crisp, modish suit, his cravat tied neatly, his eyes as blue as a sunny day.

"It is you!" he said. "I wasn't certain—you look quite different, you know."

She smiled up at him. "I didna recognize ye, at firrrst! Wull ye nae join me?"

He sat down opposite her. "Have you enjoyed your rest? I didn't know how much it was needed. I'd almost forgotten what it was like to sit and talk to a pretty girl."

"I suppose ye've been keeping yersel busy, then?" There was a hint of acid in her well-modulated voice and he looked at her in bewilderment.

"Busy?"

"Wi' girrrls, and a'."

Carey laughed. He'd slept for a solid week, then begun arrangements to provision the new field hospital he was to staff. The few girls he'd met were either married to soldiers at the front or would sell themselves for a pack of Players. He had little interest in that sort.

There was no point in revealing his heretofore unexciting encounters.

"Paris could spoil a man," he lied cheerfully, pushing a blond lock back with a boyish gesture. "And you? What have you been doing since I saw you last?"

What had she been doing? Sitting here, watching lovers pass! Seeing little families, cooing over a babe in arms! Growing older every day! That's what! But she didn't intend to let him know it!

"I hae enjoyed my stay," she said evasively.

"Are—are you waiting for someone?"

Carey made a move as if to rise and she put out a hand, stopping him.

"I—He sent worrrd that he canna coom. I hae the day free—"

"Then perhaps we could spend it together."

"It wad be nice—"

Her smile, he thought to himself, was like a miracle, a reflection of the sun, erasing the willful lines around her mouth. Good God, she was beautiful! The old alarm sounded in his mind, saying, "These are not normal times—don't get involved."

He silenced it ruthlessly. What the hell! This was Paris! No harm in enjoying a young lady's presence on a summer afternoon! It would be over soon enough, and they'd be back to the grim reality of war.

Carey lifted a finger for the waiter, ordered a drink, then reached across the table and took Denise's hand. It trembled for a moment in his own, like a small white butterfly.

"Liane," he said. "Nora, Jo. Are they having a good time, too? I think of you all, often."

Denise's lips tightened a little as he included the others, but she answered in a few short syllables, describing their activities.

"And what happened to Gus?" he asked. "Don't tell me you brought him to Paris."

At his mention of the militant gander, Denise was smiling again. Jo and Nora had driven miles to find a still-occupied farm, giving the goose to the farmer on one condition: that he be allowed to live out his natural lifetime. Two wool blankets, a pair of boots, and a case of hardtack had been thrown in to cinch the deal.

"To Gus," Carey laughed, raising his glass in a toast.

"To Gus."

The thought of the goose brought back memories of the heartrending days at the front, and her brow wrinkled a little.

"We—we hae been concerned aboot the new assignment. Where we're tae be sent—"

"Let's not think about it now! Let's think about ourselves, the day, the sunshine—"

"Aye," she said, her smile returning. "Aye!"

They walked a long way, each extremely conscious of the other. Peter Carey the man, Denise found, was a far cry from Peter Carey, surgeon. And Denise, animated and lovely, was not the cross, tired young woman he'd considered an interloper in his hospital.

They found a small park, where pert French maids pushed baby carriages and children romped along its winding paths. Peter settled down, his back against a tree near the cobbled street, and watched Denise.

She'd captured a ball that rolled across the grass toward the roadway, returning it to its owner, a little white-clad boy. He immediately accepted her as a participant in his game, throwing it ineptly toward her. She ran to catch it and toss it back; her hair escaping into ringlets, her eyes sparkling with delight. Just so, she had played with Rory—

Again, Peter Carey felt a stirring of unease at the feelings she unleashed inside him. He forced himself to remember this was just for today—

Then the ball rolled toward the street again. Denise ran after it, not seeing a cariage that had rounded a corner, the horses at a fast pace—

Carey was on his feet, overtaking her in a single bound, catching her around the waist and pulling her back as the carriage thundered by.

"That was a bloody stupid thing to do," he said harshly, turning her to face him. "Dammit, woman! You might have been killed!"

His words cut off as he frowned into the white face so close to his, and he groaned, crushing her to him, his mouth seeking hers.

"Ah, Denise! Denise!"

Denise swayed in his arms, faint—not from fear, but from something far more compelling. Her pulse was hammering in her ears until she couldn't think. Her knees were so weak that she leaned into him for support, feeling a heat that burned through her new green gown.

"Peter—"

A child's shriek interrupted her and they sprang guiltily apart. They had attracted an audience, and the little boy was crying, pointing to his forgotten ball, which rested against the opposite curb.

Red-faced, Peter Carey retrieved it.

They left the park and the French nursemaids with their knowing smiles and walked some more.

"It is growing late," Peter said finally. "Perhaps I should return you to your hotel."

"I suppose sae."

Then, looking at her flushed cheeks, Peter Carey knew he couldn't let her go, not yet. He threw all his scruples to the breeze, slamming the lid on his warning alarm.

"Or maybe," he said huskily, "you would consent to dine with me. Have you ever eaten at La Tour d'Argent?"

She would love to. And she had not.

At the famous, though unpretentious, "Tower of Silver," Carey ordered the diner de la maison, with its three marvelous courses: Potage Tour d'Argent, Sole Cardinale, and the dish upon which the reputation of the house had been built—Caneton a la Presse. The proprietor, Frederic Delair—called Frederic the Great of Paris—served them himself, solemnly presenting them a certificate stating that the duck they would eat was number 28,613.

Though Denise retained the certificate as a souvenir, she could never recall the taste of what was reputed to be the most fabulous cookery in the world. She was still a little dazed from her earlier sensations. Peter Carey was in similar case. Their conversation was carefully light, with long pauses that seemed like chasms between them.

Finally, they finished their meal and left La Tour d'Argent. Carey was determined to return the girl to her hotel—and as quickly as possible, before things got out of hand. He saw Denise to the suite she shared with the others and thanked her, fighting a desire to kiss her once more. He was rescued when Liane opened the door unexpectedly.

"Dr. Carey!" Liane gasped. Then she was standing on tiptoe, arms around his neck, kissing his cheek. "Nora! Jo! Come see who's here!"

The other girls came, crowding around Carey. Grinning, he kissed each of them in turn. "You cannot imagine," he said fervently, "how I have missed you—all of you!"

In the presence of numbers, his wariness relaxed, and he talked volubly of their upcoming assignment. It would appear they were being sent back to the vicinity of Ypres—

"Maybe," Liane said prayerfully, "we can see Gus on the way!"

That night, after he had gone and they were all abed, Denise lay with her fists clenched and her face hot. She'd thrilled through the entire evening from that earlier kiss, wondering if it meant—anything. And evidently it hadn't. For he'd kissed them, every one, and he said he'd missed them all. As far as she was concerned, he could gae tae hell!

She rose and found her handbag, seeking a paper certifying the Caneton a la Presse as number 28,613. She would throw the domned thing away! Crumpling it in her hand, she held it for a long time, then replaced it once more, tears wetting her cheeks as she returned to bed.

"I dinna care," she said stoutly, pummeling her pillow.

"I dinna care!"

Dr. Peter Carey, making his way home with his hands jammed in his pockets and a pipe jutting from his mouth, was equally perturbed. For today, he'd learned something new about himself and young Denise Dugal.

He discovered he cared too much.

chapter 27

Peter Carey needn't have been concerned about an awkward relationship with the lovely Scottish lass. She was crisply cool and professional as they traveled to Ypres. There, to protect himself, he demoted her from surgical assistant to nursing. It was better this way, not seeing so much of her, and now he had sufficient staff.

A small group of American medical personnel had been sent to work with Dr. Carey, to experience the rigors of life in a field hospital under wartime conditions. There were four doctors at his service.

"All of them married," Jo reported gloomily, "and one of them's a grandpa!"

"I wadna wish a rrromance wi' a doctor," Denise sniffed. "They're deadly dool!"

"Not Dr. Carey," Liane said loyally. Denise shot her a look that sent her scurrying away.

Along with the American physicians had come a small skeleton crew: two ambulance drivers and their aides, and several big-eared, buck-toothed young orderlies and a grumpy records clerk.

Nora, bumped from her position as ambulance driver, was furious. She'd taken pride in her ability to keep the trucks running with makeshift repair; in being able to drive over rugged terrain. Jo was equally despondent, certain that she was assigned to nursing only because she was a woman.

Discrimination, that's what it was.

Except for Liane, it was an unhappy group that set up cots and medical trays—and waited.

A battle was in the making. They had arrived in late July. The noise of intense artillery bombardment growled and hammered against the distant sky.

"This one," Peter Carey said morosely, "is going to be a bitch!"

In two weeks, more than three million shells were spent against the enemy. Then, the night before the jump-off, there was a torrential rain. The battlefield became a quagmire, British soldiers wallowing through the mud, blasted by shellfire.

By nightfall of the first day, there were 31,850 casualties—and only five hundred yards had been gained.

The thunderstorms continued for the next ten days. Shell holes and trenches filled with water; the hospital with wounded. The ambulances running back and forth to the front were often mired to the hubs; the drivers appearing more like clay figures than men.

In mid-August, the weather cleared briefly. Again, the British advanced five hundred yards, but at a terrible cost. Now the skies were filled with aircraft;

the whining of their motors drowned in the thunderous noise of battle on the ground.

In surgery, the doctors worked at full speed, trying to patch mangled bodies into some human semblance. Many of the less grievously wounded were taken directly to the hospital tent with crisp instructions.

"Bullet wound. Right shoulder. Not septic. Remove, cleanse, and bandage."

Denise performed these less crucial surgeries with Nora's help. Her nerves were frayed by the direct responsibility, her back and arms ached, and sometimes she felt a hopelessness that made her sick inside. This was hell. It would go on like this forever. The war would never end.

On November 20, the third Battle of Ypres wound down; its gears frozen by ice sealing the battlefield. Another 244,897 British soldiers had been lost in an advance of only nine thousand yards.

With a number of patients being moved to the coast for shipment, there was at last time to eat, to sleep, to read letters from home. And there were many of them. Em and Arab wished them to know they were hard at work, knitting sock, mittens, and scarves at the Episcopal church, two days a week. Jo's mother, Missie, had joined the campaign to sell Liberty Bonds. Shy Petra Wang, mother of Liane, was helping at a Red Cross canteen—

"We're proud of you," Em wrote. "At first we were concerned that the atmosphere would be less than genteel—"

Jo, reading the letter aloud, stopped to whoop at that remark, then continued.

"—less than genteel. But now that we're involved, we are more informed. Women have had to change

in these troubled days. Arab and I are determined to
keep up with the times."

That statement brought a great deal of giggling and
loving speculation.

"Can you imagine Aunt Em with her ankles showing?" Jo asked.

"Or wearing britches?" Nora said wryly, looking
down at the trousers she wore, tied at the waist with
tent cord to keep them up.

"Or haein' t'tak a mon's clothes off?" Denise added.

"Or handle a bedpan?"

"Or gie an enema—"

The suggestions went from bad to worse as the
girls rocked with laughter, the thought of two faded
little ladies in such predicaments was almost too
ludicrous to bear. It was Liane who brought them to
their senses.

"I think we ought to read the book again," she said
softly, "Missie's book, about their lives when they
were young. Then, they were ahead of their time—"

It was true. They sobered, and opened more mail.

Included was a box of Christmas gifts from Arab
and Em, who had taken the warning to ship early
quite seriously. Inside, they found presents which
provoked more laughter: dainty purchased underclothing for each; semisheer gowns and pegnoirs.

Em and Arab, indeed, were keeping up with the
times—if not with the weather that held two armies
rigid in its freezing grip.

Nora yanked a cap over her pinned-up hair, pulled
on a man's army issue coat, gathered up the wrappings and carried them outside to burn. In the stack
was an unopened letter, mislaid in the confusion; a
letter that was of extreme importance to at least one

member of their group; a letter that none of them would ever see.

It was addressed to Denise Dugal.

You might be able to see your little brother sometime, her mother had written. *We've finally heard from him. He's somewhere in France* . . .

Nora was freezing. Too cold to even think of checking the trash she carried, she threw the wadded bundle into a trench filled with used bandages and other gruesome relics from surgery, and touched a match to it. Then she headed back toward the hospital tent.

An ambulance stood beside it. She frowned a little. It had been unloaded, and should have moved out some time ago.

She walked around the machine, seeing a sight that took her back to Maggie's miracle on the road to Paris. A stalled truck, a pair of feet belonging to someone working under it—but these boots were certainly not Johnny Looper's! Good Lord! They must be size fourteens at least!

"Sonofabitch!" The curse came from beneath the truck, and Nora grinned to herself. Lying down on the ground, she nudged herself under the machine.

"What's the trouble, buddy?"

The man did not look at her. He was scowling at the undercarriage, a bleeding knuckle at his lips.

"Trying to tighten up the universal," he said crossly. "Damn wrench slipped!"

Nora reached for the wrench. "Gimme," she said in her husky little voice "Lemme give it a try—"

Effortlessly, she fitted the tool to exactly the right spot, and gave it a turn.

"There," she said with satisfaction. "Done."

"You're one helluva mechanic," he said as they

worked their way from beneath the vehicle, sitting up, preparatory to getting to their feet. "Wish I could trade—"

He stopped short, confused at seeing a small freckled face with dancing gray eyes.

"Goddamn! You're a girl!"

"I been told so," she grinned.

He blushed painfully. "I figured you was one of them weak-kneed, bedpan-carrying jackasses they got working in the hospital tent—"

Nora's grin spread. Evidently he held the same opinion of the orderlies that she and the other girls did. But she didn't intend to let him off so easily.

"I work in the hospital," she said. "I carry bedpans. Ain't too sure about my knees. But the rest—"

Now even his ears were flaming. "You got me all wrong. I was talking about the guys. Awww, hell!" He stuck out a massive grease-stained paw to engulf Nora's small hand, shaking it solemnly.

"Name's Otto Muehller. Most folks call me Mule."

Nora was equally formal. "Glad t'meetcha, Mule. I'm Nora Murphy."

"Yes," he said helplessly. "Well!"

Simultaneously, they realized how they must look, sitting flat on the frozen ground, shaking hands like a pair of idiots. They both began to laugh and he stood, helping her to her feet. Pulling a grease rag from his pocket, he meticulously removed a smudge from her freckled nose.

"There," he said.

Mumbling an incomprehensible excuse, Nora fled to her tent. At the door, she turned and looked back. He was still standing there, watching her.

And she liked what she saw.

No wonder they called him Mule! He was a giant

of a man, looking like he'd been rough-cut from an enormous tree. His hair was sort of a dusty brown, his eyes an electric blue. And standing close to him, smelling grease and oil and pipe tobacco, she'd felt an irresistible attraction—

It couldn't be! She shut her eyes and thought of Jacques, his slender elegance, his scent of soap and cologne; his soft eyes and gentle breeding. Her hand went to the ring she wore on a chain, trying to remember him, to call him back—

Instead, she watched a big square man in greasy coveralls, who lit a curved pipe, took a puff or two, then slowly walked away.

chapter 28

In late November, just as operations ended at Ypres, word came of a successful battle at Cambrai to the south. Tank brigades had forced their way through the forward German position, followed by five infantry divisions; 180 tanks were soon out of action; 65, victims of enemy fire, the others ditched because of mechanical failure.

"They got to find somebody with know-how to work on them things," Mule Muehller said hotly.

Nora agreed.

Even with faulty equipment, the tank attack had won a gain of ten thousand yards with a loss of only four thousand men.

Unfortunately, a counterattack by the Germans, on November 30, won it all back again.

Christmas was a time of doldrums. The hospital was still overflowing with patients and there was little time for rest. The word filtering in was bad. Reconnaissance planes had reported massive movement toward the German trenches. The German General Ludendorff was preparing for a new offensive in the spring.

Depression reigned at the field hospital. And tempers were short.

"One would think your General Pershing would begin to take some action," Peter Carey said angrily to Frank West, one of his American colleagues. "Good God! He's been sitting down there at Chaumont for three months! What the hell's he waiting for?"

"Perhaps," West said quietly, "he doesn't wish to make as many mistakes as your General Haig."

Peter Carey grinned ruefully. "Touché," he admitted. "I suppose I'm rather grim, tonight. After all, it's Christmas Eve, and we've had one hell of a day."

"And we're finished here, unless we're called out for some complication. I've been saving a bottle for a celebration. How about hitting my quarters for a drink?

Carey was silent, his thoughts evidently far away. West persisted.

"What do you say," West persisted. "We've earned it."

"Sure," Carey said with a forced grin. "Why not?"

As they walked towards West's tent, he could hear a sound of singing. There was no piano, here, but he knew the girls had provided some sort of festive atmosphere. He thought of the previous year; the way they'd sung carols, the patients joining in.

And in his memory, Denise stood out like a star—

It was just as well he had another invitation, he decided. His emotions were pretty unstable tonight, and he just might make a fool of himself.

Denise waited all evening for Peter Carey to appear. Tonight, all the girls had taken pains with their appearance; she, more than most. Not because of Peter Carey, she insisted to herself. But because—

She couldn't think of a reason.

The evening ended and it was time for sleeping medications. The girls moved from bed to bed, soothing restless, hurting men, occasionally depositing a kiss as a holiday token. Liane and Jo would remain on duty. Denise went to her tent, her mouth tightening as she heard a burst of laughter from the American officers' tent, recognizing Carey's laugh among the others.

She felt a mingled rage and hurt. Surely he'd known there'd be a party for the patients! How dared he snub them for a—a gaggle of rrrowdy Yanks!

She went into her tent and closed the flap, too miserable to sleep. Even Nora had someone! She'd left the party tae gae a-walking wi' her latest swain!

And there was only one explanation for Nora's popularity. It was plain the lass had the morals of an alley cat!

Nora, walking quietly beside the mammoth man, his boots crunching on the frozen surface of the ground, was chiding herself for accepting his invitation. And she was frightened.

For a time, her heart had been frozen. And at last, it was beginning to thaw. She wasn't sure that she wanted it to.

She cast a sidelong look at Mule Muehller. No one could be more different from Jacques! There was

just—too much of him! He seemed to blot out the
stars. The hand that reached to steady her was big
and square, permanently ingrained with grease. He
did not have Jacques's courtly manner—

But then, he'd grown up so differently—

She thought of the life he'd described in their few
stolen minutes of conversation. He was the youngest
of a huge German Lutheran family. His brothers
farmed and his sisters married farmers, all living in
the vicinity of a town called Elk Creek, Nebraska.

"Little town," he had told her. "Boethe's Hard-
ware and Mortuary, Eversole's General Store—A
little park with a pavilion..."

It sounded nice.

He'd joined the army for two reasons. First, his
family was German, and he felt he owed it to America.
Second, he'd always had a passion for motors, and
figured this was a good place to learn.

"I want to build tractors," he had said dreamily,
"farm machines."

His grandfather had died in the fields, pushing a
plow. There had to be a better way—

She found herself sharing his dream. She had
studied his rough drawings, her enthusiasm mounting.

"Hey," she had said, "what about this? If you take
a look at the drive train, you might—"

"I'll be damned," he said over her shoulder. "Think
you got it!" He had picked her up and whirled her
around, laughing up into her face. "That's what's
been bothering me! Nora, girl, we're one hell of a
team!"

Then, his face turning red, he set her on her feet.
But the melting operation had already begun.

She'd been fighting with herself ever since. She
liked Mule Muehlller! Liked him more'n she'd ever

liked another man. But likin' wasn't love—was it? Then why did the feel of those square hands spanning her waist, his warm breath on her cheek, make her go trembly all over—like now?

"Are you cold?"

If she said she wasn't, he might guess at the turmoil going on inside her.

"A little bit, I reckin," she said.

An arm as big as a truck tire and twice as tough went around her, gathering her in against the heated, solid wall of him.

"Didn't think," he apologized. "Gets damn cold in Elk Creek. Guess you're not used to it, coming from California."

"I reckin not."

"Hey," he said, "look at that!" He was pointing to the sky over no-man's-land, high above the occasional flashes of exploding shell. "You suppose that's the one?"

"You mean that star?" she asked, sighting along his finger, totally confused.

"Sure. Hell, it's Christmas Eve, and that's east, ain't it?"

For a moment, she thought he was kidding her. Then, seeing the rapt expression on his face, she knew he wasn't. And she loved him for it.

"I s'pose it could be."

His arm tightened. "You know what my ma used to say? She said that at midnight on Christmas Eve, the animals talk to each other. Once, I sneaked out to the barn in the middle of the night but, dammit, I went to sleep in the haymow."

Nora grinned, seeing a squarely built red-cheeked little boy keeping vigil on a cold and lonely night.

"Did you git a spankin'?"

"Got a cold. Spent the next week in bed with a mustard plaster on my chest. Burned like hell."

Now they were both laughing. Then their laughter died in a sudden awareness of each other. His face came closer to hers, and she felt a flutter inside, as of wings.

"Nora—"

Dear God, he was going to kiss her. And she had to stop him! She wasn't ready—

"Tell me some more about your family," she stammered. "Bet yer wonderin' what they're doin' tonight—"

"I know," he said quietly. "First, they go to the schoolhouse, for the school tree. Then, they go singing carols at all the farms. And, finally, they wind up at the house for the biggest damn feed you ever saw, Ma sitting at one end of the table, Pa at the other, and maybe twenty or so kids and grandkids in between. Uncle Karl'll be there, Aunt Greta, Pastor Ludwig—"

The list went on, and Nora listened enviously. She had never known a real home. First there had been a room over Nell's bar in San Francisco. When Nell died, they'd moved to the Courtney mansion. She'd sort of grown up on the fringes of other people's lives.

"We always have our big meal on Christmas Eve," Mule continued. "The next morning, there's church. Then in the afternoon, Pa hitches up the sleigh and we visit around—"

"I think I'd kinda like all that," Nora said wistfully.

Mule Muehller looked down at the girl beside him. He'd decided right off that she was the one for him. He'd take a lot of kidding for bringing home such a sawed-off little runt, but who the hell cared?

He'd fallen like a ton of bricks the minute he saw her, with her cute little face drifted with freckles.

It had been even better to discover she was someone he could talk to. But some innate sensitivity told him to go slow. Something, maybe a shadow in those big gray eyes, told him this girl had been hurt.

"I'd like to have you there," he said now. "I'd like to take you to the school tree and to church and show you off. Ma—Ma would like you—"

"Oh, Mule—"

She didn't move, but he could feel her retreating.

"Too soon, huh?" he asked hoarsely.

"Yes," Nora said. "There was somebody—"

Was?

"He's dead?" Mule Muehller asked in a gentle voice. Her eyes told him the answer.

He shrugged his massive shoulders and grinned crookedly. "Well, then, I just wait, I guess. Didn't have a right to say anything, anyhow, with the war going on—"

The war! A place where you fell in love, and love died on the battlefield.

Nora stood on tiptoe and kissed Mule Muehller. "Please ask me again. And, Mule—take care of yerself! Don't let nothin' happen to you—ever."

Denise, unable to sleep, had thrown on a coat and stepped out of the tent she shared with the others. She saw Muehller and Nora returning from their walk. The big man's arm was around the wiry little girl.

It was just as Denise had thought.

She didn't want to share the tent with Nora just yet. Face set, she walked away, fuming at the state of affairs that kept her here in this godforsaken, terrible place. Turning back, she rounded a tent and ran

smack into a man's arms. For a brief space, she
struggled, remembering the furtive Dr. Butts—

"My word!" It was Peter Carey's voice, slightly
slurred, but unmistakable. "What have we here? Ah,
a redheaded wildcat!"

"Let me gae, Dr. Carey," she hissed. "Ye're droonk!"

He mulled it over for a moment. Perhaps he was.
He didn't know, because he'd never been a drinking
man. If he was it felt damn good—and so did the girl
he held tightly in his arms.

"Sae, I'm droonk," he said, mocking her accent.
"But I hae coom tae gie ye a kiss for Chrrristmas,
lass—"

Before she could stop him, he pulled her more
tightly against him, tipping up her face. His mouth
found hers and burned there, melting her resistance.
She answered his kiss with her own, her body moving against him, seeking to be closer—closer—

And then a shell exploded in the distance, with
such a concussion that she jumped away from him.
For a moment, she stood stunned—and then she
fled, his mocking laugh following her.

She entered her tent, hands pressed to her hot
cheeks, and Nora stirred sleepily.

"Denise?" she asked, yawning "where have you
been?"

" 'Tis nae yer business," Denise snapped. "I dinna
wish to discoos my prrrivate affairs wi' the likes o'
you!"

Nora did not feel like quarreling tonight. She
turned her face to the tent wall. All she wanted to do
was sort out her own confused feelings.

Denise jerked off the festive gown she'd worn for
this Christmas evening, and tossed it into a corner,

then donned her flannel gown. Climbing into her cot, she pulled the rough blanket under her chin.

This was the most miserable Christmas Eve she'd ever spent. And tae top it off, she'd been kissed by a mon i' nae condition tae rrrecall it i' the morning!

chapter 29

Peter Carey did recall kissing Denise Dugal. Unfortunately, he could remember little else. They had been swapping lewd jokes in the American officer's tent. Good God! He might have said anything!

Or done anything!

For the next few days, he stayed apart from Denise, eyeing her only when she didn't see him looking. She was unchanged, cool, crisply efficient.

Maybe he'd behaved himself like a gentleman.

Meanwhile, horror stories were drifting from the south. The Germans were reported to be massing for an all-out attack. There were tales of a new kind of gas, more devastating than chlorine or phosgene; a gas that blistered a man inside and out—

And then, on March 21, the German guns opened fire on the lines along the Somme. And the rumors of their new weapon proved to be true.

For two hours, the enemy lobbed gas shells into the British trenches. The battlefield was fogbound, and the mists became a poisonous shroud. When the gas attack ceased, trench mortars began pounding, and the Germans moved in on blinded troops, appearing like apparitions through the fogbank. Exploding British ammunition dumps added to the nightmarish scene, capricious pinwheels of fire destroying aid stations, artillery horses, narrow-gauge railheads.

The British retreated.

And word came that Paris was under fire. Morale in the hospital sank to a new low. Then British positions only a few miles distant were deluged with the new mustard gas. The humid weather held it to the ground. It was followed with a barrage of high explosives—and finally, nine German divisions.

Peter Carey waited for the order to evacuate as aid stations behind the line were either captured, destroyed, or in the process of pulling back. Ambulances bumped along the rutted terrain, depositing patients wherever they might be cared for. Once again the hospital was working at peak capacity; wounded being transferred from surgery to tent. Outside on blankets lay men with blinded eyes and blistered lungs, retching, coughing their lives out.

There was nothing to be done for them, except give them the open air and space they craved—

From the hospital grounds, the shell-shattered sky looked like a scene from hell. Low along the horizon, the deadly gas was saffron, streaked with a sickly green. The mortar range was three to three and a half miles, and several landed close enough to vibrate the earth, the tents quaking with the force of the explosion.

And the girls worked on.

"Are ye nae afeart?" Denise asked Jo.

Jo, bandaging a soldier's wounded shoulder, looked up briefly, her face white with fatigue.

"No. I suppose it's because we've seen so much. It can't be much worse."

"Aye," Denise said softly. She moved to another cot and bent to soothe a boy who was suffering from shock. His eyes were wild and crazed. But he couldn't move.

His legs were gone below the knee.

Peter Carey was in a quandary. The evacuation orders had arrived, and the situation was impossible. There were too many seriously wounded to transport. Most of them would die if they were moved. He discussed it with Dr. Stacey, and they both determined to stick it out, no matter what came.

But there were the other members of the staff to consider.

Carey called a meeting, explaining his decision. Those patients with the best chance of recovery should be transported. The Americans were relieved of duty, and should probably return to their headquarters. The girls—

"Just a damn minute," West barked. "You're telling us to get the hell out, when we're needed here?"

"You're all family men," Carey pointed out. "While Stacey and I—"

"Forget it!" West spat. "We're staying!"

Peter Carey drew himself up. "That was not a suggestion, Major, but an order—"

"And since when does a Yank take an order from a Limey bastard?" West said insolently. "I think you forget we whipped your tails a little over a hundred years ago——"

Carey was livid. "Then, if you're such mighty warriors, where the hell's Pershing when we need reinforcements?"

"Damned if I know," Major West admitted. "But, right now, that doesn't apply. You're not getting rid of us so easily."

A look at the other American faces showed they were with the major in his decision. Carey glowered for a minute, then grinned.

"Hell," he said, "stay, and welcome!" He shook hands all round, the turned to the girls.

"You will go with the ambulances. I would suggest you take ship at Calais and go to your people in England—and stay there."

"And if we dinna choose——," Denise began.

"I didn't give you a choice," Carey shot at her. "I gave you an order! I've never believed a field hospital was a place for women, and now I'm convinced of it! You're under my protection here, and whether you like it or not, you're going! Now, pack your things!"

The girls left his presence and walked to their tent, without a word exchanged. Inside, Jo doubled her fists and hammered at her cot.

"Ooh! I'm so mad I could fight! That damned, high-and-mighty boorish stuffed shirt! I could strangle him!"

"And ye'd hae muckle help," Denise said grimly.

"I like Dr. Carey," Liane put in uneasily, "but it doesn't seem right to leave now——"

"Listen tae wee Goody Two-shoes," Denise hissed.

Nora held up a warning hand. "Dammit, we gotta

stop this! Fightin' among ourselves ain't gonna help none. Me, I'm stayin', hell er high water!"

"Me, too," the others said, almost in unison.

"Then we gotta figger out how—"

The ambulances were loaded. Mule Muehller, having heard of Carey's directive, was delighted. "You're gonna ride up front with me, ain't you, Nora?" he asked.

"I hafta stay in back with the patients, Mule. Gotta do my job."

"But I thought you said Liane—"

"Her, too. Lissen, you big dumb Dutchie! We got one man bossin' us around, and that's one too many. Just shut up an' drive, okay?" To take the sting out of her words, she stood on tiptoe and kissed him. Mule was not only mollified, but delighted. He reached for her and she stepped away.

"Hey," she said, "don't fergit that spot about a half-mile down the road. Take that chuck hole slow an' easy-like. Don't want my sick guys jounced around—"

At the same moment, Denise was giving similar instructions to the other driver.

"Dinna hit the boomp tae harrrd. We wadna want the patients tae soofer—"

The loading accomplished, the girls climbed into the rear of the vehicles, two to each. And when the trucks slowed according to instructions, they left the same way: Denise and Nora landing on their feet, Jo skidding to a sitting position, and Liane rolling end over end.

They picked her up and dusted her off, laughing all the way back to the compound, where they slipped, unseen, into their tent. Their plan was to wait until the vehicles were long gone, then go about their regular duties as though nothing had happened.

Jo twisted to look, ruefully, at the shredded seat of the men's trousers she wore. "I'll have to change."

"I will, too," Liane said. "I'm a mess."

Denise moved to a chest and began tossing out clothing. "I think we ought tae dress like ladies—"

"But we'll ruin those things," Jo cried as Denise stuffed her best blue gown into her hands. "Blood-stains—"

"Hark!" Denise said sharply.

Her tone silenced Jo. There was a moment of quiet—except for the rumbling of nearby fighting, staccato bursts of fire; the ka-room of an exploding shell.

"The men hae been i' battle," Denise said. "And noo the battle cooms tae them. I am thinking tae lift their sperrits! Tae show Dr. High-and-Mighty there is a place for woomen at the Frrront! If yer gown is o' mair importance—"

Jo's blue eyes snapped, "Hell, no!" she grinned. "Get dressed, and let's go!"

Dr. Peter Carey, dashing in to reassure the abandoned patients, skidded to a halt. Four daintily garbed females moved among the cots, tending men who seemed calm despite approaching disaster.

Damn them! How did they get back here? He had seen them board the ambulances, with his own eyes!

He opened his mouth to shout at them, then thought better of it. What the hell! There was nothing he could do about it now. And, sometimes, silence was the better part of valor.

He backed out of the tent, and made his way back to the surgery. And he caught himself whistling along the way.

Despite the encroaching enemy, spirits were lighter all round—except for Nora's. She had stayed behind and she was glad of it.

But when Mule Muehller reached the coast and discovered she was missing, he was going to be mad as hell.

——————————— *chapter 30* ———————————

Nora underestimated Mule Muehller's feelings. Certain that she would soon be bound for England, he knew he couldn't let her go without some kind of commitment. He could still feel that unexpected kiss, and hoped it meant she was getting over whatever the hell had been bothering her. All the way to Calais, he planned his proposal.

Maybe he would just say "Nora, I've waited long enough. How about us getting hitched as soon as this war is over?"

Or, maybe, it should be more romantic. "Nora, I love you! You're the prettiest girl I ever saw. And you're one helluva good mechanic. I've been thinking on starting a tractor company. Maybe we could be partners, if we was married—"

Or he could do what he really wanted to do, grab her up and kiss her until she couldn't think, and

carry her off to a preacher before she caught her
breath.

There was no opportunity to try any of the
approaches. When he reached Calais, she was gone—
and so was her friend Liane.

He remembered her careful instructions about the
hole in the road. Slow down, she'd said. She'd known
exactly what she was going to do when she kissed
him!

Mule Muehller was slow to anger. When he did
lose his temper, rage built inside him like steam in a
boiler. He fueled it with her sins.

She had as much as lied to him. Mule, with his
strong family background, put a premium on honesty.

She had not behaved in a womanly fashion. In his
home, the woman ruled the household, the man
made the decisions. Not only had Nora pulled the
wool over his eyes, but she'd disobeyed the doc, who
was, after all, the boss here.

Most of all, it was the kiss he couldn't forgive.
She'd kissed him only so that he would drop his
guard. He'd dreamed about the kiss all the way to
Calais—and he dwelled on it all the way back.

Reaching the hospital, he jammed the truck to a
halt and strode into the tent.

Nora, her arms filled with folded blankets, saw
him coming. He looked bigger than she remembered,
his body square and solid, his jaw thrust forward, his
eyes like blue chips of ice.

Oh, lordy, she thought. He's madder'n I figgered.

She'd known he'd be upset with her, and had
dreaded his return. But she hadn't expected anything
like this.

"Mule," she said with a false smile, "yer back!"

He didn't speak, but took the blankets from her

and plopped them on an empty cot, his big hand closing around her upper arm.

"Mule! Let me go! I'm on duty!"

The other girls watched, openmouthed, as he dragged her toward the door. Denise stepped forward, blocking his path.

"See here, ye canna joost—"

One hamlike hand swiped her out of his way, and he left the hospital, propelling Nora along with him. With the girls in the ward, their tent would be empty. It was as good a place as any for what he intended to do—

He shoved Nora inside. Still not releasing her, he sat down on a cot and pulled her over his knee, face down. Nora, sensing his intentions, yelped.

"Damn you, Mule Muehller! If you dare—!"

For answer, his large hand came down in a stinging smack.

"Mule!"

Another smack, another. And finally, she was sobbing with pain and fury. He set her aside and walked toward the tent opening. Nora flew after him, pounding on his back with her fists.

"Damn you!" she squalled. "Damn you! Damn you!"

She might as well have been banging on a wall. Then he was gone, not having uttered a word.

Nora backed to her cot and sat down. She hastily rose again, rubbing her tender backside. She wasn't ever gonna forgive him, she swore to herself. Never!

Mule went directly to Dr. Carey for his instructions. It appeared, Carey told him, that the British were holding now, in an S-shaped line curving around Ypres. Still it would be wise to continue moving as many patients as possible to the coast.

He didn't mention the girls.

Mule Muehller didn't ask.

In late April, the British general shortened and straightened his lines. Now, the German guns were left far back, with an area of war-torn muddy cratered earth to traverse. Only small, scrap-piled Ypres remained. On the night of April 29, the enemy ceased its attack.

In the two battles, 56,639 Germans and 21,128 Allied soldiers were killed; 250,000 Allied and 181,000 Germans choked the hospitals.

Though the patient load was greater than it had ever been before, Jo Blaine was pulled from her nursing duties to serve as interpreter for the German wounded. Normally cheerful and outgoing, she was often in a state of depression. The boy, Wilhelm, asked her to write a letter to a sweetheart he would never live to see. Karl refused to give his last name, preferring to be listed as dead. Once a handsome man, he was now a monster; half of his face blown away. Sigfreid—

"Oh, for God's sake," Denise snapped. "These are Gerrrmans yer talking aboot! Bluidy murrrderers! I dinna see why we maun nurse them back tae health!"

"They're human beings," Jo said sturdily. "And some of them don't like war any better than we do!"

"Sae we mend them and send them hame tae fight again," Denise sniffed.

"These men won't be going home," Jo reminded her. "They'll be going to prison camps. Most of them don't even want to get well!"

As time passed, even Denise softened. It was obvious they all felt the same pain, the German prisoners perhaps more than others.

War took place in the trenches, in hand-to-hand

combat, in the raveled skies. It did not enter the hospital tent, where a Tommy called for aid for a German soldier in pain; where a slum-side Britisher spread-eagled in casts gratefully accepted a smoke held to his lips for him, then jerked his head toward a German on the next cot.

"Give me chum 'ere a drag. Looks like 'e bain't a arf rum sort—"

Denise would never understand men!

In the meantime, the hospital was like a gigantic clearinghouse, patients pouring in and dribbling out; some to go home, some to wait out the war in barbed-wire enclosures—

And others sent to join the dead in Flanders Field.

The German gains, though stopped, had been demoralizing. Then came word that the enemy had crossed the Vesle, taken over the pivotal rail and road hub at Soissons, and were on their way to Paris.

One ray of hope lightened the gloomy news from the south.

The Americans, under General Pershing, had finally entered the war. They had driven the Germans back from Château-Thierry, from Vaux, from Belleau Wood—

The frantic pace at Ypres had slowed. Once more, the field hospital had its affairs under control. Major West had been called back to AEF headquarters for consultation. The remaining doctors were able to handle the workload, and the girls, after working twenty-four-hour shifts, now had regular scheduled hours.

Jo, still worn and tired, was able to find a time for writing. It did not come easily now, and she threw her pencil across the tent.

"I've been trying to put it all together," she said, vexed. "And this is all I've got!"

Denise looked at a map of lower Belgium and upper France, covered with thin delicate lines leading out from Paris.

"It leuks tae be a spider's web," she said, confused.

"It is," Jo said petulantly. "And here we are!" She jabbed a finger at the top of the map. "All we know is what we hear! We lost ground here, and they say we won! How do we know what's really happening—and where the hell's the spider?"

Denise had to agree with her. All they knew, in their insular position, was what came by word of mouth. They might not know when the domn bluidy war was ended!

June heat settled down to simmer over the ravaged boglands of Ypres. And with the heat, Major West returned, grinning from ear to ear.

He and his men were to be transferred to a field hospital at Toul, an American base.

"Good show," Peter Carey said, stepping forward to shake his hand. "But we will miss you sorely."

"I hardly think so," West laughed. "My commander requested you be attached to our service there, and the B.E.F agreed. You can expect your replacements here within the week."

Denise felt a sinking sensation in the pit of her stomach. Peter Carey was leaving. Not that she cared, of course—but they would be left among strangers. Nora was equally stunned. She and Mule Muehller were still not on speaking terms, but she'd thought one day—if he apologized—she would accept.

Oddly enough, it was little Liane who spoke up.

"You are leaving us here, then?"

"Hell, no," West laughed. "You come as part of the package! I insisted on the whole team! What would we do without our brave Florence Nightingales?"

He reached out and hugged Liane and Jo, then looked bewildered.

Nora and Denise had both burst into tears and fled the room.

chapter 31

Toul proved to be a far cry from the tiny besieged hospital at Ypres. Here, there was a city. It was a small city, true, enlarged by thousands of tents and hastily thrown-up barracks, but, to the girls, it looked like heaven.

The very atmosphere of a country at war had changed, a parade of Yanks pouring from the boats to be sent to Toul, Nancy, Liverdun, Gondrecourt, and Neufchâteau. And the Yanks were unlike the war-weary grim-faced Tommies. They were brash, cocky, their overseas caps set at an angle as they looked over the girls of Alsace-Lorraine.

Here, there were cafes and *buvettes*, their tables set in the open air. One could purchase *choucroute*— sauerkraut—the main dish of the country, garnished with breaded veal cutlets or sausage. There were kugelhofs—Alsatian oven-baked buns—and Strasbourg apple tarts served with thick cream and sprinkled with cinnamon.

"I think I hae deed, and gane tae heaven," Denise sighed.

Liane giggled. "They think they have, too." She pointed out a group of American soldiers growing happy on beer, which the Alsatians claimed to be the finest brew in France.

"Dinna leuk their way," Denise hissed. "We dinna want a prrroblem!"

She had good reason for her warning. They had been put up in a hotel until the hospital was properly set up. And every night, the Fokkers came over, shelling and strafing. Searchlights roved the sky, and antiaircraft batteries barked back, neither side doing much damage. But the alarm would sound, and all hotel guests must leap from bed and run for the *abri* in the basement. The lights would go off, and no woman was safe in the darkness. The previous night, Denise had been severely pinched. She flailed out in the direction of a man's chuckle and connected. But it did not prevent her from being pinched again.

Now, she was frowning. Liane had attracted the Yanks' attention. One of them had risen, stein in hand, and was coming to their table. She turned her head, wishing they'd stayed at the hotel with Jo and Nora—

"I be damned!"

A familiar voice jerked her around, her eyes widening. A small, natty soldier stood before her, his cap at an impossible angle, his face split in a grin.

"Johnny! Johnny Looper!"

"Old Lucky Looper himself," he said, his eyes sparkling. "Knew it was you, soon as I saw that hair. And—look at Liane here! Grew up, didn't she."

His bold blue eyes ran up and down Liane's figure, and she blushed. Denise cut in quickly, too quickly—

"I'm glad tae see ye, Johnny."

She had his attention again, his gaze steady on hers.

"Are you? Last time I saw you, I didn't figure you ever wanted to lay eyes on me again."

She flushed. "I didna mean it, Johnny. And I hae—hae changed. I hae thocht o' ye often—"

The devilish brows went up, and he grinned again. "Ye hae?" he said, mocking her. "Then gie us a kiss, for auld lang syne!"

Denise stood and leaned forward, aiming a chaste kiss at his cheek, but he maneuvered so that he captured her mouth, his hands tangled in her hair, holding her like that for a long time.

Liane gasped, and a cheer sounded from the neighboring table, Looper's buddies lifting their steins in a mock salute.

"How the hell does he do it?" one marveled loudly. "A babe in every town—"

Looper turned toward his companions and bowed from the waist, while Denise turned as red as her hair. She hadna minded the kiss—it hadna been a' that unpleasant. But he had been showing off for his rrrowdy friends.

"Hey," he said now, "how about you two joining us? I can vouch for them guys. They don't bite—"

"I dinna think sae—," Denise began.

"Then I'll join you." He sat down, rested his chin on his hands, and surveyed them.

"Yer prettier than they are."

Denise had to laugh. "Johnny, ye fule!"

"Only where a pretty woman is concerned,' he replied promptly.

He talked steadily for an hour or more; telling of his adventures. He had transferred to the infantry, where he had, of course, performed many heroic deeds. Actually, it was he who had fired the first shot at Château-Thierry; he, who had led his men through the corpse-choked splintered remnants of Belleau Wood. Single-handedly, he had taken on a battery of machine guns, firmly entrenched at Chemin des Dames—

His wild tales, interspersed with foolish anecdotes, kept them entertained until, finally, they had to leave. They'd promised Jo they'd return to the hotel before dark, when German planes would again harrass the area.

"But I'll be seeing you again, won't I?" Looper asked, his bold blue eyes betraying an anxiety.

"We'll be moving tae the hospital i' aboot a week," Denise said. "I—I dinna know."

"Well, hell, I only got two-three days leave. Look, I won't make no passes or nothing. We can just walk around, sort of see what's going on—"

And show his friend he has a—a babe, Denise finished in her mind. He suddenly looked vulnerable, harmless. Lucky Johnny Looper, a' talk and nae show! He'd be gangin' back tae the lines, and 'twas a wee favor he wanted—

"Tomorrow?" she asked quietly. "Here?"

His face beamed like the sun. "You betcher sweet boots," he said with feeling.

He walked them back to the hotel, swaggering, with a girl on each arm, nodding to everyone he knew. And it seemed he knew them all, old hands and new arrivals alike.

"There goes Lucky Looper." It was a common refrain, and it was clear he believed it himself.   In the following days, Denise enjoyed—and was grateful for—Johnny Looper's company. As he'd promised, he made no advances. It was enough to strut through the streets of the little village with the loveliest girl he'd ever met, on his arm; enough to know that he was envied by his friends—and also that this was exactly what they expected of Lucky Looper.

On the third day, the last day of his leave, Denise dressed in her very best and took a long time with her appearance. For some stupid reason, she felt she owed it to him. He had been an entertaining companion, never attempting to take advantage of her.

Did she want him to? That thought worried her. She'd discovered a yearning inside, a need to be held, to be admired, to be important to someone.

But the mon wasna Johnny Looper. He wad be tall, wi' brrroad shoulders, a goldy-saft beard when he didna shave; blond hair that fell o'er eyes as blue as seawater—

As though she had conjured him up, Peter Carey appeared as they returned to the hotel on that last evening. A strange American officer was with him. She saw Carey point her out, and the officer shook his head, making an unheard comment.

It was evident they were discussing her, and they had nae richt!

Holding her head high, she swept into the hotel on Looper's arm. He saw her to the room she shared with the others, and she sensed, rather than saw, that Peter Carey had mounted the stairs behind them.

"I been behaving myself, ain't I? Like I promised." Johnny Looper's voice was husky, his eyes questioning.

"That ye hae!"

"Then, since I'm heading for the trenches, d'you suppose you—"

Denise held out her arms, feeling him tremble as he hugged her. And she kissed him, warmly and willingly—even though she had to bend a little in the process.

"Miss Dugal!" Peter Carey's voice was icy in the hallway. Looper jerked back in surprise, anger washing over his features, then a kind of humorous resignation. No sense in mixing it with a British officer. And, after all, he'd got more than he'd expected. If it bothered the big fella—let him eat his heart out!

Adjusting his cap to its devil-may-care angle, he went whistling down the stairs.

Carey glared at Denise, unable to stop his words of recrimination. "I have no control over your private life," he said frostily, "but you know it is against the rules to fraternize with enlisted men, especially—"

"I wasna frrraternizing," she said, anger tinting her cheeks.

He ignored her interruption and continued, "—especially with men of that stripe."

"I dinna ken what yer talking aboot! How dare ye crrriticize a mon ye dinna know!"

"I was just told what manner of man he is," Carey said firmly. "His reputation for being a—a rounder—is well known."

"And yer's is lily-white?" she snarled. " 'Tis worse tae gie a soldier a good-bye kiss—than tae be grabbed i' the darrrk by a common droonk?"

Her words set him back on his heels. "I only came to tell you we're ready to move out in the morning," he said stiffly. "Privates Muehller and Stone will drive you to the hospital site."

With a jerky bow, he turned and strode toward the stairs. Denise stood where she was for a long time, and finally unclenched her fists. Her nails had cut small half-moons into her palms. Why did the mon a'ways mak her sae angry!

She entered the room and informed the others of their upcoming departure. Luckily, they were too excited to notice that she was upset. They were pleased to be going back to work. After the harried days at Ypres, time was beginning to hang heavy on their hands. They packed, chattering with excitement. It was a long time before they got to bed.

There, Denise finally gave in to tears, trying to tell herself she was crying for Johnny Looper. She had just dropped off to sleep when German planes passed over, the alarm sounded, and they had to run for the *abri* in the basement.

She was pinched and prodded, but could only feel grateful for the darkness that hid her swollen eyes.

chapter 32

The members of the hospital team moved toward the front with an American convoy. The girls marveled at the trucks and equipment; the huge guns, still glistening from American factories. The doughboys marched in long columns, to the cadence of nonsense songs. "K-K-K-Katy," they sang. "I'll be waiting for you at the k-k-k-kitchen door," or, "Mademoiselle from Armentières, parlay-voo—"

Jo, in the back of a swaying truck, scribbled happily, filled with pride in her countrymen. "Look at them," she said happily. "There's nothing like them in the whole world."

"Ye hae nae seen a Scots rrregiment wi' their plaids and bagpipes," Denise said sourly.

Jo shrugged. Wow, Denise was in a bitch of a mood today! And talking to Liane and Nora was like talking to a wall!

Liane was thinking of the soldiers, too, wondering how many of them would return from the fray they were entering into so lightheartedly. And Nora was conscious only of the fact that Mule Muehller was behind the wheel of their vehicle.

The road was a horror, deeply rutted with the passing of armor and marching feet, the roadsides matted, vegetation crushed where vehicles had pulled out for repair; but on the horizon, the undulating landscape was golden with blooming mustard, echoing the sun in an azure sky. Here and there were small farms, grape vines carefully pruned and trellised. A little village was quaint with gingerbread—

Yet, war waited in the distance. And, soon, its muttering sounded over the convoy's approach.

The hospital was set at the edge of desolation. From its site, the earth forward to the lines outside St. Mihiel was a gigantic trampled area. Men and machines had been on the move in rain and in snow. Here was a limber, sunken to its hubs. Evidently it had not been considered worth salvaging. There was a tank that had not seen battle, burned from the inside out, possibly due to a fault in production.

And there was the hospital, clean, new; several large tents and a small brick building, evidently once a school or church. Trucks lined the area in front of the compound; new trucks, covered with canvas and marked with the red cross that identified them as ambulances.

Even more astounding was the presence of American women. A sour, gray-haired woman with a no-nonsense bearing introduced herself as Mrs. Bent, in charge of the Red Cross aides.

She would assign them to their billets. They were, of course, subject to certain rules. There would be no fraternization with patients or male hospital personnel. She would set their schedules. For those on day shift, lights out would be at—

"Mrs. Bent!" Denise interrupted the woman who looked at her in shocked disapproval. "How lang hae ye been at the Front?"

"I fail to see where it matters. I have been trained—"

"And we have experience," Jo put in quietly.

The woman's face was red with irritation. "I will not tolerate insubordination," she said. "You will obey orders, while you are in my charge."

"We are only assigned here," Jo said stubbornly. "We're with VAD—"

"You are still in my charge!" The woman's eyes were like flint. "And if you flout my authority, it will go hard with you!" She turned to a quiet girl who stood beside her, seemingly shocked at the turn of conversation.

"Rachel, you will take these young ladies to their quarters. And I wish the group broken up. Miss Dugal will room with you, Miss Blaine with Jennifer Adams. I would suggest Miss Wang with—Barbara Haynes, and Miss Murphy can share with Doris Van Slack—"

The girls stood stunned. They had come this far together, and now they were to be separated. Denise opened her mouth to speak, and Mrs. Bent glared at her.

"You are all dismissed!"

They followed the girl called Rachel, too bewildered at the turn of events to protest further. Only when they reached the little square outbuilding that was to be their new home did anyone speak.

"The bitch!" Denise exploded. "The bluidy bitch! I wullna stond for this kind of trrreatment!"

"Nor I," Jo said. "I'm going back and tell her off!"

Rachel moved to block her way, her eyes watering, her face terrified.

"You can't do that," she whispered, her eyes darting to see if the outburst had been overheard. "Mrs. Bent won't like it. You'll just get in trouble—"

"I dinna gie a domn!" Denise said.

"Please." Rachel wrung her hands. "Oh, please, don't!" She sought for something to dissuade them. "You'll like the others, I promise! Just—try!"

Tired, disheartened, they finally agreed to accept Mrs. Bent's edict—until they could work out something better. Entering the building, they were introduced to their future companions, who were equally upset at the new arrangements; two of them, women ambulance drivers, absolutely furious.

Doris Van Slack and Jennifer Adams had signed up for Red Cross work together. Both girls were debutantes, and had volunteered "to do our bit for our boys." Their driving uniforms had been expensively tailored to fit their chic persons, complete with pastel chiffon scarves to tuck in at the throat. They could hardly wait to show them off—

And now, they were being parted, forced to room with women they did not consider their social equals.

Jo took an immediate aversion to fluffy-headed Jennifer Adams.

"I don't like this any better than you do," she said bluntly. "I prefer a roommate who can carry on an intelligent conversation!"

Jennifer gasped and backed away before the small dark-haired girl with blazing blue eyes. "I suppose we can manage," she said feebly.

Nora was out of her depth with Doris Van Slack. An extraordinarily beautiful girl, she was haughty and cool, of obvious breeding. Nora was tongue-tied, feeling her own origins were apparent: her mother illegitimate; the adopted daughter of a madam; her father a handyman. She felt like an inferior specimen in Doris Van Slack's eyes.

Liane had lucked out. She liked Barbara Haynes, a horse-faced woman with lank brown hair and a dedication to nursing. They were going to get along—

Denise was frantic. It was clear that Rachel was Mrs. Bent's toady, a yes-woman, with the spine of a jellyfish. She knew that whatever she did would be spied upon and reported to the officious woman-in-charge.

Maybe if she had a talk wi' Peter Carey—

Nae, she couldna do that, nae matter hoo miserrrable life here became!

They were taken on a tour of the hospital facilities; everything clean and new, no patients as yet. And as they returned to their quarters, Nora noticed Doris Van Slack preening, eyeing all the soldiers in the compound with inviting glances. And, suddenly, she stopped short.

"Look at that gorgeous hunk of man," she breathed. "I understand he's one of the drivers. We go in pairs, you know, in case there's a problem. I hope I draw him! I think I'll ask old Benty—"

Nora followed her gaze and met Mule Muehller's eyes, then looked away.

The next morning, she saw Mule and Doris together, looking over one of the ambulance trucks. Her lip curled as she imagined the conversation.

What does that do? Oh, isn't it cute?

But her heart felt squeezed, and she was a little nauseated.

Something I ate, she told herself.

In the days that followed, she discovered two

things. Miss Doris Van Slack, despite her inviting glances and her eye for a good-looking man, was an icicle; an out-and-out prude. An innocent story sent her into the vapors; a mention of sex was indecent. Someday, she would probably make a nice man very unhappy!

The other thing was that Doris and bubble-brained Jennifer Adams were Mrs. Bent's pets. Maybe she and Jo could use that bit of knowledge to their advantage.

She was still pondering on it when she ran into Jo. To her surprise, steady, sensible Jo burst into tears.

"I can't take much more of that Jennifer," she wept.

"She's got a brain the size of a pea! And besides that, she's nutty as a fruitcake! She sleeps with a damn rag doll! Says it makes her feel safe! And she burns a candle all night because," Jo raised her voice to a mincing baby talk. "'Mommy always let me, so I wouldn't be afraid of the dark.' A black cat crossed her path the other day, and she kept me awake all night, sure something awful was going to happen—"

Jennifer was superstitious, and Doris was a frigid prude! Nora began to grin.

"Listen, Jo," she said, "I've got an idea!"

--- *chapter 33* ---

That evening, Jo gave Nora a box of white candles she'd filched from Jennifer's supply. Nora went to the line of trucks. Those at the rear were the dilapidated vehicles she and Jo had driven at Ypres. Careful to remain unobserved, she squatted down and thrust a candle inside the soot-blackened exhaust. She inspected it.

Perfect!

She continued until they were all sufficiently blackened, repacked them carefully, and returned them to Jo, who hid them under her cot.

Step one.

Leaving the trucks, she cast a yearning eye toward the burned-out tank. She'd been wanting to inspect the thing, see what made it tick, but not right now. First things first. She looked at a list she'd made.

Her next move was to locate an old tin in the

dump near the cook tent. In her chest was a ball of twine, saved from Christmas packages of previous years. A wounded sapling provided the resin she needed—

Mrs. Bent had a blackboard in her office, probably to set up a duty roster. Nora faced the lion in her den with a question as to when operations were expected to begin.

Remembering Maggie Murphy's beginnings as a thief on the streets of Liverpool, she grinned as she palmed the chalk.

In the room she shared with Jennifer Adams, Jo put all the objects Nora produced to good use. She carefully drew a pentagram on the floor and set a small folding table to one side, draping it with a black shawl and lining the black candles in a row.

The can with its resin twine she placed carefully under her own cot, with a loop she could slip over one finger.

Jo had been taken care of. Now, it was Nora's turn. She really had no idea where to begin her own campaign. Leaving her quarters, she stepped outside. In the distance, she could see Jennifer and Doris returning from a walk.

Probably rakin' us over th' coals, Nora thought angrily. Well, sticks and stones could bust her bones, but words would never hurt her, as Maggie always said—

She turned to go in—too quickly, and there was a twinge in her shoulder. She had injured it once in lifting a patient, and it still was tricky. This time, it came as a surprise, and she clapped a hand to it, moaning involuntarily.

"Are you all right, Miss Nora?"

It was one of the orderlies the Americans had brought with them to Ypres. They were both big-eared, bucktoothed, and shy. She had never got their names straight. This one was either Tom or Tim. But—hadn't he voiced his hopes of becoming a doctor one day? Nora stifled a smile.

"My shoulder," she whimpered. "I think I done dislocated the damn thing—"

"Maybe you ought to see Dr. Carey," he said hesitantly.

"But if it ain't out of place, I'd feel silly," she said. "If it is—I bet you could tell!"

He looked both smug and frightened. "I might be able to—let me see—"

"Not out here in the open. Could you—come in my room? Nobody's there." When he hesitated, she moaned again. "Oooh! It hurts like hell—"

Nervously, he followed her into the small building. "I could get in trouble for being here," he said. "If your roommate came in—"

"Oh, she won't," Nora said airily. Her eyes fell on Doris's chiffon scarf, thrown carelessly across her cot. "Tie that thing on the doorknob, and she'll go away. It's a signal we got—"

He obeyed, then shyly probed her collarbone and shoulderblade. "I don't feel anything out of place."

Nora could hear footsteps in the hall and recognized Doris Van Slack's prancing gait. Recklessly, she unbuttoned her blouse and pulled it down to reveal a smooth, freckled shoulder.

"Course you don't," she whispered hurriedly, "not through all that cloth. Hell, don't be bashful. Yer gonna be a doc—"

The door banged open suddenly to reveal an angry Doris, her crumpled scarf in her hand. "Who—?"

she began. She stopped, wide-eyed at the incriminating scene before her.

"I was just—," the red-faced orderly stammered. Nora reached and put her fingers to his lips.

"It's all right," she said. "I'll see you some other time. And, thanks—"

Standing on tiptoe, she kissed him, buckteeth and all. His ears flaming crimson, he fled. And Nora turned on Doris.

"What th' hell's th' matter with you?" she asked. "Didn't you see the scarf? Didn't you know enough not to barge in?"

Doris opened her mouth and closed it. For a pretty girl, she certainly bore a resemblance to a fish, Nora thought. A cold fish at that. She decided to be magnanimous.

"Well, mebbe you didn't know," she said in a forgiving tone. "You never been in the perfession. My ma allus used a scarf on th' knob as a signal. My Grammaw learned her, I guess. She was a madam. It kinda runs in the family. But let's make a deal, huh? You don't walk in on me, I don't walk in on you—"

Within the hour, two social butterflies hit Mrs. Bent's office. The room also served as her sleeping quarters, a cot and washstand separated from her desk by a screen. She had been in bed. Without her glasses, and with her hair awry, she'd lost every vestige of authority. And she was certainly not prepared for the deluge that struck her.

Nora Murphy was a prostitute.

And Jo Blaine was a witch.

"Now, girls," she said with the fawning tone she adopted with her blue-blooded volunteers, "I am sure there's some mistake."

She listened, horrified, as Doris raged through a wild tale about scarves tied on doorknobs and three generations of the world's oldest profession.

"I told her to get out," Doris panted, "that I was afraid I—might catch something! And she said not to worry, she was careful."

Oh, dear God, Mrs. Bent thought. Oh, dear God!

Then it was Jennifer's turn. She'd gone into her room, ready for bed after her walk, and there was this—this witch! There was an—an evil symbol on the floor, and she was burning black candles.

"She was trying to call up the devil," Jennifer sobbed, "saying m-magic words and waving her hands. And when she did, there was this—this horrible sound, like a—ghost."

"Go back to your rooms," Mrs. Bent said helplessly, "and I will—"

"I will not go back there," Doris said primly. "Never!"

"And neither will I!" Jennifer said hysterically. "It was awful—awful—"

Mrs. Bent sent for an orderly, telling him to set up two extra cots in the office for one night, then she crossed the compound to the small house where the girls resided, opening the door to Jo's room without knocking.

There was no sign of the satanic orgy Jennifer described, only a single white taper burning near her cot. On the other, Jo Blaine struggled up, yawning.

"Jennifer? Oh—Mrs. Bent. Is something wrong?"

The woman was nonplussed. How do you accuse a young woman of evil practices when there is no evidence? When she most certainly had been asleep? She glanced around again, finding nothing. Finally, she pointed a trembling finger at the white taper by Jennifer's bed.

"What is that?"

Jo Blaine was round-eyed and innocent. "That? That's Jennifer's candle. She's afraid of the dark, you know. That's why she sleeps with her doll." She yawned again. "Sorry, I can't quite wake up. A black cat crossed Jennifer's path, yesterday, and I was up all night with her—"

"Just—just go back to sleep."

Mrs. Bent backed out and closed the door, going to the room Nora shared with Doris. Nora was not in bed. Her face was white, chalk white, in truth, and she had a small charcoal brazier burning, a pot of water atop it. She was assiduously applying hot packs to her shoulder.

Confronted with Doris's accusations, Nora's pain-racked face was a mask of confusion. It was true that the orderly—Tom, or Tim, had been trying to put her shoulder in place. She had asked him to, hating to bother Dr. Carey with it.

"The scarf on the door?" Mrs Bent prompted.

"I dunno. Mebbe she forgot and left it there. She leaves them around all over the place."

Mrs. Bent followed Nora's sweeping gesture. It was true. A rainbow of scarves filled the room, draped over the bed, drawer knobs, a table—

"I'm some worried about Doris," Nora said in a guilty whisper. "I think she's—sick. She's got a—a kind of thing about—sex." On the last word, her voice was almost inaudible. "She's allus lookin' at men, and she keeps bringin' up things like—"

"Never mind," Mrs. Bent said hastily.

She left Nora and returned to her office, her mind fully made up. Though she'd had misgivings about

Jennifer and Doris being able to fulfill their duties, she'd swallowed them, thinking of the debutantes' position in the social register. They did not belong here at the front, and she intended to tell them so.

Much to her surprise, they agreed with her.

chapter 34

Doris and Jennifer left for AEF headquarters with the first available transportation. Mrs. Bent had not yet recovered her aplomb when Nora Murphy and Jo Blaine appeared at her desk.

Since the two who had gone were ambulance drivers, they wished to be transferred from the nursing staff to those positions.

The woman tried to pull a cloak of authority around her shoulders.

"I hardly think—"

Jo laid several sheets of papers in front of her. They were letters commending the girls' driving skills, and their work in the field near Ypres, suggesting them as replacements for those who had disaffected. They were signed by both Peter Carey and Major Frank West.

As Mrs. Bent still hesitated, reading over the typed words, Jo turned to Nora.

"I slept so well last night," she sighed, "without that damn candle burning—"

"Me, too," Nora agreed. "I always stayed awake, worryin', waitin' fer Doris to come in. If she was carryin' on with one guy, it wouldn'ta been so bad. But when it's anything in pants—"

"I wonder what they would have done in the field?" Jo said thoughtfully.

Nora shrugged. "I dunno. Reckin Jennifer'd come unglued after dark, without her candle and her dolly. Doris—hell—she mighta raped the other driver."

Slam!

Mrs. Bent slapped the letters on the desk, her face afire. "Consider yourselves transferred to ambulance duty," she barked. "You will be assigned to number five. Now—get out of my sight!"

Outside, the girls began to laugh, tears of mirth streaming down their cheeks.

"Didja see her face?" Nora gasped. "The ol' bitch! And those letters, Jo! How the hell did you get them to sign—"

Jo wiped at her eyes. "Simple. I sneaked into her office while she was getting Doris and Jennifer off, typed the papers, then took them to Carey and the major. I said it was something Mrs. Bent needed their signatures for. They signed them without reading—"

"Men!" Nora said feelingly, "God bless 'em!"

Returning to their quarters, Jo reorganized their sleeping arrangements. If Mrs. Bent kicked up a fuss, they'd deal with it at the time. For now, she moved her things and Nora's into one room. Barbara and Rachel could share, or they could each have a room to themselves if they wanted. Denise and Liane would be roommates.

"Ye didna ask me," Denise exploded. "I hae a rrright tae my ain choice—"

"You do," Jo said promptly. "Barbara, Rachel, or Liane. But you've been so bitchy lately, I don't think anybody but Liane could stand you."

They faced each other for a long moment, the two cousins who had started out such good friends. Denise started to rail back at her, then stopped herself. It was true, and she wasn't too certain why she was compelled to be so hateful.

It was Mrs. Bent, she thought. Denise, spoiled and pampered, had never been ordered around in all her life. And it was Rachel, the sniveling little spy she'd been forced to room with. It was the war itself, and she was—she had to face it—homesick.

And it was Peter Carey! Peter Carey with his insoofferable actions! He was a bigoted, boorish mon—

Denise packed her things and moved in with Liane.

To the east, the British army had pushed off at Amiens, crossing no-man's-land in a quarter of an hour, routing the Germans. To the British right, the French pushed as far as Fresnoy. The Canadian infantry, preceded by Mark V Star tanks, pressed forward. Australian troops leapfrogged ahead with two solid tank battalions, sixten small Whippet tanks, and a brigade of cavalry.

The tide of the battle seemed to be turning. At last, there was a glimmer of hope.

And the convoys moving to the lines intensified. The road leading past the hospital was choked with troops, weapons carriers, supply trucks. The Nineti-eth Division was coming in to replace the First

Division of regulars, whose weary straggling retreat was in marked contrast to the attitude of the newcomers. Americans fresh to the front leaned out of their trucks to shout good-natured suggestive remarks to the girls who watched them pass.

"Wait right there, sweetheart. I'll be back—soon as I twist the Kaiser's tail."

Or, "Oh, you kid! Save me a kiss, babe!"

The foot soldiers marched in cadence, singing their marching songs—

". . . You may forget the gas and shells—You'll never forget the Mad'moiselles—Hinky dinky parlay voo . . ."

And with the convoys, came the planes: German Schlastas, raking the roads with machine gun fire and light bombs; Fokkers engaging British SE-5As, Sopwith Camels, and French SPADS so that the Schlastas were free to do their worst. Puffs of dust rose to the heavens as fire stitched the roads and geysered with exploding shells, doing little but impeding the progress of the convoys. More harm was generated in the skies as planes circled and maneuvered, not a day passing without one or more going down in flames.

Nora and Jo could name then all. And Nora's fingers itched to tinker with the engines—engines perfect enough to turn a man into a bird.

As the convoys passed, patients dropped out for emergency treatment. A soldier suffering from an old wound that had not healed properly. Several casualties of the Schlasta's strafing. Infections picked up from obliging mademoiselles. Blistered feet that had turned septic. A suspicious case who had somehow managed to cut off his trigger finger.

There was always something. It was some time before Nora found a free hour to accomplish what she'd been wanting to do—take a look at the burned-out tank.

She crossed the field to where it sat, a dead and blackened monster of war, one tread slipped and awry, and began poking around it curiously.

Hell! Its machinery wasn't any more complicated than a truck or a tractor. Having seen the things in motion, moving inexorably, like doom itself, she'd somehow expected more. And she could see right off what had happened; a problem with carburetion! There were ways the thing could be improved. Growing a little excited, she poked at the tank's innards, getting covered with soot and rust, and not caring.

"Think you can fix it?"

Nora whirled, pushing her hair back with a soot-black hand, smearing her forehead in the process.

It was Mule Muehller, wearing an uneasy, apologetic grin.

"You ain't got no right sneakin' up on me like that," she blurted angrily.

"Didn't sneak," he pointed out. "Walked. Hell, it's a free country, ain't it?"

She looked at his honest, open face; the big square body like a warm wall to lean against; and finally at his huge hands. They brought back the memory of the day in her tent at Ypres, when he had dared to—

"Sure, it's free," she snapped. "And you can have it all t'yerself! I'm heading back."

As she tried to pass him, he reached out and grasped her arm, pulling her to face him.

"Nora," he groaned, "Nora—dammit, don't do this to me!"

"Ain't doin' nothin'," she said, fighting the whispery feeling that ran through her, turning off her defenses, one by one. "Ain't done nothin'!"

"The hell you ain't! My God, girl! I can't eat, can't sleep! I spend all day watching for you. Then you go by with your nose in the air, like somethin' smells bad, and I—"

"You wasn't watchin' when that Doris was around," Nora sniffed.

"I wanted to teach her something about trucks," he said, smoothing back his dusty brown hair with a harried expression. "Damfool woman! Didn't know a gas line from a water hose."

Nora felt a grin twitching at the corners of her mouth. The big, dumb ape hadn't even guessed Doris was making a play for him!

Men!

"Then I reckin yer wantin' to apologize for what you done back in Ypres?"

"Hell, no! I ain't sorry I walloped you, and, by God, I'd do it again! Man finds the girl he wants to marry, he's gotta be able to trust her!" His face was twisted in a ferocious scowl that somehow reminded her of her Grampa Sim.

Man finds the girl he wants to marry!

The words rang in Nora's head. And suddenly everything came right. Jacques had been her great, romantic love. With him, she wasn't a freckled little straw-haired girl, but a lady.

And that, she thought ruefully, might have been pretty damn hard to live up to.

She still loved Jacques, and she'd never forget him. But this man she could spend her life with.

"Mebbe it's me that ought to apologize," she said, ducking her head and staring at her feet. "I should of told you we was goin' back. I was scared you'd try to stop me."

"Ain't gonna tell you what you can do, or can't do,"

he said promptly. "Just—whatever it is, you gotta be honest with me."

She looked at him then, seeing the kindness in his blue eyes, the gentleness of him that only a man his size could afford to display. She felt suddenly shy—like a young girl with her first love, and exposed—her feelings naked in the sunlight.

"Mule," she said nervously. "I done figgered what happened to this thing." She gestured toward the tank. "It was in the carburetion. A spark—"

He laughed and picked her up, setting her inside the cockpit of the ruined tank. Then he climbed in beside her and took her in his arms.

"Lemme tell you," he said teasingly, "about sparks!"

He began with a kiss. Soft and tender at first, it graduated into flame. Trembling against his hard muscled body, Nora drew away to catch her breath.

"Lordy," she said in wonder. "Oh—lordy! I didn't know—"

"That was just a spark," he grinned down at her. "Now, lemme tell you about fire—"

He kissed her again. This time, it became a conflagration, searing through her; producing an ache that needed to be satisfied. Nora clung to him, a vine against a sun-warmed wall, seeking to grow closer—closer, feeling big gentle hands that touched her, and intensified the fire in her veins. They belonged together, she thought dazedly, belonged—

Finally, he put her from him, groaning a little with the effort.

"We stop here, Nora. War's gonna be over soon. And then—"

War. Nora's mind faltered its way back to reality. She had forgotten where she was, and what was happening in the world outside.

"It's gonna be right for us," Mule Muehller continued. "A church wedding first. And then—"

Right for them! Memory came flooding back. Recollections of a room at the top of Paris; Jacques Leceau; of lying in his arms, loving him.

And this man wanted honesty above all things. She couldn't live a lie, let him think he was getting a virginal bride. Her eyes brimmed with tears, but she forced herself to speak.

"Mule, I gotta tell you—"

He put a soot-covered palm over her mouth. "You talk too much. Lemme finish. Reason I want a church wedding, I figure it wipes out everything that ever happened. It's like we both start from there—"

He had guessed, she thought, seeing the expression in his eyes. And he was making it easier for her.

"I promise I'll be the kind of wife you want," she said passionately. "Forever and ever!"

"You'll go fishing with me?"

She giggled. What a dumb thing to say!

"Sure."

"And make love on the riverbank?"

"If nobody's lookin'."

"And help me build tractors? And have a dozen kids?"

She assented, visualizing herself at one end of a groaning table, Mule at the other, sturdy children filling the space between them. Then she was suddenly stricken.

"Dammit, Mule, I just remembered. I can't cook."

"I'll teach you," he said, pulling her close again. Then they forgot all else; touching, holding, savoring the exquisite pain of needing each other—and holding back, waiting for a new beginning that would erase the past.

The skies darkened. From Toul, the searchlights reached into the heavens, crisscrossing, and in the massive dark hulk of Toul's cathedral, the bells began to ring.

chapter 35

For a time, it seemed that the war had dwindled to an almost friendly standoff. But there was no doubt that something was building. Liane, with an ache of prescience in her bones, was perhaps more aware of it than the others.

And then it came, in a burst of fire like the end of the world.

The Allied attack started along the entire line at 1 A.M., on September 12, 1918. First, there were billowing clouds of smoke and gas, then a few scattered artillery shots, followed by the boom of larger-caliber guns. Within minutes, the volume of sound intensified, becoming a kind of ringing, metallic resonance that seemed to increase pressure on the brain, creating an intense, nerve-racking tension.

On the horizon, the flashes merged into a band of shivering light. Trees and low hills stood in silhouette against dark crimson and silver white, star-bursts of fire rising above the color band in a glorious display.

It was raining, and it was cold. Liane, standing outside her quarters, was exceedingly nervous. Nora and Jo had already been called. With the other ambulances, they were on their way to the front. Liane hugged herself for warmth and searched for something to say to Denise, who stood beside her.

"It's beautiful, isn't it? If we didn't know what was happening—"

"I see naething tae keep me frae my bed," Denise said snappishly. "We are nae set for duty until noon—"

"I think we'll be needed sooner. I don't think Mrs. Bent realizes—"

"She wull," Denise said with relish. "That wooman wi' her orrrders and schedules. 'Rememberrr yer place, girls,'" she said, mocking her, the woman's authoritative tones incongruous with a Scotch accent, "'ye are ainly nurrrses. The real worrrk is tae be doone by the doctors. Do nae overstep yer bounds.'" She halted and added savagely, "Bluidy, bossy bitch!"

"I'm sorry for her," Liane defended her. "She doesn't know how awful—"

"Aweel, I for one, wull be glad tae see her get her coomuppance!"

Denise flounced back to her room. Liane, watching her go, wondered what in the world could be wrong with her. When Nora returned from making up with Mule Muehller, all soot-stained, but with her happiness shining through, Denise had said awful things.

It was true, Liane thought, that Nora was rather a mess that night, her uniform rumpled, great black handprints in—in intimate places. But that didn't mean that Nora was a—a whore, as Denise accused her of being.

After all, Nora and Private Muehller were going to be married. And if it made Nora happy—

Liane's cheeks burned as she realized the direction of her thoughts. Brought up in a quiet household, with an inbred code of morality, she had come a long way from the idealistic child she'd been. If she loved a man, and it was wartime, how far would she go?

She couldn't answer, because she'd never been truly in love. Her Asian heritage kept her from an interest in Caucasian men. There had been Rory Dugal, of course. But that was puppy love. And she'd felt a strong link of affection for some of the longtime patients at Ypres. She was glad she'd had sense enough to recognize it for what it was: maternal feelings for helpless men—who needed her.

Someday she would go home and meet someone among her father's Chinese acquaintances. And then she, too, would be happy.

She shivered a little, still not wanting to go in, coming back to her original problem.

Denise.

They'd all been angry over what she said about Nora. And she'd picked up her gear and moved to the unoccupied room. Now, she spoke to them as little as possible. She was practically hateful to Mrs. Bent. And, as far as Nora knew, she hadn't said a word to Dr. Carey since they arrived.

It was beyond understanding. Liane wished there were some way to straighten it out.

A series of star-bursts on the horizon, the thudding of a great gun, its voice speaking over the ringing resonance that pressed against her brain, reminded her that Nora and Jo were out there, somewhere near the lines.

She prayed they would be safe.

Then, quaking with cold and damp, she went to her room, removing her wet gown and robe, donning a shirt and a pair of men's trousers.

What was coming toward the hospital compound would probably not fit Mrs. Bent's schedule. And it would be gruesome, messy work that required freedom of movement. Liane was ready.

As it neared 5 A.M., the soldiers crouched in their trenches. The night was still wild with rain and wind. They waited, huddled in their sodden clothes, for the barrage to lift.

Then it was over the top; smashing through woods; across a blasted terrain crisscrossed with enemy trenches. Fighting like demons, the raw and untried troops clawed onward.

And the ambulances began running to the rear, patients brought in by every possible conveyance; some trying to make it afoot, the lame guiding the blind.

Mrs. Bent, faced with the terrible urgency of a field hospital in an emergency, got the comeuppance Denise had wished for her.

All the teaching and instruction she'd received went out the window. There could be no schedules, no organization, with so many lives at stake! This man couldn't live! That man! Voices beat at her ears. "Please help me! Help me!" Or, "Ma'am, wouldja take a look at my buddy, here—"

The hospital filled. And there were men lying on litters in the rain and wind, men with faces of putty gray, mummy brown, the blue green of near-asphyxiation. Men lay, sat, leaned, were supported by others as grievously wounded as they.

Mrs. Bent disintegrated. And her toady, Rachel, was a quivering bundle of tears.

Denise took charge. Taking a package of cigarettes from a soldier's pocket, she lit one, handing it to the crying girl.

"Soom o' the men ootside are asking for a smoke. And they might as well hae it," she said fiercely. "Gae alang the lines, haud it for them. Tell them they hae nae lang tae wait—puir deevils. It may be theirrr last—! And ye, noo, Mrs. Bent!"

Taking the woman's elbow, she steered her to a patient lying on a litter. His arm was nearly amputated, hanging by a shred, and the pad someone had applied was dripping red.

"Haud his arm," Denise said firmly. "I maun tie off the veins—"

"You can't—"

Denise fixed her with a look. "The mon is bleeding tae death!"

The older woman was stunned into complete obedience. She did as she was told, her eyes blank with shock. Denise completed her work, then snipped the flap of skin that held the arm, free.

The thing came off in Mrs. Bent's hands. She stared at what she held for a moment, then fainted dead away.

Denise stepped over her and went on to the next patient.

Mrs. Bent woke, shaking her head free of the gray haze that enveloped her brain. She had failed, she thought, sitting up. All she had learned was useless in the face of this—gruesome reality. She rose and stumbled to Denise's side.

"I am all right now," she said. Then, in a piteous, uncertain voice, "Tell me what to do."

Denise looked at her. The woman was deathly pale, her hands shaking. It was clear she was not yet recovered enough to be of use.

"The litters. We hae emptied soom for rrreturn tae the front. They maun be washed—"

Mrs. Bent went out into the darkness. The empty litters had been aligned to one side of the surgery. They were all blood-soaked, crimson turning to a pinkish tinge in the rain. Here and there were bits of flesh adhering.

Fighting nausea, she carried pails of water, sloshing grimly until the litters were usable again. Only then did she notice the pile of debris at the corner of the building; blood-soaked bandages, clotted clothing that had been cut away; amputated parts. The smell of gore and raw flesh was overpowering.

Mrs. Bent disgraced herself further. When her retching ceased, she returned to Denise. Her hair was wet and straggling, her face was green, but her eyes were steady once more.

"I am ready to help now," she said. "I am quite myself again. And—Miss Dugal—thank you."

—————————— *chapter 36* ——————————

Within two days, the American army had liberated two hundred square miles of French territory. A new line was established as the troops took over old German positions. The trenches were booby-trapped and infested with lice, but there was no other alternative. Enemy planes buzzed overhead constantly, spitting fire. The Americans answered them back with their own guns: stump-mounted heavy Maxims left behind.

The roads had been completely destroyed. Abandoned German ammo dumps, in the middle of no-man's-land, had to be raided and then destroyed.

And the line had to be held.

There was a mammoth exchange of troops in the days following the Yanks' successful invasion. New, green recruits coming forward, seasoned fighters moving to the rear. There, they would be given five days of rest; five days in which to gorge on local cheese, sausage, and beer.

Then, they were slated for a new battle in the Meuse-Argonne.

The sheer weight of numbers at the field hospital began to lift. The more grievously wounded died. Others, as they were able, were transported to Base Hospital No. 2 at Mesves. And some of the walking wounded, those with shell splinters and minor ailments, were shunted toward the Meuse. Within ten days, though the beds were filled, the state of emergency had lifted.

Mrs. Bent quietly returned to her scheduling of shifts. She had asked for an appointment with Dr. Carey, but it was some time before he was able to see her. After their conversation, Peter Carey sent for Denise.

Her first reaction was one of anger. He had nae right tae summon her sae summarily. And she had a pretty good notion of what it was all about. Auld Bent had been biding her time, waiting tae tattle about her actions after the attack. She could just imagine what she did!

Miss Dugal defined my rules, insisting on performing care beyond a nurse's capabilities.

The auld bat!

Well, she wadna dignify the wooman's accusations wi' an answer. She'd onie doone what maun be done i' the situation. If he hadna the wit tae figurre it oot for himsel, then—tae hell wi' him!

She yearned to run to her quarters, to put on a dress and arrange her hair. Then she would have felt braver in facing him. But his summons allowed no leeway. She had to wear the stained shirt and trousers she'd been working in. Her face was flushed, her hair in disarray—

She had no idea that when she walked into Peter Carey's office, he thought she was the prettiest thing he ever saw.

"Please close the door," he said quietly.

Feeling the magnetism that seemed to leap between them, she halted, frozen to the spot. His words broke the spell, and she remembered she was probably in for a lecture.

The door closed with a slam.

"Aweel?" she said, her head high.

Carey, his head bent, shuffled some papers on his desk. Then he shoved them away, with a decisive gesture.

"Mrs. Bent has been talking to me—"

Denise's body went taut, her eyes flashing. "I am cerrrtain she has—"

Carey, feeling the animosity bristling from her, cleared his throat uncomfortably.

"It's about your duties. She asked that I make a special point of telling you—"

"Then, domn it, mon," Denise exploded, "get on wi' it! Say what ye hae t'say! I canna stond here a' day while ye muddle aboot!"

Carey's mouth settled into a straight line. There was no getting along with this woman! No matter what he said, she was always ready to fly at him like a bloody virago! He'd made a promise to Mrs. Bent, however, and he'd keep it, by God! Then all he wanted was for the girl to get the hell out!

"She has asked me to put in for a special commendation," he said stiffly. "She says your work during the emergency was above and beyond the call of duty, and suggested I thank you personally—on behalf of myself and the staff."

Denise stared at him, open-mouthed. Her magnificent body began to sag as tension left her. Her face was pale. It was like watching a candle flickering out. And her eyes—

Her eyes filled as she swayed, catching hold of the back of a chair.

"Denise—"

He rounded his desk, catching hold of her arms. She lifted her tear-dewed face and his concern became something more.

"Denise—don't—"

And then he was kissing her, finding the sweetness of her mouth beneath the salt of tears, feeling the thud of her heart against his own, the rounded curves beneath the stained uniform pressed so closely to his.

When she drew away on a sob, his inner alarm sounded again. He did not intend to be drawn into an emotional entanglement, especially not with a hot-tempered woman who fought him at every turn. He had his own plans for his life and those plans did not include a girl who was both beautiful, ambitious, and prickly as a brier.

Carey got his emotions under control and seated her in a chair.

"Now," he said gently, "what upset you? What did I say?"

"I dinna know," she said woefully. "I dinna know."

He hesitated, seeking for words to put them back on an impersonal basis. "I'd like to tell you that I was wrong when you first came to Ypres; wrong about all of you. You have been—an excellent team. In fact,

I'm also considering commendations for the other girls. Your help has been invaluable—"

Her head was bowed, the tears still flowing. He felt a wrenching pain in his chest and forgot his warning signal.

"Oh, God, Denise! Please—"

He moved toward her, and as he moved, the door opened. Dr. Stacey poked his bald, age-spotted head inside.

"One of the ambulances is back. We've got a tough one; a head wound. West said to call you."

Carey lingered for a moment in indecision, then ran out on his way to surgery. Denise stood up and, still blind with weeping, made her way back to her quarters.

Why had she made sooch a fule o' hersel, and afore Peter Carey o' a' people?

It was only that she had been braced for a confrontation, and his praise had caught her short.

She scrubbed at her eyes, remembering how it had been at home. There, she had been the only daughter; Denise the beautiful, the family's greatest pride. She'd only disappointed them in discouraging the local suitors—then leaving home.

It had been their fault, she thought dismally. Her parents, her brothers. They'd brought her up to think the world lay at her feet.

And for four lang years, she had been naebody! She'd set oot tae mak her marrrk at twenty-three. And noo, she was twenty-seven. A lass who could tak off a mon's arrrm wi'oot a qualm, but went a' trembly at a kind word, a comforrrting kiss—

And that was a' it had been. She maun remember that! He thocht nae more o' her than he did of Liane, Nora, and Jo.

He'd made that verrry plain.

She wished she'd stayed hame, where she was luved and pampered. Where she could stay a lass forever, and could do nae wrong. Maybe that was why she didna like Mrs. Bent. She saw hersel i' the future, lonely and unluved.

Denise looked about the bare room she occupied alone. She had ainly hersel tae blame. The things she'd said aboot Nora had been unkind, blurted in a moment o'—jéalousy. And once spoken, they could not be called back.

Palm pressed to lips that still pulsated from Peter Carey's kiss, she sat for a long time, recognizing her loneliness.

Then she rose and moved her gear back to the room she'd shared with Liane.

chapter 37

Liane Wang wasn't too happy with her former roommate's return. She was exhausted, having been called to fill in for Denise. And she hadn't come back for a long time. Liane had to go on duty again within a few hours. She needed some time to rest and to think. She had a problem, one that was too ridiculous to consider.

She had fallen in love with a hand.

The hand was attached to a long, rangy body, with a face she hadn't seen. The man's whole head was swathed in bandages that left only a mouth and nose for breathing. And there was a strong chance that, beneath the wrappings, he was blind.

"They'd brought him in for surgery this very day. She made her rounds and stopped to take his pulse as a matter of course. And, looking at his hand, she'd had a strange sensation, her heart beginning to beat

much too fast. It was as if she recognized the long,
brown fingers, so different from most of the patients'.
They were oddly ridged with callus; the ends spatu-
late, nails worn away, A working man.

But what kind of work, she wondered.

It didn't matter. What troubled her was the impact
she received just from holding that limp, unconscious hand. It was as if it had touched her, caressed
her in loving ways. And her head hurt with the
strange humming that had accompanied her too-
perceptive childhood. It had been a long time since
she'd felt this way. There was always too much
confusion, too much pain crying out around her.

Maybe, she told herself, her nerves had suffered
during the last onslaught of wounded. Or else, she
was weird like Luka, as Denise had said. For a third
alternative, this could just be one of the dumb things
expected of her. Stupid, clumsy Liane.

Berating herself for her own faults, she had no idea
that she had outgrown her childish impulsiveness
and her coltish awkwardness long ago; or that many
of the patients followed her with their eyes, seeing a
lovely oval face and silky shining hair.

Lying on her cot, she fought for sleep that wouldn't
come. Her mind kept returning to the man in bed
23. It was impossible that they'd met before. His
name was Steve Long, and even that was unfamiliar
to her. The face beneath the bandages might be
pock-marked, ugly, with a crooked nose or a weak
chin. She had no way of knowing. Yet she had an
irresistible urge to return to the ward and sit by his
bedside.

It was insane!

Insane or not, she endured a sleepless hour or
two, then returned to her work, drawn, despite

herself, to the patient in 23. He was still unconscious. According to Mrs. Bent, he had a severe head
wound which might have damaged the optic nerve.
Only time would tell.

During that time, he would probably be transferred to a base hospital. And she would never know
why she'd had the strange reaction to this one man
out of many.

Change dressings; dispense medications. Bed 43,
patient chilling; bed 15, amputee, feverish and crying;
bed 31, shell shock. Violent.

Liane went through all the motions, medicating,
soothing, as she had done so many nights before,
knowing that one or more of her patients would not
live to see another day.

Finally, there was that time of comparative quiet
Liane had grown to expect; silence broken only by
the snores and moans of sedated sleepers. Rachel sat
sleepily at a small desk, chin in hands, but Liane
found a folding chair. She drew it up in the narrow
hallway between beds 23 and 24. She smiled a little
to herself, noting that the man's long narrow feet
extended beyond the foot of the cot. How tall he
must be—

For a long time, she sat quietly, fingers laced
together in her lap. The man lay still, one arm free of
his covering, his throat and upper chest exposed.

He's brown all over, Liane thought, a little surprised. Impulsively, she put her hand on his. Her
flesh was dark, but with a creamy Asian tint. It
glowed against his brownness with a strange
opalescence—a moonstone against fine leather.

An odd comparison!

Then she forgot comparisons as the hand turned

palm upward, fingers curling to grip her own.

She began to tremble as the feeling of prescience—
of something remembered—flowed through her again.
Her voice was unsteady as she whispered, "Mr.
Long?" Then, uncertainly, "Steve?"

The figure didn't move. But a small sound issued
from the unbandaged hold that was his mouth.

"Dar——," the sick man said hollowly. "Dark—"

Liane remembered what Mrs. Bent had said. That
it might be dark for him forever. Tears ran down her
cheeks, but her voice was steady as she said, "Of
course it's dark. It's the middle of the night. Now,
sleep—"

In a few minutes, his rough brown fingers relaxed
their hold. But Liane did not relinquish hers until
she heard Rachel's frantic call.

"Liane!"

The amputee in bed 15 would cry no longer. He
had died, his face still wet. Liane touched a finger to
his cheek. Tears were a part of life. And they would
go on and on. He was only a boy, and somebody,
somewhere, would cry for him.

She drew a blanket over his face and calmed
Rachel. The girl had never become accustomed to
death, and probably never would. Sending Rachel
for two orderlies to remove the body, she returned to
Steven Long's bedside.

"Please, God," she whispered, "let this one live."

Dawn came, and Denise and Barbara came
to take their turn at duty. Denise was unusually subdued, not even balking when Mrs. Bent
complained about her long absense the previous
day.

"I'm sorry tae hae caused ye trooble," she said

mildly. Then, checking the charts with Liane before she departed, Denise was almost apologetic.

"I hope ye dinna mind my cooming back tae yer room. I hae been lonely."

Her words penetrated Liane's mind, making her forget her own concerns for a moment. It was alien to Denise's nature to apologize to anyone.

"Of course I don't mind," she said generously.

Together they went down the lists; this man was critical; that one had required additional medication in the night. And, of course, there was the amputee—

The roster completed, Liane fought a compulsion to remain. It would be impossible. Mrs. Bent would surely ask her reasons. And, those, she didn't know herself.

"Would you keep special watch on bed 23?" she asked Denise. "And if you need me—call me—"

Denise looked at her curiously. Bed 23 had ainly coom in yesterrrday. His head was wound with bandage like a moommy! If she didna know better, she'd hae thocht wee Liane was smitten. But there was nae way.

Probably, she thought indulgently, the child had ane o' her odd, fey notions aboot the mon.

"I wull," she promised, amusement rich in her tone.

Liane blushed and fled.

Her rest that day was sketchy and fraught with erotic dreams; dreams of a disembodied brown hand that stroked her, lovingly, intimately. She woke herself moaning, her pillow clutched against her emptiness, and sat up, appalled at herself.

Liane had never been overly obsessed with men. She only knew that there would be one someday, and that she would be a good and faithful wife. But this—this was alien to her nature.

Her face crimson, she sat up, hugging her knees, wondering whatever in the world had happened to her.

It was Nora, she thought. Nora and her romantic adventures had put such things into her mind. But what did one do to erase them?

Tired and confused after her interrupted rest, she finally rose and went to relieve Denise. As they went over the day's problems together, Denise winked at her conspiratorially.

"Dinna worrit aboot twenty-thrrree. He's been wide awake and asking for ye—"

"But he couldn't! He doesn't know—"

Denise shrugged and left, still wondering what the deevil there was between those twa—

Liane, suddenly shy of bed 23, left it until last. Steve Long was still lying in the same position, looking as if he hadn't moved since morning. She stepped backward, prepared to slip away.

"Who's there?" A muffled voice did not conceal a soft, lazy drawl. "It's you, ain't it? The night lady?"

"I'mthenightnurse," Liane said, so flustered she ran the words together. "Myname'sLiane—"

His brown hand lifted, a graceful gesture that halted her.

"Whoa up! Run that by agin—"

Her face flaming, she repeated her words more slowly.

"That's what I thought you said." She had the feeling that beneath the bandage he was grinning. "Been waitin' for you."

"Last night—I don't see how you knew I was—"

"Couldn't see," he said. "And you told me it was

night. After that, I slept pretty good, I guess. This mornin'—I reckon I could take it better."

Then he knew about his sight, that he might be blind. Liane felt a lump in her throat, feeling the strange buzzing in her head that opened a tiny peephole into the future.

"You're going to be all right." Her voice rang true with certainty. "I know it!"

"I'll be goldanged," he said, with a kind of wonder. "Somethin' tells me mebbe you do!"

The brown hand lifted, searching the air until she reached to touch it, then it folded over her own. When it finally relaxed, she knew he slept—and that beneath the beehive bandage he was smiling.

---————— *chapter 38* ————————

Long before dawn of the next morning, the ambulances set out for the front again. They had driven the track so often that it was almost memorized. After they reached the original front, there would be no road, just a winding path past bombed-out entrenchments, villages reduced to rubble, the remnants of ancient oaks pointing skeletal fingers at the sky. The earth looked like the face of the moon, cratered, deeply rutted, ancient, dead—

And death was here. All around the little convoy. In the trenches, in rags and tatters caught in charred coils of barbed wire. And it was silent in no-man's-land. Far ahead the sky vibrated with light, but here there was no sound.

Only the laboring engines of the ambulance trucks as they struggled across the devastated war-torn land.

Nora and Jo, as always, were at the tail of the convoy. Outranked by Mac Hill, the lead driver—naturally, a man—they had been placed there for their own protection. It was too easy to wander off the path in the darkness. There were still mines, unexploded shells—perhaps even a wounded German lying low to open fire.

In their position at the rear, the little ladies would be safe. And this was as it should be in wartime, the men taking the brunt of danger.

"Egotistical jackass," Jo had muttered when Mac issued his instructions.

Nora's description was much more colorful.

After that, they amused themselves on the long, difficult drives by inventing new and more interesting names for Hill. And, finally, Nora discovered that she could irritate the man by lagging behind. On the final short spurt into the first-aid collecting stations, she would speed up and be waiting patiently in line when he came to reprimand her.

"Dammit—pardon me, ladies—but where the hell— I'm sorry—were you? You've got to keep up!"

Nora would smile. "We're here, ain't we, Mac? Where the hell were you?"

Today, they'd dropped back farther than ever. Nora had been talking about Mule Muehller, driving his vehicle somewhere along the line; her plans for the future, the children they would have. Her eyes were shining as she steered around obstacles, her mind only half on her driving. It was some time before it dawned on her that she was monopolizing the conversation. She blushed.

"You'll find somebody, someday, Jo."

"Not me," Jo laughed. "I'm going to be the best doggone reporter the world has ever seen. No man's going to tie me down. Oh, maybe when I'm old—"

"Look, Jo!" Nora braked to a stop and pointed.

Above, two planes were dogfighting; tracers stitching the sky with red embroidery. They were only dark silhouettes against the lightening heavens as they looped and dove at each other like vicious hawks.

"Which one is ours?" Jo asked, craning her neck. "I can't tell."

"I can't either," Nora confessed. Then she gave a muffled cry. "Oh, my God!"

One plane fluttered in the sky, going into a spin—

"Pull out," Nora shrieked, "git your nose up—"

For a moment, the plane leveled, then it drifted downward, wings tilting upward, down—

"He's goin' to try t'land," Nora said, awed, "in this!"

She gestured at the broken, shell-torn space around them; the litter and debris of battle. "There ain't no place—"

There was a bumping sound in the distance, a rending of wood and metal. The girls stared into the darkness. There were no flames.

"He's down," Nora said briskly. "Guess he made it." She touched the gas to move ahead and Jo caught at her arm.

"The pilot may be hurt," she said. "We ought to go and see."

Nora looked at the pitted ground. Hill would be furious if they ventured out of the caravan's path. It was one thing to drive a proven track, another to venture into unknown territory. There was no telling how far away the plane had fallen. A mile, maybe two. And if Mule Muehller reached the collecting site with the others and she didn't appear at a reasonable interval—he would be wild.

"Could be it's a damn German," she said uncertainly. "Ain't sure we—"

"And it could be one of our boys," Jo said promptly. "Can't let him die because we're scared!"

The girls stared at each other. Both of them were big-eyed, pale. Nora broke first.

"Dammit, who's scared?" she asked crankily. "Let's go."

"The boss man won't like it," Jo said. She gestured ahead. The other ambulances were not in sight.

Nora forced a grin. "Who the hell cares," she asked nonchalantly. It was only Mulc who had her worried. And she wasn't married to him—yet.

She jammed her foot on the accelerator and rocked the truck out of the ruts, heading off into no-man's-land.

It was a eerie journey. They crept alongside a line of trenches. Here, the scent of death was heavy, gaggingly so. As the skies lightened, they saw bodies strewn haphazardly. The truck ran over something that gave beneath its wheels—and they were afraid to look back. The sun's first light glinted off a rifle. It pointed at them from a trench. Behind it was a crazily tipped German helmet. The enemy who wore it had no face.

Nora swallowed. "You all right, Jo?"

Jo's world had tilted and spun for a moment. It seemed forever before she heard her own voice answer—"Yes."

And, finally, they found the wreckage of the plane. The undercarriage had been torn away, wings ripped free of the fuselage. It had landed on the only clear spot in the ruined area. Luck had been with the pilot.

And the markings on the body of the craft identified it as German.

"Oh, hell," Nora said, braking. "This damn wild ride fer nothin'!"

They sat for a moment, staring at the mangled plane. Then Jo said quietly, "The pilot might still be alive. Maybe we ought to take a look—"

"If he's dead, we can't help 'im. If he's alive, we'll probably git our butts shot off. I reckin we oughta let well enough alone."

"But if he's hurt?" Jo persisted. "We can't just go off and leave him here to die."

Nora shut off the engine. "Yer the boss," she said tersely. "Let's go."

The plane was an Albatros D-III, known to the Allies as a Vee-strutter. It was one of the more deadly weapons the Germans had turned against their enemies, equipped with two belt-fed and synchronized machine guns. Walking toward the craft, the girls felt naked and exposed. At any moment, those guns might start to chatter—and it would be the end.

"Don't think there's nobody in there," Nora said nervously. "Mebbe he already took off—"

Reaching the wreckage, they climbed to look into the cockpit. The plane, already tilted, tipped a bit more. And the seat was empty; blood-spattered, but empty.

Climbing down, they circled the craft. And Jo found the man's trail, blood flecks against seared grass; dark spots on scorched earth; marks that appeared as if he had dragged himself along.

"This way," Joe said excitedly. The tracks led to a crater. They could not see over its rim.

Nora regarded the shell hole thoughtfully. Just because the man was hurt didn't mean he wasn't still dangerous. She stopped Jo from running on ahead. They would split, each approaching the hole from a different side. No sense in actin' like idjits!

It was silent as they crept forward, as silent as a grave, which Jo thought, shivering, it just might be. It was likely the pilot had just crawled this far to die—

Reaching the edge of the crater, she peered over the edge. The man was there, sprawled against the side; his face was dead white, his eyes closed. His gray uniform was blood-soaked, and there was a pistol in one limp hand.

He was surely dead! Jo moved on, forgetting caution. One boot dislodged a clod of earth, and it bounded into the crater. A pair of astonished blue eyes opened wide—

Then there was a spanging sound as he fired in instant reaction. Jo tumbled backward and sat down, not too sure she hadn't been hit.

Nora, to his other side and just above, leaped into the shell hole. She landed on him as he lifted the gun to fire again, the bullet exploding harmlessly in a gout of earth. The German pilot dropped the gun, moaned, and lapsed into unconsciousness.

Nora kicked the Luger away from his nerveless fingers, then picked it up, training it on its owner.

"Jo," she called, her voice trembling with fear. "Jo? You okay?"

Jo's answer was no steadier. "Missed me," she said.

"Wasn't for want of tryin'," Nora said. The gun, pointing at the enemy, was shaking. "Oughta blow his damn brains out!"

Jo slid into the crater and approached the wounded man nervously. "Just keep him covered. Let me see how bad he's hurt."

He was badly hurt, indeed. A bullet wound in his chest might have punctured a lung. His shoulder was dislocated, one leg broken, the bone piercing the flesh.

"Think he'll make it?" Nora asked.

Jo shook her head doubtfully. "Looks pretty bad."

"Then mebbe we oughta leave him. Just go on about our bizness—"

Jo's eyes clouded with tears. "I couldn't, Nora! Just—look at him!"

He was truly a beautiful man, in spite of his pallor. His hair was golden, haloed in the early morning light. Wide-shouldered, slim-hipped, he might have been a god straight from the pages of a volume of mythology on Jo's shelves at home. His mouth was sensitive, twisted a little with pain.

"Oh, hell," Nora said. "Reckin yer right. I couldn't leave him, neither!"

Jo fetched a first-aid kit from the ambulance, and packed his chest wound with gauze. The shoulder would have to remain as it was. She was afraid to try to put it into place, for fear it would intensify his bleeding. The leg would require surgery. For now, she applied a rough splint to protect it from further damage.

Finally they placed him on a litter and managed to remove all of it, litter and man, from the shell hole. "Wish to God Mule was here," Nora panted as they carried the man toward the ambulance. "This feller must weigh two hunderd er more!"

"We'll make it," Jo said, gritting her teeth.

They reached the truck and were forced to lower

the litter to the ground for a moment. Both of the
girls were soaked with perspiration, their bodies
trembling with strain. They wiped grimy faces and
stretched aching backs. "I'm ready," Jo said finally.

They bent to the litter, lifting it, and the German
moaned.

"*Das tut mir weh—*"

"*Tun Sie es noch einmal,*" Jo answered in his own
tongue.

His eyes opened again, eyes pure and blue, filled
with a child's surprise at his own pain. The expression faded as he began to focus, seeing two figures in
the hated olive drab of the enemy. He remembered,
now. Remembered falling from the skies; remembered
crawling from the plane, fighting his Luger from its
holster, prepared to kill himself—preferring death to
capture. Something had happened. He had lapsed
into unconsciousness, though he recalled firing—

It didn't matter. What mattered was that he had
botched his original plan. He had no desire to live in
his present state—a shattered hulk, a prisoner.

Perhaps he could taunt his captors into ending it
for him.

"*Schwein,*" he managed weakly. "Dirty American
pigs!"

"He speaks English," Jo said in astonishment.
"You hear that?"

"I be damned," Nora said.

At the sound of feminine voices, German ace Kurt
Kellerman's blue eyes widened even further.

Mein Gott! Fräuleins!

Not only was he a prisoner, but he'd been captured by a pair of women! He tried to move and was
pushed back, gently. A liquid was forced between his
clenched lips; some kind of medication that numbed

his senses, hazed his brain. Then his litter was lifted into the ambulance, and he blacked out completely; a blessing as the vehicle bounced and jounced across a rough terrain to join the rest of the convoy.

chapter 39

The return to the track seemed longer to Jo than the trip out into the blasted territory. She was acutely conscious of the man in back; of the damage the drive could do to his terrible wounds. Each horrendous bump brought a moan from her, and she bit her lower lip until it bled.

"Can't you take it a little easier, Nora?"

"You wanna drive?" Nora asked angrily. "You know we gotta ketch up with the others as quick as we can. What the hell's the matter with you?"

"It's just—"

Jo looked over her shoulder, and Nora caught the meaning of her gesture.

"Him? Dammit, you know the sooner we git him to the hospital, the better off he'll be. Now, shut up and lemme drive!"

They reached the blasted tree they'd marked when

they left the track. Turning into the trail, Nora
positioned the wheels to avoid the deeper ruts.

"Hang onta yer hat, kid," she said grimly. "I'm
gonna let 'er rip."

When they pulled into the collecting station, the
other ambulances were loading their last patients.
Mule Muehller was in a towering argument with
Mac Hill, waving his arms and shouting when Nora
parked at the end of the line. Two soldiers immediately began lifting litters into the truck, and Nora
walked up behind the quarreling men.

"Don't give a damn what you think," Mule was
bellowing. "I'm loaded, and I'm heading out! Them
girls have run into trouble, and by God—"

"If they did, it was because they didn't stick with
the rest of us," Mac Hill snarled. "I'm in charge, and
I say we stay together! You'll keep your place in
line!"

"The hell I will!"

Nora tapped Mule on the shoulder. He spun around,
his face black with fury that faded into an expression
of surprise and relief, then returned again.

"Where the devil have you been?" he exploded.

"Run over some barb wire," Nora said demurely.
"Had t' fix a flat."

"That settles it," Mule growled. "I'm riding tail,
from here on out, case you have any more problems." He thrust out his massive jaw. "You got any
objections, Hill?"

Mac Hill took one look at the pugnacious Mule,
and decided he did not.

They were late returning, due to the time the
missing ambulance cost the convoy. Reaching the
hospital, Jo stayed beside the German's litter until it
disappeared into surgery. Knowing there was no way

of guessing how soon he'd be cared for, she went to the quarters she shared with Nora.

"I'm worried about him," she told Nora glumly. "Do you think they'll take his leg off? And that chest wound! What do you think his chances are if his lung—?"

Nora threw a pillow at her. "For God's sake! Half of them guys we brung in are in bad shape! And that feller's a damn Kraut! I gotta git some shut-eye! What th' hell's got inta you, Jo?"

Jo Blaine did not know.

After a sleepless hour, she rose and went to the hospital. Denise and Rachel were on duty, and she asked if a wounded German had been brought in from surgery.

"Half a dozen," Denise told her, intent on changing a dressing. "They're segrrregated, o'er yon." She gestured toward one end of the tent. Jo hurried to the designated row of cots, her heart beating a little faster.

He wasn't there.

She followed Denise who was rushing frantically to make all the newcomers comfortable. "This is a big, blond man," she said tremulously, "with blue eyes. Quite—quite nice-looking. He has a chest wound, and injured leg, and—"

Finally her red-haired cousin turned on her.

"He is there, or he isna! He may nae hae been brocht in frae surrrgery, I dinna know! As for his leuks, they a' leuk alike, these Gerrrmans! Noo, let me be aboot my worrrk!"

Guiltily, Jo returned to her quarters. When she finally slept, she dreamed the injured man was calling her—that he was in pain, needing her. She bent above him, in her dream, and he reached up to take her shoulder, shaking her—

"Jo!" It was Nora's voice, Nora's hand that roused her. "Jo! We've overslept, dammit! Hurry! We're pulling out in fifteen minutes—"

Jo pulled on her clothes and ran outside. The trucks were lining up, ready to move. She still had five minutes and hot coffee would be waiting in the mess tent. She passed it by, and rushed into the hospital, going to the line of cots against the wall—

And he was there, his face like carved marble, in sedation, only a flicker of pain about the sensitive mouth to show he lived.

A card at the foot of his cot identified him as Kurt Kellerman.

Kurt!

Jo gently drew back the sheet that covered him, her eyes filling with tears as she saw his leg was intact. They had not removed it, then. His upper torso was heavily bandaged. There was where the trouble would be—

"Jo?"

Liane stood beside her, her almond eyes puzzled, a tray of medications in her hands. "What are you doing here? The ambulances are just leaving. I thought—" She paused, looking uncertainly from Jo to the man on the cot.

Jo seized her arm. "I'm going," she said in a choked voice. "Liane—look after him—please—"

"Why, yes. Of course—"

But Jo was gone, flying out to join the line of trucks that would trundle across no-man's-land, bringing back the sad wreckage of war.

Liane watched her go, then shook her head. Her eyes were troubled as she looked down at the wounded

German. It was clear Jo had an interest in him. But how could she possibly know him? He'd just been brought in. There was no way—

She turned her gaze to bed 23, remembering that it was possible to fall in love with a man's hand.

But this was a German! The enemy!

Poor Jo!

Liane went about her work. Then, as the pressure slackened, she returned to the side of her own special patient. He'd slept since she came on duty, and she'd found herself wishing he would wake. It was a rather selfish wish, she told herself. The man needed all the rest he could get in order to mend. He seemed to have shifted his position, however, because two long brown feet had found their way from his covering. She smiled at the way they projected over the foot of the bed, then pulled the blanket down, tucking them in.

"Howdy," came a muffled voice from the swathed face. "It's you, ain't it? My favorite gal?"

"It's—it's Liane," she stammered, her face pink.

"I figgered as much. Reckon I'd know you anywhere."

"I—don't see how—"

"Easy. You smell like flowers, and yer purty. Give me yer hand—" His groped in the air, and she put her fingers in his, thrilling at his touch. Then he pulled her toward him. "Bend down. I'll tell you what you look like—"

Trembling a little, she obeyed. His long brown fingers touched her hair. "Black," he said in his soft drawling voice. He traced the oval of her face. "Little bitty thing, ain't you?" He sounded amused. He followed the line of her brows, touched her lids—

"Brown eyes," he said happily. "Just what I thought! Not black brown, but goldy brown! Right?"

His hands moved to her lips, a gentle fingertip touch.

"Sweet," he said.

She felt her mouth begin to quiver, and backed away.

"Maybe I don't look like you say at all," she said, trying to calm the butterflies that fluttered in her throat. "I don't see how you can tell—?"

Steve Long burst out laughing. "Easy. Asked the feller in the next bed. He kin see."

Liane couldn't help joining in, and he sobered instantly. "You sound like bells," he said quietly, "on Christmas mornin'. Liane—You got a minute? I'm homesick as hell. I'd jest like to talk to somebody—'

She scanned the room. The patients were all as quiet as they could be under the circumstances. She brought her little folding chair and pulled it up close. And he began to talk, in that gentle, lazy drawl that seemed to wrap around her heart, making it a willing prisoner.

He left home in May, sailed out of New York— now, there was a town—in June, then hit the trenches on the twelfth of September. Must of marched right by here, come to think about it.

Where was home? Liane had the impression that, beneath the bandages, he was grinning. He was just an old country boy, a cowboy, he reckoned. He had his own little spread in New Mexico, outside of Tularosa.

Tularosa? A little bitty old town, founded by Mexicans back in the mid-1800s, when the Injuns were still on the warpath. Nope, its name didn't have nothing to do with roses. It was taken from the word *tular* and meant full of reedy places—

A swamp?

Again, he was laughing. Hell, no! New Mexico was anything but. The Tularosa Basin was kind of a desert, with prickly pear, mesquite, yucca—tarantulas, rattlesnakes, and scorpions—and damn little shade. It wasn't very wide but it was a couple hundred miles long. The Franklin and Organ, San Andres and Oscura mountains to the west. To the east, the Hueco, Sacramentos, Sierra Blanca, and Jicarilla. The Jumanos Mesa was its northern boundary. To the south the basin merged with the Chihuahua Desert of Mexico.

"It sounds—fascinating," Liane murmured.

"Yep. It's mebbe the most beautiful place in the world—and ugly as hell."

He talked on, telling of the malpais country near Carrizozo, where a volcanic eruption had covered the land with a jumble of black lava rock; of an ocean of white gypsum between Tularosa and the Organ Mountains, as pure as snow.

"It kin be a hundred fourteen on top," he said. "Dig down a foot, and it's like ice—and, hell, you oughta see it under a moon—"

As he talked, she could see the mountains above the valley, Sierra Blanca, pine and aspen to the snow line; the Sacramentos, great masses of pink and purple under a setting sun; the Organs, harsh and haunted, ridged and wrinkled, lifting rocky spires and turrets to the sky. And the sleeping lady—a formation above the small, fairly new city of Alamogordo, that had served as landmark through the ages.

And on the desert floor, cactus blooming with waxen, dew-filled cups; yucca rising ten feet into the air with creamy, ghost blossoms; the whips of ocotillo tipped with red. And to balance their beauty, thorns, rabbit brush, lechuguilla, alkali flats—

A rough and rugged land, with people to match;

shootings, outlaws, range wars. It was a wonder the early settlers survived, but they did—

Survivors!

Now Liane knew why she could picture the type of setting he described. It was very like that which Aunt Missie had depicted in her book. Tamsen, Em, and Arab had made their way through this country, to reach the little border town of Magoffinville—now called El Paso!

Liane heard Rachel calling. It was time to prepare the morning charts. She and Steve Long had talked together for hours. And for the first time, she realized he still held her hand. It had seemed so natural for her fingers to be gripped in his—

"I've got to go," she whispered. "But, Steve—," she stumbled a little over his name, "tonight, when I come on duty, I'll bring a book with me. There's some of it I'd like to read to you—"

Forcing herself from his side, she remembered Jo's German, his cot lined up along the wall with the other enemy wounded. She had forgotten her promise to watch over him. If anything had happened in these last hours—

Hurrying to his side, she checked his pulse and respiration. He was still unconscious, but, thank God, he was still alive.

And so was Steve Long, who would live, but might not see the country he loved so much with his own eyes ever again—

chapter 40

Kurt Kellerman had actually been conscious for some time. When the little nurse approached, he feigned sleep. He needed time to think, to remember what happened, and to devise a plan to escape if it were possible. He could recall very little, actually.

He had been wounded, had crash-landed, and managed to drag himself away from his wrecked plane. After that, everything was lost in a haze of pain. He remembered deciding to shoot himself, firing at someone else—then a realization that he had been captured by women.

That, of course, might have been delirium. *Gott!* He hoped that it was. He could be the laughingstock of the *Schlachtstaffeln* if it were discovered. Yet, there was a face strongly implanted in his mind. Not this young woman, with her Asiatic features, but another—with black, tumbled hair and eyes of so dark a blue, like shadows in a mountain lake, a voice that was sweet, yet crisp with authority.

Yet he seemed to remember that voice speaking to him in his own tongue.

It had to be just a fever dream. Perhaps someone he had met at home, in Westfalen—

But he knew he had met no one like her. Never in his life.

The nurse checked his pulse. He tried to breathe slowly, evenly, though it felt as if the engine of his plane were sitting on his chest. Then she moved away, leaving him to his concerns.

Within a few moments, she was back again, and there was someone with her.

"You see, he's doing well," the little nurse said. "He's still unconscious—"

"I don't think he is! I think he's playing possum."

Kurt Kellerman's eyes flew open as he recognized the crisp, sweet voice. And he saw what he feared most to see. Rumpled black hair, dark blue eyes set above rosy cheeks; a small girl in a too-large man's uniform.

"See," she said to the other girl, "I told you." Then, to Kurt himself, *"Wie geht's?"*

How are you! She had spoken in German, so even that had not been a dream. How to answer that? I am wounded, I am in pain, I have suffered the indignity of capture by women, and I will be sent to a prison camp if I survive? *Gott in Himmel!*

"Why did you not shoot me," he asked in slow, distinct English. "I would have preferred to die like a man."

Jo's eyes crackled with blue lightning. "We did not shoot you for the same reason we did not shoot these others," she gestured at the pain-filled world around her, Germans and Allies alike. "I would suggest you try to live like a man!"

"I am not a coward, *Fräulein*," he said hotly.

"Then prove it."

"I am a soldier, *Fräulein*. A pilot—"

She put her hands on her hips and glared at him. "Am I supposed to bow? Or kneel? I'm a reporter—and an ambulance driver. So what?"

"What I'm trying to say," he gritted, "is that I prefer death to dishonor! It is something a woman would not understand! Especially a woman of a decadent nation—"

Jo's face was suddenly livid with anger, her fists doubled at her sides. Liane, frightened, caught at her arm and she pulled away, glaring at Kurt Kellerman.

"That's enough, Buster," Jo rasped, in a voice that was alien to her own ears. "I wish to hell we'd left you in that damn hole!"

Kellerman was too stunned to answer as, back stiff, she marched away.

From the next bed sounded a guttural voice, speaking in German.

"These American females," it said, "have a too-high opinion of themselves. When we have conquered the world, we will show them what they are good for. There is only the one thing—"

"I do not know you," Kellerman said coldly. "Your name, sir?"

"*Oberleutnant* Wilhelm Von Heiser—"

"Then, Herr Von Heiser, I will promise you this! You will behave like a gentleman with these young ladies, or I shall kill you myself."

There was silence in the German end of the ward, and Kurt Kellerman was left alone with his thoughts.

He had a lot to think about.

Again, Jo was unable to rest during her off-duty hours. She spent the day in a state of barely suppressed fury. A woman wouldn't understand! Damned stupid pigheaded men! She'd spent these last four years dragging back broken, twisted hulks, trying to save their darned lives! And some of them, losing an arm or a leg, just up and died because of their—their damned pride!

Catch a woman doing that? Hah!

And a decadent country! Just because women in America weren't treated like—cows! Because they had minds of their own, and were capable of using them!

At least, she'd be able to put Kurt Kellerman out of her mind, now. She wouldn't be seeing his face in her dreams, and worrying about him being sent off to prison camp. In fact, the sooner he went, the better—

She seethed instead of sleeping. And when Denise, just coming off duty, poked her head in the door that night, she was still awake.

"Joost wanted tae tell ye, I dinna fault ye," Denise beamed. "Yer Gerrrman is a gorrrgeous mon! I'd gie ye a rin for yer money, lass, if they wasna moving them oot i' the morning—"

Jo sat upright on her cot. "Moving who out? What are you talking about?"

"The Gerrrmans. Ye didna know? They're taking them awa tae the prison hospital, tae gie us mair space for our ain."

"But they can't! If his wound opened—"

"I canna help it," Denise said testily. "The orrrders came frae Perrrshing himsel. Dinna scowl at me!"

Oh, dear God, Jo thought numbly. Dear God!

Denise went to her own room. Jo rose and dressed and hurried to the hospital tent. Kurt's features were no longer carved in marble, but flushed, his cheeks bright red, his eyes glassy.

He was, however, still in command of his senses. He held his good hand toward Jo Blaine.

"I am glad you came. I wish to apologize for my words of this morning. It was churlish and ungrateful of me. I am sorry—"

Jo's face softened. Kurt Kellerman was certain he'd never seen eyes so deep and so lovely. Or a voice as sweet as she said, "It's all right. Just get well—"

Then the man in the next cot made a pointed remark about her virginity. He spoke in German, but the ugly words were unmistakable. Jo, understanding the language, turned crimson, and Kellerman lunged upward, managing to get his good leg off the cot and onto the floor.

"I said I would kill you," he shouted in his own tongue.

"No," Jo screamed. "No!" She caught at him. "Liane, help me!"

It took both girls to subdue him. As he lay back, drained from his sudden spurt of activity, Liane checked his bandaged chest. Thank God, it had not started bleeding again! And they didn't dare risk another such incident.

The man in bed 22 was in a coma, and had been near death for some time. It was Liane's suggestion that the cots be switched. Kellerman would probably be safer among the enemy than with his own comrades.

Sending Rachel on an errand, they managed the move in secret. Rachel was a dull girl, with little interest in the patients. She would probably never know the exchange had been made.

And, after all, Jo thought, shivering, it would only be for a night—and then he would be gone.

The move effected, Jo went to her quarters and tried to rest again. Finally, she rose and returned to the hospital. Kellerman lay quietly on his cot, next to Liane's friend, Steve Long. His fever had risen, and they'd had to sedate him.

Jo would be leaving with the ambulance within the hour. She would probably never see Kurt Kellerman again. And she knew that she cared. She cared very much.

Wrapped in her own misery, it was some time before she noticed Liane. The girl's eyes were red. She had been crying.

She had just lost another patient; the man they had moved earlier in the day. He hadn't a chance of survival, but it was heartbreaking, anyway. Apparently, he had no one in the world to mourn him; no next of kin. There was only Liane to cry for him.

Jo looked toward the cot where the man still lay, his face covered. She remembered noting his injuries when they moved him: a bandaged chest, a splinted leg.

Her voice trembling with excitement, she asked to see his records.

Poring over them, comparing them to Kurt Kellerman's, she decided there just might be a chance.

"Liane," she said, "you've got to help me!"

She outlined her plan.

They altered the records, switching the cards at the foot of both cots. When the orderlies came, it appeared to be one of the enemy they carried away. The sleeping Kurt Kellerman would awaken to discover his name was now David Stone. Liane was to caution him against speaking his own language. If he became delirious, she was to sedate him—heavily.

"And then what?" Liane asked, still overcome with

the immensity of what they had done. "Suppose they send him to another hospital—or off to the States?"

"Before that happens," Jo said confidently, "I'm going to help him escape."

"Jo, you can't! You—you could be shot for that!"

"You just watch me," Jo grinned.

Now that they had gone this far, there was no turning back. Rachel would never be the wiser. Mrs. Bent looked only at charts and records.

That left Barbara—and Denise.

Barbara was a dedicated nurse. Kurt Kellerman was in no condition to survive transfer to a prison hospital, and she would recognize that fact. But Denise—?

Jo remembered her words. *I'd gie ye a rin for yer money, lass, if they wasna moving them oot ...*

"Don't worry about Denise," Jo said grimly. "I have a notion she'll fall in line, though I'm none too happy about her reasons for doing it! You'll see her before I do—just explain to her and to Barbara what we've done."

Nora poked her head inside the tent. "Jo, dammit, yer holdin' up the whole line—"

"Coming."

Jo Blaine took one last look at Kurt Kellerman's sleeping face and hurried to join Nora at her post. So far, so good, she thought wryly. But where in the hell did she go from here?

chapter 41

In the quiet hours, Liane returned to Steve Long's side. She had brought her copy of *The Survivors* by Melissa McLeod—the pseudonym her Aunt Missie had chosen when she wrote the story of her family's background.

Settling herself by Steve's bed, one hand in his, she opened the book with the other, prepared to read. Steve Long was a little leery of the whole procedure. He was a man of action, not a reader, his liking for fiction confined to tall tales around a campfire on the range at night.

To his amazement he was immersed in the tale to the point that he was disappointed when the reading ceased and Liane closed the book.

"It's time to prepare the charts," she said. "If you want, I'll read some more when I'm on duty again."

"If I want!" Steve groaned. "Dammit, yer leavin'

me high an' dry!" Then he uttered his first word of complaint since entering the hospital. "I wish t'hell I could see t'read!"

Liane touched his bandaged face, gently. There was that humming in her head again that sometimes came with a flash of foresight. Her face lit with a beautiful glow as she caught a glimpse of the future.

"You will," she said softly. "You will!"

Steve Long almost believed her.

Neither of them knew that Liane's voice reached other ears as she read in the night. Kurt Kellerman, waking from his drugged sleep had, in spite of himself, been pulled into the story. The alien setting enchanted him, the personalities of the girls especially struck him. He visualized gentle Liane as Em McLeod; the mercurial redheaded day nurse as Arabella—

And Jo Blaine, with her flashing blue eyes and tumbled dark hair as—Tamsen.

He would have been surprised to know that Steve Long had already cast small, shy Liane in that role.

Just prior to duty change, ambulances driven by military police arrived. The German wounded were moved from cot to litter, and transferred to the covered vehicles. Liane, together with a burly sergeant, checked the names off, one by one.

Kurt Kellerman, listening for his own name, was stunned to learn he had died during the night.

Liane, glancing toward Kellerman's cot, saw that he was awake. Dear God, she thought, don't let him say anything! He seemed about to speak. An almost imperceptible gesture of her hand silenced him.

What the devil, he wondered, was going on? This was no honest mistake. The nurse, Liane, knew of his presence and was concealing her knowledge.

Whatever the reason, it was a reprieve.

The ambulances were finally gone. Liane stood for a moment, in indecision. She wished Kellerman had not been sedated the previous night. It should be Jo who talked to him.

Finally, she made her way to his cot, bending down to whisper to him.

His name was now David Stone. He was not to speak in German, no matter what transpired, not even in his sleep. He must remember that, or they would all be in trouble.

"I do not understand," he said haltingly. "Why are you doing this for me?"

Liane was still trembling with fright. She'd forced herself into a state of false calm while talking with the military police. She had put her own integrity on the line in covering for a man who was an enemy— who was responsible, in a way, for hurting men like—Steve. Now, she was on the ragged edge of tears.

"I am doing nothing for you," she said sharply. "I am doing it for Jo!"

His blue eyes widened, the pleasure in them twisting inside her like a knife. Dear God, Jo loved this man and he loved her! What in the name of heaven had Jo got herself into!

"But what about the—others?" he asked. "The nurses, the doctors—him?" He gestured toward Steve Long in the next bed, then to a patient at his other side.

"Steve won't say anything. That one," she pointed, "can't speak. I can handle Barbara. Rachel won't know the difference. The doctors only know the patients from the charts. And Denise—"

"Yes?"

"She'll go along with us," Liane said, flushing.

"But it wouldn't hurt to—sort of flirt with her. She likes—attention."

"I believe I can manage that," he said dryly. "In fact, perhaps our friend Steve might wish to share in the effort. If she were asked to continue on with the tale you were reading—

"Or was that a labor of love?"

Liane went crimson. She had believed him to be asleep, had thought the night's tender scene to have been unobserved. Here she'd risked everything to save that—that damn German's neck, and he'd spoiled her most private moments. She spun, and walked off, fuming.

Finally, she had to admit that it was not a bad idea. Though she'd wanted to be the one to read the book to Steve, it might keep Denise pacified. She'd noticed Denise was attracted to Kellerman. Maybe, if he returned her interest, it might bring Jo to her senses.

Then Liane stopped short. What if, instead, her Scottish cousin managed to intrigue Steve Long? If she did, Liane would die!

Then she had to laugh. Denise would have no time for a man who might be blind, a cowboy from New Mexico—or a man without a face. Even Liane had no idea what was beneath that swath of bandage. Steve might look like a—a horse, for all she knew.

But she loved him, no matter what!

There! She'd said it!

Kurt Kellerman watched her go, realizing he'd upset her. He'd only meant what he said in a teasing way. He realized that the little Liane felt for Steve Long—what he was beginning to feel for Jo Blaine—

Jo, the blue-eyed, dark-haired girl who had worked out this arrangement to keep him here.

Why had she done it? Surely, the ruse would be

discovered in time. And then the girls would surely be in trouble, accused of harboring an enemy.

Gott in Himmel!

Whatever happened, he thought, his jaw set, he must play the part they had set for him. Though where in the hell this thing was going to end, he had no idea.

chapter 42

Denise was only too glad to go along with the charade. Her life had become a dreary grind of tending the wounded, changing dressings, emptying bedpans. Hiding out a German soldier, right under the nose of the impeccable Dr. Carey, added a bit of spice to her daily rounds. And Kurt Kellerman, now David Stone, was a verrry handsome mon! 'Twas true that Jo Blaine was sweet on the mon, but she, Denise, could be wi' him a' the day.

Naething could coom o' their rrrelationship, of course, wi' the mon being a Gerrrman, but it was guid tae be admired, and leuked at as a wooman.

And she enjoyed reading her Cousin Missie's book. She read dramatically, telling of Tamsen's sacrifices for her sisters.

"I hae a'ways," she said modestly, "thocht mysel tae be verrry akin tae Tamsen—"

"Indeed," Kurt Kellerman lied. Steve Long grinned beneath his bandages.

And Denise read on.

Within the next few days, it was evident there was a tug of war in progress, with both Jo and Denise vying for Kurt Kellerman's attention. Denise had been wearing the trim VAD uniform while on duty. Now, she blossomed out in the garments she'd bought during her last trip to Paris. Jo, coming in from an ambulance run, clad in fatigues covered with mud and blood, felt her blood begin to boil.

"If I had known this was a formal gathering, I would have dressed for it," she said, her words dripping with ice.

"Dinna fash yersel," Denise said with overdone politeness, "ye leuk—sweet, doesna she, Kurt? Like a wee dirrrty lad. Nae a' woomen can get awa wi' wearing a mon's breeks—"

Jo, eyes crackling with blue fire, moved toward Kellerman's bed, ignoring Denise. "You are feeling better?"

He reached to take her hand, and Denise intervened. "Ye mauna touch my patient. A' that muck—," she surveyed Jo from head to toe, "is unsanitarrry!"

"You go to hell!" Jo said. She stamped out, and Denise looked after her in feigned surprise.

"I dinna ken what hae got intae the lass!"

War, thought Kurt Kellerman, was hell. But it just might be preferable to being torn between two women.

In the middle of the night, as the ambulances formed up to wend their way toward the front again, Nora got the shock of her life. Her assistant driver, who climbed gingerly into the cab, was dressed in a blue velvet traveling suit, complete with an ornate hat.

"Lor' lumme!" In her astonishment, Nora fell back on one of Maggie's favorite expressions. "Don't tell me we're goin' t'Buckingham Palace fer tea!"

Jo looked her up and down, disdainfully. "Not all women want to dress like men," she said.

Nora pursed her lips in a soundless whistle and put the truck in gear. She didn't know what had happened to put Jo in this kind of mood—and she damned sure wasn't gonna ask!

Normally, Doctors Carey and West attended only to surgery, the other American doctors on call for emergencies in the wards. Now, the offensive along the Meuse-Argonne Front had pulled much of the German concentration to that area. Here, along the lines established by the St. Mihiel salient, there was only a holding action. Carey had time, at last, to check on a few of the surgical cases that had given him concern.

He entered the hospital tent, reading over the charts. There were two in particular he wanted to take a look at: a head injury, which might have resulted in blindness—ah, here it was, Steve Long, bed 23—and another with a chest wound he'd considered fatal. The man's name was what? Stone—David Stone.

His brows shot up as he studied the record. Stone still lived. It as something of a miracle. Bed 24, too, an odd coincidence; the two he wanted to see were side by side.

He turned and scanned the room, his heart skipping a beat as he saw Denise Dugal. She sat on a chair, evidently reading aloud. Carey walked along the line of cots, surprised to find she was seated between cots 23 and 24. And she wasn't wearing the proscribed uniform, but something totally unsuitable for her occupation.

A faint frown between his brows, he approached her. Her head was bent, the flaming hair piled high to reveal an unexpectedly defenseless neck, stray curls burning against its creamy whiteness.

For a wild, undisciplined moment, he wondered what it would be like to kiss that spot, just below the hairline. Then he fought the notion back and sought for a professional mien.

"Miss Dugal?"

Denise jumped, dropping the book. It slid from her lap to the floor, and she picked it up, her face flushed.

"Aye, Dr. Carey?"

"I would like to examine these two patients, please." He turned to the man in 23. "Mr. Long, how are you feeling?"

"Like takin' on a cougar," Steve said cheerfully. His hand went to his bandages. "Know I'm an ugly sonofabitch, but hell, Doc, how long do I have to stay in hidin'?"

Carey laughed. "Any headaches?"

"Nope."

Carey patted the feet that stuck over the end of the cot. "I think we shall probably have an unveiling tomorrow morning. You—do know the possibilities, regarding your sight."

"Yep," Long said laconically. "I ain't sweatin'."

A brave man, Carey thought. Though he seemed totally relaxed, his hands were clenched, his knuckles white. He was a magnificent specimen, straight out of a western novel. Blindness to a man of his caliber would be a hell of a thing—

"Tomorrow morning, then." Peter Carey moved on to the next bed.

Denise, frozen with fear, had not moved. Dr. Carey intended to examine Kurt Kellerman. They would be found out. Her mouth was dry as Carey spoke to her.

"Would you mind moving aside a little. I need more light—"

He drew back the sheet and inspected Stone's chest wound. It was healing nicely. Then he took a look at the fractured leg. It, too, was doing well.

He straightened. "Well, that's it, I suppose, until tomorrow—"

He left the hospital tent, a confused and bewildered man.

He was not always good with faces and names, but he knew his injuries. David Stone's lung had been completely destroyed by a massive puncture. The man in bed 24 had taken a bullet. It evidently missed any vital organ. Stone's leg had been crushed near the hip joint. This patient's leg was broken below the knee—a compound fracture. He closed his eyes, trying to remember, picturing himself at his operating table; this man— also a magnificent specimen, as he recalled Stone was not—lying there, semiconscious, his lips 'compressed—

Only once had a sound escaped him—

"Mein Gott!"

The patient in bed 24 was a German! And the German patients had been shipped to a prison hospital several days before.

Somehow, there had been a switch. And someone had to be responsible. He thought of Denise, sitting by the man's bed, reading aloud. Surely she did not have time to give all her patients equal treatment. He recalled how pale she'd appeared when he moved to examine Stone, how jerky and uncoordinated her movements had been—

But she couldn't have fallen in love with a German soldier. The fool, he thought angrily, the silly, addlepated fool!

Carey recognized some of the fury that seethed inside him as jealousy, and forced himself to calm down. He did not return to his surgery, but went to his own quarters where he sat on the side of his bed, hands clasped between his knees.

What was his duty, here? The war would soon be over. The man was bedridden and harmless. Should he go to Major West with what he knew? And if he did, would it be due to his idea of ethics—

Or because he hated the man because of a girl—

He did not know. In the name of God, he did not know!

In the hospital tent, Denise was both relieved and depressed. Peter Carey had not discovered their deception. But he had treated her like—like a piece of furniture. "Move, I need more light!" Had he forgotten how he had held her in his arms?

She wished that she could!

On the morrow, she wad ignorrre th' mon! She might e'en prrretend tae be smitten wi' th' lad he thocht was David Stone! That should prrrove she didna gie a domn!

Kurt Kellerman relaxed his tense muscles. Through the examination, his mind had been on Jo—and what might happen if his identify were discovered.

And Steve Long was quieter than usual. Tomorrow, his bandages would be removed and he would know if he were doomed to a sightless life.

In any case, he wanted Liane to be beside him when it happened. And he prayed that Liane's would be the first face he would see.

chapter 43

When Liane came on duty that night, Steve told her what he faced the next morning.

"I was wonderin' if you'd mind hanging around after yer shift's over. I'd kinda like you to be there."

"I'll stay," she said shakily. "If you want me—"

"Hell, yes." His hand groped for hers. "I never been sick in bed afore. Never had nobody take care of me like you been doin'. Right now, I feel like a bull calf lookin' fer its ma—"

She knew this was as close as he'd ever come to a confession of fear. She wanted to put her arms around him, hold him tight, promise him that everything would be all right.

In truth, she was as frightened as he was, perhaps more. Terrified that he would never see again—and afraid that he might. He knew the color of her hair, her eyes. They had been described to him. But did he know that she was more Chinese than Caucasian? And would it make a difference?

"Course," he drawled, "when they take these here rags off, you gotta brace yerself. I never won no beauty prize, but I never skeered no babies, neither—"

"And I—I'm different than you think, Steve. "I look like—"

"I know. Ugly as a mud fence." Beneath the bandages, she knew he was grinning. "Sort of a cross between a horned toad an' a kangaroo rat, right? Well, lemme tell you, lady, after this last week, anybody's gonna look good!"

"I hope so," she said. "Oh, Steve—I hope so."

"Well, we'll soon find out. But right now, I don't wanna think about it. You got that book? My buddy in the next bed awake?"

He was. Liane found the place Denise had marked and read for a long time. When she tired, Steve countered with a tale of his own: a story of Tularosa's past.

The men of Tularosa had gone to do battle with Indians. The women vowed to build a church, should they return safely. And they kept their vow, building a great adobe structure in which the village still worshiped—the Church of St. Francis De Paulo—

"Are you a Catholic?" Liane asked.

Steve Long grinned. "Nope—reckon I'm—nothin'. Ain't sayin' I don't believe in anything. Sometimes, ridin' the range in early evenin', I see one of them sunsets that looks like a path right up t'heaven, an' I figger there's somethin' bigger'n me. How about you?"

"I—I guess I'm not anything, either," Liane said faltering. She thought of the two sides of her: strict Protestantism come down from her Gran-gran, Em, and her Chinese grandfather's Buddhist heritage, pulling her both ways.

"Well, I reckon there's somebody listens if we pray hard enough," Steve said rather wistfully.

Liane knew that he was still thinking of the morrow; wondering if he would see—

Her own eyes filled with tears. "Excuse me for a moment," she said, "I'll be back—"

She left the hospital tent and stood outside, head leaned against the canvas wall, tears streaming down her cheeks, hugging herself against the cold. The ruined earth stretched before her, sheeted with black ice as far as the horizon. A minor shelling had begun in the distance, and the sky shivered with light, a star-burst flaring above it like an unfolding flower. Through her tear-blinded eyes, it might have been a sunset—a stairway leading to eternity.

"Please," she said aloud, "please, God, let Steve see!" And inside her mind was a small unspoken prayer. "Let him like what he sees—"

It was a long night. The ambulances returned in the early morning hours, Jo coming immediately to the hospital tent. Her blue dress had one blood-stained sleeve, and her skirts were draggled with mud, but to Kurt Kellerman she was beautiful, so unlike the women he'd known; women who bore many children, who baked and stitched and scrubbed the front steps every morning.

He thought of his country, its picture-postcard beauty: black forests and rilling streams—a sameness, its women performing the same duties from generation to generation.

While Jo Blaine—Jo was like the people of Liane's book, part of a strange and varying land of mountains, deserts, forest, and thorny vegetation; a land of

dust, wind, rain, sun, and snow. A land that somehow shaped its women to its own pattern.

Life with Jo Blaine would never be dull, passive—
Mein Gott! What was he thinking! He was the
enemy. He would be found out, taken to a prison
camp—and he would never see her again.

"A penny for your thoughts," she said now, teasingly.

Kurt Kellerman raised his blue gaze to hers, too
quickly to erase the yearning in them. She caught
her breath.

"Kurt—"

"My thoughts," he said, trying to pull himself
together. "I was thinking that this deception cannot
go on. Perhaps we can say it was a mistake, a
confusion, therefore you will not be blamed—"

"Forget it," Jo said firmly. "We won't be caught.
And we'll work this out somehow."

"But I do not see a future. One day I shall be
recovered—"

"And then," Jo grinned, "I'm going to help you
escape!"

His eyes welled with tears, astonishing him. He
had not cried since he was a small boy. It was not a
manly thing to do.

"I am ashamed," he said.

"Oh, Kurt," Jo whispered, her own eyes watering
in sympathy, "don't ever be ashamed—of anything."

She brought his hand to her cheek, torn through
with an agony of love and pity. "I love you, Kurt,"
she said.

Her impulsive words surprised her, and she broke
off with an indrawn breath. Kurt Kellerman was even
more startled.

"*Ach—Gott!*" It was a cry from the heart. "There
can be nothing ahead for us! Nothing!"

"There is this." Jo bent, touching her mouth to his. He responded hungrily, one arm going around her, pulling her down to him.

"Don't let me hurt you," she whispered.

"Hurt me? You have destroyed me, little Jo—"

A few moments later, looking up from the shelter of Kurt's arms, Jo realized that she probably had. Denise stood staring at them, her face shocked and angry.

"I just—" Jo stammered. "We—"

"I hae nae interrrest in yer affairrrs," Denise said coldly. "I ainly ask ye tae rrremember this is a hospital, nae a bawdy hoose!"

"Denise, you're misjudging—"

"Am I, noo? Pairhops ye and Norrra are birrrds of a faither, nae better than ye should be—"

Jo stamped her foot, sputtering impotently, then fled, bumping into Peter Carey on the way out.

"What's all this about," the astonished doctor asked.

"Naething," Denise said loftily. "Naething at a'."

Carey shrugged and made his way to his patient, Denise following. Liane was sitting beside Steve Long. Peter Carey frowned. Wasn't she supposed to be on night duty? Then he saw something in her eyes—hope and fear, commingled. She had an interest in this patient, he realized. Softhearted little Liane. She'd always suffered for them all—

Well, if she were sufficiently concerned to be here when she should be sleeping, she might as well assist—

"Liane will help me," he told Denise. "You may go on about your business."

Denise walked away, still upset at the scene she'd witnessed earlier, stinging at Peter Carey's abrupt dismissal. And Carey moved to the head of Steve Long's cot.

With a pair of surgical scissors, he carefully removed layer after layer, revealing a strong, unshaven chin, a shock of dark hair over a tanned forehead. Liane could see the terrible scar beginning at the temple, lost in the bandage still covering the eyes, reappearing at the jawline.

"Now," Carey said, "I'm going to ask you to close your eyes. Do not open them until I tell you to. You may see—nothing. Or you may see a blurred image that will right itself, eventually. That is what we are hoping for."

"Liane?" Steve Long's voice was hoarse, and the girl moved to take his hand. He drew her towards him, and Carey suddenly understood.

"Stand here—where he can see you. Now, Long—are you ready?"

"Yes."

Carey lifted the last of the covering away, holding his hand to shield the light.

"Now," he said, "tell us what you see."

Liane drew in a shuddering breath at the sight of Steve's face; lean and masculine, carved in dark brown leather. The black-lashed lids fluttered, then opened to reveal startling gray eyes, the color of a stormy sky. He blinked once, then again. Then, finally, on a sigh of ineffable relief, he breathed—

"Liane!"

"You see me?"

He looked at the small earnest face above him, still shimmering a little, true, but a perfect oval with straight silky hair and golden eyes—a complexion like a yucca blossom, neither white nor cream—

"I see you," he said.

Then she was sobbing. He reached up and gathered her close. Peter Carey cleared his throat.

"I'll just have another look at Stone here, until you are—ready."

He could have saved his breath. Neither of them heard a word he said.

chapter 44

That first day, Steve Long was allowed to sit up. The next, he was walking. There seemed to be no dizziness—except when Liane was near—and, except for the scar, no lasting effects.

"You must have a head like a mule," Carey said admiringly. "You had one helluva wallop. Should have killed you."

Long rubbed his scalp, his gray eyes twinkling. "Solid bone," he said. "But I got th' disposition of a mule. Get my head sot on somethin', that's the way I'm goin'."

His statement gave Peter Carey the opening he'd been looking for. The word was that there would be another big push on the St. Mihiel front soon. The hospital should be emptied in preparation, and they were shipping out all ambulatory patients on the morrow. He could send Steve Long along with them

353

to the base hospital—but, within a week, they'd probably have him back in the lines. His other option—

In Carey's opinion, the war would soon be over. Long had already done his duty. If he wished, Carey would sign to send him back to the States—

"To sit out the rest of it?"

"Well," Carey said uncomfortably, "I suppose so, but—"

"Sorry, Doc. Never welshed on a bet, or turned my back on a scrap. Reckon I'll finish what I done started."

Carey sighed, and tapped his stubborn patient on the head. "You're right," he said. "Solid bone. Better tie up any loose ends. You'll leave for Mesves, tomorrow."

After he had gone, Steve Long lay cursing himself for being seventeen different kinds of fool. He could have been leaving this miserable damp climate and heading home; home, where it was still warm at this time of year, dust devils swirling from ground to sky.

Instead he was slated for a base hospital—then a return to the lines. And all because he was muleheaded. A month ago he wouldn't have had second thoughts. But now, there was Liane.

It was going to hurt like hell to leave her. And if he was sent to the front again—and his luck ran out—

Damn! Damn! Damn!

He said nothing to Liane when she came on duty. In the quiet hours of the night, she read for them again. He listened with only half his mind, wondering how he would tell her.

"I'll have to stop here," she said at last. "The records—"

"Wish I could stick around to hear the end of the story," Steve said quietly.

Liane closed the book, looking at him in alarm. "What do you mean?"

As gently as possible, he told her what Dr. Carey had said, seeing her small face shrivel as he spoke. "I'll be coming back through," he added hurriedly.

"Back to the front?"

"I reckon so."

Liane did not cry. Numbly, she went throught the motions of filling out charts to be read by Denise and Barbara. On Steve's chart, she wrote *To be transferred to Mesves*.

She stared at the words for a long time.

When the ambulances arrived to transport Steve and a hundred others to the base hospital, Liane was waiting to say good-bye. Jostled in the crowd of walking wounded, Steve stepped to one side, drawing her with him. He wanted to take her in his arms, to kiss her, to ask her to wait. But it wouldn't be fair to her. And if he held her, he'd never let go—

"That book," he said hoarsely, "it have a happy endin'?"

"I—I suppose it does."

"I reckon I'll just hang onta that thought. Most stories do."

"Yes—"

A sergeant was calling off names. "Lehigh—"

"Yo!"

"Lester—"

"Here."

"Long! Long! Where the hell are you—?"

"I got to go," Steve said, squeezing her hands until he feared he'd hurt her. "But I'll be comin' back. And don't you fergit it!"

She watched him climb into the truck, her eyes huge and blind with pain. Then she hurried to her quarters, lying down, her hands pressed to her temples. She'd always hated the humming in her head that sometimes brought visions of the future. Today, she would welcome it. But she felt too deeply—too deeply—and there was nothing, nothing but a rain of tears that did not wash away her grief.

There was no more reading in the hospital tent. Liane did not realize Kurt Kellerman's interest in the book. She was too emotionally exhausted to do anything but drift through her duties like a tired child. Denise, on the other hand, did not go near Kellerman's bed. She was angry at him, at Jo—at Dr. Carey—at Liane and her departed love. In fact, she seemed unable to get along with anyone. She knew she was being impossible, but no matter how she tried, she couldn't stop herself.

She attempted to reason it out, coming back to the same conclusions she'd drawn before. She had lost these good years of her life, and had no one.

Nora had Mule Muehller, Liane her Steve, and Jo her damned German!

It wasn't that she cared about Kurt, though he was certainly a handsome man. But it would have been nice to be first with someone—anyone. And it would show Peter Carey somebody cared!

Barbara was Jo's friend. Rachel was so dumb! Denise was left with nobody to talk to but dried-up Mrs. Bent. Oddly enough, she found her to be starved for attention. She'd been flattered until the woman, an affectionate hand on her arm, had coyly suggested that Denise call her by her first name.

And her name was Alabaster—

From that time on, Denise kept to herself. It was

strange that anyone could be so lonely in a crowd. If
ainly she could keep frae being sooch a cat!

She finally managed to blame her problems on the
United States Army. Since they'd become attached to
the hospital here, there'd been no letters from home.
One day, they'd all arrive in a bunch, and her
disposition would improve—

Just knowing someone cared.

Luckily, they were all kept busy. A new enemy
had reared its head in their midst. The ambulances
coming back from the front were laden with cases of
Spanish flu. These had to be segregated. The officers
and nurses gave up their quarters, moving once again
into flimsy tents that billowed in the icy winds,
slapped with a rain that was half sleet. And as the
wounded and sick were brought in, other troops
moved forward to take their places. There was a
dizzying, constant turmoil.

Walking, head down, to her tent, Denise was
surprised to hear her name. It was a man's voice,
ringing joyously in the icy air.

"Denise! Hey, doll! Wait up!"

Johnny! Johnny Looper!

Denise didn't wait, but ran to meet him. They
collided, laughing, hugging each other, both talking
at the same time.

Finally, he held her at arm's length, looking at her
with admiring eyes. Her cheeks were bright, her
eyes shining with pleasure at seeing him.

"Well," he said, swaggering a little, "looks like you
missed the old man—"

"Oh, I hae, Johnny! I hae!"

"You damn well better. I went AWOL, hopin'
you'd still be around."

"Oh, Johnny!"

"It's okay. My unit's up the road a ways, and I got a guy to cover for me. Hell, if I'd known you'd be so glad t'see me, I'd of flat deserted."

Glad? If he only knew how glad! Johnny was someone who really cared, who wasn't mad at her! She threw her arms around him and kissed him again.

"Miss Dugal!"

She whirled to see Dr. Peter Carey. His face was hard with disapproval. Domn the mon! Was he spying on her? He—

Her thoughts froze as she saw the man beside him. A Scot! His kilt was flying in the wind, his knees were blue with cold, but he was definitely one of her own people! How she'd missed the sight of plaid and sporran!

"This gentleman is an envoy from the British," Carey said coldly. "I had thought it would please you to speak with him for a few moments—"

"Aye," Denise said breathlessly, "oh—aye—"

"Then I will leave the two of you to converse— while I have a talk with this young man." Peter Carey's blond brows were drawn together, his mouth tight. "If you will come with me, sir!"

"Yes, sir!" Johnny Looper saluted, his back stiff. He followed Peter Carey to the officer's tent, and Denise's heart sank. Johnny was AWOL, and it was her fault. Carey was certain to discover it. Dear God, what would happen to him—

"Sae yer name's Dugal," the Scot said genially. "I'm o' the Duncans, mysel."

"I am pleased tae mak yer acquaintance," Denise said mechanically, her mind still with Johnny.

The Scot was looking at her curiously. "Do ye hae a brother i' th' sairvice, pairhops?"

She shook her head. "My aulder brothers are tae auld, the wee one tae yoong—"

"There was a Dugal in my rrregiment, spittin' image o' ye! Rory Dugal. Died a herrro at the Somme. A brrraw laddie, he was, puir boy."

The blood had left Denise's face, her lips were blue, and she was shivering uncontrollably. The Scot looked at her in alarm. "Hae I gie ye bad news? Was the lad yer kin?" He grasped her arm and looked around frantically for Carey. "We maun get ye set doon, lass—"

"It—it's naething." Denise's voice sounded far from her own ears. "I hae been exposed tae the Spanish flu—'tis a chill. I maun gae t'my bed—"

He released her and she ran to her tent, still shaking like a leaf. Nora and Jo were sleeping. She quelled an impulse to wake them, to spill out her grief.

Nae, this was her ain business, a prrrivate thing. She seated herself on her cot, trying to control her chattering teeth.

"It canna be," she kept telling herself. "It canna be!" Rory was ainly a lad—

Yet she had not seen him in four long years. And lads grew up. She doubled over the ache in her middle. Ahh, God—Rory! How could she e'er hae thocht things would stay th' same at hame?

This war! This bluidy war! The domn Gerrrmans! She wished she were a mon! She would kill them a'! And that included Kurt-bluidy-Kellerman! Though sleet still slanted against the tent, her chill had gone. Now, she felt hot, anger boiling, raging, seething inside her!

How long she sat there, she would never know. It was full dark when she rose from her cot. Taking a pistol from the center pole where it hung in its holster, she checked it for ammunition. It was loaded, ready to use.

She walked stiffly across the compound and entered the hospital tent. Rachel paid no attention, but Liane looked at her in surprise.

"What is it? Did you forget something? Denise— are you ill?"

Passing Liane like a sleepwalker, she went to Kurt Kellerman's bed. The pistol was concealed in her apron pocket, the safety off. Still keeping the weapon hidden, she raised the barrel, pointing at his head.

It didna seem right. He was sleeping, and wadna know. He should be made tae soofer—and the bitch that brrrocht him here, alang wi' him.

Denise watched him for a moment, then turned and walked, zombie-like, into the night.

Liane looked after her, disturbed.

There was something wrong with Denise—terribly wrong. Perhaps she should go and check—

"Liane," Rachel called plaintively, "this man's bleeding again. I need some help."

Denise would have to wait.

chapter 45

Jo Blaine, dreaming of Kurt Kellerman, was deep in blissful sleep when Nora shook her shoulder with a hand like ice, bruising in its grip.

"Ouch," Jo mumbled. "Leggo, dammit. I'm awake!"

She sat up, yawning. Surely it wasn't time to drive the route. It seemed she'd only got to sleep. It was so cold outside, and her blankets were warm—

It wasn't Nora standing above her, but Denise, her face ghastly in the glow of a carbide lantern, eyes darkly circled, her mouth drawn—she looked—scary.

"What the devil? What is it, Denise? An emergency? Here—sit—"

Denise backed away from her reaching hand. "Wake Nora. She maun hear what I hae tae say—"

"I'm awake," Nora said crossly. "How th' hell kin a body sleep with somebody shinin' a light in their face?" She reached for her clock and stared at it

361

gloomily. "A hour to go, yet. Awright, what's on yer mind. It better be good—"

"'Tis ainly fair tae let ye know. I' the morrrning, I'm gaeing tae Dr. Carey, and tell him ye're harrrboring a Gerrrman."

Jo gave a small cry, and Nora leaped to her feet: a pugnacious little figure in her white flannel gown. "Yer—what? I'll see you in hell, first!"

"And hoo are ye gaeing tae stop me?"

"Yer crazy as a bedbug," Nora gasped.

"Nae," Denise said, "I hae joost coom tae my senses."

"Denise," Jo's voice was choked, "Denise, I don't know what's got into you. But I beg you—"

"I hae made oop my mind. Ye forrrget this mon is an enemy. It is my duty—"

"Duty be damned," Nora barked. "Denise, if you do this, yer a—a bitch."

Surprisingly, Denise yawned. "I think I'll lie doon," she said in a vague voice. "I hae warrrned ye."

She stumbled to her cot and Nora turned to Jo, who still sat, pale and frightened.

"Getcher clothes on," she rasped. "I won't stay in this tent one more minute with this—this hellcat! Let's git over an' talk to Liane."

Within a few minutes, the girls were walking toward the hospital tent, heads down against the stinging sleet.

"She won't go through with it, will she?" Jo asked, hopelessness in her voice. "She wouldn't dare."

"Wouldn't she?"

"But why?" Jo whispered. "Why?"

"I dunno. Jealous, mebbe. Or just plain mean."

"What do you think they'll do with Kurt."

"Prison camp."

Jo thought of what she'd heard about the barbed wire enclosures, insufficient rations, men dying like flies of the Spanish flu. She had talked to several military police, collecting material for an article.

"We can't let it happen! Oh, God, Nora! What are we going to do?"

"Right now," Nora said, "we're goin' to talk t'Kurt about it. See what we can come up with."

They talked first to Liane, surprised at her reaction. The old Liane would have wept. This one turned into a small spitting ball of fury, fists doubled, cheeks splotched with red.

"Damn her! I should have known! She came in here and stood by Kurt's cot, looking like she wanted to kill him—! I'm going to go tell her off—"

They restrained her with difficulty. It would do no good. And the ambulances were due to leave shortly.

"I'm not going," Jo said stubbornly. "I've got to tell Kurt."

Kurt Kellerman took the news stoically. He had rather expected it. His wounds were healing, and he would soon be shipped off to Mesves, where his identity was certain to be discovered. His only fear was for the women who had protected him.

"Jo," he said softly, "once you gave me a promise. You said that you would help me to escape. I will need an American uniform, a pair of crutches. I will try to make it through the front lines—"

"You can't do that," Jo said in horror. "It's blowing sleet out there—"

"I can do what I must."

Nora looked toward the receiving desk. Rachel was fast asleep, her head on her folded arms. "Let's get movin'," she said sourly. "Ain't much time."

A short while later, a pallid soldier, whose uniform

hung loosely on his gaunt frame, was helped from the hospital tent and into the rear of an ambulance. Jo crawled in beside him, tucking a blanket around his shivering frame. "I'll come back with you," she whispered, "as soon as I can."

They went through their normal routine, the engines idling to warm. Mule Muehller, on the way to his truck, managed to catch Nora long enough to steal a kiss. Mac Hill walked along the lines, checking out vehicles and drivers.

"You girls dressed warm?" he asked, stamping his feet to warm them. "This is one helluva—'scuse me, ladies—cold night!"

He went on, his breath blowing clouds of steam as he peered in each window, and then he was out of sight. Jo slid from her seat beside Nora, and climbed in the back of the ambulance. The vehicle shuddered as Nora put it in gear—and they were on their way again.

Though this night was different from all others. On this night, Jo's buoyant girlhood had come to an end.

Kurt Kellerman reached out to her in the darkness, drawing her beneath the blanket that covered him, tucking it in around her. She leaned her head against his shoulder, feeling no desire, no surge of passion; just a need to be near him—always.

This, perhaps, would be all they'd have.

"Kurt, are you sure—?"

"I have no choice, *Liebchen*."

His chest wound could open with the strain of walking on crutches. He must cross the line of fire between the American front and the German. And he was likely to die at the hands of either. She closed her eyes against a vision of Kurt dead, sleet slashing down to cover his upturned face. And she would not know. There would be no one to tell her—

"Do not cry, little one. For my sake."

Jo wiped her eyes on her sleeve and tried to smile. Twisting a little, she reached into her pocket and pulled out a folded scrap of paper.

"This is my address in California, for when the war is over. If you will let me know—"

"I will let you know."

"Oh, Kurt!" She threw her arms around him, bursting into an abandoned, heart broken weeping. "I can't let you go! I can't!"

"Liebchen!"

His mouth found her face, kissing her tears away, moving on to her lips. They clung together like two lost children, and the miles ticked away beneath them—too fast, too fast.

Nora, behind the wheel, was in a quandary. The first-aid station would be milling with people. She could not let Kurt Kellerman out at that point. Ideally, she should trundle off the road, cross as much of the rough terrain as she could, and find a spot there.

But she no longer brought up the rear of the convoy. Mule Muehller was right behind her. She could handle him, but his relief driver might not be too keen on helping a German escape.

Visibility was poor, and it was some time before she realized Mule's vehicle was no longer in sight. She slowed, dropping back, and it did not appear. It was clear he was stalled somewhere, probably fixing a flat. She yelped with glee, then settled down to her driving.

Nearing the aid station, she searched for the right spot to turn off. There! The ambulance bumped and jounced over the frozen, ruined ground as she pointed it toward the trenches. The land ahead of her lit up with sulferous flashes, and off to one side something was burning with a phosphorescent fire.

She stopped the ambulance and waited, giving them time for a moment's farewell. Finally, she could wait no longer. She climbed down and went to the rear.

"We gotta hurry," she said hoarsely. "They're gonna come lookin' fer us—"

Jo emerged first, her face looking white and chilled. Then Kurt followed, painfully hitching his crutches under his arms. He and Jo looked at each other for a long moment and then he turned away, crippling toward the front lines.

Nora led Jo to the truck and helped her in. The arm she held was lifeless—like a rag doll. They sat for a moment, watching until Kurt topped a rise, a tall black silhouette haloed against a sky that shivered with light, his crutches balanced carefully. Making his way downward, he slowly disappeared. They could see his shoulder, his head—

Then nothing.

Jo made no sound as Nora turned the ambulance around and made her way back to the road. She didn't turn toward the collecting station, but went back the way they'd come, discovering Mule's truck along the side of the track.

She hopped out of the cab. Mule was squatting beside a wheel with a lug wrench, swearing up a storm, his assistant driver sitting warm in the cab.

"Figgered you had trouble," Nora sang out, "so I come back. Need a hand?"

"Not now," Mule grunted. "Wouldn't you know I'd draw a sonofabitch that doesn't know how to change a tire? Hell, I'm half froze, and I've skint my knuckles off!"

A hug and a kiss warmed him and revived his spirits. He was ready to go, and Nora climbed back in her truck and turned around.

If Mule knew how glad she was he had that flat, he'd kill her.

At the collecting station, the wounded were soon loaded and they made their way back to their base. In all that time, Jo was silent. Nora, wisely, let her be. It was only when they had reached the compound and Nora shut the engine off that Jo said a word.

"I'm never going to forgive Denise for this. Not ever. I wish to God she'd just—go away, and I never had to see her again."

Those, Nora thought grimly, were her own sentiments, exactly!

---------------- *chapter 46* ----------------

Denise, exhausted by her terrible anger, had slept.
And she had dreamed. In her dream, she was a leggy
teenager, playing wi' a wee Rory, beside the singing
burn. The sky was blue, with small puffs of cottony
clouds, the mountain still frilled with snow above
fields purple with heather. The little lad ran laughing
after a collie, twining his fists in its golden coat. Then
the chase was reversed as the dog ran after the boy.

"Rin, Rory," she called in her dream. "Rin!"

The animal tugged at the child's breeks playfully,
then bounded off again, Rory after him.

"Tak care, Rory," she called. "Rory! Rorrry!"

She leaped to her feet, screaming. The lad had
fallen into the burn. She could see his wee red head
bobbing as he was swept downstream.

And she screamed again.

This time it woke her. She lay still for a moment,

unable to orient herself. Then the events of the previous day came back to her. The nightmare had been real. It didna matter what the cause, wee Rory was gane, lost forever.

And she had a thing to do.

Rising, she dressed and went out into the compound. Nora and Jo should have returned by now. They were nowhere in sight. Probably, she thought bitterly, with their German murderer. It made no difference. She maun do what she maun do.

She went directly to the surgery. Dr. Carey was occupied, an orderly told her.

She would wait.

It was nearly noon before he was free. He led her into his small office, his face still set and angry.

"This had better be important," he said abruptly. "If it's about your—friend, he is in the supply tent under guard and will remain there until I get in touch with his superiors."

"'Tis nae that," she said firmly. "I wish tae reporrrt that we are harborrring an enemy i' the hospital. He hae assumed the name o' David Stone. He wasna sent awa wi' the other prrrisoners, because—"

She stopped short. He knew this already! The mon knew, and he had done naething!

"Why didn't you report this before," he asked quietly.

"I prrromised the girrrls—"

"And that promise no longer holds?"

Her cheeks were splotched with red, but her head was high. "I hae tae do my duty," she retorted. "Joost as I expect ye tae do yours!"

Peter Carey stared at the girl. How the hell had he ever seen her as attractive? And here she'd been disturbing his sleep for four long years! He had a few words for her. Vindictive, vixenish little bitch! He wondered what the German had done to arouse her vengeful nature.

But she was right. He had a duty. He'd just hoped nobody would point it out to him. He rose, shoving back his chair and slapped his hat on his head.

"All right," he said wearily, "let's go."

At the hospital, they discovered David Stone was missing. Another patient already occupied his cot. And Barbara Haynes, knew nothing about it. His cot was empty when she came on duty. She assumed he died in the night.

"They did it," Denise shrieked. "Jo and Nora teuk him awa—"

Carey sent for the others. They lined up before him, their expressions rebellious.

"I just got t'sleep," Nora said crankily. "Liane was on duty all night. What the hell's th' big noise about."

He questioned them. They knew nothing. Only that a man by the name of David Stone had been a patient.

"I believe he had a chest wound, didn't he?" Liane asked innocently.

"They're lying," Denise raged. "We maun searrrch the compound, send oot patrrrols—"

"Are you telling me how to handle my affairs, Miss Dugal?" Carey asked coldly.

"Nae—"

"Then let us consider the evidence. A man is missing. To all concerned, his name was David Stone. There is nothing to back up your accusations, therefore—"

"What if the mon's a spy! What if he has classified inforrrmation—"

Carey's mouth quirked in a mirthless grin. "Like what? The square footage of our hosptial tent? Availability of medical supplies? And, supposing that you are correct, that he is an enemy—and a spy—there's no way in God's world the man could survive to reach his people!" He paused, startled—

"Miss Blaine—Jo! Someone catch her—"

Jo Blaine had fainted dead away.

Denise moved to help and Nora planted herself squarely in front of her. "You touch her," she spat, "an' I'll knock yer damn head out from atwixt yer ears! And that's the last word I'm gonna say t'you, ever—'cep'n you better find another place to sleep!"

She turned her back and helped the now-recovered Jo to her feet and out the door. Denise looked at Liane. "I had tae do it," she said helplessly. "If ye knew—"

Liane gave her a withering glance and walked away.

"I am wondering, Miss Dugal," Peter Carey said, "if you wouldn't be happier with a transfer to another unit? I would be glad to oblige."

Carey's cold-eyed rejection was the last straw.

And it was all because of Kurt Kellerman! A German. One of the race who had killed her brother, maimed Sean Murphy. For God's sake, couldna Nora remember? And Liane's Steve—how dared they forget!

"I wull think on it," she said arrogantly, "and let ye know. Noo, I maun get back to worrrk."

She spent the remainder of the day in the hospital tent. Barbara Haynes was evidently in on the story, because she was cold, speaking only when spoken to. When her shift ended, Denise stayed on. She would not return to the tent when Nora and Jo were there.

Liane, coming in for evening duty, ignored her—as if she weren't there.

She had twa choices, Denise thought miserably, and neither o' them did she wish tae tak.

She could tak the transferrr the doctor offered, but then they wad think they'd drrriven her awa.

Or she could gae hame.

Hame wi'oot Rory, wi' her parents greeting, would be mair than she could bear—

Thinking of her parents, her anger swelled again. Rory dead, and the Gerrrman off scot-free! She wished she had kilt the mon last night! She wished she could kill them a'!

The thought stopped her in her tracks.

Maybe there was a third choice, after all.

It was several hours until the ambulance convoy would leave. She went to the tent she shared with the others. Either Jo and Nora were asleep or they didn't intend to acknowledge her presence. She rummaged in the darkness, finding by feel the shirt, trousers, and boots she'd worn at Ypres. They were British issue, but they would do for now. Finally, she removed the sheet from her bed and left the tent.

There was no place to effect the change she wanted. Finally, she climbed into one of the empty ambulances. There, shivering with cold, she cut the sheet into strips and bound her breasts tightly, thickening her waist. Pulling on the clothing she'd procured, she strapped the pistol on her hip, then took surgical scissors to her hair.

It fell, lock by shining lock, until there was nothing but a smooth red cap—like any lad. Gathering her shorn curls into a small bundle, she climbed from the vehicle and ran her fingers inside the exhaust, drawing them through what was left of her hair, drabbing its color.

And now she was ready for the next step.

Fighting the wind, she went straight to the supply tent. Johnny Looper and his guard were kneeling on the floor, shooting craps, a half-empty bottle between them.

"I hae coom for the prrrisoner," she said in a deep, boyish voice. "I am tae take him tae Dr. Carey."

Looper spun at the sound of the familiar accent, almost losing his balance. He saw a tall young man with girlish features, cap set tightly over close-cropped dark hair. But that voice! No matter how disguised, he'd know it anywhere!

"D——," he stammered, "d-d-d——"

The new comer silenced him with a hand movement. The guard, loathe to cease his game, looked at the young soldier suspiciously.

"You got a paper, or something?"

"I dinna need a paper," Denise said sharply. "Nae when I hae this—"

She pointed the pistol at Johnny Looper, who stood promptly. She moved him ahead to the door, then turned as an afterthought.

"I was also asked tae brrring a complete kit for a mon who is gaeing back tae the lines. Can ye gather it for me? The mon is aboot my size."

The guard moved reluctantly to do her bidding, and within a few moments she and Looper were out and into the compound. He stopped.

"Denise? It is Denise, isn't it? What the hell—"

She jabbed at him with the pistol. "Move!"

Looper had always been one to hedge his bets. Maybe the tall young man was Denise, maybe it wasn't. Whichever, he wasn't about to argue with a gun. He moved ahead of her—past the hosptial tent—on down to the first ambulance in line, near the road.

The wind howled around the flapping canvas coverings, sleet peppering the stretch of black ice before them as she fought open the door.

"Get in," she said harshly. "Ye're drrriving."

Johnny hopped in behind the wheel, a grin splitting his face from ear to ear. "I be damned," he whooped, "it is you, ain't it, doll? And you pulled it off!"

It would be another story in his repertoire. Lucky Johnny Looper, on the eve of being shot for desertion, kidnapped by a gorgeous babe and escaping to safety. Maybe, he grinned to himself as he put the truck in gear and began to roll toward the road, he might even hint at a little smooching along the way.

Hell, he wouldn't have to hint! If she wasn't after him, she wouldn't have gone to all this trouble.

"Well," he said happily, "we done it. We're home free! What you say we stop up the road a ways?"

"I agrrree."

"Hot damn!"

But when he finally pulled over, she climbed out, pointing that damned gun at him again. "Ye wull stay where ye be, Johnny. I'm maun change—"

When she returned, she had traded the British issue for American. He stared at her in confusion. "I don't get it—"

"Simple," Denise said quietly. "My name is Denis, Denis Dugal. That's hoo ye'll intrrroduce me tae the rrregiment, as a rrreplacment."

Seeing the look of horror growing on his face, she asked, "Did ye ne'er hear o' Sapper Dorrrothy Lawrence?"

"The Limey broad that got herself to the trenches—just fer the hell of it?"

"I plan tae do the same," Denise said serenely. "Except that I plan tae kill Gerrrmans."

------------------------ *chapter 47* ------------------------

When the ambulance convoy went out that night, Mac Hill's was missing and there was hell to pay. He woke Dr. Carey, insisting that it had been stolen by a deserter, and was probably headed for southern France.

Carey immediately thought of the prisoner in the supply tent, and headed there with fire in his eye. The guard was asleep and hard to waken. An empty bottle provided the reason for his stupor, and Carey slapped him awake.

He had not neglected his duty, the man insisted drunkenly. Carey himself had sent a soldier for Looper. No, it wasn't anybody he recogized. Hell, how could he remember what he looked like? Tall—thin—had a gun.

The man was so sure of his facts, Carey finally had to believe him. It was probably one of Looper's chums. And, after all, the prisoner was no great loss. The American ambulance, however, was.

To their surprise, the ambulance was found; not going away from battle, but headed toward it, just short of the front lines. Evidently Johnny Looper had decided to rejoin his unit. Carey put the incident from his mind.

It wasn't until evening of the next day that Denise Dugal was reported missing.

Mrs. Bent was first. She did not like to have to report her girls, but Denise Dugal had become quite insubordinate. She had not worked half of her shift the previous day, and this day she hadn't shown at all. Perhaps if he spoke to her—

He promised he would, then had second thoughts. She was probably sulking in her tent. He would give her one more day to shape up, then give her the choice of transfer or going home.

His next visitor was little Liane Wang, her small face terror-stricken. Denise seemed to have disappeared. Her cot had not been slept in. She couldn't find her anywhere.

"She has to be on the hospital grounds," he said, comforting her. "I'll check it out."

When she had gone, he sat with his head in his hands. Women! He had enough trouble without this! Where the hell was the girl?

A wild thought entered his head. Looper! She was certainly cozy enough with the man! Could she have gone off with him?

No!

The ambulance had been headed toward the battle zone. Certainly no place for a romantic tryst. She had to be here someplace.

Wearily, he jammed his hat on his head and went

looking, cursing the cold, the stinging sleet—and Denise Dugal.

He did not find her.

He called the girls together again. Had Denise said anything that might have given them a clue. Was she homesick, for instance. Would she be capable of catching a ride with a passing convoy heading south, then making her way to the coast—and home to Scotland.

"I figger she's capable of anything," Nora said angrily.

Carey sighed as he studied all their faces: Nora's angry, Jo's cold and frozen, Liane's frankly concerned. "Do you suppose we should contact her family? I could send a courier to wire—"

"It would only worry them," Liane said softly. "There's nothing they could do. Maybe we should wait. She'll turn up." She looked at him pleadingly for affirmation. "I know she will—"

"Of course," he said soothingly, "of course—"

That night, the girls sat together in guilty silence. Carey's mention of Denise's family had taken them back in time, back to a willful, ambitious girl surrounded by love and affection—whose only dream was to build an exciting life of her own.

"If anything happens to her, Aunt Ramona would die," Jo said ruefully. "I remember saying I wished I didn't have to see her again—"

"She wasn't all that bad," Nora added. "Wrongheaded and spiteful and jealous, but—"

"I think she felt like she was outside," Liane said quietly. "She never had to try to get along with anybody. She grew up thinking she was somebody special. Maybe it's sort of our fault."

"I'll never forgive her for what she did to Kurt," Jo said. "I don't care what the rest of you think!"

"Maybe she had a reason, something we don't know about—"

"Hah!"

"We can't just forget about her," Liane persisted. "Remember Dr. Butts? Maybe there's somebody around here like him—only worse. Remember the girl at Nancy?"

Again they were silent. When a pretty young VAD was found dead, mutilated in a field, word had spread through their ranks like wildfire. They'd caught the soldier who did it, a harmless-looking ex-patient with a grudge against nurses, but for a long time the girls had clung together and were careful crossing the compound after dark.

"But look how Denise handled Doc Butts," Nora said. She began to laugh. "I'll never forget the look on his face—"

The others joined in. "It was her idea to keep Gus," Jo added. "And, then, I remember when she—"

She stopped, all of them realizing what they were doing at the same time.

They were talking as if she were dead—

In spite of their various grudges against the red-haired girl, a general atmosphere of gloom pervaded their daily activities. A day passed. Another.

And then their mail caught up with them. It had been stacking up in some British area for almost a year, and they should have been delirious with joy. But the pile of letters for Denise put a damper on their pleasure.

They read their letters to each other, starting with the earliest postmarks, giggling over the admonitions they received. Maggie instructed Nora to tie a woolen sock around her neck on cold nights, to ward off sore throats. Em's spidery, old-fashioned handwriting stated that she hoped they were getting to bed at an early hour, and she included a recipe for sunburn lotion. Though it turned one green, it was quite efficacious, and washed off easily.

Missie's letters to Jo were euphoric essays on the advancement of women, due to the war.

"I guess we'll be behind the times when we get home," Jo giggled.

They read on and on, interested in the disparity between their world and the one they'd left behind. Finally, Jo paused.

"Listen to this. It's postmarked later than the others, and there's something I don't understand—"

The tone of her voice silenced them all, and they listened as she read an excerpt from her mother's letter.

"Your aunts are terribly concerned over the news from your Aunt Ramona. Arab says she should go to her but, of course, travel is impossible at this time— and at Arab's age, it would be unwise. Our thoughts and our prayers are with her."

The reference ended there. The next paragraph had to do with women working on the assembly line.

"What do you suppose is wrong," Liane asked. "Do you think Ramona is—sick? She couldn't have heard—"

"About Denise? No, it's something else. And I'm going to find out what it is!"

Jo moved to Denise's stack of mail, and began shuffling through it, finally opening an envelope.

"You can't do that!" Liane gasped. "You can't read Denise's—"

"The hell I can't," Jo said grimly. "Just watch me!"

The letter she selected was written in a man's hand—Uncle Denis, she assumed correctly. And it contained the answer.

Rory Dugal had been killed in the last battle of the Somme.

"No!" Liane whispered, remembering the bright-faced laughing boy who had been her first love. "Oh, no!"

"There's more," Jo said.

She read on. Ramona had not been well since Denise left. Now, she felt she'd lost both a daughter and a son. It would help if Denise came home—even for a visit. The unsentimental, brawny Scot's letter was out of character, a mixture of sorrow, anger—and pleading.

All their eyes were wet by the time Jo finished reading.

"Then that's where Denise went," Jo said in a choked voice. "Home."

"I don't think so." Nora was still troubled. "This is the first mail we got. Hell, she couldn't have knowed—"

"Maybe she did," Liane said excitedly. "There was a Scot here to see Dr. Carey—"

"The doc would have mentioned it if he said anything. And he didn't talk to Denise."

"But he did," Liane said. "Out on the compound. I saw them. I remember looking at his knees!" She paused, blushed, and stumbled on. "It was so cold. And they were purple—"

Normally they would have teased her, but not

today. At the moment they could only think of Ramona, her son dead, her daughter—God knew where.

They decided to call on Dr. Carey again.

Carey Heard them out, turning a pencil in his fingers as he recalled a bit of chance conversation. He'd been so damned upset over Denise's behavior with that bloody, cocksure Looper bastard that he'd paid little attention to the Scottish officer's words.

There had been a Dugal in his regiment, the man said. He'd mentioned it to the young VAD, asking if the lad might be a relative. He was not; however, the Scot feared he might have upset the young lady. She seemed to be a lass of tender sensibilities.

Carey had laughed. "About as tender as a trench mortar," he had snorted, "and as prickly as a roll of barbed wire! Forget it, man!"

They had gone on to a discussion of the progress of the war, and Denise wasn't mentioned again.

Carey recounted the story, damning himself for a flaming, insensitive jackass. A few words might have drawn the facts from Denise. Instead, he'd accused her of breaking promises, offering her a transfer to another unit, cut her away from anyone she might have talked to.

Her behavior had been beyond comprehension. But, then, so had his! He was so damned jealous—admit it, Carey!—of Looper, that he was ready to condemn anything she said or did. So blooming protective of his own precious freedom that he denied his own feelings toward the girl.

He'd been a fool! A damned bloody fool! The pencil snapped in his hands, and he looked down at the two pieces of it, dully.

"I think she's gone home," he said at last. "Surely,

someone will be hearing from her. But for now—we ought to wait, in the event that—"

"That she isn't there," Jo said quietly. "It would be terrible for Ramona if—"

The others completed her unfinished sentence in their minds. It would be terrible for Ramona to learn she'd lost two of her children, instead of one—

Days passed, and no word came.

chapter 48

Denise did not think of the cousins she'd left behind. Crouched in the bottom of a trench, she was conscious only of her own misery. There had been a gas attack a short time earlier. Johnny had drilled her in the use of her gas mask, but it hadn't been necessary after all. The canisters had fallen short, and a blast of rain and sleet had reduced its spread.

Still, her nostrils and eyes were stinging, her tender flesh pink and inflamed.

The front was not what she'd thought it would be. Just a time of dreary waiting. Occasionally a patrol would go out. Sometime it would return, sometimes not. Johnny Looper had gone twice, somehow managing to keep her out if it—just as he had managed to provide a little privacy for her, creating a small room inside the trench with tarpaulin walls.

Her cheeks reddened as she remembered the

things he had done for her—at the expense of his
self-respect. Johnny was a man who thrived on admiration, and he had deliberately damaged his own
reputation for her sake.

She thought of that night in the ambulance. How
stunned he'd been when she explained what she
wanted to do. Finally, she broke down and told him
about Rory. He put his arms around her and held her
while she sobbed.

Then he said, "I ain't gonna do it, doll! I'm taking
you back."

Her scorn settled what tears could not.

She pulled back from him, her lip curled. "I
thocht ye were the grrreat herrro! Lucky Johnny
Looper! The mon who's afeart o' naething in the
worrrld! I didna expect a wee snivellin' cowarrrd i'
ye!"

"Now, wait a damn minute," Johnny said hotly, "I
can take care of myself—"

"But ye canna tak carrre o' me?"

"Hell, yes! Ain't nothing I can't do!" He stopped
short, preparing to repudiate his words, but she
threw her arms around him.

"Oh, Johnny, I thank ye! I thank ye!"

Johnny Looper was hooked, and there was no way
he could wriggle out of this one.

They drove on, as close to the trenches as they
dared, then left the ambulance. The sky ahead of
them was blood red, the noise horrendous as they
stumbled across pitted, shell-pocked earth. Denise,
freezing, blinded by lashing sleet, stumbled off the
path—and tripped. She tried to get to her feet and a
flare of shellfire revealed the gruesome thing she'd
fallen over.

It was a man, what was left of him frozen like a

bundle of dry twigs inside the remnants of a German uniform.

"Och," she cried. "Johnny—"

He was beside her, lifting her, ignoring the horrid object that had tripped her up.

"You gotta stay on the track, doll—"

"But I canna see!" Her voice was plaintive, like that of a child, and she hated herself for it.

"Get behind me and hang on."

She followed Johnny Looper, casting an occasional furtive glance behind her. Guid lord! She'd been oop tae her elbows in surrrgery! She'd watched men dee. But she hadna touched anything like that afore— She shuddered.

"You okay, kid?"

"Joost cold," she said. Then she felt guilty again. Johnny was taking the brunt of the weather and guiding her. There was sae much she had tae learrrn!

The sky ahead was a pyrotechnical display. To the right, something burned with a phosphorescent glow. And the noise, always the noise—

She stumbled along, confused by bursts of color, deafened by sound, bumping against Johnny as he stopped short. A sentry, his weather gear glazed with ice, had appeared, ghostlike, out of sleet.

"Halt!" It was a peremptory command. "Advance, and give—good God! Looper! Where the hell have you been?"

Johnny swallowed his impulse to brag about his capture and escape. He'd been worried all along about protecting Denise once they met up with his unit. The Lawrence dame had got away with a stint in the trenches—and then, again, maybe she hadn't— but he intended to hide Denise's identity for her own sake. And here was his first test.

"Around," he said vaguely. "This here's a new replacement. S'posed to join our outfit and got lost in the shuffle. Denis Dugal, here. Denis, this is Tim Boggs."

Boggs extended his hand and Denise looked at it for a moment, then belatedly held out her own. She couldn't remember shaking hands with a man before. She had a lot to learn.

The sentry pointed. "You'll find your bunch over there, Looper. Gil Hutchins been covering for you. Sarge ain't caught on." He slapped Denise's shoulder. "Glad t'meetcha, Dugal. Carry on—"

Then they were moving forward again. From the trenches ahead came a crackling of small-arms fire. "Enemy patrol," Johnny said, unconcerned. "Keep yer head down—"

Denise emulated his crouch as they approached the line, then straightened up at a light piping whistle. Looper whirled, grabbed her by the waist and pitched her forward. She went into the trench, face first, Looper landing on top of her.

Finally he sat her upright. She fought for breath, her hand going to her bleeding face.

"Why the deevil did ye do that?" she hissed, when she could breathe. "Guid lorrrd! Ye a'most kilt me!"

"Daisy cutter," he said tersely. "Comes in low and spreads. We was damn lucky to—"

His voice was drowned out in a thunderous roar followed by an explosion some distance away.

"That was a coal box," he instructed her. "Least-ways, with them, you got a idea what hit you."

"Then—this is a full-scale attack?"

He began to laugh. "Hell, no. This goes on all the time. This is pretty quiet."

"But what arrre we supposed tae do?"

"Whatever we're told," he said gaily. "Mostly set and wait. Right now, let's git some of that blood and muck offa yer face, doll."

He wet a handkerchief from his canteen and washed her battered cheek, finishing the job with iodine. It stung, and Denise clenched her teeth, determined not to utter a word of complaint.

Then he spread a groundsheet and they huddled together against the trench wall, waiting for the morning.

When it came, it was gray and cold, mist rising from the no-man's-land before them. There was activity in the trench, men calling out to each other, belching, making rude noises, to the accompaniment of crude remarks that reddened Denise's cheeks.

"You gotta git used t'that, kid," Johnny said sympathetically. If this was the worst that happened, he thought, she'd be okay. But he was scared the troops would discover he had a girl here. Scared as hell—

She looked okay to him, of course. But he hadn't seen her like this in the light.

A man just down the line relieved himself against the wall, and Denise turned away. Johnny squinted his eyes and grinned, recognizing him.

"Hell, Hutchins, ain't you got no manners? Whyn't you find yerself a bush—"

"Heard they was all t'other side the German lines," Hutchins voice came back. "To fur t'walk. That you, Looper? Hell, figgered you was either dead er in jail. Didn't think we'd have t'see yer ugly mug agin!" He came toward them, fastening his fly, peering through the fog, catching a glimpse of what looked to be a feminine face.

"Who you got there, a lady friend?"

Damn, thought Looper, it ain't gonna work!

"This here's Gil Hutchins," he explained to Denise. "Old buddy of mine. Gil, shake hands with Denis Dugal, new guy, just come in."

Hutchins, embarrassed at his first impression, tried to kid his way out of it.

"Figgered it was a woman, being it was you. Knowed you didn't go in fer pretty boys—"

To Denise's acute embarrassment, Johnny slipped an arm about her waist. "Kind of a shortage of women up here," he said cheerfully. "Hell, you know me! Old Lucky Looper's bound to try anything once—"

Gil Hutchins stared at him with disbelieving eyes. "You gotta be kidding—"

Then he saw the fatuous look Looper had turned on his companion.

"Shee-yut," he said disgustedly.

He walked away.

"Why did ye do that?" Denise raged. "It wasna funny! The mon thinks—"

"Just what I want him t'think," Johnny said with satisfaction. "Gil's got a big mouth. It'll be all along the line in no time."

"But, Johnny," she wailed, "why!"

"You ain't exackly the rugged type, doll. You ever seen yerself walk?" Looper took a few mincing steps, swinging his hips from side to side. "This way, they'll still think yer a guy, except kinda—" He waved a limp wrist.

"I dinna mind what they think o' me! But—" she stopped, helplessly. "Ye joost lost a frrriend."

"Look, babe, its' a joke. Just a joke, see? And nobody can put one over like Johnny Looper. Hell, relax and enjoy—"

"I willna let ye do it!"

His forced grin faded. He folded his arms and glared at her. "It's already done, kiddo. Now, if you wanna, I'll take you back to the hospital. If you don't, then yer gonna do what I say. You got it?"

"Aye, Johnny."

"Then keep yer damn mouth shut."

Once begun, Johnny Looper played his part to the hilt. He strung ground sheets to make a little cubicle of privacy for Denise. A sign, painted in iodine, proclaimed the small tentlike structure as "Lucky Looper's Lovenest." Above those words, in foot-high letters, he wrote KEEP OUT.

As he had guessed, word of his idiosyncracy passed rapidly along the trench. Most of his former friends pointedly ignored them. A few sniggered behind their hands. Several threatened to punch him in the nose, but he paid no attention to their bad-mouthing, seeming serene with his young male companion.

Only Denise knew what it cost him. The swaggering, bragging little man had become something of a hero to his companions. There was nothing Johnny Looper couldn't do, nothing he hadn't done. The tales of his improbable adventures had been told and retold, amplified and magnified until he'd achieved a certain raffish fame. He'd even begun to believe the stories himself.

Now, all that was ended. He and Denise were left pretty much to themselves. In the improvised tent, Denise sat, knees drawn up, face on her folded arms, thinking how much she owed him.

She had to think of Rory, she told herself dully. Rory, who had been murdered by those monsters out there. She must think only of vengeance.

Oh, Lorrrd, if they wad ainly do something! Each day, a few wounded were carried out and passed back to the collecting stations. Three men had been killed down the line, the exploding shell sending them into fragments that plastered the trench walls. Was that what they were all here for? To sit and wait while the enemy picked them off, one by one?

The food was cold and rancid. Clothing was never dry from the eternal mist and rain, frozen to one's body, perhaps, but always damp. Boots were heavy with mud that would not scrape away. And at night, huge corpse-rats scuttered along the trench floor.

And the sky always shivered with light. Denise tried to remember when skies stood still, with tiny painted clouds above serene hills; when the air smelled of flowers and the rippling burn—and not of burned powder, and putrefaction.

And then the gas had come, a saffron cloud along the horizon. If the canister had nae fallen shorrrt, they would a' be dead, blue-faced alang the line; an arrrmy of dead men.

Johnny parted the curtain behind which Denise sat hidden, shouting at her to come and look.

She followed his finger to the horizon. The saffron cloud had deepened, mingled with purple smoke.

"It didn't fall short," Johnny shouted in her ear, "it's ours! They're softening them up, doll! We're moving out! I just got the word—"

Fresh troops would be coming up to take their places. Then more. They would leapfrog ahead. Right now, they must see to their guns.

He went over them carefuly, attaching bayonets, grinning as he pretended to parry, then stab through an enemy. And, finally, with the others, they watched and waited, a long line of excited, determined men.

"There it goes," Looper said in a hushed voice. "The barrage—"

It was dark now. The sky glowed solidly crimson, stabbed with flame from the Allied batteries. Balls of silver and red rose high into the heavens, exploding into showers of stars. Rockets joined them, turning night into day.

Denise's throat was dry as she listened to Looper's instructions. Whistles along the line would signal the attack. He would be the first over the top. She would follow behind him.

"You got that. Behind me! And stay behind me. If anything happens to me, find the nearest hole and jump in! Don't try to do nothing stupid, y' hear?"

He looked at her, worry in his eyes, and she realized what an encumbrance she'd become.

"Johnny, dina let anything hoppen tae ye! I couldna bearrr it!"

His eyes darkened, and for a moment he looked like a stranger. "We get out of this, doll, you figger I got a chance? You know what I mean."

"Aye, Johnny, ye've got a chance."

He grabbed her suddenly and held her close, and she bent to kiss him, eyes closed, pretending for a moment that he was—someone else.

"Hot damn!" he shouted happily. "Hot damn!"

Then a nearby whistle blew and he was over the top and running in a crouch. Denise scrambled from the trench and ran, bent low, behind him.

---------------- *chapter 49* ----------------

Earlier that same day, Liane felt the old familiar humming in her head that preceded a revelation.

Something was going to happen. She felt it in her very bones. She tossed and turned, trying to get some sleep after her long shift, and sleep wouldn't come.

"Liane," Nora mumbled from her cot, "what the hell's got inta you? Yer jumpin' around like a frawg on a hot rock. Ever time I start to drop off—"

"Oh, simmer down, Nora," Jo said acidly. "I can stand one of you making racket, but not both! When I get home, to my own room, I'm going to sleep for a week—"

Liane rose and pulled on her clothes. She would go over to the mess hall for a cup of tea. Maybe that would help. Crossing the compound, her strange sensation increased. Maybe, she thought hopefully, I'm coming down with flu.

Even flu would be preferable to this. It was not a good feeling, something ugly floating at the edge of her conscious mind, trying to get in. It was as if she should warn someone of impending disaster.

Except she didn't know who to warn, or what to caution them against.

There was a table in the mess tent. Sometimes the doctors sat there when off duty. To her surprise, Dr. Peter Carey was there at the moment, his face in his hands. Seeing her, he called out, inviting her to sit with him.

She was reluctant for a moment, wanting to puzzle out whatever was bothering her. Somebody else conversing wouldn't help. Then she noticed how tired he seemed, his blue eyes shadowed, and lines about his mouth. He often looked like that when he lost a patient.

Maybe he needed to talk.

He did.

He pushed a fresh cup and a pot of tea toward her as she sat down, then rubbed wearily at his temples.

"I've got the damndest headache," he admitted. "Like I'm waiting for something horrible to happen. Glad to have someone to talk to. Maybe I can get my mind off it."

"I know what you mean," she told him.

"You, too?" He cocked a blond brow. "Well, it is good to have company, even in misery."

Then both of them burst out with the same question at the same time.

"Have you heard from Denise?"

They laughed at their duet, then quieted, thinking ¹e missing girl. "I don't know what to do," Carey said. "Sometimes I think I ought to wire her people. Then I cannot bring myself to it. I suppose—it's on my conscience."

"Mine, too," Liane said in a small voice. "I—I think I hated her for a while. But if I'd known about Rory—" Her eyes filled with tears, and Carey guessed, rightly, that she'd been fond of the boy herself.

"What was Rory like?"

"Like Denise, a lot. He seemed to be—brighter than most people, always laughing. He was—very nice."

"And what was Denise like?"

He really cares, Liane thought, seeing the shadow in his eyes. She found herself telling him of Denise's background; the spoiled only daughter in a brawling family of sons, who wanted more out of life.

"I don't think she really did," Liane said softly. "She just wanted to be somebody—herself—and she didn't know how. She—she was awfully lonesome, and we didn't help much."

"I didn't either," Carey said morsely. He told her of his treatment of Johnny Looper, and of the way he'd shamed Denise when she came to him with the story of the German. "If I'd only admitted I knew about it anyway, tried to talk to her, instead of accusing—

"Oh, hell!"

He had his face in his hands again, and Liane was at a loss. The stiff British doctor had always seemed like a minor God to her. Yet he had feelings like everybody else. Finally, she put a small hand on his arm.

"Remember," she whispered, "none of us knew. We thought she was just being—bitchy."

That word coming from Liane's innocent lips surprised him into laughter.

"I suppose we did," he said, finally sobering. "But that doesn't excuse my part in it. And, now, I've got this damned, bloody feeling—"

"About Denise?"

"I don't know," he said worriedly. "I just don't know."

Finally he rose, saying he had to get back to surgery. Liane decided to return to work. They were short-staffed, due to Denise's departure, Mrs. Bent now forced to take a stint in the day. She would be glad to be relieved. As to sleep, perhaps Liane could catch a catnap later. If she didn't, it wouldn't be the first time she'd worked a straight twenty-four hours.

But there was still that—that damned humming in her head! She pitched into her daily activities with a vengeance, trying to erase the sound, and was so intent on what she was doing that she didn't see the man who entered the tent.

Her first inkling that anything was amiss was Barbara Haynes's giggle. And Barbara was not a giggler. Liane finished adjusting a patient's pillow, then turned to look at her friend. She was whispering to someone—a tall, lanky man, who towered over her.

Liane's heart stopped beating, and she felt a suffocating sensation in her chest. It couldn't be—

And then he turned to face her.

"Steve," she cried, "oh, Steve—Steve—"

She ran toward him, sending a tray of surgical supplies crashing to the floor. He caught her up in ⌐rms, lifting her high into the air. She looked ⌐o a smiling, clean-shaven face, a scar at one side leading from temple to jawline; seeing flint gray eyes that twinkled like stars.

"Put me down," she said, blushing, knowing they were the focal point of all eyes. "Steve—"

"You ain't no bigger'n a minute," he said fondly. "Damn, I been lookin' forward to this—" He set her down and she smoothed back her hair with a flustered hand.

"What are you doing here, Steve. You're not—you're not—"

"On my way back to the trenches? Damn right. Gotta git this war over with, 'cause I've got somethin' else in mind—"

"Steve—" She looked at him helplessly, not knowing what to say. Was this the reason for the premonitaion that had haunted her all day? No, this was good, not a feeling of doom impending—

But he was going back to the front. Dear God, if something happened to him—!

Barbara gave her a gentle push. "Go on. Get out of here. The man's got to get back to his unit. Why don't you walk to the road with him? I can handle things until you get back."

So soon! Liane swallowed hard, and went for her coat.

It was raining, an icy rain. And as they walked together, they were silent. There was so much to say, and so little time. Finally, Steve Long stopped, turning her to face him.

"I got no right to say this now. But if I was to come back and ask you—ask you if you could mebbe put up with a broke-down cowpoke fer the rest of yer life, what wouldja say?"

She looked into eyes no longer merry. Now they were deep and still and waiting. And she thought

how she'd fallen in love with him, a little piece at a
time. First, a callused brown hand, dark against a
hospital sheet; then two large feet that overhung the
edge of a cot; his slow, soft drawl. And finally, this
beloved face—

Liane swallowed hard. There was something he'd
have to know before she answered. "Steve, I'm three-
quarters Chinese. Your folks might not like me. My
grandfather is a—a Buddhist. He keeps to the old
ways."

"And I'm a fourth 'pache," he said promptly, "along
with a quarter Mex, and the rest Texas. My grampaw
chews t'baccy, an' Grammaw smokes a pipe. Reckon
that means we're in-com-pat-ible?"

His mischievous grin was back, and she was halfway between laughter and tears.

"If you're asking me to marry you, the answer is
yes!"

With a wild rebel whoop, he lifted her into the air
again, then pulled her down to kiss her soundly. The
passing convoy had a view of the proceedings, and
they responded with a resounding cheer.

Finally, Steve set Liane down. "May all our kids be
polky-dotted!" he drawled. Then he was running, his
long legs scissoring, to catch up with his men.

Liane stood in the rain, watching until he was out
of sight, then slowly made her way back to the
hospital tent. This should be the happiest moment of
her life, but she was frightened. What if something
happened to Steve; if this happiness were suddenly
snatched away?

She thought of Nora, after Jacques's death. She
w̶ ̶ beginning to live again. And Jo, poor Jo, with
̶ ̶e that hadn't a chance from the beginning.
̶ ̶heard her crying in her sleep.

I'm not like Nora, she told herself. For me, there could never be another man. And I'm not brave, like Jo. If Steve were killed, there would be nothing ahead—nothing.

She returned to duty, and worked straight on through the night. There was still the humming in her head—a feeling that something bad was going to happen, and she had no idea what it was.

chapter 50

Liane's headache was shared by someone else. Denise's head was pounding as she ran, following a small dark silhouette that zigzagged across a moonscape, silhouetted by the fire-bright sky ahead. She was barely conscious that other figures ran beside her, stumbling over the rough terrain, some of them silent, others cursing, a few yelling like banshees.

"We'll get yuh, you bastards!"

"Here's one fer the Yanks!"

And a terrible, blood-chilling rebel yell—

And Denise added her own voice to the tumult. "A Dugal!" she cried. "A Dugal!"

She might have been one of her own ancestors, kilt-clad, the rifle in her hand a broadsword, the sound of bagpipes skirling behind her—

"For Rory," she screamed into the night. "For Rory—"

A chattering sound cut throught the din, silencing her. Figures were falling around her, and Johnny had turned back.

"Down," he shouted. "Down!"

Denise fell flat, Johnny Looper beside her.

"Machine gun," he panted. "Nest, to the right. You okay?"

"Aye."

She was all right, but someone moaned near her, a groan that ended in a gurgling sound. Farther away, a voice called for help, small, monotonous, dying away into a whisper. And Looper cursed through clenched teeth.

"Damn the sonsabitches t'hell," he snarled. "I'm going after 'em!"

"Johnny—"

"You stay here," he said. "Play dead. I'll be back—"

She watched him wriggling along on his stomach like a snake, freezing occasionally, the moving on again. Time stood still. Seconds were minutes, minutes hours as she held her breath, looking across a landscape bathed in a white light, dotted with hummocks that were—or had been—men.

Johnny, she prayed, be carrreful—Johnny—

There was a wet warmth seeping through her clothing; the blood of the man next to her, running in rivulets as if seeking life.

Denise was nauseated, but she daren't move.

Johnny rounded a hummock, rising to a crouch. She held back a scream, certain he'd been seen. But at that moment, one of the hummocks rose. Ah, God! The man had no legs! He was trying to walk on—what was left!

Another burst of gunfire and he was virtually cut in two.

The spot where Johnny had been standing seemed to erupt in flame.

"John-n-ny!"

Denise was sitting up now, forgetting his instructions. And Johnny was loping toward her. She went suddenly weak in relief.

"Got 'im," he panted. "Grenade. Come on, let's go—"

About half of the hummocks dotting the earth rose to their feet. Now there was no anger, no euphoria. Many of them had left a buddy, wounded, dying, or dead.

They moved on in grim silence.

Their path lay through a ruined village, reduced to rubble by fire from both sides. Here, a few chimneys were left standing stark against the white-lit sky; heaps of crumbled stone bulked along both sides of the road.

And, here, there was a sniper.

Denise's first inkling came when a bullet spanged off a ruined wall beside her, stinging her cheek with a peppering of shattered rock. She fell, lying close to the wall, hoping to hide in its shadow. And the sniper brought down another running man, sending the rest scrambling for shelter.

Denise lay very still, figuring the angle of fire. It had been downward. Carefully, she moved her gaze from a still-standing chimney to another—and there she saw him, evidently on a ledge of some sort, a silhouetted head, the long line of his rifle as he aimed—

She sat up, her back against the wall, and took a

careful bead on the man. 'Tis ainly a squirrrel, she told herself. I maun think o' him as a squirrrel—

She pulled the trigger and the rifle clattered down into the cobbled street, the sniper following.

It seemed to take forever for him to fall. Denise felt sick inside, unable to move—

Then Johnny was helping her to her feet, grinning from ear to ear. "By God, doll, you done it! Dammit, you done it good!"

Gil Hutchins was right behind him. He was tight-lipped, his eyes hard, but he thrust out a congratulatory hand.

"Thanks," he said. "He got Tim. Reckon you evened the score."

"I kin pick 'em," Johnny boasted.

Gil Hutchins gave him a disgusted look and walked away.

It didn't matter. She'd make Johnny proud of her. He hugged her briefly, and then they were moving out again.

A cold drizzle had begun. The ground grew slippery underfoot. As the bombardment ahead intensified, the earth seemed to convulse beneath Denise's feet, the sky pulsing with lurid light.

Then it ceased so abruptly that the silence was shattering. The artillery had judged, correctly, that the first waves would have reached the trenches—

The going was difficult now, shell holes gaping everywhere, bits of smoking shrapnel sizzling in the rain. Somewhere along the line, there was an explosion. A mine? Planes fought overhead, tracers arching against the night. On the ground, the air was thick with smoke, the smell of powder—and a faint residue of mustard gas that burned the lungs. Ahead was the barbed wire, great coils slack against the sky. And beyond that—the German lines.

"This way," Johnny Looper shouted. "Over here—"

There, the wire had been cut by an earlier patrol. They had left a grim reminder behind them. The body of an American soldier was hopelessly entangled, riddled by German fire.

Johnny ran through the gap, Denise following him. But she turned to look at the soldier, sick with grief and anger—

And she lost sight of Johnny Looper.

Surely he had gone straight ahead! She hurried on, calling his name in a low tone. "Johnny?"

Suddenly, she felt her footing go. She was sliding downward—the domned mud! Frantically, she fought for balance, but to no avail. She landed with a thump in the bottom of a hole.

Scrambling to her feet, rifle still in her hands, she looked wildly for a handhold, some way to pull herself out of her predicament.

Then she realized that she was not alone.

Against the opposite wall leaned a German soldier, looking at her with a stunned expression. His rifle lay at his feet, and he seemed frozen with shock at her sudden appearance.

There was no time to think. With an involuntary reaction, she sprang forward, thrusting him through with her bayonet. Then she leaped back, horrified at what she'd done. He fell sideways, seeming to take forever, his blue eyes still fixed on her with that look of horror and surprise.

Should she pull the bayonet free? Oh, God, she couldna! She drew back against the far side of the hole, hands over her mouth, unable to suppress a little whimpering sound.

"Johnny—"

And there he was, reaching a hand to her. "Gil saw you fall. I came back—"

His words choked off as his body jerked. A spray of blood covered Denise's face. And then Johnny Looper slowly toppled into the dugout.

Denise squatted beside him, automatically doing all the right things, checking for a pulse, a heartbeat. There was none. The bullet had gone through his heart from the rear, severing his spine.

"Johnny," she whispered, "oh—Johnny!" The whisper rose to a scream. "John-e-e-e-e!"

Ahead, there was a crackling of fire as fresh German troops entered the line of defense. And enemy artillery began to pound again, raking the land between the trenches to prevent a further assault.

Denise huddled in the dugout, Johnny Looper cradled in her arms. Against the opposite wall the German soldier hung, pinioned, his eyes still staring. And now the rain fell steadily, intermingled with chunks of mud from exploding shells.

I hae kilt the mon, Denise thought miserably. Joost as I hae kilt Johnny. If he hadna coom back for me, he would yet be alive. Lucky Johnny Looper! His luck had rin oot, and all because of Denise Dugal.

"I'm sorrrry," she wept. "Forgie me, lad. I didna mean this tae hoppen! Coom back! Coom back, sae I can keep my prrromise tae ye—"

The shells pounded. Rain, mud, noise! The heavens riven with man-made lightning and terrible, killing stars. And all the while the dead German soldier looked on. It was too much! Too much!

Denise put bloodstained palms over her ears and screamed, a thin, high mindless wail—

And then Johnny Looper was Rory. Wee Rory. And he was so wet and cold.

O' course, she thought. Rory fell i' the burrrn. She maun warrrm him.

In the morning, the drizzle had been replaced by swirling mists. The mists semed to take human form, and she talked to them.

"It's Rory, Mama," she explained. "He's sae cauld. Pairhops a cup o' tea—"

By evening, her voice had died to a mumble, and then it was silent. She lay curled about Johnny Looper's body, protecting it, her face like death. It had begun to sleet again, icy particles hissing on a howling wind.

Above and ahead, the battle raged, the Germans slowly being pushed from their positions and retreating to the rear.

chapter 51

Once again the small hospital was a scene of carnage; bleeding, dying men brought in by the hundred. Liane worked without sleep, studying the faces of new arrivals, afraid of what she would find. Once, turning back a sheet, she discovered a man with dark hair and a long, disfiguring scar, the other side of his face blown away.

She nearly collapsed until she saw the length of him: a short man, with hands that were pudgy and pale.

Steve was never far from her mind.

Nora and Jo were pulled from their ambulance duties and pressed into nursing. With Denise gone, they were urgently needed. They were both unhappy about the assignment, but saw that it was necessary.

There were just too many wounded to handle.

Mule Muehller, driving toward the collecting station on the third day, was glum and moody. Nora should be driving that truck just ahead. He missed the hell out of her. It had been good just to know she was there, waving a saucy hand at him, or leaning out to look back with a perky grin.

He loved that girl! He settled down to a dream of a little town in Nebraska, a small white frame church—and Nora coming up the aisle.

His folks, he thought happily, were going to love her—

He was so engrossed in his thoughts that he failed to see the desolation around him. It wasn't until they pulled up to the collecting station that he came back to the present, leaving behind green fields and meadows, a sandy creek where wild grapes grew.

Turning up his collar against the chill, he climbed down from his truck to lend the medics a hand—only to find there was some sort of a hullabaloo.

They had brought in a shell shock case, found in a dugout with a couple of bodies, a German—and one of their own. They'd checked the boy for wounds, a young medic said, stammering with excitement, and he—she—turned out to be a girl.

Mule Muehller was normally calm and slow thinking, but this one hit him right between the eyes.

"Where is she," he asked hoarsely, "I wanna see her!"

"So does everybody," the medic smirked. "You'll have to wait your turn."

Then Mule Muehller had a fistful of his uniform, lifting the sputtering man a foot off the ground. His other hand was doubled into a hamlike fist, prepared to swing.

"I think I know who it is, you damn fool," he

roared. "Keep yer dirty thoughts to yerself! Now, where the hell is she—"

A short time later, Mule Muehller's ambulance roared off down the track to the hospital. It contained a single patient. Mac Hill saw him pulling out and squalled like a scalded cat. He'd probably get busted again, over this, but he didn't give a damn!

Mule, jaw set, settled down to his driving.

He reached the hospital in record time, and burst into the large tent.

"Nora—Jo—Liane! C'mere!"

"Holdjer horses, Mule," Nora said reasonably, "can't you see we got our hands full?"

"I got Denise out here," he yelled. "Drop what yer doing!"

Liane did.

Unfortunately, it was a bed pan.

The girls clustered around the ambulance as Mule climbed in, carefully passing a litter down to their waiting hands.

"Oh, my God," Jo said, "look at her—"

Denise's cropped hair shone above a chalk white face, eyes sunken in purple sockets, lips blue. The uniform she wore was spattered with blood; her shirt, replaced in haste, buttoned crookedly. She was thin, almost emaciated—

Liane burst into tears.

"What the devil's going on?" Peter Carey, taking a brief break to rest his eyes and hands, had come up behind them. The girls stepped away, revealing the litter and its burden.

Carey's face went gray. Then he was beside Denise, on his knees, checking her pulse, lifting an eyelid. He noted her extreme pallor, the cold moistness of her skin—the thready pulse. She was breathing shallowly, irregularly.

"Shock," he said, getting to his feet. "Nora, get a cot set up in my office. Immediately. Jo, get extra blankets, hot-water bags. Muehller, give me a hand with the litter. Liane, inform Major West I will not return to duty today."

Within moments, his commands had all been obeyed. Jo brought Denise's flannel gown, and they washed and dressed her, placing her on the cot with her feet elevated and hot-water bottles tucked beneath her blankets.

"Get back to your duties," Carey said in a shaky voice. "I'll take care of her for now."

When they had gone, he pulled a chair close to the girl's bed. Her short locks curled softly above a face of incredible purity.

She looks like a blessed angel, he thought to himself, forgetting her willfulness and the stormy sessions they'd had in the past.

His eyes were filled with tears, and his shoulders shook with a man's harsh sobs as he bent above her.

"My love," he said in a voice he didn't recognize as his own.

"My own dear love."

For several days, Denise lingered in a coma. She did not want to return to consciousness. She lived in a dream in which she was warm and snug in her own bed on a highland farm. She could see a blue sky through the crisp yellow curtains blowing at her window, and hear her brothers laughing and playing outside—

She should get up, she knew. But it was good lying here. Her mother would come in a moment and bring her a tray with tea and scones.

"You just sleep, honey," she would say. "Just—sleep."

"I don't think she wants to live," Carey told the girls worriedly. "I wish to hell I knew what happened out there!"

Surprisingly, another patient provided the key.

A seasoned soldier with the name Gil Hutchins at the foot of his cot caught at Liane's skirt as she passed by.

"I got to talk to you," he said hoarsely.

He'd heard about the girl they'd found at the front. And he knew who it was. In fact, he saw it happen— he'd turned in time to see him—her—disappear, and had called out to Looper.

"Hey, pal. You just lost lover-boy." He pointed at the dugout. "Down there, case yer interested—"

Johnny turned back, and Gil saw him get it. He'd killed the bastard that shot him. And then he'd gone on, to be wounded about half an hour later. He looked ruefully down at his foot. Only half of it remained. His military career was over, he supposed.

But that was beside the point. He wanted to apologize to the little lady for—thinking what he thought. Just tell her that. She'd understand.

Liane went to Dr. Carey. He flinched at hearing Looper's name, then set his jaw and went to talk to Hutchins. He learned of Denise's stay in the trenches, how Looper had led them to believe they had a—an unusual relationship; how she had shot down a sniper in a blasted village, and then the events of that last day.

"I want her to know I'm sorry," the man went on. "Hell, me and Looper was buddies! Might of knowed it was a woman, knowing him—"

Peter Carey somehow managed to keep his feelings from showing. He'd been right in thinking there was something between Denise and the cocky little man. But hearing it through someone else's lips put a seal to it.

And it hurt! It hurt! And he had nobody but himself to blame.

The important thing now, was to get Denise well. Leaving her in Liane's care, he rode with Mule's ambulance to the collecting station, talking with the drivers who brought Denise in.

The next day, Gil Hutchins was taken to Carey's office on a litter, then lifted to a chair, his injured foot propped before him. Carey knelt beside Denise and shook her gently.

"Denise, do you know where you are?"

She opened glazed green eyes and closed them again.

"Denise," Carey asked sternly, "where is Johnny? Johnny Looper."

"John—ny?"

Memory came back to her expressionless face. It seemed to break apart before his eyes. "Johnny!" She sat up, nervously plucking at the blankets, then sank back, her eyes wide with horror.

"I kilt him—"

"No, you didn't." Gil Hutchins leaned forward. "I saw it happen, and I got the bastard that done it."

"But it was my fault—my fault—"

"Don't never think that, lady. I've knowed Johnny a long time. He—was just a accident, lookin' for a place to happen. Hell, he's been shot up, beat up, and he always come back laughing, looking for more. His time was bound to come. Nobody believed that 'lucky' crap but him!"

Denise begin to shiver, shaking with chills almost strong enough to break her bones. Peter Carey put his arms around her, holding her face against his chest.

And, finally, the tears came, flooding her cheeks, soaking his shirt front, as he murmured endearments as one would to a child.

Gil Hutchins looked anywhere else he could look. He felt like a damned Peeping Tom, but he was trapped. He wiped at his eyes, wishing to hell he was back in the trenches. He'd loved 'em and left 'em in his time, but this mushy stuff got to him.

chapter 52

Denise slept naturally for the next ten or twelve hours. When she woke, she found her hand in Peter Carey's. He slept beside her in a chair, looking absurdly young with the lines smoothed from his face by sleep, blond hair falling over his forehead, golden lashes curling like a girl's.

Her eyes slanted sideways, recognizing her surroundings. She had no idea how she'd come here. Her last memory was of Johnny, blood—the dead German's blue eyes watching her—

Carey, sensing her tremor, came instantly awake. "What is it, love—"

Love! Her eyes widened. She seemed to remember him saying it before—in a dream.

"I dinna know," she said numbly, trying to control her quivering nerves.

"Would it help to talk about it?"

"I think it would."

She told him about Rory, not noting his lack of surprise, and about helping Johnny Looper to escape, joining his unit as a soldier.

"He—he was my friend. He leuked after me, kept me safe. And he gae oop his rrreputation tae do it."

"I know," Carey said quietly. "Hutchins told me. He'll pass the word to anyone who matters."

"He hae a big mouth," Denise said with a forlorn grin. "Johnny says—'

She was weeping again, and he drew her to a sitting position, seating himself behind her so that her head rested on his shoulder.

"Go ahead. Cry it out. I know you loved him."

"Luve had naething tae do wi' it," she said angrily. "I liked him! I liked him mair than anyone I e'er knew! He was—kind."

Which I was not, Carey thought sadly.

As though she, too, had the same thought, she stiffened in his arms. "I would like tae gae back tae my ain bed, wi' the other girrrls, if they wull hae me."

"Of course they will. Maybe when you're stronger—"

"I want tae gae noo—"

He stood, sighing. Clearly, she wanted no part of him. Perhaps it would be for the best.

That afternoon, she was moved from the warm office to a cold tent. Alone at last, she wished she could erase the time between now—and when she last slept here. She could feel her body coming back to life, a tingling sensation, like warmth after frostbite. And she knew she would be unable to remain in Peter Carey's presence without giving herself away.

She luved him. There was nae sense in fighting

her feelings. Luved him sae much her heart hurrrt, and her head went all fuzzy. His words o' affection had been naething but comforrrt, as he wad hae gien tae any ailing child—

He knew her tae well tae carrre about her i' that way; knew her mean jealous naturrre, how she betrrrayed her friends—

He likely thocht she had slept wi' Johnny Looper.

And he didna know the worrrst, that she had kilt twa men.

Nora, Jo, and Liane found Denise Dugal vastly changed. She'd lost her old sparkle, her arrogant, head-high way of dealing with things. She apologized to each of them in turn, asking forgiveness from all of them but Jo.

To Nora, she said, "I'm sorrry I hae said ugly things aboot ye. 'Twas my envy speaking. I hope ye can forget my hatefulness."

To Liane, she apologized for treating her like a child.

And to Jo, she said humbly that she had been wrong. "Ye canna forgie me, and I dinna blame ye. I wull prrray for your mon's safe-keeping."

And, surprisingly, level-headed Jo burst into tears and hugged Denise tight. They cried together, and were once again friends.

It was Gil Hutchins who relieved Denise of a great deal of her worry. In several days, he hitched on crutches to visit her in her quarters, and they talked together for a long time.

He told her of his friendship with Johnny Looper, relating one fantastic exploit of Looper's after another. Denise found herself laughing, in spite of herself, Johnny's face with its cocky grin replacing the memory of the body she'd held in her arms.

"He couldna hae doone that," she cried, after a tale in which Johnny supposedly slipped behind the German lines for a liaison with a general's mistress. "I dinna believe it!"

"Ain't too sure I did, either," Gil grinned, "but it made a damned good story."

They talked of Johnny, they talked of the trenches, and finally the day the troops went over the top.

"I kilt a mon," she said drearily. "Twa o' them, i' fact. And noo I know ye canna rrreplace ane life by taking anotherrr."

Seeing the shadow in her eyes, Gil hastened to reassure her. 'Mebbe yer takin' too much credit fer what you done. Hell, I fired at the same time. Reckon Johnny did, too. Any one of us might have did it!"

Her expression lightened for a minute, then dulled again. "There was the mon i' the hole wi' us. I stabbed him tae death."

"You didn't even do that!" He was grinning again. "Hell, he prob'ly got done in by a patrol! I heard the medics wondering why the hell you bothered. Guy'd been dead a couple days, and was almost froze."

"Ye—ye are making that oop—?"

"Didja see any blood?"

She closed her eyes, remembering. The German had leaned against the wall, with a look of horrified surrpise at her sudden appearance. She ran him through. He fell sideways. His expression hadn't changed—

And she could recall no bleeding.

"Oh, Gil! Thank ye! Thank ye!"

She kissed him impulsively, just as Peter Carey started to enter the tent.

He backed away, hating himself for his jealous

nature. He had no responsibility for the girl. She could kiss whomever she wished.

But he didn't have to watch it, to feel it tearing at his middle like a pain.

He did not return to the tent again.

When the girls thought Denise was strong enough, they gave her her letters from home. She wept over them, and wrote Ramona a long letter, filled with warmth and love, telling her she would soon be back—and saying nothing of her recent adventures.

Within a few days, she returned to the hospital routine, a quarter day at first, then a half—and finally managing a full shift, carefully avoiding a chance meeting with Peter Carey. She was walking to her quarters after a long day when she heard her name called.

Carey was running to catch up with her. He took her arm in a strong grip, as if he thought she would pull away, and glared at her.

"You shouldn't be working," he scolded her. "In fact, I recommend you return home."

"I canna," she said honestly. "Not yet. Leuk at me!"

He did, seeing her short-cropped hair now growing into soft, fiery curls above a pale face that was no longer rosy and bright.

"You've been avoiding me," he frowned. "Why?"

"I thocht ye had been avoiding me," she said.

He released her and shoved his hands in his pockets. "I suppose I have," he said gloomily. They walked together for a time and then he stopped, his face firm with decision, and turned her to face him.

"Why did you insist on going back to your tent

when you were ill? Was my presence so—so revolting? Did I say something, do something—?"

"Ye didna."

"Then, why?"

She drew herself up, returning his gaze in her old arrogant fashion.

"If ye maun know, I cannot bearrr yer wishity-washity ways. Ye hate me, then ye luve me, then ye hate me again. I dinna wish tae be hurrrt any mair!"

She stamped her foot, then looked at him in horror, realizing she'd given herself away.

And then she promptly burst into tears.

"Denise!" Carey gathered her resisting body close, feeling it finally relax and settle against him. "I never meant to hurt you. Oh, God, I never meant to hurt you!"

He led her back to his office and shut the door. She saw that her cot was still there, rumpled now, the pillow dented.

"I've been sleeping there," Peter Carey said. "It was the only way I could feel close to you. Does that tell you anything?"

"Peter—"

"Wait," he said quietly. "You sit here." He placed her in his chair behind his desk, then went to sit on the foot of the cot, trying to put as much distance as possible between them.

"I want to tell you a story, Denise. Then I'm going to ask you a question, but I want you to know what you're in for before you answer."

Haltingly, he told her a tale of a little boy, growing up in a big house in London. From the time he was born, it was settled that he would be a doctor. He became one, though he had other dreams.

Then the boy, now grown up, fell in love.

He fell in love with the most beautiful girl in the world. She, too, had dreams. And they were far removed from his own, so he tried to keep from loving her.

And that had now become impossible.

He was quiet for a long time, studying his hands. And finally Denise broke the silence.

"Yer drrreams, canna ye tell me what they are?"

"I want to doctor animals, not people! I want to be a veterinarian, to live on a farm, to have a wife and a dozen children!" He looked at her a bit defiantly, as though waiting for her scorn.

"I wull hae a farm when I wed," she whispered. "'Tis a bonnie place, wi' meadows o' heatherrr and brrracken, above my father's place. There, the burn sings a' the day, and wee birrrds nest i' the grass. The hoose is sma, but—"

Carey's face lit with hope. He made a move to rise, and she put out a staying hand.

"I hearrrd ye oot, mon. Noo ye maun hark tae me! "A wooman gaes wi' the hoose. She is wullfu', hot-temperrred, wrrrong-headed, and she has a jealous heart. But she is wulling tae try—"

He was standing now, his arms outstretched. "I'll take her like she is," she said, his eyes shining. "Come here, love!"

She surveyed the distance between them, and extended her own arms.

"It might be wiserrr," she smiled, "tae meet somewhere i' the middle!"

It was to be a point of argument for the rest of their lives. Who took how many steps in reaching whom. And who had actually done the proposing.

At the moment, there was no need for thinking. They met, catching each other in a violent embrace, their kisses frantic, desperate, as they tried to make up for lost time.

Finally, he pulled her down to the cot. They lay together, savoring the sweetness of just touching.

"I think I have loved you forever," he said, tracing the lines of her mouth with a wondering finger. "Let's not wait! I'll put in for leave and take you home to Scotland. We'll get married there, and then—"

"Nay," she said in a small voice. "I dinna want that."

Carey sat up, frowning down at her. "Don't tell me you've already changed your mind!"

"I hae the richt tae plan my ain wedding!"

"Then, dammit, what do you want!"

"I want tae be wed herrre, i' the kind o' place I met ye. And I dinna want tae wait."

Then he was kissing her again, holding her in an agony of love. They had waited far too long to find this awesome thing between them, and he knew just how she felt.

Almost—but not quite.

From a dizzying height halfway between heaven and earth, Denise had managed to hang on to a shred of practicality.

They couldna wait. They couldna. For if they did, she was bound tae boggle it a' ane way or another.

chapter 53

The news of Peter and Denise spread rapidly through the hospital, displacing war as a topic. For days there had been rumors of negotiations for peace. But after four long years of nightmare, no one could believe it would ever end.

Romance, however, was something else. It was here and now, in Denise Dugal's blushing face and Peter Carey's obvious happiness. There was a stirring of new life in the hospital tent. One man who insisted he wished to die—and probably would have, considering his aversion to living as a cripple—decided to wait awhile.

If there was gonna be a wedding, by God, he didn't intend to miss it.

Liane and Nora were as excited about the coming marriage as if it were their own. Nora began to wish she and Mule hadn't decided to wait. Liane thought of Steve, wondering where he was, if he were well, guiltily glad that her foreboding had not been connected with him.

Jo, too, was happy for Denise. She went through the coming days smiling, hiding the pain that ate away at her inside. Always in her mind was the vision of a tall man on crutches—a sick man—climbing over a rise, silhouetted against a battleground he must make his way through.

Peter Carey said Kurt wouldn't live to make it. And what he said was probably true. Jo knew she would have to face up to the fact that Kurt Kellerman was dead.

She also knew, with the straightforwardness she'd inherited from both her parents, that Kurt was the only man she'd ever love.

She must get back to her writing again. Must begin thinking about a career. That was all that was left to her.

Though the girls argued with Denise, suggesting she be married in Paris—or at least go there to purchase a trousseau, Denise held her ground.

The wedding would be a simple ceremony, performed in the hospital tent by the American chaplain. And she intended to wear her VAD uniform.

"You can't," Nora gasped. "Dammit, you only git married once!"

Denise only smiled serenely, and went ahead with her plans.

On the evening of November 11, Peter Carey donned his uniform and went to the hospital tent. Major West was already there, along with Chaplain Donovan. Mule Muehller had driven miles and brought back leaves to decorate a makeshift altar and festoon the canvas walls. A table had been set up. Somehow, the mess hall had managed a wedding cake and a wide range of cold rations cut up and transformed into hors d'oeuvres. To one side, a wash basin filled with ice contained Major West's contribution, a number of bottles of excellent champagne.

Carey entered, blinking at the festive scene, and a cheer went up, followed by whistles and catcalls and remarks that turned his clean-shaven face red.

"Glad you ain't operatin' on me t'night, Doc! Reckon you ain't too steady—"

"He's got better things t'do than carvin' on yer beat-up carcass," another patient scoffed.

"Trade places with yuh, Doc! Yer bed's gonna be warmer'n mine—"

He smiled back, his stiff British upbringing long gone. He was finally beginning to understand these Yanks with their ribald humor. They were heroes, all—

And right now, he was scared. Scared as hell!

Mrs. Bent peeked her head inside the tent. "She's coming," she said archly. "Get ready—"

A hush fell over the room, and a legless man drew a mouth harp from under his pillow. The strains of "In the gloaming," filled the room as Liane, Nora, and Jo entered the tent, clad in their uniforms, their faces glowing.

Then, finally, the wedding march.

Big Mule Muehller had been chosen to give the bride away. He was trembling like a leaf, but Denise stood tall, proud, serene, her eyes fixed on her husband-to-be. She moved toward him, light haloing her short curls and burnishing them with fire. She was lovelier than he had ever seen her. And she was wearing a neat VAD uniform, the same type of thing she'd worn when he first saw her. His breath caught in his throat as everything blurred before him.

The dress became a wedding gown, the hospital tent a cathedral. And he knew it would have been the same if they were in a field—in Paris—or his mansion in London, their marriage as beautiful, their vows as strong and meaningful—

"Do you, Peter, take this woman—"

Carey answered, in a dream.

"Place the ring upon her finger, and repeat after me—"

Ring!

Good God! He hadn't thought about a ring! There was a brief pause as he stared frantically at his own bare hands—then Nora Murphy moved forward. She lifted a chain from her neck and slipped a ring from it, handing it to him.

He fumbled a moment, then slid it on Denise's slim finger.

"With this ring," he repeated after the chaplain, "I thee wed—"

And within a moment they were pronounced man and wife. Somehow the legless man managed to produce a sound like the skirl of bagpipes from his mouth harp as they turned triumphantly to face their captive guests.

Jo and Liane were frankly crying, and for the wrong reasons.

They were crying for Nora, who had given up her last reminder of Jacques Leceau.

Mule Muehller was not an intuitive man, but he guessed there was some significance in what his love had done. He was watching her eyes as she paused, only for an instant. He'd seen the shadow in them.

Then her mouth set, decisively, and she removed the chain.

And with it, he knew she'd removed a barrier, the tiny bit of Nora that he'd been unable to reach.

As the imitation bagpipes skirled, he reached out and gathered Nora to his side.

Carey and Denise cut the wedding cake, to a great deal of good-natured kidding.

"Watch 'im with that knife, lady. Hell, no tellin' what he might cut off—"

Champagne corks popped, and food and drink was passed around, the bridesmaids serving. There was a lot of teasing laughter. It was almost impossible to envision the room as a hospital ward.

But it grew late. It was time for medications, sleeping pills. The couple were preparing to make their departure when a messenger came in, his whole bearing crackling with excitement.

He handed a slip of paper to Major West, who read it and shouted, an incomprehensible war whoop.

"Listen!" he said gleefully. "Dammit, just listen to this!"

He paused for a moment, then said portentously, "On the wedding day of Dr. and Mrs. Peter Carey, at the eleventh hour of the eleventh day of the eleventh month—

"An armistice was signed—"

The room, for a moment, was silent as death. Then someone let out a wild rebel yell. It was followed by pandemonium. Men who had been too weak to speak above a whisper cheered at the tops of their lungs. Boys who would be lifelong cripples shouted exultantly.

They would be going home!

The legless man with the mouth harp tore into

"The Star-Spangled Banner" with gusto, and soon many of them were singing over the noise.

It was over—Over There. Finally over. There were mothers waiting, wives, children, sweethearts—

And there were some who would be doomed to wait forever.

Jo slipped outside, leaning against the tent wall, tasting the tears she'd been holding back. Denise had her doctor, Nora would have her gigantic Nebraskan, Liane her—cowboy. If only—

There was no point in thinking about what might have been. She still had her mother, her father, her lame step-brother at home. And she had her writing.

Peter and Denise escaped from the tent under cover of the new excitement. Laughing, absorbed in each other, they did not see Jo. She watched them go, then wearily turned toward her own tent.

At least the war was over. And that was something to be happy for.

Denise and Peter reached his office—which was to be their honeymoon cottage. They entered and he closed the door, both of them suddenly strangely shy.

"I wish I had known the war would end," he blurted. "We would have waited a couple of days. A hotel in Paris, with carpets—a bath—"

"Ye dinna know me, Peter. I prrrefer my honeymoon at hame—"

Her gesture encompassed the small cubicle, with its desk, chair, and cot.

"We dinna need the trrrappings—"

He looked at her, soberly. "I love you, girl!"

"And I luve ye."

They were at an impasse. "Denise—"

"Peter—"

They had both spoken at once. They began to laugh.

"I suppose I should step outside, while you get— comfortable?"

"I couldna be comforrrtable, knowing ye were cauld." She was frowning a little. "Hoot mon, dinna ye ken what tae do—?"

He did. One long step took him to her. He undid the fastenings of her uniform, letting it fall to the floor. She kicked it away, feeling his lips on her shoulders, burning there—

"Domn it, mon," she panted, "maun I tak the lead in a' we do? Ye are sae slow—"

From that moment on, she lost her will. Peter Carey was inexperienced in marriage, but he knew his anatomy. Her underthings were torn, rather than removed, drifting like a snowstorm to join the gown. Then she was lifted in strong muscular arms, dropped on the cot. And, finally, he was beside her, over her, inside her.

She closed her eyes against ecstasy far beyond imagining, seeing the shivering skies of war, the star-burst of shell, rockets drifting—

But the war was over and ended, she thought blissfully.

This—this life as Peter Carey's wife and love—was a new beginning.

chapter 54

June 7, 1919, San Francisco

Liane Wang stood in an upstairs bedroom of Em Courtney's gracious old mansion. She was clad only in a white petticoat, her ivory shoulders bared.

Through the window, she could see the guests arriving; a few in automobiles, many in horse-drawn carriages. Looking out upon the city, she saw the changes that had been made in these last years. New buildings had sprung up. Smoke from factories curled into the air.

How different it must have been when Tamsen, Em, and Arab first came here! She wished, ruefully, that she might have seen it then.

She wished Tamsen could be present for her wedding. There had been so many lately, she thought, sighing.

All of them but Jo—

Jo had been wonderful through it all. Maybe she

was quieter, her eyes not so bright, her laughter not so infectious. But she'd handled it well.

Far better than I could, Liane thought.

First, there had been Denise's wedding, somehow appropriate for those terrible war years. For the armistice to have been signed on that same day was a wonderful coincidence.

And after her wedding, there had come the waiting; waiting until the hospital was emptied of patients, then for space available, with all the soldiers going home.

They'd gone first to Scotland, where Ramona greeted her daughter and her new husband with open arms. Leaving Denise and Peter, the rest went on to Luka's in England to collect Maggie and Sean before taking ship for the States.

They broke their journey in Nebraska, Mule Muehller meeting them in Omaha. Nora had flown into his arms like a hummingbird—

Liane smiled, thinking of the meeting between the matriarch, Gerda Muehller, and Maggie Murphy. Both ladies were equally domineering, and it had been a clash of wills until they discovered neither could get the better of the other.

Gerda had been a peasant's daughter, attaining status only after coming here with her sternly moral husband. Maggie had been a street girl, living off her wits on the docks at Liverpool.

"Ain't never lost me touch," Maggie said happily. "'Ere." She proffered Gerda's lapel watch, which she had lifted as a lark.

"How did you do that?" her red-faced hostess sputtered.

"Easy," Maggie said grandiosely. She proceeded to show her.

In turn, Gerda milked twenty cows morning and night, and could produce a dozen apple pies at the drop of a hat. The two women developed an admiration for each other that was to be long-lived.

They formed an additional bond through the union of their children, Sean and the senior Muehller cut out of the wedding plans. The two men walked the property, Muehller pointing out the status of his corn crop, Sean describing how he'd lost his leg in the war.

The wedding was held at a small white frame church, the men going together in the farm truck, the bride arriving with the women in a brother-in-law-to-be's Model-T.

They had a flat on the way.

When the bride walked down the aisle, a tiny girl in virginal white, her tip-tilted nose and freckles barely showing beneath her veil, no one would have guessed she'd insisted on helping Jo change the tire—except maybe Mule, who looked a little startled as he slipped a ring on a soiled, small hand.

Liane could remember only bits and pieces of the ceremony: the way Sean's peg leg tap-tapped as he led his daughter down the aisle; how Maggie had looked at her husband, eyes filled with adoration; the open church windows, Green fields rolling to the horizon, and birds twittering in a tree heavy with leaf, punctuating the promises Nora made in a soft, clear voice.

And then it was over, the two of them coming down the aisle, Nora radiant with love.

It was beautiful. But no more beautiful than Denise's wedding—nor than her own would be.

Only Jo—

"Liane, may we come in?"

The door opened to admit Liane's mother, Petra Wang. She carried a freshly pressed gown that had been her own. It swayed on its hanger like a ghost. Em Courtney was with her, her faded face soft with the thought of what was to come. And Arab, rounder than Em, a little withered, but with traces of her beauty still showing through.

How like Arab Denise is, Liane thought suddenly.

And behind them, Jo, smiling as though this might be her own wedding day, God bless her—

They helped her into the wedding dress, admiring her, arranging its folds, settling the veil that was now almost an ivory.

"A beautiful bride," Em said mistily. "Like your mother," she smiled at Petra—"and—a lot like Tamsen."

I wish I were, Liane thought. I wish I were. Tamsen had courage—

Finally, someone laid a mist of flowers in her arms. Liane looked down at them, dizzy with the scent.

"The music's beginning," Em said distractedly. "Would you like one of us to wait with you?"

"No," Liane said with a forced smile. "I think I'd like—to be alone."

They left, and she braced herself to stop her trembling. All morning, she'd filled her mind with other thoughts to keep from facing that of the ceremony.

She must think of Steve.

She tried, and couldn't summon up his face. He was a stranger! And she was giving her life into his care, going off to a harsh land of sun and wind and poisonous things that crawled—

Dear God, she was out of her mind! Em, Arab, and her mother had tried to talk to her, to dissuade her. Why hadn't she listened!

"Liane—"

Jo's gentle tap on the door was a signal. Liane could hear the music swelling below. Missie Blaine, her matron of honor, would be going down the stairs. The Jo—

Stiffening her spine, Liane went to the head of the circular staircase. Her father, Lee, waited there to take her arm.

Jo, already in position, saw Liane's face; a beautiful sleepwalker, she might have been headed for the guillotine.

The Liane saw her husband-to-be, and the numbed expression was gone; replaced with a kind of glory.

Jo relaxed, knowing it was going to be all right. It was going to be all right for all of them.

Her hand went to her bosom, feeling the crackle of a note she had concealed there.

Liebchen, it read, *I am well. I will come for you when I can. I pray to find you waiting. You are my salvation, and my love—*

It was signed *Kurt Kellerman.*

She had only just received Kurt's letter. And she had wanted to confide in Liane. But, today, Liane should think only of Steve.

She would not tell the others until he arrived.

Nora would have her problems with Mule's close family ties. Liane was moving into a life that would often be bewildering and strange.

But perhaps she, Jo, had the hardest road of all. Almost ten million men had died in the war. More than six million had been crippled or invalided for life. In her country, Kurt would be the enemy; she in his.

She shivered a little, then it was as if Tamsen was standing beside her; Tamsen, who had overcome so many obstacles. Jo turned, expecting to see her never-forgotten face—but there was no one there.

I wish I had her courage, she thought. They needed it, all of them. And none of them would ever be Tamsen, but there was a little bit of her in each of them.

"Do you take this woman—" the minister asked.

"I do," Steve answered in his lazy drawl.

"And you, Liane Wang, do you take this man—"

"I do."

Brown hands slipped a ring on Liane's finger, hands she had fallen in love with before she ever saw his face.

"I now pronounce you man and wife."

And it was done.

The triumphant recessional began, and the young couple took up their positions at the door. Em kissed them both, then turned to the groom's parents, a dark, lanky man with high cheekbones, and his wife, face lined and worn from days of dust and sun.

"I love weddings, don't you?" Em enthused, trying to put them at their ease. "I only wish—my sister Tamsen had been present."

Liane felt that humming feeling in her head—this time, not an unpleasant sensation, just a feeling of being touched by a loving thought.

She stood on tiptoe, and her tall groom leaned down to hear her.

"I think she is," Liane whispered. "I think she is."

Steve was not about to disagree. Last night, they'd finished the last chapter of Missie's book, together. If there was ever a survivor, it was Tamsen Tallant—and there had to be some part of her still here—

He slipped an arm around the small girl who was going to a strange and lonely place as his wife—just as Tamsen, married on a San Francisco wharf, had sailed to Russian Alaska with Dan Tallant.

Steve looked at Em, brave in her widowhood, at Arab, equally courageous. And he knew with all his heart that this was the proudest day of his life.

His sons would bear his name. But his daughters would inherit the blood of the McLeods.

Postlude

On the waterfront, a setting sun painted the sky with rose, gilding the waves that lapped gently against the docks. A warm wind from the land smelled like flowers. The beauty of the evening wasn't lost on two men fishing from a small boat.

"Look at that," one man sighed. 'Never woulda noticed it before the war. Now I can't see enough of it."

"This is the life, all right," his friend agreed.

They returned to their fishing, sitting together in the silent camaraderie of those who have shared experiences best not spoken of.

The light faded, and soon the sky was black as velvet, stars piercing it here and there, the moon beginning to rise. There was a shift of wind, a cool sea wind that brought mists rising from the docks, swirling in phantom shapes.

"We better pack it in," the first man said.

The other agreed, and they reeled in their lines, setting their backs to the oars. Then one made an odd choking sound.

"Jee—sus!" he said.

"What the hell?" The other followed his friend's shaking finger. It pointed at the dock.

"Didja see that?"

"I don't see nothing, damn it—!"

"There was two people there! I seen 'em! A girl in a white dress, her hair down—barefooted! And a man, a tall feller."

"Well, they ain't there now." The speaker looked worriedly at his friend. "You still see 'em?"

"No, I guess it was the fog—"

"Or maybe you was at the front too long!"

"Yeah, maybe."

Still, they looked around furtively as they beached their boat, then hurried toward the shabby hotel they called home, one limping badly, half supported by the other.

And wisps of mist swirled on the dock as fog moved in, covering the sleeping sea with a blanket of eiderdown. Wisps that took many forms. They might have been errant spirals of fog, created by wet winds. Or they might have been a bride and groom, recently come from a wedding, setting sail on a new adventure.

From somewhere in the heart of San Francisco, church bells rang out: a silvery paean of peace. Then even that voice was muffled by the fog.

And all was still.

ROMANCE...ADVENTURE ...DANGER...
by Best-selling author,
Aola Vandergriff

___**DAUGHTERS OF THE SOUTHWIND**
by Aola Vandergriff   (D30-561, $3.50)
The three McCleod sisters were beautiful, virtuous and bound to a
dream—the dream of finding a new life in the untamed promise of the
West. Their adventures in search of that dream provide the dimensions
for this action-packed romantic bestseller.

___**DAUGHTERS OF THE WILD COUNTRY**
by Aola Vandergriff   (D30-562, $3.50)
High in the North Country, three beautiful women begin new lives in a
world where nature is raw, men are rough...and love, when it comes,
shines like a gold nugget. Tamsen, Arab and Em McCleod now find themselves in Russian Alaska, where power, money and human life are the
playthings of a displaced, decadent aristocracy in this lusty novel ripe
with love, passion, spirit and adventure.

___**DAUGHTERS OF THE FAR ISLANDS**
by Aola Vandergriff   (D30-563, $3.50)
Hawaii seems like Paradise to Tamsen and Arab—but it is not. Beneath
the beauty, like the hot lava bubbling in the volcano's crater, trouble
seethes in Paradise. The daughters are destined to be caught in the turmoil between Americans who want to keep their country. And in their own
family, danger looms...and threatens to erupt and engulf them all.

___**DAUGHTERS OF THE OPAL SKIES**
by Aola Vandergriff   (D30-564, $3.50)
Tamsen Tallant, most beautiful of the McCleod sisters, is alone in the
Australian outback. Alone with a ranch to run, two rebellious teenage
nieces to care for, and Opan Station's new head stockman to reckon
with—a man whose very look holds a challenge. But Tamsen is prepared
for danger—for she has seen the face of the Devil and he looks like a man.

___**DAUGHTER OF THE MISTY ISLES**
                                   (D30-974, $3.50, U.S.A.)
by Aola Vandergriff   (D30-975, $4.50, Canada)
Settled in at Nell's Wotherspoon Manor, the McCleod sisters must carve
new futures for their children and their men. Arab has her marriage and
her courage put on the line. Tam learns to live without her lover. And even
Nell will have to relinquish a dream. But the greatest challenge by far will
be to secure the happiness of Luka whose romance threatens to tear the
family apart.

Don't Miss These Other Fantastic Books By HELEN VAN SLYKE!

___**ALWAYS IS NOT FOREVER**

(A31-009, $3.50)
(In Canada A31-022, $4.50)

Lovely young Susan Langdon thought she knew what she was doing when she married world-famous concert pianist Richard Antonini. She knew about his many women conquests, about his celebrated close-knit family, his jet-paced world of dazzling glamor and glittering sophistication, and about his dedication to his career. Here is an unforgettably moving novel of a woman who took on more than she ever counted on when she surrendered to love.

___**THE BEST PEOPLE**

(A31-010, $3.50)
(In Canada A31-027, $4.50)

The best people are determined to keep their Park Avenue cooperative exclusive as ambitious young advertising executive Jim Cromwell finds when he tries to help his millionaire client get an apartment. In this struggle against prejudice, the arrogant facade of the beautiful people is ripped away to expose the corruption at its core.

___**THE BEST PLACE TO BE**

(A31-011, $3.50)
(In Canada A31-021, $4.50)

A NOVEL FOR EVERY WOMAN WHO HAS EVER LOVED. Sheila Callahan was still beautiful, still desirable, still loving and needing love—when suddenly, shockingly, she found herself alone. Her handsome husband had died, her grown children were living their separate and troubled lives, her married friends made her feel apart from them, and the men she met demanded the kind of woman she never wanted to be. Somehow Sheila had to start anew.

___**THE HEART LISTENS**

(A31-012, $3.50)
(In Canada A31-025, $4.50)

Scenes from a woman's life—the rich, sweeping saga of a gallant and glamorous woman, whose joys, sorrows and crises you will soon be sharing—the magnificent tale ranging from Boston of the roaring twenties through the deco-glamour of thirties' Manhattan to the glittering California of the seventies—spanning decades of personal triumph and tragedy, crisis and ecstasy.

___**THE MIXED BLESSING**

(A31-013, $3.50)
(In Canada A31-023, $4.50)

The sequel to THE HEART LISTENS, this is the story of beautiful young Toni Jenkins, the remarkable granddaughter of Elizabeth Quigley, the heroine of the first book, torn between her passion for the one man she desperately loved and loyalty to her family. Here is a novel that asks the most agonizing question that any woman will ever be called upon to answer.

The *BEST* of Romance
from WARNER BOOKS